BIGGLES
STORY
COLLECTION
II

CAPTAIN W. E. JOHNS

A Red Fox Book

Published by Random House Children's Books
20 Vauxhall Bridge Road, London, SW1V 2SA

A division of The Random House Group Ltd
London Melbourne Sydney Auckland
Johannesburg and agencies throughout the world

Biggles Flies East Copyright © W. E. Johns
(Publications Ltd) 1935
Biggles Flies West Copyright © W. E. Johns
(Publications Ltd) 1937

1 3 5 7 9 10 8 6 4 2

Biggles Flies East first published by Oxford University Press 1935
Biggles Flies West first published by Oxford University Press 1937

This Red Fox edition 2001

Printed and bound in Great Britain
by Bookmarque, Croydon, Surrey

Papers used by Random House Group Ltd are natural,
recyclable products made from wood grown in sustainable forests.
The manufacturing processes conform to the
environmental regulations of the country of origin.

The RANDOM HOUSE Group Limited Reg. No. 954009

www.randomhouse.co.uk

ISBN 0 09 942706 0

CONTENTS

1. Biggles Flies East   7

2. Biggles Flies West   241

Red Fox would like to express their grateful thanks for help in preparing these editions to Jennifer Schofield, author of *By Jove, Biggles*, Linda Shaughnessy of A.P. Watt Ltd and especially to the late John Trendler.

BIGGLES
FLIES EAST

Foreword

The careers of most of those who served in the Great War* for any length of time resolve themselves, in retrospect, into a number of distinct phases, or episodes, rather than one continuous period of service in the same environment. For example, an artillery officer serving in France might find himself, a month later, acting as an aerial gunner on the Italian Front, and after seeing service in that capacity for a while would be sent home to England to get his pilot's wings. Later, when he qualified, he might be rushed off to fill a vacancy in another theatre of war—possibly Salonika or East Africa.

Each of these periods was quite unlike the others; it represented a different climate, a different set of faces, and an entirely different atmosphere.

The career of Captain James Bigglesworth, M.C., D.F.C. (known to his friends as 'Biggles'), was no exception, as those who have read his already published war experiences will agree. But there was one period that has not so far been mentioned, and the reasons have been twofold.

In the first place Biggles, far from taking any credit for the part he played in this particular affair, regards the whole tour of duty with such distaste that even his

---

* The First World War 1914–18. Principal contenders, the Allies: Britain, France, Russia, Italy, Serbia, Belgium, Japan (1915), Romania (1916), USA (1917). Against the Central Powers: Germany, Austria-Hungary, Turkey and Bulgaria (1915).

friend, the Honourable Algernon Lacey (who, it will be remembered, served with him in No. 266 Squadron when it was stationed at Maranique, in France), seldom if ever referred to it. Just why Biggles should feel this way about what were undoubtedly vital affairs of national importance is hard to see, but the fact remains. Like many other successful air fighters, he was a law unto himself, and intolerant of any attempt to alter his point of view—which may have been one of the reasons why he was successful.

Secondly, the Official Secrets Act* has been tightened up, and as one of the principal actors in the drama that is about to be disclosed was alive until recently—not only alive, but holding an important position in the German Government—it was thought prudent to remain silent on a subject that might have led to embarrassing correspondence and possibly international recriminations. This man, who at the time of the events about to be narrated was a trusted officer of the German Secret Service, in the end met the same fate as those of his enemies who fell in his hands—blindfold, with his back to a wall, facing a firing party in the cold grey light of dawn. Whether or not he deserved his fate is not for us to question.

There is little more to add except that Biggles, at the time, was a war-hardened veteran of twelve months' active service. He had learnt to face the Spandaus** of the German Fokkers without flinching, and the *whoof, whoof, whoof* of 'archie'*** bursting around his machine

---

* Official Secrets Act. An agreement which, when a British subject signs, forbids him or her to disclose confidential information prejudicial to the State.
** German machine-guns were often referred to as Spandaus, due to the fact that many were manufactured at Spandau, Germany.
*** Anti-aircraft gunfire, a Royal Flying Corps expression.

left him unmoved. He afterwards confessed to Algy that it was not until his feet had trodden the age-old sands of the Promised Land that he learnt to know the real meaning of the word Fear.

When he went there he was, like many another air warrior, still a boy; when he came back he was still a boy, but old beyond his years. Into his deep-set hazel eyes, which less than eighteen months before had pondered arithmetic with doubt and algebra with despair, had come a new light; and into his hands, small and delicate—hands that at school had launched paper darts with unerring accuracy—had come a new grip as they closed over joystick and firing lever. When you have read the story perhaps you will understand the reason.

1935   W.E.J.

The word 'Hun' as used in this book, was the common generic term for anything belonging to the enemy. It was used in a familiar sense, rather than derogatory. Witness the fact that in the R.F.C. a hun was also a pupil at a flying training school.

W.E.J

Chapter 1
How it Began

I

Captain James Bigglesworth, R.F.C.*, home from France on ten days' leave, stopped at the corner of Lower Regent Street and glanced at his watch. 'Ten to one; I thought it felt like lunch-time,' he mused, as he turned and strolled in the direction of the Caprice Restaurant, the famous war-time rendezvous of R.F.C. officers in London. At the door he hesitated as a thought occurred to him, and he contemplated dubiously the clothes he was wearing, for he was what would be described in service parlance as 'improperly dressed', in that he was not in uniform but civilian attire. The reason for this was quite a natural one.

His uniform, while passable in Flanders, where mud and oil were accepted as a matter of course, looked distinctly shabby in London's bright spring sunshine, and his first act on arrival had been to visit his tailor's with a view to getting it cleaned and pressed. This, he was informed, would take some hours, so rather than remain indoors he had purchased a ready-made suit of civilian clothes—to wear while his uniform was being reconditioned, as he put it. It was an obvious and pardonable excuse from his point of view, but whether or not it would be accepted by the Assistant Provost

---

* Royal Flying Corps 1914–1918. An army corps responsible for military aeronautics, renamed the Royal Air Force (RAF) when amalgamated with the Royal Naval Air Service on 1 April 1918.

Marshal or the Military Police, if he happened to run into them, was quite another matter. So he hesitated when he reached the fashionable meeting-place, torn between a desire to find someone he knew with whom he could talk 'shop', and a disinclination to risk collision with the A.P.M. and his minions who, as he was well aware, kept a vigilant eye on the Caprice.

'What does it matter, anyway? At the worst they can only cancel my leave, which won't worry me an awful lot,' he decided, and pushed open the swing doors. There were several officers and one or two civilians lounging round the buffet, but a swift scrutiny revealed that they were all strangers, so he selected a small table in a secluded corner and picked up a menu card.

He was still engrossed in the not unpleasant task of choosing his lunch when, out of the corner of his eye, he saw some one appear at his side, and thinking it was only a waiter he paid no immediate attention; but when he became conscious of the fact that some one was in the act of settling in the opposite chair he looked up with surprise and disapproval, for there were plenty of vacant tables.

'Good morning, Captain Brunow,' said the newcomer, easily, and without hesitation.

'Sorry, but you're making a mistake,' replied Biggles curtly, resuming his occupation.

'I think not,' went on the other coolly. 'Have a drink.'

Biggles eyed the speaker coldly. 'No, thanks,' he answered, shortly. 'I have already told you that you are making a mistake. My name isn't Brunow,' he added, in a tone that was calculated to end the conversation forthwith.

'No! Ha, ha, of course not. I quite understand. In the circumstances the sooner a name like that is forgotten the better, eh?'

Biggles folded the menu and laid it on the table with deliberation before raising his eyes to meet those of his *vis-à-vis*. 'Are you suggesting that I don't know my own name?' he inquired icily.

The other shrugged his shoulders with an air of bored impatience. 'Don't let us waste time arguing about a matter so trivial,' he protested. 'My purpose is to help you. *My* name, by the way, is Broglace—Ernest Broglace. I—'

'Just a minute, Mr Broglace,' interrupted Biggles. 'You seem to be a very difficult person to convince. I've told you plainly enough that my name is not Brunow. You say yours is Broglace, and, frankly, I believe you, but I see nothing in that to get excited about. As far as I am concerned it can be Dogface, Hogface, or even Frogface. And if, as I suspect, your persistent efforts to force your company upon me are prompted by the fond hope of ultimately inducing me to buy a foolproof watch, a bullet-proof vest, or some other useless commodity, I may as well tell you right away that you are wasting your time. And what is more important, you are wasting mine. I require nothing to-day, and if I did I shouldn't buy it from you. I trust I have now made myself quite clear. Thank you. Good morning.'

Broglace threw back his head and laughed heartily, while Biggles watched him stonily.

'For sheer crust, your hide would make elephant-skin look like tissue paper,' went on Biggles, dispassionately, as the other showed no sign of moving. 'Are you going to find another table—or must I?'

Broglace suddenly leaned forward, and his manner changed abruptly. 'Listen, Brunow,' he said quietly but tersely. 'I know who you are and why you're in mufti*. I know the whole story. Now, I'm serious. The service has outed you, and there is nothing left for you but to be called up as a conscript, be sent to France, and be shot. What about earning some easy money — by working for people who *will* appreciate what you do?'

Biggles was about to make a heated denial when something in the face opposite seemed to strike a chill note of warning, of danger, of something deeper than he could understand, and the words he was about to utter remained unsaid. Instead, he looked at the man for a moment or two in silence, and what he saw only strengthened his suspicions that something serious, even sinister, lay behind the man's uninvited attentions.

There was nothing very unusual in the stranger's general appearance. Of average height and built, he might have been a prosperous City man, just over military age, possibly a war profiteer. His hair was fair, close cut, and began high up on a bulging forehead. His neck was thick, and his face broad and flat, but with a powerful jaw that promised considerable strength of will. But it was his eyes that held Biggles, and sent a curious prickling sensation down his spine. They were pale blue, and although partly hidden behind large tortoiseshell glasses, they held a glint, a piercing quality of perception and grim determination, that boded ill for any one who stood in his path. Biggles felt an unusual twinge of apprehension as they bored into his own and he looked away suddenly. 'I see — I see,' he said slowly.

There was a sound of laughter from the door, and a party of R.F.C. officers poured into the room, full of

---

* Civilian clothes worn by someone who usually wears a uniform.

14

the joy of life and good spirits; some made for the buffet and others moved towards the luncheon-tables. Biggles knew one or two of them well, and they gave him the excuse he needed, although he acted more upon intuition than definite thought.

'Look here,' he said quickly, 'I know some of these fellows; perhaps it would be as well—'

'Exactly. I agree,' replied the other, rising swiftly to his feet. 'I shall be here between tea and dinner—say about 6.30. The place will be empty then.' With a parting nod, he walked away quickly and was lost in the crowd now surging through the entrance.

Biggles sat quite still for some minutes after he had gone, turning the matter over in his mind. Then he made a quick, light meal and joined the crowd at the buffet. He exchanged greetings with Ludgate of 287 Squadron, whom he knew well, and drew him aside. 'Listen, Lud,' he said. 'I want to ask you something. Did you ever hear of a chap named Brunow?'

'Good gracious! yes; he's just been slung out of the service on his ear, and about time too. He was an awful stiff.'

'What was it about?'

'I don't know exactly, but I heard some fellows talking about it in the Alhambra last night. I believe he was hauled up on a charge of "conduct unbecoming an officer and gentleman", but I fancy there was more to it than that. Anyway, he was pushed out, and that's the main thing.'

'Did you know him personally?'

'Too true I did. I was at the same Training School with him.'

'Was he anything like me—in appearance, I mean?'

Ludgate started. 'Well, now you come to mention it,

15

he is, a bit; not so much, though, that any one knowing you would make a mistake.'

'I see. Thanks, laddie—see you later.'

'Where are you going?'

'Oh, just for a look round,' replied Biggles airily. Which was not strictly true, for he looked neither right nor left as he strode briskly along Coventry Street and down St Martin's Lane into the Strand, where he turned sharply into the Hotel Cecil, the Headquarters of the Air Board.

After the usual wait and interminable inquiries, he at length found himself outside a door, bearing a card on which was neatly printed:

AIR STAFF INTELLIGENCE

Major L. Bryndale

He tapped on the door, and in reply to the invitation to enter, walked in and found himself facing a worried-looking officer who was working at a ponderous desk littered with buff correspondence-jackets and memo-sheets.

'I'm Captain Bigglesworth of 266 Squadron, home on leave, sir,' began Biggles.

'Why are you not in uniform?'

'That is one of the things I shall have to explain, sir, but I have something else to tell you that I think you should know.' Briefly, but omitting nothing of importance, he described his recent encounter in the restaurant.

The Intelligence Officer looked at him long and earnestly when he had finished, and then, with a curt, 'Take a seat, don't go away', left the room, to return a few minutes later with a grey-haired officer whose red tabs bespoke a senior Staff appointment.

Biggles rose to his feet and stood at attention.

'All right, sit down,' said the Staff Officer crisply. 'Have you seen this fellow who accosted you before to-day?'

'Never, sir.'

'Describe him.'

Biggles obeyed to the best of his ability.

'You know about the Brunow affair, I suppose?' asked the other when he had finished.

'Vaguely, sir. I ascertained, subsequent to my conversation with Broglace, that he had been dismissed from service recently.'

'Quite.' The General drummed on the table with his fingers. 'Well,' he went on, 'this may lead to something or it may not, but I think we should follow it up. Your leave is cancelled with effect from to-day and you will be posted to this department for special duty forthwith. I'll see that your leave is made up later on. In the meantime, I want you to try to get inside this fellow's confidence; find out just what he is up to, and report back here tomorrow. Meet him to-night as he suggests.'

'Very good, sir.'

'And I think it would be a wise precaution if you employed the next few hours making yourself thoroughly acquainted with Brunow's history, so that you can assume his identity if necessary. Major Bryndale will give you his dossier.' Then, turning to Major Bryndale, 'I'll leave Bigglesworth with you,' he said, and left the room.

At ten-thirty the following morning Biggles was ush-
ered by Major Bryndale into the more spacious office
of Brigadier-General Sir Malcolm Pendersby; his face
wore a worried expression, for although he was not
exactly nervous, he was by no means pleased at the
turn events were taking.

The General glanced up as he entered. 'Well, Bigglesworth—sit down—what happened yesterday after you
left us? Did the fellow turn up?'

'He did, sir,' answered Biggles, 'and it certainly looks
as if—well—'

'Tell me precisely what happened.'

Biggles wrinkled his forehead. 'To tell the truth, sir,
it isn't easy. You see, nothing definite was said, and
no actual proposition made. It seemed to me that Broglace had something to put forward, but was being very
careful.'

'As indeed he was bound to be if he is engaged in
espionage,' put in the General dryly.

'Quite so, sir. As I was saying, it was all very indefi-
nite; his conversation consisted chiefly of hints and
suggestions, but if I may judge, the position at the
moment is this. Broglace thinks I am Brunow; he knows
Brunow has been cashiered*, and somehow or other
knows quite a lot about his history. For example, he
knew quite well what I only learnt yesterday from
Brunow's dossier—that he is of Austrian extraction and
was in the Argentine when war broke out. He knows,
too, that although his financial interests are—or were—
British, his sympathies, by reason of his parentage,
may be with Germany and the Central Powers. He is

---

* Dismissed from the Armed Forces with dishonour and disqualified
from entering public service.

working on the assumption that Brunow's disgrace has embittered him against the British—an assumption that I took care not to dispel—and that he might be induced to turn traitor.'

'But you say he made no definite offer.'

'That is quite true, sir, but it struck me that he was trying to convey his idea by suggestion rather than by actual words, in the hope that I would make the next move. He dare not risk going too far, in case he was making a mistake.'

'How did you leave matters?'

'I told him in a half-hearted sort of way that there was nothing doing, but at the same time tried to create the impression that I might be persuaded if it was made worth my while.'

'Excellent! Go on.'

'That's all, sir. Naturally, I didn't want to lose touch with him, in case you decided to arrest him, so I have made a provisional appointment—'

'Arrest!' The General opened his eyes in mock astonishment.

'Why, yes, sir,' faltered Biggles, puzzled. 'I thought that if there was a chance of him being a spy, you would arrest him on—'

'The General waved his hand. 'Good gracious, Bigglesworth,' he cried, 'we don't work like that. If the man is indeed a spy he will be far more useful to us at large than in the Tower of London*. Once we know his game we can use him to our advantage.'

'I am afraid that's rather beyond me, sir,' confessed Biggles, 'but I've done what I could, and that is the

* During the First World War, the Tower of London was used to house spies, prior to their trial. Some were later executed at the Tower.

end of it as far as I am concerned. May I now continue my leave?'

'Not so fast—not so fast,' replied the General quickly. 'Who said you had finished? This may be only the beginning. Pure chance seems to have placed a card in our hands that we may not be able to use without you, and I should like to give the matter a little consideration before reaching a final decision. Help yourself to cigarettes; I shan't keep you long.' He gathered up some papers on which he had been making notes and left the room.

Nearly an hour elapsed, however, before he returned, a period that left Biggles plenty of time to ruminate on the position—an unlucky one from his point of view—in which he found himself.

The General's face was grave when he returned and sat down at his desk, and he eyed Biggles speculatively. 'Now, Bigglesworth,' he commenced, 'I am going to have a very serious talk with you, and I want you to listen carefully. While I have been away I have examined the situation from every possible angle. I believe that Broglace's next move will be to make a definite offer to you, provided you do not give him cause for alarm. If our assumption is correct, he will suggest tentatively that you work for him, which means, of course, for Germany; I would like you to accept that offer.'

'Accept it?' cried Biggles incredulously.

The General nodded slowly. 'In that way we could take full advantage of an opportunity that seldom presents itself.'

Biggles thought swiftly. 'What you mean, sir, is that you would like me to become a German spy, working for the British,' he said bluntly.

The General looked rather uncomfortable. 'Without

20

mincing matters, that is precisely what I do mean,' he said gravely. 'Obviously, I cannot detail you for such work, but it is hardly necessary for me to remind you that it is the duty of every Englishman to do his best for his side whatever sacrifice it may involve. That is why I am asking you to volunteer for what may prove a very difficult and dangerous task. I have looked up your record, and you appear to be unusually well qualified for it, otherwise I would not contemplate the project seriously for one moment. Major Raymond, the Intelligence Officer attached to your Wing in France, speaks highly of your ability in this particular class of work; you have helped him on more than one occasion. Frankly, to handle an affair of this sort with any hope of success would be beyond the ability of the average officer. Still, the final decision must be left to you, and I should fail both in my duty and in fairness to you if I tried to minimize the risks. One blunder, one slip, one moment's carelessness—but there, I think you appreciate that, so there is no need for me to dwell on it. Well, how do you feel about it?'

Biggles thought for a moment or two. 'To pretend that I view the thing with favour would be sheer hypocrisy,' he said rather bitterly, 'but as you have been good enough to point out my obvious path of duty, I cannot very well refuse, sir.'

The General flushed slightly. 'I quite understand how you feel,' he said in a kindly tone, 'but I knew you would not refuse. Now let us examine the contingencies that are likely to arise, so that we shall know how to act when they do . . .'

Chapter 2
Algy gets a Shock

I

Lieutenant Algernon Lacy, of 266 Squadron, stationed at Maranique, in France, acting flight-commander in the absence of Biggles, his friend and flying partner, landed his Sopwith Camel* more carefully than usual, and taxied slowly towards the sheds, keeping a watchful eye on a shattered centre section strut as he did so. On reaching the tarmac he switched off his engine, climbed stiffly to the ground, and walked towards the Squadron Office to make out his combat report. He was feeling particularly pleased with himself, for he had just scored his third victory since Biggles had departed on leave.

He pushed open the door of the flimsy weatherboard building, but seeing Major Mullen, his C.O.** in earnest conversation with 'Wat' Tyler, the Recording Officer, would have withdrawn had not the C.O. called him back.

'All right, Lacey, come in,' he said. 'I was waiting to have a word with you, although I am afraid it is bad news.'

Algy paused in the act of pulling off his gauntlets and looked at the Major with a puzzled frown. 'Bad news?' he repeated, and then, as a ghastly thought

---

* A single seat biplane fighter with twin machine-guns synchronised to fire through the propeller. See cover illustration.
** Commanding Officer

struck him, 'Don't tell me Biggles has crashed,' he added quickly.

'Oh, no; nothing like that. You've been posted away.'

'Posted!'

'To Headquarters Middle East—in Cairo.'

Algy stared uncomprehendingly. 'Posted to Middle East,' he repeated again, foolishly. 'But what have I done?'

'Nothing, as far as I am aware. I can only tell you that this posting has not come from Wing Headquarters, or even General Headquarters in France. It has come direct from the Air Board.'

'But why?'

'I am sorry, Lacey, particularly as I hate losing a good officer, but it is time you knew that the Air Board is not in the habit of explaining or making excuses for its actions. You are posted with effect from to-day, and you are to catch the 7.10 train to Paris to-night. You will have to take a taxi across Paris in order to catch the 11.10 from the Gare de Lyon to Marseilles, where you will report to the Embarkation Officer at Quay 17. Your movement Order is ready. That's all. I'll see you again before you go.'

Algy sat down suddenly, and, as a man in a dream, watched the C.O. leave the office. Then, as the grim truth slowly penetrated his stunned brain, he turned to Wat in a cold fury. 'So that's all the thanks—' he began, but the Recording Officer cut him short.

'It's no use storming,' he said crisply.

'Wait till Biggles gets back; he'll have something to say about it.'

'Biggles isn't coming back.'

Algy blinked. 'Not coming back! Suffering rattlesnakes! What's happened? Has the Air Board gone balmy?'

'Possibly. I can only tell you that Biggles is posted to H.E.'

'Home Establishment,' sneered Algy. 'My gosh! that proves it. Fancy posting a man like Biggles to H.E. He'll set 'em alight, I'll warrant, and serve them right, too. Does the Air Board imagine that fighters like Biggles grow on gooseberry bushes? Well,' he rose despondently and turned towards the door, 'that's the end of this blinking war as far as I am concerned. I've no further interest.'

Wat eyed him sympathetically. 'It's no use going on like that, laddie,' he said quietly. 'That sort of talk won't get you anywhere. You do your job and put up a good show, and maybe you'll be able to wangle a posting back to 266. We shall miss you, and Biggles— I need hardly tell you that. Oh! by the way, I'll tell you something else, although you're not supposed to know.'

'Go ahead; you can't shock me any more.'

'You'll have a travelling companion, some one you know.'

'Who is it?'

'Major Raymond of Wing Headquarters. He's also been posted to Headquarters Middle East.'

'Good! I shall be able to tell him what I think of the Air Board.'

'And finish under close arrest. Don't be a fool, Algy. We're at war, and no doubt the Air Board knows what it's doing.'

'Maybe you're right,' agreed Algy sarcastically, as he picked up his gauntlets and left the office.

II

Ten days later, tired and travel-stained, he stepped out of a service tender at Kantara, Palestine, the aerodrome to which he had been sent on arrival in Egypt. No explanation for this further move had been asked or given; he had accepted his instructions moodily, and without interest. Kantara, Almaza, Heliopolis, Ismailia, Khartoum, or Aden, it was all the same as far as he was concerned—at least, so he had told Major Raymond when they had parted company outside Middle East Headquarters in Cairo. Where Raymond had gone Algy did not know, for he had not seen him since.

'Take my kit to the Mess Secretary's office until I fix up my quarters,' he told the driver, and then swung round on his heel as he heard his name called. Major Raymond, in khaki drill uniform, was walking briskly towards him.

'Hello, Lacey,' he cried cheerily, 'so we meet again.'

'Hello, sir,' replied Algy in surprise. 'I didn't know you were coming to Palestine, too. I'm feeling very homesick, so it's a treat to see some one I know. Why couldn't they have sent us along together, I wonder?'

'Never wonder at anything in the service, Lacey,' smiled the Major. 'Remember that there's usually a method in its madness. I had to attend an important conference after I left you in Cairo, but I got here first because I flew up—or rather, was flown up. Are you very tired?'

'Not particularly, sir. Why?'

'Because I want a word with you in private. I also want you to meet somebody; it is rather urgent, so I would like to get it over right away.'

'Good enough, sir,' returned Algy shortly.

The Major led the way to a large square tent that stood a little apart from the rest. 'This is my headquarters,' he explained, with a curious expression on his face, as he swung aside the canvas flap that served as a door.

The tent was furnished as an office, with a large desk, telephone, and filing cabinets, but Algy noticed none of these things. He was staring at a man dressed in flying overalls who rose from a long cane chair and walked quickly towards him, laughing at his thunderstruck expression.

'I don't think an introduction is necessary,' observed Major Raymond, with a chuckle.

Algy's jaw had sagged foolishly and his lips moved as if he was trying to speak, but no words came. 'Biggles,' he managed to blurt out at last. 'Why the—what the dickens—oh, Great Scott, this has got me beaten to a frazzle.'

'Let's sit down; it's too hot to stand,' suggested the Major. 'And now let us try to work out what has happened, and why we are here,' he went on, when they were all comfortably settled. 'I'm by no means clear about it, so the sooner we all know the real position the better. You probably know more than anybody, Bigglesworth, so you had better do the talking.'

Biggles smiled rather wanly as he leaned back in his chair and unfastened his overalls, exposing the R.F.C. tunic he wore underneath. 'If you'll listen I'll tell you all I know,' he said quietly.

Briefly, he told them of his encounter with Broglace, and his subsequent conferences at the Air Board. 'You see,' he explained, 'I realized that the General was quite right when he said that it was up to every one to do his best. I hated and loathed the idea, but what could I do? In the end I told him that I would go on with the business on the understanding that no one knew except himself and two persons I should name, the idea being that those two persons should act as liaison officers with me. I have only one life to lose, and I want to hang on to it as long as I can, so I didn't feel inclined to make my reports through strangers, even though they were officers of the British Intelligence Service. Sooner or later a counter-spy would get hold of the tale, and then the balloon would go up as far as I was concerned.

'Mind you, the question of going to Egypt or Palestine hadn't been raised then; that came later. Anyway, I agreed to go on with the thing if I could work with two people I knew I could trust absolutely. The General agreed, and when I named you he was quite pleased, because, as he said, apart from the question of trust, you, Algy, would be valuable because you could fly, and you, sir, because you were already on the Intelligence Staff. Now you know why you were posted.

'The next move came when I saw Broglace that evening. When he realized that I was ready to talk business he put his cards on the table and made me an offer of high wages if I would join the German Secret Service, and that showed me just where I stood. I said I'd think it over, went back to the General, and asked him what I was to do about it. He told me to accept, but if possible get to this part of the world, where the war was going to pieces as far as we were concerned, because the place was rotten with German spies—due chiefly to the activities of a Hun named El Shereef. Our people only know him by his Arab name; they very badly want to get a slant on him, and that was to be my job. They suggested that when I got here—if I did—I should get in touch with our leading Intelligence

27

Agent, Major Sterne. He's a free-lance, and as far as I can make out tears about the desert on a camel, or on horseback, pulling the wires through Arab chiefs and tribesmen. El Shereef and Sterne are the two big noises out here, apparently, and each has been trying to get at the other's throat for months.

'I said I'd try to get out here but would prefer to play a lone hand; I didn't like the idea of working under anybody, not even Major Sterne, although they say he's brilliant. Well, to make a long story short, I saw Broglace and told him I was prepared to fall in line with him. He wanted me to go to Belgium, but I shot him a line about being well known, and sooner or later was bound to bump into somebody who knew me. He quite saw the wisdom of my protest, and asked me to which other theatre of war I would prefer to go. I told him Palestine, and that was that.'

'But how on earth did you get out here?' asked Algy curiously.

'Ah, that would make a story in itself,' replied Biggles mysteriously. 'Broglace gave me a ring, a signet ring with a hinged flap that covered a peculiar device, and told me it would work like an oracle. And he was right. It did. I'd flown home on leave, as you know, so I went and got my machine, and instead of flying to France, went straight to Brussels. Broglace thought I'd stolen it—but that's by the way. It was a sticky trip, believe me, with Huns trying to shoot me down all the way, but I got there. As soon as I landed I was taken prisoner, but I flashed my ring and it acted like a charm. You should have seen the Huns bowing and scraping round me. I was pushed into a train for Berlin, where I had to go through a very dickens of a cross-examination from a kind of tribunal. It put the wind up me properly, and I don't mind admitting it. Then I was sent on to Jerusalem, where I reported to the Intelligence people, who posted me to Zabala under Count von Faubourg, who is O.C.* of the German Secret Service on this particular sector of the front.

'I got there two days ago, and was sent out on a reconnaisance this morning to get my general bearings.'

'But how on earth did you manage to land on our side of the lines in a Hun machine?' asked Algy in amazement.

'I didn't say anything about a Hun machine. I'm flying a British machine, a Bristol Fighter**. The Huns have two of our machines, a two-seater—the Bristol—and a Sopwith 'Pup'. They must have forced-landed over the wrong side of the lines at some time or other, and been repaired. Anyway, I slipped over right away to try to get in touch with you in order that we could make some sort of plan, and fix a rendezvous where we could meet when I have anything to report. I fancy the Boche*** idea is that I shall land over here and take back any information I pick up. That's why I'm still wearing a British uniform, although I have a German one as well.

'I daren't stay very long, or they may wonder what I'm up to. While I've been waiting I've jotted down some suggestions on a sheet of paper; I'd like you both to read them, memorize them, and then destroy it. Algy, I imagine you will be exempt from ordinary duty; the Major will be able to arrange all that. As a temporary measure I have decided on the oasis of Abba Sud as an emergency meeting-place. It's well out in the

* Officer Commanding.
** Two seated biplane fighter with remarkable manoeuvrability, in service 1917 onward. It had one fixed Vickers gun for the pilot and one or two mobile Lewis guns for the observer/gunner.
*** A derogatory slang term for the Germans.

desert, a good way from either British or German forces, so it should be safe. Here it is.'

He crossed over to a large wall-map that hung on the side of the tent, and laid his finger on a small circle that bore the name Abba Sud. 'I want you to hang round there as often as you can, and watch for me,' he went on. 'I may be flying a British machine, or a German, and in either case I will try to fire a red Very* light to let you know it's me. Then we'll land, talk things over, and you can report to Major Raymond. Now I must go. We're in touch, and that's a load off my mind. We shall have to settle details later to suit any conditions that may arise; it's all been such a rush that I haven't been able to sort the thing out properly yet.'

He rose to his feet, fastened his overalls, and held out his hand. 'Good-bye for the present, sir. Cheerio, Algy.'

Algy sprang up in a mild panic. 'But you're not going back—to land behind the Hun Lines?' he cried aghast.

'Of course I am.'

Algy turned a trifle pale and shook his head. 'For God's sake be careful,' he whispered tersely. 'They'll shoot you like a dog if they spot what you're doing.'

'I know it,' returned Biggles calmly, 'so the thing is not to get caught. You keep your end up and it will pan out all right. Remember one thing above everything. Trust nobody. The spy system on this front is the best in the world, and if one whisper gets out about me, even in the Officers' Mess here, I'm sunk. Cheerio!' With a final wave of his hand he left them.

As he walked swiftly towards the aerodrome where

* A coloured flare fired as a signal from a special short-barrelled pistol.

he had left his machine he paused in his stride to admire a beautifully mounted Arab who swept past him, galloping towards the camp. The Arab did not even glance in his direction, and Biggles thought he had never seen a finer example of wild humanity.

'Who's that?' he asked a flight-sergeant, who was going in the direction of the hangars.

The N.C.O.* glanced up. 'Looks like Major Sterne, sir, coming in from one of his raids,' he replied casually. 'He's always poppin' up when he's least expected.'

'Thanks, flight-sergeant,' replied Biggles, and looked round with renewed interest. But the horseman had disappeared.

Deep in thought, he made his way to his machine and climbed into the cockpit. The engine roared. For a hundred yards he raced like an arrow over the sand and then swept upwards into the blue sky, turning in a wide circle towards the German lines.

* Non-commissioned officer, e.g. a corporal or sergeant.

Chapter 3
Biggles gets a Shock

During the short journey to Zabala, which besides being the headquarters of the German Intelligence Staff was the station of two German squadrons, one of single-seater Pfalz Scouts and the other of two seater Halberstadts, he pondered on the amazing chain of circumstances that had resulted in the present situation. That the work to which he had pledged himself would not be to his liking he had been fully aware before he started, yet curiously enough he found himself playing his part far more naturally than he had imagined possible. At first, the natural apprehension which the field-grey uniforms around him inspired, combined with the dreadful feeling of loneliness that assailed him when he found himself in the midsts of his enemies, almost caused him to decide to escape at the first opportunity; but when the dangers which he sensed at every turn did not materialize the feeling rapidly wore off, confidence grew, and he resolved to pursue his task to the bitter end.

But for Hauptmann* von Stalhein he would have been almost at ease. Of all the Germans he had met during his journey across Europe, and in Zabala, none filled him with the same indefinable dread as von Stalhein, who was Count von Faubourg's chief of staff. The Count himself was simply a rather coarse old man of the military type, brutal by nature and a bully to those

* Captain.

who were not in a position to retaliate. He had achieved his rank and position more by unscrupulous cunning, and the efforts of those who served under him, than by any great mental qualifications.

The other German flying officers he had met were quite normal and had much in common with British flying officers, with the possible exception of Karl Leffens, to whom he had taken a dislike on account of his overbearing manner—a dislike that had obviously been mutual.

Erich von Stalhein was in a very different category. In appearance he was tall, slim, and good-looking in a rather foppish way, but he had been a soldier for many years, and there was a grim relentlessness about his manner that quickly told Biggles that he was a man to be feared. He had been wounded early in the war, and walked with a permanent limp with the aid of two sticks, and this physical defect added something to his sinister bearing. Unlike most of his countrymen, he was dark, with cold brooding eyes that were hard to meet and held a steel-like quality that the monocle he habitually wore could not dispel. Such was Hauptmann Erich von Stalhein, the officer to whom Biggles had reported in Zabala and who had conducted him into Count von Faubourg's office for interview.

Biggles sensed a latent hostility from the first moment that they met, and felt it throughout the interview. It was almost as if the man suspected him of being an imposter but did not dare to question the actions of those who had been responsible for his employment. Whether or not von Stalhein was aware that he, as Lieutenant Brunow, had previously served in the British R.F.C. he did not know, nor did he think it wise to inquire. Of one thing he was quite certain, however, and that was that the German would watch

33

him like a cat watching a mouse, and pounce at the first slip he made.

Another thing he noticed was that all the Germans engaged in Intelligence work wore a signet ring like the one that had been given to him by Broglace; it appeared to be a kind of distinguishing mark or identification symbol. The Count wore one, as did von Stalhein and Leffens; he had also seen one or two other officers wearing them. His own, when opened, displayed a tiny dagger suspended over a double-headed eagle, with a small number 117 engraved below. Just how big a part it played in the German espionage system he had yet to learn.

If he had been sent to Zabala for any special reason he had not yet been informed of it. The Count, his Chief had merely said that he would be employed in the most useful capacity at the earliest opportunity, but in the meantime he was to make himself acquainted with the positions of the battle fronts. Nevertheless he suspected that his chief duty would be to land behind the British lines, for the purpose of either gathering information or verifying information that had already been acquired through other channels. In this he was not mistaken.

Of El Shereef he had seen no sign—not that he expected to. The name was almost a legend, hinted at rather than spoken in actual words. Still, there was no doubt that the man existed: General Pendersby had assured him of that. He could only keep his ears and eyes open and wait for some clue that might lead to the identification of the German super-spy.

At this period of the war the German Secret Service in Palestine was the most efficient in the world, and of its deadly thoroughness he was soon to have a graphic example. Quite unaware of this, he reached Zabala without incident, and after making a neat landing, taxied into the hangar that had been reserved for the British machines. He did not report to the office at once, but went to his quarters, where he changed into his German uniform. Naturally the British uniform was not popular, and for this reason he invariably wore overalls when he was compelled to wear it. Having changed, he made his way slowly to the Officers' Mess* with a view to finding a quiet corner in order to study a German grammar he had bought, for his weak knowledge of the language was one of the most serious difficulties with which he was faced, and for this reason he had worked hard at it since his arrival in German territory.

He had not been seated many minutes when an orderly entered and handed him a note from the Count requesting his presence at the Headquarters office immediately. With no suspicion of anything unusual in his mind, he put the book in his pocket, picked up his cap, and walked down the tarmac to the old Turkish fort that served both as his Chief's headquarters and as sleeping quarters for the senior officers, while the courtyard and stables had been converted, by means of barbed wire, into a detention barracks for prisoners of war.

He knocked at the door and entered. The Count was leaning back in his chair with the collar of his tunic unfastened, in conversation with von Stalhein, who half sat and half leaned against the side of the desk. A fine coil of blue smoke arose lazily from the cigarette he was smoking in a long amber holder, and this, with the rimless monocle in his eye, only served to accentuate his effeminate appearance; but as he took in these

* The place where officers eat their meals and relax together.

35

details with a swift glance, Biggles thought he detected a sardonic gleam in the piercing eyes and experienced a twinge of uneasiness. He felt rather than saw the mocking expression that flitted across von Stalhein's face as he stood to attention and waited for the Count to speak.

'So! Here you are, Brunow,' observed von Faubourg easily. 'You went out flying this morning—yes?' He asked the question almost casually, but there was a grim directness of purpose about the way he crouched forward over his desk.

Biggles sensed danger in the atmosphere, but not by a quiver of an eyelid did he betray it. 'I did, sir, acting under your instructions,' he admitted calmly.

'Why did you land behind the British lines?' The easiness had gone from the Count's manner; he hurled the question like a spear.

Biggles turned stone-cold; he could feel the two pairs of eyes boring into him, and knew that if he hesitated he was lost. 'Because I thought it would be a good thing to ascertain immediately if such landings could be made with impunity,' he replied coolly. 'The occasion to land in enemy country might arise at any time, and it seemed to me that a preliminary survey of the ground for possible danger was a sensible precaution.'

The Count nodded slowly. 'And is that why you visited the Headquarters tent of the British Intelligence Service?'

Biggles felt the muscles of his face grow stiff, but he played his next card with a steadiness that inwardly amazed him. His lips parted in a smile as he answered carelessly and without hesitation, 'No, sir. I had no choice in that matter. I was sent for—it was all very amusing.'

'How?'

'The idea of being invited into the very place which I imagined would be most difficult to enter. I am afraid I have not been engaged in this work long enough to lose my sense of humour.'

'So it would seem. Why were you sent for?'

'Because I had said in the Officers' Mess that I was a delivery pilot*, and he—that is, the officer who sent for me—was merely interested to know if I was going to Heliopolis as he had a personal message for some one stationed there.'

'What did you say?'

'I told him I was sorry, but I was not going near Heliopolis.'

'Anything else?'

'Nothing, sir. The matter ended there and I came back.'

'Who was the other officer with Major Raymond?'

The words reacted on Biggles's tense nerves like an electric shock; there seemed to be no limit to German knowledge of British movements. 'No wonder we are getting the worst of it,' was the thought that flashed through his mind, as he answered with all the nonchalance he could muster, 'I've no idea, sir. I saw another officer there, a young fellow, but I did not pay any particular attention to him. If I thought anything at all I imagined him to be an assistant of some sort.'

'You knew the other was Major Raymond, who has just arrived here from France?'

'I know now, sir. I was told to report to Major Raymond: that's how I knew his name. I knew nothing

* The pilot who delivers aeroplanes to service squadrons from the manufacturers or repair depots.

about his just having arrived until you told me a moment ago.'

'Have you ever seen him before?'

'Not to my knowledge.'

'He didn't recognize you?'

'Oh, no, sir—at least, I have no reason to suppose he did. He was quite friendly.'

The answer apparently satisfied the Count, for he looked up at von Stalhein with a look which said as plainly as words, 'There you are: I told you so. Quite a natural sequence of events.' But von Stalhein was still watching Biggles with a puzzled smile, and continued to do so until the Count told him that he might return to his quarters, although he must remain at hand in case he was needed.

Biggles drew a deep breath as he stepped out into the blazing sunshine. His knees seemed to sag suddenly, and his hands turned ice-cold although they did not tremble. 'My word! I've got to watch my step and no mistake; these people have eyes everywhere,' he reflected bitterly, and not without alarm, as he walked slowly towards his quarters.

Chapter 4
A Meeting and a Duel

He had just finished dressing the following morning when his presence was again demanded by Count von Faubourg. His mind ran swiftly over his actions since the last interview, and although he could think of nothing he had done that could be regarded as a suspicious action, it was with a feeling of trepidation that he approached the fort. 'It's this beastly ever-present possibility of the unknown, the unexpected, turning up, that makes this business so confoundedly trying,' he thought, as he knocked on the door.

As he entered the office he instinctively looked round for von Stalhein, but to his infinite relief he was not there. Moreover, the Count seemed to be quite affable.

'Good morning, Brunow,' he called cheerfully. 'I have a real job for you at last.'

'Thank you, sir,' replied Biggles, with an enthusiasm he certainly did not feel. 'I shall be glad to get down to something definite.'

'I thought perhaps you would,' answered the Count. 'Now this is the position. We have received word that a large body of British troops, chiefly Australian cavalry, has recently left Egypt. There is a remote chance that they may have gone to Salonika, but we do not think so. It is far more likely that they have been disembarked and concealed somewhere behind this particular front in readiness for the big push which we know is in course of preparation. You may find it hard to believe that twenty thousand men can be moved, and hidden, without our being aware of their destination, but such unfortunately is the case. The British have learnt a bitter lesson, and they are acting with circumspection. I want you to try to find those troops. If they are in Palestine, then it is most likely that they are somewhere in the hills—here.'

He indicated an area on his large-scale wall-map. 'Search there first, anyway,' he continued. 'The fact that our reconnaissance machines have been driven off every time they have attempted to approach that zone suggests that our deductions are correct; if you will take one of the British machines you will not be molested. If you cannot find the camp from the air it may be necessary for you to land and make discreet inquiries.'

'Very good, sir.' Biggles saluted, returned to his quarters, put on his British uniform and his overalls, and then made his way to the hangar where the British machines were housed. He ordered the mechanics to get out the Sopwith Pup,* and then glanced along the tarmac as an aero-engine came to life farther down. A silver and blue Pfalz Scout** was taxi-ing out into position to take off, and he watched it with interest as its tail lifted and it climbed swiftly into the shimmering haze that hung over the sandy aerodrome.

'That's Leffen's machine; I wonder what job he's on,' he mused, as he climbed into his cockpit, started the engine, and waited for it to warm up. But his interest in the other machine waned quickly as he remembered the difficult work that lay before him, for the task was one of the sort he had been dreading.

* Single seater biplane fighter with a single machine gun synchronised to fire through the propeller. Superseded by the Sopwith Camel.
** Very successful German single-seater biplane fighter, fitted with two or three machine guns synchronised to fire through the propeller. See cover illustration.

To report the position of the Australian troops to the Germans, even if he discovered it, was obviously out of the question; yet to admit failure, or, worse still, name an incorrect position that the enemy would speedily prove to be false, was equally impossible.

'I'd better try to get word to Raymond and ask him how I am to act in cases of this sort; maybe he'll be able to suggest something,' he thought, as he pushed open the throttle and sped away in the direction of the British lines. For some time, while he was in sight of the aerodrome, he held steadily on a course that would take him over the area indicated by von Faubourg, but as the aerodrome slipped away over the horizon behind him he turned north in the direction of Abba Sud.

A few desultory bursts of German archie blossomed out in front of him, but he fired a green Very light, the 'friendly' signal that had been arranged for him by headquarters and the German anti-aircraft batteries, and they died away to trouble him no more.

He kept a watchful eye open for prowling German scouts, who would, of course, shoot him down if they failed to notice the white bar that had been painted across his top plane for identification purposes, but he saw nothing, although it was impossible to study the sky in the direction of the blazing tropical sun. 'I hope to goodness Algy is about,' he thought anxiously, twenty minutes later, as he peered through his centre section in the direction of the oasis.

He searched the sky in all directions, but not a sign of a British machine could he see, and he was about to turn away when something on the ground caught his eye. It was a Very light that curved upwards in a wide arc, and staring downward he made out an aeroplane bearing the familiar red, white, and blue marking standing in the shade of the palms that formed the oasis.

'By jingo, he's down there,' he muttered in a tone of relief, as he throttled back and began to drop down towards the stationary aeroplane. A doubt crossed his mind about the suitability of the sand as a landing surface, but realizing that the R.E.8*—for as such he recognized the waiting machine—must have made a safe landing, he glided in and touched his wheels as near to the trees as possible.

Somewhat to his surprise, he saw two figures detach themselves from the shadows and walk quickly towards him, but when he identified them as Algy and Major Raymond he smiled with satisfaction and relief. 'This is better luck than I could have hoped for,' he called, as he switched off, and hurried to meet them.

'I had an idea you'd be over to-day, so I got Lacey to bring me along,' returned the Major as he shook hands. 'Well, how are things going?'

'They're not going at all, as far as I can see,' answered Biggles doubtfully. 'I'm supposed to be looking for this fellow El Shereef, but I haven't started yet, for the simple reason that I haven't the remotest idea of where to begin; I might as well start looking for a pebble in the desert. I'm scared stiff of making a boob, and that's a fact. Do you know that by the time I got back yesterday the Huns knew I had been to see you?'

'Impossible,' cried the Major aghast.

'That's what I should have said if it had been any one else, but you wouldn't have thought so if it had been you standing on the mat in front of the Count, and that swine von Stalhein,' declared Biggles, with a

* British two-seater biplane designed for reconnaissance and artillery observation.

marked lack of respect. 'I don't mind telling you that I could almost hear the tramp of the firing party when the Old Man pushed the accusation at me point blank. I went all groggy, but I lied like a trooper and got away with it. That's what I hate about this spy game: it's all lies; in fact, as far as I can see, nobody tells the truth.'

'I'm sorry, but it's part of the game, Bigglesworth,' put in the Major quickly. 'What excuse have you made for getting away this morning?'

'No excuse was necessary; I've been sent out on a job, and that's why I'm so glad to see you.' In a few words he explained his quest.

The Major looked grave. 'It's very difficult, and how the Huns knew about these reinforcements is more than I can imagine,' he observed, with a worried frown. 'No, by Jove! There is a way,' he added quickly.

'I'm glad to hear that,' murmured Biggles thankfully.

'The Australian troops are hidden in the palm-groves around Sidi Arish, but they are leaving there to-night to take their places in the support trenches. You can report their position at Sidi Arish when you get back, and it will be quite safe; von Faubourg will get a photographic machine through by hook or by crook, and he will see that you are correct. The chances are that he will launch a bomb raid to-night, after midnight, by which time the Australians will have gone. In that way we can kill two birds with one stone. You'll put your reputation up with von Faubourg, and consolidate your position, and the Huns will waste a few tons of bombs.'

'Fine! We couldn't have planned a better situation,' declared Biggles delightedly. 'And look here, Algy, while I think of it. I have been wondering how you could get a message through to me in case of emergency. There's only one way that I can think of and

43

it's this, although it mustn't be done too often. Behind our aerodrome at Zabala there's a large olive-grove. You could fly over low at night and drop a non-committal message, cutting your engine twice in quick succession as a signal to let me know that you've done it.'

'It sounds desperate,' observed Algy doubtfully.

'It is, but it would only be done to meet desperate circumstances.'

'Quite, and I think it's a good idea,' broke in the Major. 'I've only one more thing to say. I'm afraid you won't like it, but an idea has been put up to me by H.Q., although they have no idea, of course, of the means I might employ to carry it out. As you are probably aware, the German troops along a wide sector of this front get their water by a pipe-line that is fed from the reservoir just north of your aerodrome.'

'I've noticed the reservoir from the air, but I didn't know it watered the troops. What about it, sir?'

'Can you imagine what a tremendous help it would be to us in making preparations for the next big attack if that water-supply failed?'

'I hope you are not going to ask me to empty the water out of the reservoir,' smiled Biggles.

'No, I was going to ask you to blow it up.'

The smile disappeared from Biggles' face like magic, and he staggered. 'Great goodness!' he gasped; 'you're not serious, sir?'

'Would I be likely to joke at such a juncture?'

'But you can't make troops die of thirst.'

The Major's brow darkened. 'My dear Bigglesworth,' he said firmly, 'how many times am I to remind you that we are at war? Either we go under, or Germany. The Germans wouldn't die of thirst anyway; they would merely be seriously inconvenienced.'

'But am I not taking enough risks already, without

44

going about blowing things up?' complained Biggles bitterly. 'It sounds a tall order to me.'

'On consideration you may find that it is not so difficult as you imagine. I can supply you with the instrument, a small but powerful bomb—in fact, I brought it with me on the off-chance. You could conceal it in your machine, and hide it when you got back; put it in a safe place until you are ready to use it. Then all you would have to do would be to touch off the time-fuse, set, say, for half an hour, and return to your quarters. That's all.'

'All! By Gosh! and enough, too,' cried Biggles. 'All right, sir,' he added quickly, in a resigned tone. 'Get me the gadget and I'll put it in my machine; I'll see what I can do.'

A small but heavy square box was quickly transferred from the back seat of the R.E. 8 to the underseat pocket of the Pup, and Biggles prepared to take his departure. 'It's going to be jolly awkward if the Huns want me to collect information, as I expect they will,' he observed thoughtfully. 'I wish you could arrange for some dummy camps, or aerodromes, to be put up so that I can report—' He broke off abruptly and stared upwards.

The others, following the direction of his eyes, saw a tiny aeroplane, looking like a silver and blue humming bird, flash in the sun as it turned, and then race nose down towards them.

Biggles recognized the machine instantly, and understood exactly what had happened. 'It's Leffens,' he yelled, 'the cunning devil's followed me. He's spotted me talking to you. Swing my prop, Algy—quick.'

He leapt into the cockpit of the Pup as the silver and blue Pfalz roared overhead, with the pilot hanging over the side staring at them.

In answer to Biggles' shrill cry of alarm Algy darted to the propeller of the Pup, and at the word 'contact', swung it with the ability of long practice. The engine was still hot, and almost before he could jump clear the machine was racing over the sand, leaving a swirling cloud of dust in its wake.

Biggles, crouching low in the cockpit, was actuated by one overwhelming impulse as he tore into the air, which was to prevent the Pfalz pilot from reaching Zabala and there denouncing him. That Leffens was flying at such an out-of-the-way spot by pure chance he did not for one moment believe; he knew instinctively that he had been followed, possibly at von Stalhein's instructions—but that was immaterial. The only thing that really mattered was that Leffens had seen him at what could only be a pre-arranged rendezvous with British R.F.C. officers, and he had no delusions about how the man would act or what the result would be. He knew that if he was to continue his work—and possibly the whole success of the British campaign in Palestine hung on his efforts—Leffens must not be allowed to return to Zabala.

Nevertheless, it looked as if he would succeed in getting back, and indeed he had every opportunity of doing so, for his flying start had given him a clear lead of at least two miles. But suddenly he did a curious thing: he turned in a wide circle and headed back towards the oasis. It may have been that he felt safe from pursuit; it may have been that he did not give Biggles credit for acting as promptly as he did; or it may have been that he wished to confirm some detail on the ground. Be that as it may, the fact remains that he turned, and had actually started a second dive towards the oasis when he saw the Pup zooming towards him like an avenging angel. He turned back sharply on his original course and sought to escape, but he had left it too late, for the Pup was slightly faster than the Pfalz.

Biggles pulled up the oil pressure handle of his Constantinesco* synchronizing gear and fired a short burst to warm his guns. His lips were set in a thin straight line, and with eyes fixed on the other machine he watched the gap close between them. He had no compunction about forcing a combat with Leffens. Quite apart from the fact that the German disliked him, or possibly suspected him, and was therefore a permanent source of danger, he now knew too much. Yet he was by no means a foeman to be despised, for six victories had already been recorded against his name in the squadron game-book**.

Biggles' hand closed over his firing lever, and he sent a stream of bullets down the wake of the fleeing scout. The range was, he knew, far too long for effective shooting, but the burst had the desired effect, and his lips parted slightly in a mirthless smile as he saw the Pfalz begin to sideslip.

'He's nervous,' was his unspoken thought, as he began to climb into position for attack.

But Leffens was looking back over his shoulder and started off on an erratic course to throw his pursuer off his mark. But it availed him little; in fact, in the end such tactics proved to be a disadvantage, for the manoeuvre caused him to lose speed, and with the Pup roaring down on his tail he was compelled to turn and fight.

With the cold deliberation of long experience, Biggles

---

* The synchronizing gear for machine-guns which interrupts the firing mechanism ensuring that the bullets do not hit the propeller blades but pass safely between them.
** Record of all enemy aircraft shot down by squadron members.

waited until he saw the stabbing tongues of flame leaping from the Pfalz's Spandau guns, and then he shoved the joystick forward with both hands. Straight down across the nose of the black-crossed machine he roared like a meteor, and then pulled up in a vertical Immelmann turn*. It was a brilliant move, beautifully executed, and before Leffens could grasp just what had happened the Pup was on his tail, raking the beautifully streamlined fuselage with lead.

But the Pfalz pilot was by no means beaten. He whirled round in a lightning turn and sent a stream of tracer bullets in the direction of the Pup. Biggles felt them hitting his machine, and flinched as he remembered the bomb under his seat, but he did not turn.

The German, unable to face the hail of lead that he knew was shooting his machine to pieces about him, acted with the speed of despair and took the only course left open to him: he flung joystick and rudder-bar over and spun earthward. But if he hoped by this means to throw Biggles off his tail he was doomed to disappointment: not for nothing had his opponent fought half a hundred such combats. The spin was the obvious course, and for a pilot to take the obvious course when fighting a superior foeman is suicidal, for the other man is prepared for the move and acts accordingly.

Leffens, grasping the side of his fuselage with his left hand, and still holding the machine in a spin, looked back, and saw the Pup spinning down behind him. He knew he could not spin for ever. Sooner or later he would have to pull out or crash into the sun-baked surface of the wilderness.

* The manoeuvre consists of a half roll off the top of a loop thereby quickly reversing the direction of flight. Named after Max Immelman, successful German fighter pilot 1914–1916 with seventeen victories, who was the first to use this turn in combat.

Biggles knew it, too, and waited with the calculating patience of the experienced air fighter. He saw the earth, a whirling band of brown and yellow, floating up to meet him, and saw the first movement of the Pfalz's tail as the German pilot kicked on top rudder to pull out of the spin. With his right hand gripping the firing lever he levelled out, took the silver and blue machine in his sights, and as its nose came up, fired. The range was too close to miss. The stricken Pfalz reared high into the air like a rocketing pheasant as the pilot convulsively jerked the joystick into his stomach; it whipped over and down in a vicious engine stall, and plunged nose first into the earth. Biggles could hear the crash above the noise of his engine, and caught his breath as a cloud of dust rose high into the air.

He passed his hand over his face, feeling suddenly limp, and circled round the wreck at stalling speed. In all directions stretched the wilderness, flat, monotonous, and forbidding, broken here and there by straggling camel-thorn bushes. The thought occurred to him that the German pilot might not have been killed outright, and the idea of leaving a wounded man in the waterless desert filled him with horror.

'I shall have to go down,' he muttered savagely. 'I don't want to, but I shall have to; I can't just leave him.'

He chose an open space as near as possible to the crash, landed safely, and hurried towards the shattered remains of the German machine. One glance told him all he needed to know. Karl Leffens was stone dead, shot through the head. He was lying in the wreckage with his right hand outflung. His glove had been thrown off, and Biggles caught the gleam of yellow metal. Stepping nearer, he saw that it was the signet

49

ring, shining in the sunlight. Automatically, he stooped and picked it up and dropped it in his pocket with a muttered, 'Might be useful—one never knows.'

Then he saluted his fallen opponent. 'Sorry, Leffens,' he said in a low voice, 'but it was either you or me for it. Your people threw the hammer into the works, so you can't blame anyone but yourself for the consequences.' Then, making a mental note to ask Algy to send out a burying party, he took off and returned to the oasis. But of the R.E.8 there was no sign, so he turned again and headed back towards Zabala.

On the way he unfolded his map and looked up the position of Sidi Arish, and smiled grimly when he saw that it was on the fringe of the area pointed out to him by von Faubourg. 'I hope the Old Man* will think I have done a good morning's work,' he murmured, as he opened his throttle wide and put his nose down for more speed.

* Slang: person in authority, the Commanding Officer.

Chapter 5
The New Bullet

It may have been fortunate for Biggles that by the time he reached Zabala a slight wind had got up and was sweeping low clouds of dust across the sandy expanse that served as the aerodrome, and that its direction made it necessary for him to swing round over the sheds in order to land. But it was not luck that made him look carefully below, and to left and right, as he skimmed in over the tarmac in order to see who was about. Thus it was that his eyes fell on von Stalhein standing alone on the lee side of the special hangar. There was nothing unusual about that, but with Biggles the circumstances were definitely unusual, for on the floor of his cockpit reposed an object that could hardly fail to excite the German's curiosity if he saw it. It was the explosive charge provided by Major Raymond.

It was not very large; indeed, it would have gone into the side pocket of his tunic; but the bulge would have been conspicuous, and it was not customary for airmen to fly with bulging pockets while canvas slots and cavities were provided in aeroplanes for the reception of such trifles as Very pistols, maps, and notebooks.

Consequently Biggles deliberately overshot and finished his run on the far side of the aerodrome in a slight dip that would conceal the lower part of his machine from watchers on the tarmac. He reached far over the side of the cockpit and dropped the bomb lightly on the sand with confidence, for as far as he knew that part of the aerodrome was seldom visited by any one, and the small object would hardly be likely to attract attention if a pilot did happen to see it.

It was as well that he took this precaution, for von Stalhein was waiting for him outside the hangar when he taxied in. Biggles nodded casually as he switched off, and without waiting to remove his flying kit set off in the direction of Headquarters 'Just a minute; where have you been?' von Stalhein called after him.

'I have been making a reconnaissance over the Jebel-Tel country—why?' replied Biggles carelessly.

'Did you see anything of Leffens? I believe he was going somewhere in that direction.'

'I saw a blue and silver machine—those are his colours, aren't they?'

The German's eyes never left Biggles' face. 'So! you saw him?' he exclaimed.

'I've said so, haven't I?' answered Biggles shortly. 'Is there anything particularly funny about that, if he was working in the same area? The heat made visibility bad, but I think it was his machine. I wish he'd keep away from me in the air; if the British see him hanging about without him attacking they may wonder why.'

'Did you have any trouble?'

'Nothing to speak of. But I've got an important report to make, so I can't stay talking now.' So saying, Biggles turned on his heel and walked quickly in the direction of the fort.

There was an odd expression on the Count's face as he looked up from his desk and saw who his visitor was. 'Well, what is it?' he asked irritably.

'The Australian troops are hidden among the palms around Sidi Arish, sir,' stated Biggles, without preamble.

A look of astonishment spread over the Count's face,

but it was quickly replaced by another in which grim humour, not unmixed with suspicion, was evident. 'So!' he said, nodding his head slowly. 'So! Where is Hauptmann von Stalhein?'

'On the tarmac, sir—or he was a moment ago.'

'Ask him to come here at once. That's all.'

Biggles left the room with the feeling that something had gone wrong, although he could not imagine what it was. Had the Count been pleased with his report, or had he not? He did not know, and the more he thought about it the less was he able to decide. He hurried around the corner of the sheds in search of von Stalhein, and then stepped back quickly as he saw him. For a moment he watched, wondering what he was doing, for he appeared to be working on the Pup's engine.

Biggles heard footsteps approaching, and rather than be found in the act of spying on his superior officer, he stepped out into the open and walked towards von Stalhein, who was now examining something that he held in the palm of his hand, something that he dropped quickly into his pocket when he heard some one coming.

'Will you please report to the Count immediately,' Biggles told him with an assurance he was far from feeling.

'Certainly,' replied the other. 'I shall be glad to see him,' he added, with a suspicion of a sneer, and limped off towards the fort without another word.

Biggles watched him go with mixed feelings.

'What the dickens was he up to?' he muttered in a mystified tone, as the German disappeared through the entrance to the fort. He took a swift pace or two to where von Stalhein had been standing. One glance, and he knew what had happened, for there, plain to see in the cowling, was a small round hole that could only have been made by one thing—a bullet. His heart gave an unpleasant lurch as he realised just what it implied, and his teeth came together with a click. 'That cunning devil misses nothing,' he growled savagely. 'He knows now that I've been under fire.' Then, seized by a sudden alarm, he lifted the cowling, and looking underneath, saw what he had feared. In a direct line with the puncture in the cowling there was another jagged hole in the wooden pattern that divided the engine from the cockpit. But the hole did not go right through. The bullet must have been stopped by it, in which case it should still be sticking in the stout ash board; but it was not.

'He found it, and he's dug it out with his pen-knife,' thought Biggles, moistening his lips. 'He'll know it's a German bullet,' he went on, thinking swiftly, with his brain trying to grasp the full purport of the new peril. then he gave a sigh of relief as an avenue of escape presented itself. 'It might have been fired some time ago; if he says anything about it I can say that it's always been there—was probably one of he shots fired by the Hun who brought the machine down,' he decided, turning towards the aerodrome buildings, for he did not want von Stalhein to return and see him examining the machine.

For a moment or two he was tempted to turn and jump into the machine and escape to the British lines while he still had an opportunity of doing so, but he fought back the desire, and then started as his eyes fell on two soldiers who had appeared round the corner of the hangars. He noticed that they carried rifles. They stopped when they saw him and leaned carelessly against the side of the hangar. 'Watching me, eh? You'd have shot me too, I expect, if I'd tried to get back into that machine,' he thought banefully. 'Well, now we know where we are, so I might as well go and get some lunch; it looks as if it might be my last.'

He walked unhurriedly to his room, changed, and then strolled into the ante-room of the Mess, where a number of officers were lounging prior to going in to lunch. A word or two of conversation that was going on between a small group at the bar reached his ears, and a cold shiver ran down his spine as he deliberately paused to listen. 'Leffens . . . late . . . new bullets . . .' were some of the words he heard.

In the ordinary way most of the regular flying officers ignored him, no doubt on account of his assumed traitorous character—not that this worried him in the least—but one of them, whose name he knew to be Otto Brandt, now detached himself from the group and came towards him.

'Haff you seen Leffens?' he asked, anxiously, in fair English.

Biggles felt all eyes on him as he replied, 'Yes, I saw him this morning, or I thought I did, near Jebel-Tel, but I was not absolutely certain. Why?'

'He hass not come back. It is tragic—very bad,' replied the German heavily.

'Very bad?' queried Biggles, raising his eyebrows.

'*Ja*, very bad—if he has fell. He was making test of the new bullets that came only yesterday. If he has fell in the British trench they will know of our new bullets at once, which is very bad for us.'

'Yes,' said Biggles, vaguely, in a strangled voice, wondering how he managed to speak at all, for his heart seemed to have stopped beating. He walked over to the window and stared out across the dusty aerodrome. 'So Leffens was carrying a new type of bullet,' he breathed, 'and von Stalhein has found one of them in my machine. 'That'll take a bit of explaining. Well, if they'll only give me until to-night I'll blow up their confounded reservoir, and then they can shoot me if they like.'

With these disturbing thoughts running through his head he walked through to the dining-room, had lunch, and then repaired to the aerodrome, observing that the two soldiers still followed him discreetly at a respectful distance. He was just in time to see a two-seater Halberstadt* take off and head towards the lines. Half a dozen Pfalz scouts followed it at once and took station just above and behind it.

'There goes the photographic machine with an escort,' he thought dispassionately, as they disappeared into the haze. He wondered vaguely what von Stalhein was doing, and how long it would be before he was confronted with Leffen's bullet and accused of double dealing; but then, deciding that it was no use meeting trouble half-way, he turned leisurely towards the pilot's map-room, where he studied the position of the reservoir, which was a well-known landmark. Satisfied that he could find the place in the dark, he returned to his quarters, to plan the recovery of the bomb which he had left on at the aerodrome, and await whatever might befall.

He had not long to wait, Heavy footsteps, accompanied by the unmistakable dragging stride of von Stalhein, sounded in the passage. They halted outside the door, which was thrown open. The Count and von Stalhein stood on the threshold.

'May we come in?' inquired von Stalhein, rather unnecessarily, tapping the end of his cigarette with his

---

* German two-seater fighter and ground attack biplane with two machine guns, one synchronised to fire through the propeller for the pilots use.

forefinger to knock off the ash, a curious habit that Biggles had often noticed.

'Of course,' he replied quickly. 'There isn't much room, but—'

'That's all right,' went on von Stalhein easily. 'The Chief would like to ask you a question or two.'

'I will do my best to answer it, you may be sure,' replied Biggles. Through the window, out of the corner of his eye, he saw the Halberstadt and its escort glide in, but his interest in them was short-lived, for the Count was speaking.

'Brunow, this morning you reported to me that you had located a division of Australian cavalry at Sidi Arish.' It was both a statement and a question.

'I did, sir.'

'Why?'

Biggles was genuinely astonished. 'I'm afraid I don't quite understand what you mean,' he answered frankly, with a puzzled look from one to the other.

'Then I will make the position clear,' went on the Count, evenly. 'The story I told you of the movement of Australian troops from Egypt was purely imaginary. I merely wished to test your—er—zeal, to find out how you would act in such circumstances. Now! What was your object in rendering a report which you knew quite well was incorrect?'

'Do you doubt my word, sir?' cried Biggles indignantly. 'I don't understand why you should consider such a course necessary. May I respectfully request, sir, that if you doubt my veracity you might post me to another command where my services would be more welcome than they are here?' He glared at von Stalhein in a manner that left no doubt as to whom he held responsible for the suspicion with which he was regarded.

The Count was obviously taken aback by the outburst. 'Do you still persist, then, that your report is authentic? Surely it would be a remarkable coincidence—'

There was a sharp tap on the door, and Mayer, the Staffel leader of the Halberstadt squadron, entered quickly. 'I'm sorry to interrupt you, sir,' he said briskly, 'but I was told you were here, and I thought you'd better see this without loss of time.' He handed the Count a photograph, still dripping from its fixing bath.

The Count held it on his open hand, and von Stalhein looked down at it over his shoulder.

'*Himmel!**' Von Faubourg's mouth opened in comical surprise, while von Stalhein threw a most extraordinary look in Biggles' direction.

'Brunow, see here,' cried the Count. 'But of course, you have seen it before, in reality.'

Biggles moved nearer and looked down at the photograph. It was one of the vertical type, and showed a cluster of white, flat-topped houses upon which several tracks converged. At intervals around the houses were three small lakes, or water-holes, beyond which were extensive groves of palm-trees. But it was not these things that held the attention of those who now studied the picture with practised eyes. Between the palms were long rows of horse-lines and clusters of tiny figures, foreshortened to ant-like dimensions, that could only be men.

The Count sprang to his feet. 'Splendid, Brunow,' he exclaimed, 'and you, too, have done well, Mayer. Come on, von Stalhein, we must attend to this.'

'But—' began von Stalhein, but the Count cut him short.

* Heavens!

'Come along, man,' he snapped. 'We've no time for anything else now.' With a parting nod to Biggles, he left the room, followed by the others. At the door von Stalhein turned, and leaning upon his sticks, threw another look at Biggles that might have meant anything. For a moment Biggles thought he was going to say something, but he did not, and as the footsteps retreated down the passage Biggles sank back in his chair and shook his head slowly.

'This business gives me the heebie-jeebies,' he muttered weakly; 'there's too much head-work in it for me. Well, the sooner I blow up the water-works the better, before my nerve peters out.'

Chapter 6
More Shocks

He remained in his quarters until the sun sank in a blaze of crimson and gold, and the soft purple twilight of the desert enfolded the aerodrome in its mysterious embrace. Quietly and without haste he donned his German uniform and surveyed himself quizzically for a moment in the mirror, well aware that he was about to attempt a deed that might easily involve him in the general destruction; then he crossed to the open window and looked out.

All was quiet. A faint subdued murmur came from the direction of the twinkling lights that marked the position of the village of Zabala; nearer at hand a gramophone was playing a popular waltz tune. There were no other sounds. He went across to the door and opened it, but not a soul was in sight. Wondering if the guard that had been set over him had been withdrawn, he closed the door quietly and returned to the window. For some minutes he stood still, watching the light fade to darkness, and then, feeling that the hush was getting on his nerves, he threw a leg across the window-sill and dropped silently on to the sand.

His first move he knew must be to retrieve the bomb before the moon rose; fortunately it would only be a slim crescent, but even so it would flood the aerodrome with a radiance that would make a person walking on it plainly visible to any one who happened to be looking in that direction. The light of the stars would be, he hoped, sufficient to enable him to find the small box that contained the explosive.

Resolutely, but without undue haste, he reached the tarmac and sauntered to its extremity to make sure no one was watching him before turning off at right angles into the darkness of the open aerodrome. He increased his pace now, although once he stopped to look back and listen; but only a few normal sounds reached him from the sparse lights of the aerodrome buildings, and he set about his search in earnest.

In spite of the fact that he had marked the place down very carefully, it took him a quarter of an hour to find the bomb, and he had just picked it up when a slight sound reached him that set his heart racing and caused him to spread-eagle himself flat on the sandy earth. It was the faint chink of one pebble striking against another.

That pebbles, even in the desert, do not strike against each other without some agency, human or animal, he was well aware, and as far as he knew there were no animals on the aerodrome. So, hardly daring to breathe, he lay as still as death, and waited. Presently the sound came again, nearer this time and then the soft pad of footsteps. He looked round desperately for a hiding-place. A few yards away there was a small wind-scorched camel-thorn bush, one of several that still waged a losing battle for existence on the far side of the aerodrome. As cover it was poor enough and in daylight it would have been useless, but in the dim starlight it was better than nothing, and he slithered towards it like a serpent. As he settled himself behind it facing the direction of the approaching footsteps, a figure loomed up in the darkness on the lip of the depression in which he lay. It was little more than a silhouette, but as such it stood out clearly, and he breathed a sigh of relief when he saw that it was an Arab in flowing burnous and turban. But what was an Arab doing on the aerodrome, which had been placed out of bounds for them? The man, whoever he was, was obviously moving with a fixed purpose, for he strode along with a swinging stride; he looked to neither right nor left and soon disappeared into the darkness.

Biggles lay quite still for a good five minutes wondering at the unusual circumstance. Had it been his imagination, or had there been something familiar about that lithe figure? Had it stirred some half-forgotten chord in his memory, or were his taut nerves playing him tricks? But he could not wait to ponder over the strange occurrence indefinitely, so with the bomb in his pocket, he set off swiftly but stealthily towards the distant lights.

He had almost reached them when, with an ear splitting bellow, an aero-engine opened up on the far side of the aerodrome, almost at the very spot where he had just been; it increased quickly in volume as the machine moved towards him, obviously in the act of taking off. In something like a mild panic lest he should be knocked down, he ran the last few yards to the end of the tarmac, and glancing upwards, could just manage to make out the broad wings of an aeroplane disappearing into the starlit sky. For a second or two he watched it, not a little mystified, for it almost looked as if the Arab he had seen had taken off; but deciding that it would be better to leave the matter for further consideration in more comfortable surroundings, he looked about him. No one was about, so holding the bomb close to his side, he hurried back to his quarters. 'I'd better see how this thing works before tinkering about with it in the dark, otherwise I shall go up instead of the waterworks,' he thought grimly.

He reached his room without incident, and, as far as he could ascertain, without being seen. Placing the bomb in the only easy chair the room possessed, he was brushing the sand from his uniform when a soft footfall made him turn. Count von Faubourg, in pyjamas and canvas shoes, was standing in the doorway.

Biggles' expression did not change, and he did not so much as glance in the direction of the box lying in the chair. 'Hello, sir,' he said easily. 'Can I do something for you?'

'No, thanks,' replied the Count, stepping into the room. 'I saw your light, so I thought I'd walk across to say that you did a good show this morning. I wasn't able to say much about it this afternoon because von Stalhein—well, he's a good fellow but inclined to be a bit difficult sometimes.'

'That's all right, sir, I quite understand,' smiled Biggles, picking up a cushion from one of the two upright chairs and throwing it carelessly over the box. He pushed the upright chair a little nearer to his Chief. 'Won't you sit down, sir?' he said.

'Thanks,' replied the Count. But to Biggles horror he ignored the chair he had offered and sat down heavily in the armchair. 'Hello, what the dickens is this?' he went on quickly, as he felt the lump below the cushion.

'Sorry, sir, I must have left my cigarettes there,' apologized Biggles, picking up the box and throwing it lightly on to the chest of drawers. In spite of his self-control he flinched as it struck heavily against the wood.

'What's the matter?' went on the Count, who was watching him. 'You look a bit pale.'

'I find the heat rather trying at first,' confessed Biggles. 'Can I get you a drink, sir?'

'No, thanks; I must get back to dress. But I thought

I'd just let you know that your work of this morning will not be forgotten; you keep on like that and I'll see that you get the credit for it.'

'Thank you very much, sir,' said Biggles respectfully, but inwardly he was thinking, 'Yes, I'll bet you will, you old liar,' knowing the man's reputation for taking all the credit he could get regardless of whom it really concerned. He was tempted to ask about the machine that had just taken off, but decided on second thoughts that perhaps it would be better not to appear inquisitive.

'Yes, I must be getting along,' repeated the Count, rising. 'By the way, I'll have one of your cigarettes.' He reached for the box.

'Try one of these, sir: they're better,' invited Biggles, whipping out his case and opening it. To his infinite relief the Count selected one, lit it, and moved towards the door.

'See you at dinner,' he said with a parting wave.

Biggles bowed and saluted in the true German fashion as his Chief departed, but as the door closed behind him he sat down limply and wiped the perspiration from his forehead. 'These shocks will be the death of me if nothing else is,' he muttered weakly, and glanced at his watch. He sprang to his feet and moved swiftly, as he saw that he had exactly one hour and ten minutes to complete his task and get back to the Mess before the gong sounded for dinner, when he would have to be present or his absence would be remarked upon.

He picked up the box, opened it, took out the metal cylinder it contained and examined it with interest. Down one side was a graduated gauge, marked in minutes, and operated by a small, milled screw. On the top was a small red plunger which carried a warning to the effect that the bomb would commence to operate from the moment it was depressed.

Not without some nervousness he screwed the gauge to its limit, which was thirty minutes, replaced the bomb in its box, and slipped it into his pocket. Then, picking up his cap and leaving the light still burning, he set off on his desperate mission.

The distance to the hill on which the reservoir was situated was not more than half a mile in a straight line, but he deliberately made a detour in order to avoid meeting any soldiers of the camp who might be returning from the village. He had become so accustomed to unexpected difficulties and dangers that he was both relieved and surprised when he reached the foot of the hill without any unforeseen occurrence; he found a narrow track that wound upwards towards the summit, and followed it with confidence until he reached the reservoir.

It was an elevated structure built up of several thicknesses of granite blocks to a height of perhaps five feet above the actual hill-top, and seemed to be about three-quarters full of water, a fact that he ascertained by the simple expedient of looking over the wall. Searching along the base, he found a place where the outside granite blocks were roughly put together, leaving a cavity wide enough to admit the bomb. The moon was just showing above the horizon, but a cloud was rapidly approaching it, so without any more ado he took the bomb from its case, forced the plunger home, and thrust it into the side of the reservoir. For a moment he hesitated, wondering as to the best means of disposing of the box; finally, he pushed it in behind the bomb, where its destruction would be assured. Then he set off down the hill just as the cloud drifted over the face of the moon.

He had taken perhaps a dozen paces when he was pulled up short by what seemed to be a barbed-wire fence; at first he could not make out what it was, but on looking closer he could just make out a stoutly built wire entanglement. An icy hand seemed to clutch his heart as he realized that it was unscalable, and that he was trapped within a few yards of a bomb which might, if there was any fault in its construction, explode at any moment.

Anxiously he looked to right and left, hoping to see the gap through which the path had led, but in the dim light and on the rocky hill-side he perceived with a shock that, having lost it, it might be difficult to find again.

The next five minutes were the longest he could ever remember. Stumbling along, he found the gap at last, as he was bound to by following the fence, but his nerves were badly shaken, and he ran down the path in a kind of horrible nightmare of fear that the bomb would explode before he reached camp.

'No more of this for me,' he panted, as, tripping over cactus and camel-thorn in his haste, he made his way by a roundabout course to the aerodrome. He struck it at the end of the tarmac, and was hurrying towards his quarters when he heard a sound that made him look upwards in amazement. It was the wind singing in the wires of a gliding aeroplane that was coming in to land.

It taxied in just as he reached the point where he had to turn to reach his room, and in spite of his haste, with the memory of the Arab still fresh in his mind, he paused to see who was flying in such strange conditions. He was half disappointed therefore when he saw Mayer climb out of the front seat of the machine, a Halberstadt, and stroll round to the tail unit to examine the rudder as if it was not working properly. There appeared to be no passenger, so without further loss of time Biggles went to his room, washed, brushed his clothes, and then went along to the dining-room. As he entered his eyes went instinctively to the clock. It was five minutes to eight. Dinner would be served in five minutes, and one minute later, if the bomb was timed accurately, the reservoir would blow up.

Several of the pilots nodded to him, from which he assumed that the success of his morning's reconnaissance had been made public property. Some were in semi-flying kit, and from snatches of conversation that he overheard he gathered that they had been detailed for a bombing raid which was to leave the ground shortly before midnight.

'Going to bomb the palm-trees at Sidi Arish,' he thought. 'Well, I—' His pleasant soliloquy ceased abruptly, and he stiffened instinctively as a sound floated in through the open windows. It was the low, musical cadence of an aero-engine rapidly approaching. Aeroplanes were common enough at Zabala, but not those carrying Rolls-Royce engines. Biggles recognized the deep, mellow drone, and knew that a British machine was coming towards the camp, probably an F.E. 2D.* So did some of the German pilots, and there was a general stampede towards the door.

'Put those lights out,' yelled von Faubourg, who appeared from nowhere, so to speak, without his tunic.

'Now we see der fun,' said Brandt, who stood at Biggles' elbow. 'Watch for der fireworks.'

Biggles started, for he, too, was expecting some fireworks—on a big scale, from the direction of the reser-

* Two-seater 'pusher' biplane with the engine behind the pilot and the gunner in the forward cockpit.

voir—but he did not understand Brandt's meaning. 'Fireworks?' he queried, as they stared up into the darkness.

'Der new battery on der hill is of der grandest—so! straight from der Western front, where it makes much practice. Watch der Engländer in der fireworks—ha!'

The exclamation was induced by a searchlight that suddenly stabbed in to the night sky from somewhere behind the hangars; it was followed immediately by another that flung its blinding shaft upward from a point of vantage near the top of the hill.

The pilot of the British machine, as if aware of his peril, pushed his nose down for more speed—a move that was made apparent to the listeners on the ground by the sudden increase of noise. Still visible, but with the searchlights sweeping across the sky to pick it up, it seemed to race low across the back of the fort and then zoom upwards. A hush fell on the watchers as its engine cut out, picked up, cut again, and again picked up.

Biggles felt the blood drain from his face as he recognized the signal. 'Dear goodness, it's Algy,' he thought, and itched to tell him to clear off before the searchlights found him; but he could only stand and watch helplessly.

A babel of excited voices arose from the German pilots as the nearest searchlight flashed for a fleeting instant on the machine, lost it, swept back again, found and held it. An F.E. 2D stood out in lines of white fire in the centre of the beam. The other lights swung across and intensified the picture. Instantly the air was alive with darting flecks of flame and hurtling metal from the archie battery on the hill which, with the cunning of long experience, had held its fire for this moment.

Bang—whoof . . . bang—whoof . . . bang—whoof . . .

thundered the guns as the British pilot, now fully alive to the danger, twisted and turned like a snipe to get out of the silent white arms that clung to him like the tentacles of an octopus.

A shell burst almost under the nose of the F.E., and a yell of delight rose from the Germans. 'I told you to watch der fireworks,' smiled Brandt knowingly, with a friendly nudge at Biggles, and then clutched at him wildly to prevent himself from falling as the earth rocked under their feet. It was as if the hill had turned into a raging volcano. A sheet of blinding flame leapt upwards, and a deep throated roar, like a thunderclap, almost shattered their ear-drums.

Simultaneously both searchlights went out, and a ghastly silence fell, a stillness that was only broken by the sullen plop—plop—plop of falling objects. Then a medley of sounds occurred together: yells, shrill words of command, and the rumble of falling masonry; but above these arose another noise, one that caused the Germans to stare at each other in alarm. It was the roar of rushing waters.

Biggles, who had completely forgotten his bomb in the excitement of watching the shelling of the F.E., was nearly as shaken as the others, but he was, of course, the only one who knew exactly what had happened.

Some of the officers darted off to see the damage, while others, discussing the explosion, drifted in to dinner, and Biggles, saying nothing but doing his best to hear the conversation, followed them. Some were inclined to the view that the explosion had been caused by a bomb dropped from the aeroplane, while others scouted the idea, pointing out that the machine had not flown over the hill while it had been under observation, or if it *had* flown over it before they were aware of its presence, then the delay between then and the time of the explosion was too long to be acceptable. Of von Stalhein there was no sign, and Biggles was wondering what had happened to him when the officers who had gone to the hill began to trickle back in ones or twos.

They had a simple but vivid story to tell. One wall of the reservoir had been blown clean out, and the vast weight of the pent-up water, suddenly released, had swept down the hill-side carrying all before it. It had descended on the archie battery even before the gunners were aware of it and had hurled them into the village, where houses had been swept away and stores destroyed. The earth had been torn from under the guns, which had rolled down the hill and were now buried under tons of rock, sand, and debris. The Count was on the spot with every man he could muster, trying to sort things out and collect a provisional store of water in empty petrol-cans, goat-skins, or any other receptacle he could lay hands on.

Biggles heard the story unmoved. That he had succeeded beyond his wildest hopes was apparent, and he only hoped that Algy had seen and would therefore report the incident to Major Raymond, who would in turn notify General Headquarters and enable them to take advantage of it. Thinking of Algy reminded him of the signal and what it portended, but to look for the message in the darkness was obviously out of the question. That was a matter that would have to be attended to in the morning.

He sat in the mess reading his German grammar until the noise of engines being warmed up told him that the night bombers were getting ready to start, so he went out on to the tarmac to watch the preparations.

A strange sense of unreality came over him as he watched the bustle and activity inseparable from such an event. How many times had he watched such a scene, in France, from his right and proper side of the lines. The queer feeling of loneliness came back with renewed force, and in his heart he knew that he loathed the work he was doing more than ever; he would have much preferred to be sitting in the cockpit of a bomber, waiting for the engine to warm up; in fact he would not have been unwilling to have taken his place in one of the Halberstadts, either as pilot or observer, and risk being shot down by his own people. 'It's all wrong,' he muttered morosely, as one by one the bombers took off, and the drone of the engines faded away into the distance. Lights were put out and silence fell upon the aerodrome; the only sounds came from the direction of the hill, where the work of salvage and repair was still proceeding. Feeling suddenly very sick of it all, he made his way, deep in thought, to his room, and without switching on the light threw himself upon the bed.

He suspected that he had dozed when some time later he sprang up with a start and stood tense, listening. Had he heard an aeroplane, or had he been dreaming? Yes! he could hear the whistling hum of an aeroplane gliding in distinctly now, and he crossed to the window in a swift stride, with a puzzled frown wrinkling his forehead. 'What the dickens is going on,' he muttered. 'I never heard so much flying in my life as there is in this place.' The thought occurred to him that it might be one of the bombers returning with engine trouble and he waited for it to taxi in, but when it did not come his rather vague interest increased to wonderment.

As near as he could judge, the machine must have landed somewhere over the other side of the aerodrome, near the depression in which he had dropped the bomb and from which the mysterious machine had taken off earlier in the evening. 'That's the same kite come back home, I'll warrant,' he thought with increasing curiosity, and settling his elbows on the window-sill he stared out across the silent moon-lit wilderness. But he could see nothing like an aeroplane, and he was about to turn away when a figure came into view, walking rapidly. At first it was little more than a dim shadow, but as it drew nearer he saw that it was an Arab in burnous and turban. Was it the same man . . . ?

Breathlessly he watched him approach. He wanted to dash outside in order to obtain a clearer view of him in case he disappeared, so he continued watching from the window with a kind of intense fascination while his fingers tingled with an excitement he found difficult to control. It was a weird picture. The silent moonlit desert and the Arab striding along as his forebears had done in Biblical days.

It soon became clear that he was making for the fort. Biggles watched him disappear through the entrance, and a few seconds later a light appeared in one of the end windows. He knew that there was no point in watching any longer. 'I've got to see inside that window,' he muttered, as he kicked off his shoes and stole out into the corridor.

With the stealth of an Indian, he crept along the back of the hangars until the black bulk of the old building loomed up in front of him. The light was still shining in the window, which was some six feet above ground-level, just too high for him to reach without something to stand on. He hunted round with desperate speed, afraid that the light would go out while he was thus engaged, and in his anxiety almost fell upon an old oil drum that lay half buried in the sand. He dragged it out by brute strength, and holding it under his arm, crept back to the wall of the fort, below the window from which streamed the shaft of yellow light. A cautious glance round and he stood the drum in place.

His heart was beating violently; he began to raise himself, inch by inch, to the level of the window. Slowly and with infinite care, he drew his eyes level and peeped over the ledge.

He was down again in an instant, struggling to comprehend what he had seen, almost afraid that the man within would hear the thumping of his heart, so tense had been the moment. At a large desk in the centre of the room von Stalhein was sitting in his shirt sleeves, writing. The inevitable cigarette smouldered between his lips and his monocle was in place. His sticks rested against the side of the desk.

Biggles' first reaction was of shock, followed swiftly by bitter disappointment, for it seemed that he had merely discovered von Stalhein's private office, and it was in this spirit that he picked up the drum, smoothed out the mark of its rim in the sand, and replaced it where he had found it. Then he hurried back towards his room. On reaching it he crossed to the window and looked out. The light had disappeared.

Slowly, and lost in a whirl of conflicting thoughts, he took off his uniform and prepared for bed. 'I wonder,' he said softly—'I wonder.'

What he was wondering as he sank into sleep was if a slim dandy with a game leg could change his identity to that of the brilliant, athletic, hard-riding Arab who was known mythically on both sides of the lines as El Shereef, the cleverest spy in the German Secret Service.

Chapter 7
Still More Shocks

Tired out, he was still in bed the following morning when he was startled by a peremptory knock on the door, which, without invitation, was pushed open, and the Count closely followed by von Stalhein strode into the room. If any further indication were needed that something serious was afoot, a file of soldiers with fixed bayonets who halted in the corridor supplied the deficiency.

Biggles sprang out of bed with more haste than dignity, and regarded the intruders with astonishment that was not entirely feigned.

'All right, remain standing where you are,' ordered the Count curtly. 'Where were you last night?'

'In my room, sir, where you yourself saw me,' replied Biggles instantly. 'After dinner—'

'Never mind that. Where were you between the time I left you and dinner time?'

'I stayed here for a little while after you had gone, and then as the heat was oppressive—as you will remember I complained to you—I went out and sat on the tarmac.'

'Were you with anybody?'

'No, sir, by myself.'

'In which case you have no proof that you were where you *say* you were.'

'On the contrary, I think I can prove it to you, sir.'

'How?'

'Because while I was sitting there I saw Mayer land

in a Halberstadt. You can verify that he did so. If I had not been there I could not have seen him.'

'That's no proof. Every one in the Mess knew that Mayer was flying,' put in von Stalhein harshly.

Biggles met his eyes squarely. 'I can tell you exactly how he behaved when he landed,' he said quietly. 'I couldn't learn that in the Mess.'

'Send for Mayer,' said the Count crisply.

There was silence for two or three minutes until he came.

'Can you remember exactly what was the first thing you did when you landed last night?' asked the Count tersely.

Mayer looked puzzled.

'May I prompt his memory, sir?' asked Biggles. And then, looking straight at Mayer, he went on, 'You jumped out as soon as you reached the tarmac and walked back to the empennage* of the machine. You then tried the rudder as if it was heavy on controls.'

Mayer nodded. 'That's perfectly true; I did,' he agreed.

'All right, you may go,' barked the Count, and then turning to Biggles. 'Very well, then, we'll say you were on the tarmac,' he said grimly, 'in which case you may find it hard to explain how *that* found its way to the hill-side, near the reservoir.' He tossed a small gold object on to the table.

Biggles recognized it at once; it was his signet ring. It did not fit very well, and must have fallen from his finger while he was hunting for the gap in the wire. The most amazing thing was he had not missed it. To say that he was shaken as he stared at it, gleaming

* General term referring to the tail unit of any aircraft—the tail plane, elevators, fin and rudders.

dully on the table, would be an understatement of fact. He was momentarily stunned by such a damning piece of evidence. For a period of time during which a man might count five he stared at it dumbfounded, inwardly horror-stricken.

In the deathly hush that had fallen on the room the match that von Stalhein struck to light his cigarette sounded like a thunderclap.

Biggles' brain, which for once seemed to have failed, like an aero engine when the spark is cut off, suddenly went on again at full revs. He dragged his eyes away from the unmistakable evidence of his guilt and looked at the Count with a strange expression on his face, aware that von Stalhein's eyes were boring into him, watching his every move.

'I think I can explain that, sir, although you may find it hard to believe.'

'Go on, we are listening.'

'Leffens must have dropped it there.'

'*Leffens!*'

'Yes, sir, he had my ring.'

'*Had your ring!*' The Count's brain was working slowly, and even von Stalhein dared not interrupt.

'Yes, sir; I lent it to him yesterday morning. I met him on the tarmac, just as he was getting into his machine. He told me he had forgotten his ring, and that it would mean bad luck to go back for it. So as he was in a hurry I lent him mine.'

'But I saw you wearing yours only yesterday evening,' snapped von Stalhein, unable to contain himself.

'Not mine, Leffen's,' answered Biggles suavely. 'He suggested I had better borrow his during his absence, and told me that it was lying on his dressing-table. I fetched it and have worn it ever since. I've been meaning to report the matter.'

76

'Then why aren't you wearing it now?'

'I always take it off to wash, prior to going to bed,' returned Biggles easily.

He took Leffens' ring from the drawer of his dressing-table where he had placed it when he returned from the flight in which he had shot down the rightful owner of the ring. He tossed the tiny circle of gold on to the table with the other.

Another ghastly silence fell in which he could distinctly hear the ticking of his wrist-watch. In spite of the tension his brain was running easily and smoothly, with a deadly precision born of dire peril, and he looked at his interrogators, whose turn it was to stare at the table, with an expression of injured dignity on his face.

Strangely enough, it was the Count who recovered himself first, and he looked back at Biggles half apologetically and half in alarm. 'But your ring was found on the hill-side,' he said in a half whisper. 'Surely you are not suggesting that Leffens had any hand in the blowing up of the reservoir?'

Biggles shrugged his shoulders. He saw von Stalhein feeling in his pocket and knew he was searching for the incriminating bullet, so he went on quickly. 'I am not suggesting anything, sir, nor can I imagine how it got there. I only know that for some reason Leffens disliked me; in fact, he tried to kill me.'

'*Tried to kill you?*' The Count literally staggered.

'Yes, sir; he dived down at me out of the sun and tried to shoot me down. It was a clever attack, and unexpected; some of his bullets actually hit the machine. He zoomed back up into the sun and disappeared, but not before I had seen who it was. There is just a chance, of course, that he mistook my machine for an authentic enemy aircraft.' Biggles could see that even von Stalhein was impressed.

'But why in the name of heaven didn't you report it?' cried the Count aghast.

'I most certainly should have done so, sir, had Leffens returned. After I made my report to you I went back to the tarmac to hear his explanation first. But he did not come, and assuming that he had been shot down, I decided, rightly or wrongly, to let the matter drop rather than make such an unpleasant charge in his absence. Do you mind if I smoke, sir?'

'Certainly, Brunow, smoke by all means,' answered the Count in a change of voice.

Biggles lit a cigarette. Out of the corner of his eye he saw von Stalhein drop the bullet back into his pocket and knew that he had spoken just in time. 'Have I your permission to dress now, sir?' he asked calmly. 'And I should like a few minutes' conversation with you when you have a moment to spare.'

'Certainly, certainly. But why not speak now? I shall be very busy to-day; this confounded reservoir business is the very devil.'

'Very well, sir.' Biggles swung round and his jaws set grimly. 'I have a request to make, but before doing so, would respectfully remind you that I came here under open colours, not at my own instigation or by my own wish, but at the invitation—under the orders if you like—of the German Government. But it seems that for some reason or other I have been regarded with suspicion from the moment I arrived by certain members of your staff. I therefore humbly beg your indulgence in what is to me a very unhappy position, and would ask you to post me to another station, or give me leave to go my own way.'

It was a bold stroke of bluff, and for one ghastly moment Biggles thought he had gone too far, for the last thing he wanted at that juncture was to be posted away.

But the Count reacted just as he hoped he would. 'Nothing of the sort, Brunow,' he said in a fatherly tone. 'I'm sorry if there has been a misunderstanding in the past, but I think we all understand each other now.' He glanced at von Stalhein meaningly. 'You get dressed now and hurry along for your coffee,' he went on. 'As far as I know I shan't be needing you this morning, but don't go far away in case I do. Come on Erich.'

They went out and closed the door behind them.

Biggles poured himself out a glass of water with a hand that trembled slightly, for the ordeal he had just been through had left him feeling suddenly weak. Then he slumped down into a chair and buried his face in his hands. 'Gosh!' he breathed, 'that was closeish—too close for my liking.'

Chapter 8
Forced Down

'Well, I must say that was a good start for a day's work,' he went on as he pulled himself together, dressed, and walked over to the Mess for morning coffee. 'I got away with it that time, but I shan't do it every time; one more boob like that and it'll be the last.'

With these morbid thoughts, he made his way to the olive grove where, after ascertaining as far as it was possible that he was not watched, he began a systematic search for the message he knew Algy must have dropped. It took him a long time, but he found it at last caught up in the branches of one of the grey, gnarled trees that must have been old when the Crusaders were marching on Jerusalem. It was merely a small piece of khaki cloth, weighted with two cartridges, to which was attached a strip of white rag about a yard long. A thousand people might have seen it and taken it for a piece of wind-blown litter without suspecting what it contained.

After a cautious glance around he secured it, opened the khaki rag, and removed the slip of paper he guessed he would find in it; the improvised rag streamer and cartridges he dropped into a convenient hole in the tree. One glance was sufficient for him to memorize the brief message. In neat Roman capitals had been printed:

IMPORTANT NEWS. SPEAK AT RENDEZVOUS AS SOON AS
POSSIBLE.

That was all. He rolled the paper into a ball, slipped
it into his mouth, chewed it to a pulp, and then threw
it away.

'What's wrong now?' he wondered, as he made his
way back to the tarmac. 'Why didn't he write the
message down while he was about it? No, of course, he
daren't do that: it would have been too risky; and he
would have had no means of knowing if I'd got it,
anyway.'

Still turning the matter over in his mind, and trying
to think of a reasonable excuse to go for a flight, he
reached the aerodrome. There were a few mechanics
about, most of them at work on machines, but nearly
all the serviceable aeroplanes were in the air. Of the
Count there was no sign; nor could he see von Stalhein.
Thinking of von Stalhein reminded him of his nocturnal
adventure and the mysterious Arab; he had little time
to think, but he felt instinctively that he was now on
the track of something important. That von Stalhein
might be El Shereef had not previously occurred to
him, and even now he only regarded it as a remote
possibility, for the two characters were so utterly different from the physical aspect alone that the more he
thought about it the more fantastic a dual personality
appeared to be. Nevertheless, he had already decided
to watch von Stalhein, and keep an eye open after
dark for the Arab who appeared to have access to
the Headquarters' offices; but at the moment his chief
concern was to get to Abba Sud as quickly as possible.

To fly without permission after having been warned
by the Count to keep close at hand would have been
asking for trouble, so he made his way boldly to the

fort and asked the Count if he could do a reconnaissance, making the excuse that it was boring doing nothing. To his great relief the Count made no objection, and he hurried back to the hangars in high spirits. He half regretted that he was wearing his German uniform, for it meant taking a German machine, but in the event of a forced landing on either side of the lines a German officer in a British machine would certainly be looked at askance. So more with the idea of making himself acquainted with its controls than for any other reason, he ordered out a Halberstadt in preference to a Pfalz, and was soon in the air.

He set off on a direct course for the lines, but as soon as he was out of sight of the aerodrome he swung away to the east in the direction of the oasis. Twice he was sighted and pursued by British machines, and rather than risk being attacked by pilots whose fire, for obvious reasons, he would be unable to return, he climbed the Halberstadt nearly to its ceiling, keeping a sharp look-out all the time.

He had been flying on his new course about ten minutes, and was just congratulating himself that he was now outside the zone of air operations, when his roving eyes picked out, and instantly focused on, a tiny moving speck far to the south-east. At first glance he thought it was an eagle, for mistakes of this sort often occurred in eastern theatres of war, but when he saw that it was almost at his own height he knew that it must be an aeroplane. He edged away at once a few points to the south, in order to place himself between the sun and the other machine, and putting his nose down for more speed, rapidly overhauled the stranger. While he was still a good two miles away he saw that it was a Halberstadt like his own, and his forehead wrinkled into a puzzled frown when he perceived that it was heading out over the open desert. 'Where the dickens does that fellow think he's going?' he mused, for as far as he could remember there was nothing in that direction but wilderness for a hundred miles, when the flat desolation gave way to barren hills. There were certainly no troops or military targets to account for its presence.

'I'll keep an eye on you, my chicken,' he thought suspiciously. 'It will be interesting to see what your game is.' It struck him that it might be a pilot who had lost his way, but the direct course on which the machine was flying quickly discountenanced such a theory; a pilot who was lost would be almost certain to turn from side to side as he looked for possible landmarks.

'My word! it's hot, even up here,' he went on, with a questioning glance at the sun, which had suddenly assumed an unusual reddish hue. Later he was to recognize that significant sign, but at the time he had not been in the East long enough to learn much about the meteorological conditions. But he dismissed the phenomenon from his mind as the other machine started losing height, and throttling back to half power, he followed it, still taking care not to lose his strategical position in the sun. And then a remarkable thing occurred; it was so odd that he pushed up his goggles with a quick movement of his hand and stared round the side of the windscreen with an expression of comical amazement on his face. The machine in front had disappeared. In all his flying experience he had never seen anything like it. He had seen machines disappear into clouds, or into ground mist, but here there were no clouds; nor was there a ground mist. Wait a minute, though! He was not so sure. The earth seemed to have become curiously blurred, distorted. 'Must be heat haze,' he thought, and then clutched at a centre-section strut as the Halberstadt reeled and reared up on its tail. Before he could bring it to even keel it seemed to drop right out of his hands, and he clenched his teeth as his stomach turned over in the most terrific bump* he had ever struck. The machine hit solid air again with a crash that he knew must have strained every wire and strut; it was almost like hitting water.

For a moment he was too shaken and startled to wonder what had happened; if he thought anything at all in the first sickening second, it was that his machine had shed its wings, for it had fallen like a stone for nearly two thousand feet, as his altimeter revealed; but as the first spatter of grit struck his face and the horizon was blotted out, he knew that he had run into a sandstorm, a gale of wind that was tearing the surface from the desert and hurling it high into the air.

He wasted no time in idle contemplation of the calamity. He had never before seen a sandstorm, but he had heard them described by pilots who had been caught in them and had been lucky enough to survive. With the choking dust filling his nostrils and stinging his cheeks, he forgot all about the machine he had been following and sought only to evade the sand demon. He shoved the throttle wide open, turned at right angles, and with the joystick held forward by both hands, he raced across the path of the storm. At first the visibility grew rapidly worse as he encountered the full force of it, and the Halberstadt was tossed about like a dead leaf in an autumn gale, but presently the bumps grew less severe and the ground again came into view, mistily, as though seen through a piece of brown, semi-opaque glass. As far as he could see

* A local disturbance of air currents causing rough or uneven flying. Due either to clouds, wind or changes in the air temperature.

stretched the wind-swept desert, with the sand dunes rolling like a sea swell and a spindrift of fine grit whipping from their crests. But in one place a long narrow belt of palms rose up like an island in a stormy ocean, and towards it he steered his course. From the vicious lashing of the trees he knew that the wind must be blowing with the force of a tornado, and to land in it might be a difficult matter, but with the certain knowledge that the dust which was now blinding him would soon work its way into the engine and cut it to pieces, he decided that his only course was to get down as quickly as possible, whatever risks it involved; so he pushed his nose down at a steep angle towards the trees, aiming to touch the ground on the leeward side of them.

The landing proved to be more simple than he thought it would be; he could not see the actual surface of the ground as he flattened out on account of the thick stream of air-borne sand that raced over it like quicksilver, but he knew to a few inches where it was. He felt his wheels touch, bump, bump again, and he kicked his rudder bar to avoid a clump of trees that straggled out in the desert a little way from the main group. The landing was well judged, and there was no need to open the throttle again, for his run had carried him amongst the outlying palms of the oasis. He was out in a flash, carrying two of the sandbags with which all desert-flying machines are equipped against such an emergency. Dropping to his knees, he dragged the sand into the bags with both arms and then tied them, by the cords provided for the purpose, to the wingskids.* He was only just in time, for even with these

* Semicircular hoops attached below the wings, towards the tips, to prevent damage to the wings when taxi-ing the aircraft.

anchors the machine began to drag as the wind increased in violence, so he fetched the two remaining sandbags, filled them, and tied them to the tail-skid.

'If you blow over now, well, you'll have to blow over; I can't do any more,' he thought, as, choking and half blinded by the stinging sand, he ran into the oasis and flung himself down in the first dip he reached. The sand still stung his face unmercifully, so he took off his tunic, wrapped it about his head, and then lay down to wait for the storm to blow itself out.

He was never sure how long he lay there. It might have been an hour; it might have been two hours; it seemed like eternity. The heat inside the jacket was suffocating, and in spite of all he could do to prevent it, the sand got inside and found its way into his nose, mouth, and ears. It was with heartfelt thankfulness that he heard the wind abating and knew that the worst of the storm was over; at the end it died away quite suddenly, so removing the coat, he sat up and looked about with interest. His first thought was for the machine, and he was relieved to find that it had suffered no damage, so he turned his attention to the immediate surroundings.

The oasis was exactly as he expected it to be; in fact oases in general were precisely as he had always imagined. Some things are not in the least like what artists and writers would lead us to expect; many are definitely disappointing; very few reach the glamorous perfection of our dreams, but the oasis of the desert is certainly one of them.

He found himself standing on a frond-littered sandy carpet from which the tall, straight columns of the date palms rose to burst in feathery fan-like foliage far overhead. Nearer to the heart of the oasis tussocks of coarse grass sprouted through the sand and gave promise of more sylvan verdure within, possibly water. 'In any case the water can't be far below the surface,' he thought as he hurried forward in the hope of being able to quench his thirst. He topped a rise and saw another one beyond. Almost unthinkingly he strode across the intervening dell and ran up the far side. As his eyes grew level with the top, he stopped, not quickly, but slowly, as if his muscles lagged behind his will to act. Then he sank down silently and wormed his way into a growth of leathery bushes that clustered around the palm-boles at that spot. For several seconds he lay quite still, while his face worked under the shock which for a moment seemed to have paralysed his brain. 'I'm dreaming. I'm seeing things. It must be a mirage,' he breathed, as he recovered somewhat and crawled to where he could see the scene beyond. But the sound of voices reached him and he knew it was no illusion.

In front of him the ground fell away for a distance of perhaps fifty yards into a saucer-like depression, in the bottom of which was obviously a well. Around the well, in attitude of alert repose, were about a score of Arabs, some sitting, some lying down, and others leaning against the parapet of the well from which they had evidently been drinking. But they were all looking one way; and they were all listening—listening to a man who stood on the far side of the well with his hands resting on the parapet, talking to them earnestly. It was Hauptmann Erich von Stalhein.

To Biggles the whole thing was so unexpected and at the same time so utterly preposterous that he could only lie and watch in a kind of fascinated wonder. And the more he watched and thought about it the more incomprehensible the whole thing became. How on earth had von Stalhein got there when only two hours before he had interrogated him in his room at Zabala, which could not be less than sixty miles away? What was he doing there, with the Arabs? Why was he addressing them so fervently?

His astonishment gave way to curiosity and then to intense interest as he watched the scene. It seemed to him that von Stalhein, from his actions, was exhorting the Arabs to do something, something they were either disinclined to do, or about which they were divided in their opinions. But after a time it became apparent that the powerful personality of the man was making itself felt, and in the end there was a general murmur of assent. Then, as if the debate was over, the party began to break up, some of the Arabs going towards a line of wiry-looking ponies that were tethered between the trees, and others, with von Stalhein, going into a small square building that stood a short distance behind the well. It was little more than a primitive hut, constructed of sun-dried mud bricks and thatched with dead palm fronds.

The Arabs who went to their horses mounted and rode away through the trees, and presently those who had gone into the building reappeared, and they, too, rode away. Silence fell, the blazing sun-drenched silence of the desert.

Biggles lay quite still, never taking his eyes off the hut for an instant, waiting for von Stalhein to reappear. An hour passed and he did not come out. Another hour ticked slowly by. The sun passed its zenith and began to fall towards the west, and still he did not come. Biggles' thirst became unbearable. 'I've got to drink or die,' he declared quietly to himself, as he rose to his feet and walked towards the well. 'If he sees me I can only tell the truth and say I was forced down by the storm, which he can't deny,' he added thoughtfully.

He reached the well, and dragging up a bucket of

the life-saving liquid, drank deeply; that which he could not drink he splashed over his smarting face and hands. 'And now, Erich, let us see how you behave when you get a shock,' he thought humorously, for the drink had refreshed him, as he walked boldly up to the door of the hut, which stood ajar. He pushed it open and entered. A glance showed him that the entire building comprised a single room, but it was not that which made him stagger back and then stand rooted to the ground with parted lips. The room was empty. At first his brain refused to accept this astounding fact, and he looked from floor to ceiling as if expecting to see them open up and deliver the missing German in the manner of a jack-in-the-box. He also looked round the walls for a door that might lead to another room, but there was none.

'Well, I've had some shocks in my time, but this beats anything I've ever run up against before,' he muttered. Beyond doubt or question von Stalhein had gone into the hut; only Arabs had come out. Where was von Stalhein? He left the hut, and hurrying to where the horse lines had been, saw a wide trail of trampled sand leading to the edge of the oasis. A long way out in the desert to the south-west a straggling line of horsemen was making its way towards the misty horizon; farther south a solitary white Bisherin racing camel, with a rider on its back, was eating distance in a long rolling stride that in time could wear down the finest horse ever bred. 'So you've changed the colour of your skin again, have you, Mr. von Stalhein?' thought Biggles, as the only possible solution of the problem flashed into his mind. 'Good; now we know where we are. I fancy I'm beginning to rumble your little game — El Shereef.'

As he turned away a wave of admiration for the

German surged through him. 'He's a clever devil and no mistake,' he thought. 'But how the dickens did he get here? He must have flown; there was no other way he could have done it in the time. That's it. He was in the machine I saw. Some one flew him over, dropped him at the oasis, and then went back. They didn't hear me arrive because of the noise of the wind and I was on the lee-side of them. The Arabs were waiting here for him, and now he has gone off on some job. I wonder if this place is a regular rendezvous.'

The word rendezvous reminded him of Algy and his belated appointment. 'He'll think I'm not coming,' he muttered as he broke into a run that carried him over the brow of the hill behind which he had left the Halberstadt. As it came into view he gave a gasp and twisted suddenly; but it was too late. A sea of scowling faces surged around him. He lashed out viciously, but it was no use. Blows rained on him and he was flung heavily to the ground, where, half choked with sand, he was held down until his hands were tied behind his back.

Cursing himself for the folly of charging up to the machine in the way he had, and for leaving his revolver in the cockpit, he sat up and surveyed his captors sullenly. There were about fifteen of them, typical Bedouins* of the desert, armed with antiquated muskets. A medley of guttural voices had broken out, but he could not get the hang of the conversation; he rather suspected from the way some of them fingered their wicked-looking knives that they were in favour of dispatching him forthwith, and were only prevented from doing so by others who pointed excitedly towards the

* A tent-dwelling nomadic Arab. Different groups supported both sides in the First World War.

west. Eventually these seemed to get the best of the argument, for he was pulled to his feet and invited by actions and grimaces to mount a horse, which was led forward from a row that stood near the machine. The Arabs all mounted, and without further parley set off at a gallop across the desert in a straggling bunch with Biggles in the centre.

Chapter 9
A Fight and an Escape

That ride will live in Biggles' memory for many a day. The heat, the dust, thirst, the flies that followed them in a cloud, all combined to make life almost unbearable, and as the sun began to fall more quickly towards the western horizon he prayed for the end of the journey wherever or whatever it might be.

It came at last, but not in the manner he expected; nor, indeed, in the manner the Bedouins expected. The sand had gradually given way to the hard, pebbly clay, with occasional clumps of camel-thorn, which in Palestine usually forms the surface of the wilderness proper, and low rocky hills began to appear. They were approaching the first of these when without warning a line of mounted horsemen, riding at full gallop and shooting as they came, tore round the base of the hill and swept down towards them.

Their appearance was the signal for a general panic amongst the Bedouins. Without halting, they swerved in their course and sought safety in flight; in this way one or two of the better mounted ones did eventually succeed in escaping, but the others, overhauled by their pursuers, could only turn and fight stubbornly. Their prisoner they ignored, and Biggles was left sitting alone on his horse until, stung by a ricochetting bullet, it reared up and threw him. With his hands still tied he fell heavily, and the breath was knocked out of him, so he lay where he had fallen, wondering how long it would be before one of the flying bullets found him.

He had no interest in the result of the battle, which appeared to be purely a tribal affair between locals; if his captors won, then matters would no doubt remain as they were; if the newcomers won, his fate could not be much worse, for at that moment it seemed to him that death was better than the intolerable misery of being dragged about the wilderness.

Presently the firing died away and the sound of horses' hooves made him sit up. Of his original captors none remained; those who had been compelled to fight lay dead or dying, a gruesome fact that caused him little concern. The newcomers, nearly fifty of them, were riding in, obviously in high spirits at their success.

To his astonishment they lifted him to his feet, cut his bonds, and made signals that he had nothing more to fear. They tried hard to tell him something, but he could not follow their meaning, so after a brief rest he was again invited to mount a horse and the whole party set off at a swinging gallop towards the hills. Dusk fell and they were compelled to steady the pace, but still they rode on.

Biggles was sagging in the saddle, conscious only of a deadly tiredness, when he was startled by the ringing challenge of a British sentry.

'Halt! who goes there?'

Several voices answered in what he assumed was Arabic, and there followed a general commotion, in which he was made to dismount and walk towards a barbed-wire fence which he could see dimly in the fast failing light. Behind its protective screen were a number of canvas bell tents, camouflaged in light and dark splashes of colour. Nearer at hand was a larger tent, rectangular in shape, and a number of British Tommies in khaki drill jackets, shorts, and pith helmets. A young officer, tanned to the colour of mahogany by the sun, stepped forward towards the Arabs, and another conversation ensued in which Biggles could only understand a single word, one that appeared often—*baksheesh**. Eventually the officer went back to the larger tent, and presently returned with a corporal and two men who carried rifles with fixed bayonets; in his hand was a slip of paper which he handed to the man who appeared to be the leader of the Arabs, and who, without another word, turned his horse and rode away into the night followed by the others.

Biggles was left facing the officer, with a soldier on each side of him. At a word of command they moved forward to a gate in the wire, and halted again a few yards from the large tent, in which a light was now burning.

Then Biggles saw a curious thing. A distorted shadow of a man, who was evidently standing inside the tent between the canvas and the light, leaned forward; a hand was lifted with a perfectly natural movement of the arm, and tapped the ash off the cigarette it held between its fingers. Biggles had seen the same action made in reality too many times to have any doubt as to who it was; of all the men he knew only one had that peculiar trick of tapping the ash off his cigarette with his forefinger. It was von Stalhein. As he watched the shadow dumbfounded, wondering if his tired eyes were deceiving him, it disappeared, and the officer addressed him.

'Do you speak English?' he asked curtly.

'A little—yes,' replied Biggles, in the best German accent he could muster.

'Will you give me your parole?'

'Parole?'

* Money, payment.

94

'Will you give your word that you will not attempt to escape?'

Biggles shook his head. '*Nein**,' he said harshly.

'As you wish. It would have made things easier for you if you had. Don't give me more trouble than you can help, though; I may as well tell you that I have just had to pay out good British money to save your useless hide.'

'Money?'

'Yes; those Arabs demanded fifty pounds for you or threatened to slit your throat there and then. I couldn't watch them do that even though you are a German, so I gave them a chit for fifty pounds which they will be able to cash at any British pay-office. I mention it in the hope that you will be grateful and not give me more trouble than you can help before I can get rid of you; I've quite enough as it is. What is your name?'

'Leopold Brunow.'

'I see you're a flying officer.'

Biggles nodded.

'Where is your machine?'

'It is somewhere in the desert.'

'What is the number of your squadron?'

'I regret I cannot answer that question.'

'Perhaps you're right,' observed the officer casually. 'No matter; they'll ask you plenty of questions at headquarters so I needn't bother about it now. I will make you as comfortable as I can for the night, and will send you down the lines in the morning. I need hardly warn you that if you attempt to escape you are likely to be shot. Good-night.' He turned to the N.C.O. 'All right, Corporal, take charge.'

Biggles bowed stiffly, and escorted by the two

* German: No.

95

Tommies, followed the corporal to a tent that stood a little apart from the others.

'There you are, Jerry.* No 'arf larks and you'll be as right as ninepence, but don't come any funny stuff—see, or else—' The corporal made a gesture more eloquent than words.

Biggles nodded and threw himself wearily on the camp bed with which the tent was furnished. He was tired out, physically and mentally, yet he could not repress a smile as he thought of his position. To be taken prisoner by his own side was an adventure not without humour, but it was likely to be a serious set-back to his work if he was recognized by any one who knew him. Moreover, the delay might prove serious, both on account of his non-arrival at Abba Sud, where Algy would be waiting for him, and in the light of what he had recently discovered. To declare his true identity to the officer in charge of the outpost was out of the question—not that he would be believed if he did—yet to attempt to escape might have serious consequences, for not only would he have to run the risk of being shot, but he would have to face the perils of the wilderness.

He remembered the incident of the shadow on the tent, and it left him both perplexed and perturbed. He could not seriously entertain the thought that it had been von Stalhein, yet quite apart from his unique trick of tapping his cigarette, every other circumstance pointed to it. The German was certainly somewhere in the neighbourhood, there was no doubt about that. Still, it was one thing to be prowling about disguised as an Arab, and quite another matter to be sitting inside the headquarters tent of a British post, he reflected.

* Slang: German.

96

With these conflicting thoughts running through his head he dropped off into a troubled sleep, from which he was aroused by the corporal, who told him in no uncertain terms that it was time to be moving, as he would shortly have to be on his way, although he did not say where. It was still dark, but sounds outside the tent indicated that the camp was already astir and suggested that it must be nearly dawn. He had nothing to do to get ready beyond drink the tea and eat the bully beef and biscuits which the corporal had unceremoniously pushed inside, so he applied his eye to the crack of the tent flap in the hope of seeing something interesting. In this he was disappointed, however, for the only signs of life were a few Tommies and Arab levies moving about on various camp tasks. So he sat down on the bed again, racking his brain for a line of action to adopt when he found himself, as he had no doubt he shortly would be, penned behind a stout wire fence with other prisoners of war.

From the contemplation of this dismal and rather difficult problem he was aroused by the sound of horses' hooves, and hurried to the flap, but before he reached it, it was thrown back, and the youthful officer who had spoken to him the night before stood at the entrance; behind him were six mounted Arabs armed with modern service rifles; one of them was leading a spare horse.

'Can you ride, Brunow?' asked the subaltern.

'Yes.' replied Biggles sombrely.

'Then get mounted; these men are taking you down the lines, and the sooner you get there the better, because you'll find it thundering hot presently. And I must warn you again that the men have orders to shoot if you try to get away.'

Biggles was in no position to argue, so with a nod of

farewell he mounted the spare horse, and was soon trotting over the twilit wilderness in the centre of his escort.

For a few miles they held on a straight westerly course, but as the sun rose in a blaze of scarlet glory they began to veer towards the south, and then east, until they were travelling in a direction almost opposite to the one in which they had started. Biggles noted this subconsciously with an airman's instinct for watching his course, but it did not particularly surprise him. 'Perhaps there is some obstacle to be avoided,' he thought casually, but as they continued on the same course he suddenly experienced a pang of real alarm, for either his idea of locality had failed him, or else his mental picture of the position of the post was at fault, for wherever they were going, it was certainly not towards the British lines. He spoke to his guards, but either they did not understand, or else they did not wish to understand, for they paid no attention to his remarks.

The sun was well up when at last they reached a wadi* that cut down into a flat plain, where the guards dismounted and signalled to him to do the same. For a few minutes they rested, drinking a little water and eating a few dates; then one who appeared to be in charge of the party handed him a small package, and indicating that he was to remain where he was, led the others round the nearby bend in the rock wall. This struck Biggles as being very odd, but he did not dwell on it. His first thought was of escape, and had his horse been left with him he would certainly have made a dash for it; but the Arabs had taken it with them, and he knew that on foot he would be recaptured before he

* The dry bed of a river.

had gone a hundred yards. The idea of wandering about the waterless desert without a mount, looking for a human habitation, was out of the question, so he sat back in the shade of the rock and awaited the return of his escort, who he assumed had no doubt taken his predicament into consideration before leaving him.

'Those fellows are a long time,' he thought, some time later, and moved by sheer curiosity, he walked down to the place where they had disappeared. To his infinite amazement they were nowhere in sight; nor was there, as far as he could see, a place where they could hide. He ran up the side of the wadi, and standing on the edge of the desert, looked quickly towards all points of the compass, but the only sign of life he could see was a jackal slinking among the rocks. He even called out, but there was no reply.

Wrestling with this new problem, he returned to the wadi, when it occurred to him that possibly the package that had been given to him might supply a clue, and he tore it open eagerly. He was quite right; it did. The package contained an 'iron' ration consisting of biscuits and a slab of chocolate, and a flask of water. Attached to the flask by a rubber band was a sheet of notepaper on which had been written, in block letters, three words. The message consisted of the single word, 'Wait'. It was signed, 'A Friend'.

He held up the paper to the light, and a low whistle escaped his lips as his eyes fell on the familiar 'crown' watermark. 'So I, a German officer, have a friend in a British post, eh?' he thought. 'How very interesting.'

He folded the paper carefully, put it in his pocket, and was in the act of munching the chocolate when he was not a little surprised to hear an aeroplane approaching. But his surprise became wonderment when he saw it was a Halberstadt, which was, moreover, gliding towards the plain at the head of the wadi with the obvious intention of landing. With growing curiosity he watched it approach. 'If this sort of thing goes on much longer I shan't know who's fighting who,' he muttered helplessly. 'I thought I knew something about this war, but I'm getting out of my depth,' he opined. 'I wonder who's flying it? Shouldn't be surprised if it's the Kaiser*.'

It was not the Kaiser but Mayer who touched his wheels on the hard, unsympathetic surface of the wilderness, and then taxied tail up towards the place where Biggles was standing watching him. He ran to a standstill and raised his arm in a beckoning gesture.

Biggles walked across. 'Hello, Mayer,' he said. 'Where the dickens have you come from?'

Mayer gave him a nod of greeting. 'Get in,' he said shortly, indicating the rear cockpit.

'Where are we going?' shouted Biggles above the noise of the engine, as he climbed into the seat.

'Home: where the devil do you think?' snapped Mayer as he pulled** the throttle open and sped across the desolate waste.

* The ruler of Germany.
** The controls of German aeroplanes worked in the opposite direction to the British. Thus, he pulled the throttle towards him instead of pushing it away, as would normally have been the case.

Chapter 10
Shot Down

Biggles sat in the cockpit and watched the wadi fall away behind as Mayer lifted the machine from the ground and began climbing for height. He had no flying cap or goggles, for he had been carrying them in his hand when he was attacked by the Arabs on the oasis, and had dropped them in the struggle; not that he really needed them, for the air was sultry.

So he stood up with his arms resting on the edge of the cockpit, and surveyed the landscape in the hope of picking out a landmark that he knew, at the same time turning over in his mind the strange manner of his rescue. Who was the friend in the British post? He could think of no one but von Stalhein, although he would never have guessed but for the shadow on the tent. By what means had he arranged for the Arab levies to connive at his escape? It looked as if the Arabs, while openly serving with the British forces, were actually under the leadership of the Germans. 'The more I see of this business the easier it is to perceive why the British plans have so often failed. It looks as if the whole area is rotten with the canker of espionage,' he mused. Even assuming that von Stalhein had been responsible for his escape, how could Mayer have known where he was? That he had not turned up at such a remote spot by mere chance was quite certain.

Dimly the situation began to take form. Von Stalhein, disguised as an Arab, was operating behind the British lines. That was the most outstanding and important feature, for upon it everything else rested. He may have been responsible for the sheikhs turning against the British, in spite of the brilliant and fearless efforts of Major Sterne to prevent it, although Sterne had sometimes been able to win back their allegiance with gold, rifles, and ammunition, the only commodities for which the Arabs had any respect or consideration. The Halberstadt Squadron at Zabala, while carrying out regular routine duties, was also working with von Stalhein, flying him over the lines and picking him up at pre-arranged meeting-places — not a difficult matter considering the size and nature of the country. The previous day provided a good example, when von Stalhein had been flown over to try to influence the Arabs at the oasis. Later, he must have learned that Brunow was a prisoner in British hands, and in some way had been able to arrange for him to be sent down the lines in charge of Arabs who were in his pay, in order to effect his rescue, not for personal reasons but because he would rather see Brunow behind the German lines than behind the British.

The more he thought about this hypothesis the more Biggles was convinced that he was right, and that at last he was on the track of the inside causes of the British failures in the Middle East. Thinking of the oasis reminded him that they must be passing somewhere close to it; as near as he could judge by visualizing the map, both Abba Sud and the oasis where he had seen von Stalhein must both be somewhere between ten and twenty miles to the east or south-east. He turned, and pushing his Parabellum gun* aside out of the way, looked out over the opposite side of the cockpit.

* A mobile gun for the rear gunner, usually mounted on a U-shaped rail to allow rapid movement with a wide arc of fire.

Far away on the horizon he could just make out a dull shadow that might have been an oasis, but he was too uncertain of his actual position to know which of the two it was, if indeed it was either of them. Perhaps Mayer had a map; if so, he would borrow it. He reached forward and tapped the German on the shoulder, and then sprang back in affright as the shrill chatter of a machine-gun split the air from somewhere near at hand. A shower of lead struck the Halberstadt like a flail. There was a shrill *whang* of metal striking against metal, and a ghastly tearing sound of splintering wood-work. The stricken machine lurched drunkenly as the engine cut out dead and a long feather of oily black smoke swirled away aft.

Instinctively Biggles grabbed his gun, and squinted through his slightly open fingers in the direction of the sun whence the attack had come. The blinding white orb seared his eyeballs, but he caught a fleeting glimpse of a grey shadow that banked round in a steep stalling turn to renew the attack. He turned to warn Mayer, and a cry of horror broke from his lips as he saw him sagging insensible in his safety belt; a trickle of blood was oozing from under the ear flaps of his leather helmet.

As in a ghastly nightmare, Biggles heard the staccato clatter of the guns again, and felt the machine shudder like a sailing ship taken aback, as the controls flapped uselessly. Its nose lurched downwards; the port wing drooped, and the next instant the machine was spinning wildly earthward.

Biggles, cold with fear, acted with the deliberation of long experience, moved with a calmness that would have seemed impossible on the ground. He knew that the machine was fitted with dual controls, but the rear joystick was not left in its socket for fear of the observer being hit and falling on it in a combat, thus jamming the controls. It was kept in a canvas slot in the side of the cockpit. Swiftly he pulled it out, inserted the end in the metal junction and screwed it in. Without waiting to look out of the cockpit, he pushed the stick forward and kicked on full top rudder. The machine began to respond instantly; would it come out of the spin in time? He dropped back into his seat, and snatching a swift glance at the ground, now perilously near, knew that it was going to be touch and go. Slowly the nose of the machine came up as it came out of the spin.

With another five feet of height the Halberstadt would just have managed it; she did in fact struggle to even keel, but still lost height from the speed of her spin, as she was bound to for a few seconds. Biggles pulled the stick back and held his breath; he had no engine to help him, and the best he could hope for was some sort of pancake* landing. But luck was against him, for the ground at that point was strewn with boulders, some large and some small, and it must have been one of the large ones that caught the axle of his undercarriage. The lower part of the machine seemed to stop dead while the upper part, carried on by its momentum, tried to go forward; then several things happened at once. Biggles was flung violently against the instrument board; the propeller boss bored into the ground, hurling splinters of wood and rock in all directions; the tail swung up and over in a complete semicircle as the machine somersaulted in a final tearing, rending, splintering crash. Then silence.

Biggles, half blinded by petrol which had poured over him when the tank sheered off its bearers and

---

* Instead of the aircraft gliding down to land, it flops down from a height of a few feet, after losing flying speed.

burst asunder, fought his way out of the wreck like a madman, regardless of mere bruises and cuts. The horror of fire was on him, as it is on every airman in similar circumstances, but his first thought was for his companion. 'Mayer' he croaked, 'where are you?' There was no answer, so he tore the debris aside until he found the German, still strapped in his seat, buried under the tangled remains of the plane. Somehow—he had no clear recollection of how it was done—he got him clear of the cockpit, and dragged him through the tangle of wires and struts to a spot some distance away, clear of fire should it break out. Then he sank down and buried his face in his hands while he fought back an hysterical desire to burst into tears. He had seen stronger men than himself do it, and knew that it was simply the sudden relaxation of nerves that had been screwed up to breaking-point.

Then he rose unsteadily to his feet, wiped a smear of blood from a cut in his lip, and turned to his partner-in-misfortune, for the cause of the trouble was already a tiny speck in the far distance. So swift and perfectly timed had been the attack that he hadn't even time to identify the type of machine that had shot them down.

He took off Mayer's helmet, and a long red weal across the side of his head told its own story. As far as he could see the bullet had not actually penetrated the skull, but had struck him a glancing blow that had knocked him unconscious, and might, or might not, prove fatal. He could find no other bullet wounds, although his clothes were badly torn about and his face bruised, so he made him as comfortable as possible in the shade of the rock and then went to see if he could get a little water from the leaking radiator. It was hot and oily, but it was better than nothing, so he soaked his handkerchief and returned to Mayer. Had it been possible, he would have tried to save some of the precious liquid that was fast disappearing into the thirsty ground, but he had no receptacle to catch it, so he went back to the unfortunate German and cleaned the wound as well as he could. His efforts were rewarded, for after a few minutes Mayer opened his eyes and stared about him wonderingly. Wonderment gave way to understanding as complete consciousness returned, and he smiled weakly.

'What happened?' he whispered through his bruised lips.

'An Engländer dropped on us out of the sun and hit us with his first burst,' replied Biggles. 'A bullet hit you on the side of the head and the box* spun before I could get my gun going. I managed to get her out of the spin with the spare joystick before she hit the ground, but the engine had gone, so I had to get down as well as I could—which wasn't very well, as you can see,' he added dryly. 'There are too many rocks about for nice landings; but there, we were lucky she didn't catch fire.'

Mayer tried to move, but a low groan broke from his lips.

'I should lie still for a bit if I were you,' Biggles advised him. 'You'll be better presently.'

'You'd better go on,' the German told him stolidly.

'Go on? And leave you here? No, I'll wait for you.'

'Do you know where we are?' inquired Mayer, bitterly.

'Not exactly.'

'We're fifty miles from our lines, and it's fifty miles of waterless desert, so you'd better be starting.'

'No hurry, I'll wait for you.'

* German slang for an aeroplane.

106

'It'll be no use waiting for me.'

'Why not?'

'Because I shan't be coming.'

'Who says so?'

'I do. My leg is broken.'

Biggles felt the blood drain from his face as he realized just what Mayer's grim statement meant. 'Good heavens,' he breathed.

The German smiled curiously. 'The fortune of war,' he observed calmly. 'Before you go I would like you to do something for me.'

'What is it?'

'Go and look in my cockpit and see if you can find my pistol. I shall need it.'

'No, you won't,' Biggles told him tersely, for he knew well enough what was in the other's mind.

'You wouldn't leave me here to die of thirst—and the hyenas,' protested Mayer weakly.

'Who's talking about leaving you, anyway,' growled Biggles. 'Just you lie still while I think it over.'

'If you've any sense you'll go on. There's no need for us both to die,' said Mayer, with a courage that Biggles could not help but admire.

'I'm not talking about dying, either,' he declared. 'We'll find a way out; let me think a minute.' Then he laughed. The idea of an Englishman and a German each trying to save the other's life struck him as funny.

'What's the joke?' asked Mayer suspiciously.

'No joke—but it's no use bursting into tears,' returned Biggles brightly. He walked across and examined the machine. There were still a few drops of water in the radiator, but it was poisonous-looking fluid and he watched it drip away into the sand without regret. He dug about in the wreckage until he found Mayer's map, when he sat down and plotted their position as nearly as he could judge it. As Mayer had said, they were a good fifty miles from the German lines, and farther still from the British lines, but to the south and east there were two or three oases, unnamed, from which he guessed they were very small, not less than fifteen and not more than twenty miles away. Fifteen miles! Could he do it in the heat of the day? Alone, perhaps, but with a wounded companion, definitely no. Suppose he left Mayer, and tried to find the oasis where he had seen von Stalhein; could he fly back in the Halberstadt, assuming that it was as he had left it? No, he decided, for the German would certainly have died of thirst in the meantime.

The idea of leaving Mayer to perish did not occur to him. In the desperate straits in which they found themselves, he no longer regarded him as an enemy, but as a brother pilot who must be supported while a vestige of hope remained. He regarded the crashed machine with a speculative eye, and half smiled as a possibility occurred to him. Near at hand was one of the undercarriage wheels, with the bent axle still attached; the tyre had burst, but otherwise it was undamaged. The other wheel lay some distance away in the desert where it had bounced after the crash. He retrieved it and then set to work, while Mayer watched him dispassionately.

At the end of an hour he had constructed a fairly serviceable two-wheeled trailer from the undercarriage and remains of the wing spars. He had found plenty of material to work with; in fact, more than he needed. Finally he hunted about in the wreckage for the seat cushions, smiling as he caught sight of his unshaven, blood-stained face in the pilot's reflector. He found them, threw them on the crazy vehicle, and picking up some pieces of interplane struts and canvas, approached the German.

Mayer regarded him dubiously. 'You've wasted a lot of time,' he said irritably.

'Maybe,' replied Biggles imperturbably. 'Help me as much as you can while I get this leg of yours fixed up.'

'Do what?' ejaculated Mayer. 'What are you going to do?'

'Tie your leg up in these splints, so that it won't hurt more than can be helped while I get you on the perambulator.'

'Don't be a fool—'

'If you don't lie still, I'll fetch you a crack on the other side of your skull,' snarled Biggles. 'Do you think I want to hang about here all day? Come on—that's better.'

Not without difficulty he bound up Mayer's leg in the improvised splints, and then lifted him bodily on to the trailer. He handed him a piece of fabric to use as a sunshade, and without another word set off in the direction in which he judged the oasis to be.

Fortunately the ground was flat and fairly open, but the punctured wheel dragged heavily through the patches of loose sand that became more frequent as he went on. The sun climbed to its zenith and its white bars of heat struck down with relentless force.

Nowhere could he find rest for his eyes; in all directions stretched the wilderness, colourless and without outline, a vast undulating expanse of brown and grey that merged into the shimmering horizon. The land had no definite configuration, but was an eternal monotony of sand and rock, spotted here and there with the everlasting camel-thorn. There was no wild life—or if there was he did not see it. Once he straightened his back and looked round the scene, but its overwhelming solitude made him shudder and he went on with his task doing his best to fight off the dreadful feeling of depression that was creeping over him.

The demon thirst began to torture him. Another hour passed, and another, and still he struggled on. His lips were black and dry, with a little ring of congealed dust round them. He no longer perspired, for the sun drank up every drop of moisture as soon as it appeared. Mayer was more fortunate, for he had lapsed into unconsciousness. At first Biggles had tried to keep the fabric over his face, but he soon got tired of picking it up and struggled on without it. A feeling crept over him that he had been pulling the trailer all his life; everything else that had ever happened was a dim memory; only the rocks and the sand were real.

Presently he began to mutter to himself, and eyed the sun malevolently. 'I'd give you something, you skunk, if I had my guns,' he grated through his clenched teeth. It did not occur to him to leave his companion; the fixedness of purpose that had won him fame in France kept the helpless German ever before his mind. 'Poor old Mayer,' he crooned. 'Tough luck, getting a cracked leg. Why the dickens isn't Algy here; I'll twist the young scallywag's ear for him for leaving the patrol like this.'

Mayer began to mutter in German, long meaningless sentences in which the word Rhine occurred frequently.

'When we wind up the watch on the Rhine,' cackled Biggles. 'Your watch is about wound up, old cock,' and he laughed again. He stumbled on a rock, and swinging round in a blaze of fury, kicked it viciously and uselessly. He reached the top of a fold in the ground and stared ahead with eyes that seemed to be two balls of fire searing his brain. A line of cool green palm trees stood up clearly on the skyline. 'Ha, ha, you can't catch me like that,' he chuckled. 'Mirage; I've heard about you. Thinks it can catch me. Ha, ha!'

A big bird flopped down heavily not far away and regarded him with cold beady eyes. He dropped the handle of the trailer, snatched up a stone, and hurled it with all his strength. The bird flapped a few yards further away and settled again. 'You Hun,' he croaked. 'You dirty thieving Hun. I can see you sitting there; I'll knock the bottom out of your fuselage before I've finished with you.' He picked up the handle of the trailer and struggled on.

He began to sway as he walked. Once he fell, and lay where he had fallen for a full minute before he remembered his burden, whereupon he scrambled to his feet and set off with a fresh burst of energy. He topped another rise and saw a long group of green palm fronds against the blue sky above the next dip. At first he regarded them with a sort of detached interest, but slowly it penetrated his bemused mind that they were very real, very close, and very desirable. He broke into a drunken run, still dragging the trailer, and breathing in deep wheezing gasps; the palm trees seemed to float towards him, and presently he was amongst them, patting the rough boles with his hands. The place was vaguely familiar and he seemed to know exactly where to go, so he dropped the handle of the trailer and reeled towards the centre of the oasis, croaking as he saw that he was not mistaken. In front of him was the well and the hut where, the afternoon before, he had seen von Stalhein. He had returned to his starting point. He staggered to the well, seized the hide rope in his shaking hands, dragged up the receptacle attached to it and drank as he had never drunk before. Then he refilled the makeshift bucket and ran back to where he had left Mayer. He rolled him off the trailer and with difficulty got some of the water between his parched lips, at the same time dabbing his face and neck with it. He continued giving him a little water for some time, occasionally drinking deep draughts himself; but when he felt that he could do no more for the sick man, he returned to the well and buried his face and arms in the cool liquid.

He still had the remains of the chocolate ration in his pocket, so he munched a little and felt better for it. Then he walked up to the hut, but it was empty, so he returned to Mayer with the idea of making him as comfortable as possible before going to the spot where he had left the Halberstadt, to make sure it was still there and undamaged. But suddenly he felt dreadfully tired and sat down near the trailer to rest. The shade, after the heat of the sun which was now sinking fast, was pleasant, and he closed his eyes in ecstasy. His head nodded once or twice, and he slipped slowly sideways on to the cool sand, sound asleep.

Chapter 11
A Night Flight

I

He awoke, and sitting up with a start, looked around in bewilderment, for it was night, and for a moment or two he could not recall what had happened. The moon was up; it hung low over the desert like a sickle and cast a pale blue radiance over a scene of unutterable loneliness. Then, in the hard, black lattice-like shadows of the palms, he saw Mayer, and remembered everything. The German's face was ghastly in the weird light, and he thought he was dead, but dropping on his hands and knees beside him, was relieved to hear faint but regular breathing.

Then he sprang to his feet as a strange sound reached his ears, and he knew instinctively that it was the same noise that had awakened him; it reminded him of the harsh confused murmur of waves upon a pebbly beach, afar off, rising and falling on the still night air. For a little while he sat listening, trying to identify the sound, but he could not; it seemed to come from the other side of the oasis, so he made his way cautiously through the palms to a slight rise from which he could see the desert beyond. As he reached it and looked out he caught his breath sharply and sank down swiftly in the shadow of a stunted palm, staring with wide-open eyes.

He did not know what he had expected to see, but it was certainly not the sight that met his incredulous eyes. Mustering in serried ranks was an army of Arabs;

at a rough computation he made out the number to be nearly four thousand, and fresh bands were still riding in from the desert, gathering together for what could only be one of the biggest Arab raids ever organized—for he had no delusions as to their purpose. What was their objective? Were they being mustered by von Stalhein to harass the British flank, or by Major Sterne to launch a crippling blow at the German lines of communication? Those were questions he could not answer, but he hoped that by watching he might discover. He was glad that whoever was in charge had not decided to use the oasis itself as a meeting-place, or he would have been found, but a moment's consideration revealed the impracticability of such a course; a body of men of that size could only parade in the open.

For half an hour he lay and watched them, and at the end of that time they began to move off, not in any regular order, but winding like a long sinuous snake out into the desert; and he had no need to watch them for very long to guess their objective, for the direction they took would bring them within a few hours to the eastern outposts of the British army.

'If that bunch hits the right wing of our lines of communication without warning it'll go right through them like a knife through butter, and our fellows in the front-line trenches will be cut off from supplies and everything else,' he muttered anxiously. 'I shall have to let our people know somehow.' As the tail-end of the column disappeared into the mysterious blue haze of the middle distance he glanced at the moon and made a swift calculation. 'It must be somewhere about eleven o'clock—not later,' he thought. 'At an average speed of six miles an hour, and they can easily manage that, seven hours will see them ready to strike at our

114

flank at just about dawn, which is probably the time they have fixed for the attack.'

He got up and ran back swiftly to where he had left Mayer. He was still unconscious, so he hurried round the edge of the oasis to where he had left the Halberstadt the previous day. 'If it's gone, I'm sunk,' he murmured, and then uttered a low cry of delight as his eyes fell on it, standing just as he had left it. 'Now! what's my best plan of action?' he thought swiftly. 'Shall I leave Mayer here and dash down to Kantara in the hope of getting in touch with Algy? If I do, I daren't land, for if I did every officer on the station would know that a German machine had landed on the aerodrome, which would mean that the Germans would know it too. That's no use. The only thing I can do is to write a message, drop it, and then signal to Algy and Major Raymond as we arranged. That's the safest way; they would be bound to find it on the aerodrome. But what about Mayer? I can't leave him here and risk a night landing in order to pick him up afterwards; I might run short of petrol anyway, and I don't want to get stuck in the desert again. I shall have to take him with me. But I had better have a look at the machine.'

He found it exactly as he had left it, and thanked the lucky chance that ordained that not only should he have landed at what seemed to be the little-used end of the oasis, but amongst the trees, where the machine could not be seen from the desert. After removing the sandbag anchors he lifted up the tailskid and dragged the Halberstadt into the open, a task that presented no difficulty as the slope was slightly downhill. He climbed into the cockpit, turned on the petrol tap, and then returned to the front of the machine, where he turned the propeller round several times in order to suck the petrol gas into the cylinders. The machine was not fitted with a self-starter, so he switched on the ignition and then returned to the propellor in order to swing it. Before he did so, however, he took a leaf from his note-book, wrote a message on it, and addressed it to Algy. This done, he took off his tunic, ripped a length of material from his shirt to form a streamer, and tying the message in it with a pebble to give it weight, put it in his pocket and returned to the engine.

In the warm air it started at once, and in the stillness of the desert night the din that it made was so appalling that he started back in alarm. 'Great Scott! what a row,' he muttered as he climbed quickly into his seat and began to taxi carefully to the place where he had left the German. Mayer was still unconscious and lying in the same position, so he set to work on the formidable task of getting him into the rear cockpit. This he finally managed to do with no small exertion by picking him up in the 'fireman's grip' and dropping him bodily over the side; the unfortunate man fell in a heap, but there was no help for it, and as Biggles observed to himself as he got him into a sitting position, in the seat, with the safety belt round his waist, 'He's unconscious, so it isn't hurting him, anyway.'

Before climbing back into his cockpit he looked long and critically down the track over which he would have to take off. 'If I hit a brick, there's going to be a nasty mess,' was his unspoken thought as he eased the throttle open and held the stick slightly forward. But any fears he may have had on the matter of buckling a wheel—with calamitous results—against a rock were set at rest as the machine rose gracefully into the air, and he settled down to his task with a sigh of relief and satisfaction.

It was a weird experience, flying over the moonlit

desert that in the early days of history had been the scene of wars of extermination, and the pictures of many famous Biblical characters floated up in his imagination. Below him, more than twenty centuries before, Joseph had wandered in his coat of many colours, and the Prodigal Son had wasted his money in riotous living. 'There wouldn't be much for him to spend his money on to-day, I'm afraid,' thought Biggles whimsically, as he surveyed the barren land that once, before the great rivers had dried up, had flowed with milk and honey. 'Still, maybe it will regain some of its prosperity again one day when human beings come to their senses and stop fighting each other,' he mused, as he turned his nose a little more to the north, in order to avoid being heard by the raiders, and von Stalhein in particular, who he suspected was leading them, and who would certainly recognize the drone of his Mercedes engine.

A white wavering finger suddenly probed the sky some distance ahead, and he knew he was approaching the British lines. Soon afterwards a blood-red streak of flame flashed across his vision, and he knew that the anti-aircraft gunners were at work. He was not very perturbed, for he had climbed fairly high and knew that the chances of being hit were very remote; but as the archie barrage grew more intense, he throttled back and began a long glide towards the aerodrome at Kantara. Several searchlight beams were combing the sky for him, but he avoided them easily and smiled grimly as the lights of the aerodrome came into view. 'If I was carrying a load of bombs instead of a sick German, those fellows would soon be getting what they are asking for,' he growled, and shut off his engine as he dived steeply towards his objective. White lines of tracer bullets were streaking upwards, but in the darkness the shooting was chiefly guesswork and none of them came near him, although he realized that this state of affairs was likely to change when he opened his engine and by so doing disclosed his whereabouts.

With one hand on the throttle and the message lying on his lap, he raced low over the aerodrome; when he reached the middle he tossed the message overboard, and opened and closed the throttle twice in quick succession. Then he pulled it wide open and zigzagged out of the vicinity, like a startled bird, as the searchlights swung round and every gun within range redoubled its efforts to hit him. But he was soon outside their field of fire and racing nose down towards the German lines. Once he glanced back to satisfy himself that Mayer was still unconscious. 'If he'd come round just now he might well have wondered what the dickens was going on,' he thought, 'and he might have asked some awkward questions when we got back—or caused the Count to ask some. As it is, he'll wonder how on earth he got home when he wakes up and finds himself in Zabala.'

The rest of the flight was simply a fight against the lassitude that overtakes all pilots after a period of flying, when they have nothing to do but fly on a straight course, for the comfortable warmth that fills the cockpit, due to the proximity of the engine, induces sleep, and the regular drone of the wind in the wires becomes a lullaby hard to resist. He found himself nodding more than once, and each time he started up and beat his hands on the side of the cockpit, and held his face outside the shield of the windscreen to allow the cool slipstream to play on his weary eyes.

The scattered lights of Zabala came into sight at last, and he glided down without waiting for landing lights to be put out. There was no wind, so he was able to land directly towards the sheds, and finished his run within a few yards of them. He switched off the engine and sat quite still, for now that his task was finished, and the need for mental and physical energy no longer required, he let himself go, and his aching nerves collapsed like a piece of taut elastic when it is cut in the middle.

As in a queer sort of dream he heard voices calling, and brisk words of command; but they seemed to be far away and barely penetrated his rapidly failing consciousness, and he paid no attention to them. He blinked owlishly as a flashlight was turned on his face, and felt arms lifting him to the ground. 'Mayer . . . get Mayer . . . mind his leg,' he muttered weakly. Then darkness surged up and around him as he fell into a sleep of utter exhaustion.

II

When he awoke the sun was throwing oblique shafts of yellow light through the gaps in the half-drawn curtains of his room. For a little while he saw them without understanding what they were, but as wakefulness cast out the last vestiges of sleep, he sat up with a yawn and stretched.

'So here we are again,' he thought, glancing round and noting that nothing appeared to have been touched. His hand came in contact with his chin and he started, but then smiled as he rubbed the stubble ruefully. He jumped out of bed, threw back the blinds, and surveyed himself in the mirror. 'Very pretty,' he muttered. 'A comely youth withal. Gosh! what a scallywag I look. I'm no oil painting at any time, but goodness me! I didn't think I could look quite such a scarecrow.'

119

That may have been taking rather a hard view, but his appearance was certainly anything but prepossessing. Two days' growth of sparse bristles on his chin formed a fitting background for a nasty cut in his lower lip, which was badly swollen, while his right eye was surrounded by a pale greenish-blue halo that did nothing to improve matters. A scratch across the forehead on which the blood had dried completed the melancholy picture. 'I'd better start work on myself,' he thought, reaching for his razor.

An orderly appeared while he was in the bath, and finding he was up, speedily returned with breakfast on a tray, and a broad smile which suggested to Biggles that he was in the Squadron's good books.

The Count arrived, beaming, while he was dressing, and after congratulating him on his rescue of Mayer, startled him by announcing in a grandiose voice that he had recommended him for the Iron Cross.

'It was not worth such an honour,' protested Biggles uncomfortably, for the idea of being decorated by the enemy did not fill him with enthusiasm. 'How is Mayer, by the way?'

'As well as one might expect, considering everything. The wound in his head is nothing, but his leg will take some time to get right. He has been awake a long time, and I have been with him; he had to wait for the ambulance to take him to the hospital in Jerusalem. While we waited he told me the story of what happened, or as much as he knows of it. How did you come to be taken prisoner in the first place?'

'I ran into a sandstorm and was forced down,' replied Biggles truthfully. 'I waited for the storm to pass, and was just getting back into my machine when a party of Arabs turned up and carted me off to the nearest

British post, where they held me to ransom, or sold me—or something of the sort.'

The Count frowned. 'They're unreliable these Arabs,' he said. 'I wouldn't trust them an inch. They betray either side for a handful of piastres and would cut the throat of every white man in the country if they could, or if they dared. Von Stalhein thinks a lot of them though, perhaps because he was out here before the war and knows their habits and language. That's why he's here now. Between ourselves, he's got a big show on at this very moment which—which—' He broke off abruptly as if he realized suddenly that he was saying too much. 'Come along down to the Mess as soon as you're ready,' he continued, changing the subject, as he moved towards the door. 'I want you to meet Kurt Hess.'

'Kurt Hess? I seem to have heard the name. Who is he?'

'He's our crack pilot in the East. He has scored twenty-six victories and is very proud of it, which is pardonable. He arrived this morning; he's only here for a few days, and between ourselves—' the Count dropped his voice to a confidential whisper—'he's not very pleased because every one is talking about you, and your exploit with Mayer. Perhaps he thinks, not unnaturally, that they should be talking about him.'

'I see,' answered Biggles as he brushed his tunic, and made a mental note that if he knew anything about German character he would find a ready-made enemy in the German Ace. 'I shall be proud to meet him,' he went on slowly, wondering what the Count would say if he knew that his own bag of enemy machines exceeded that of the German's.

'See you presently, then,' concluded the Count, as he went out and closed the door.

'So von Stalhein *is* leading the Arabs,' thought Biggles, 'and he isn't back yet. Well, I hope he gets it in the neck; it would save me a lot of trouble.' But even as the thought crossed his mind there was a roar overhead and a Halberstadt side-slipped steeply to a clever landing; it swung round and raced tail up towards the sheds. Before it had stopped, von Stalhein, in German uniform, had climbed out of the back seat and was limping quickly towards headqarters.

'It looks to me as if we might soon be hearing some interesting news,' mused Biggles, with a thrill of anticipation, as he went out and strolled towards the Mess.

Chapter 12
A New Pilot—And a Mission

I

There was no need to wonder which of the assembled officers was Hess. Holding the floor in the centre of an admiring group was a tall, slim, middle-aged man from whose throat hung the coveted Pour le Mérite, the highest award for valour in the German Imperial Forces. His manner and tone of voice were at once so haughty—one might say imperious—and supercilious, that Biggles, although he was half prepared for something of the sort, instinctively recoiled. 'What amazing people the Huns are,' he thought, as he watched the swaggering gestures of the Ace. 'Fancy any one of our fellows behaving like that and getting away with it. Why, he'd be slung out on his ear into the nearest pig-trough, and quite right, too. What an impossible sort of skunk he must be; yet here are all these fellows kowtowing to him as if he were an object for reverence just because he has had the luck to shoot down a few British machines. I doubt if he has ever run up against any one really hot; he'd soon get the dust knocked out of his pants if he was sent to France, I'll warrant.'

He walked across and stood on the outskirts of the group, listening respectfully, but the conversation was, of course, in German, so he could not follow it very well. He picked up a word or two here and there, however, sufficient for him to judge that the German was enlarging upon the simplicity of killing Englishmen when once one had the knack, for they had neither courage nor ability.

In spite of himself Biggles was amused at the man's overweening conceit, and his thoughts must have found expression on his face, for the German suddenly broke off in the middle of a sentence and scowled in a manner so puerile and affected that it was all Biggles could do to prevent himself from laughing out loud.

With the air of a king accepting homage from minions, the Ace moved slowly through the group until he stood face to face with the object of his disapproval; then with his lip curled in a sneer he said something quickly in German that Biggles did not understand. That it was something unpleasant he could feel from the embarrassed manner of the other Germans present.

Biggles glanced around the group calmly. 'Will some gentleman kindly tell him that I do not understand?' he said quietly in English.

But an interpreter was unnecessary. 'So!' said the Ace, in the same language, with affected surprise. 'What have we here—an Engländer?'

'He is of the Intelligence Staff,' put in Schmidt, who was Mayer's usual observer, and may have been prompted by a feeling of gratitude for what Biggles had done for his pilot. 'He's the officer who brought Mayer back last night.'

'So!' sneered Hess, with a gesture so insolent that Biggles itched to strike him. 'We know what to do with Engländers, we of the Hess *Jagdstaffel** Perhaps you

---

* A hunting group of German fighters, consisting of approximately twelve aeroplanes. Also just called a 'staffel'. The equivalent of a British squadron.

would like to hear how I make them sizzle in their seats,' he continued, addressing Biggles directly. 'I myself have shot down twenty-six—twenty-six—' he repeated the number, presumably to make sure that there could be no mistake—'like this.' He went through what was intended to be a graphic demonstration of the art of air fighting, but to Biggles it was merely comical. 'Twenty-six,' said Hess yet again, 'and by to-night it will be twenty-seven,' he added, 'for to-day is my birthday, and I have sworn not to sleep until I have sent another down like roast beef in his own oven.'

Biggles was finding it hard to keep his temper, for he knew that to fall out with the German idol would mean serious trouble. 'Excellent, *mein Hauptmann*,' he said, 'but take care you don't meet one that turns your own "box" into a coffin instead, for what would the Fatherland do without you?' The sarcasm which he could not veil was quite lost on the German, but it was not overlooked by one or two of the others, who stirred uncomfortably.

The Ace drew himself up to his full height and struck a pose. 'Do you suggest that an Engländer might shoot *me* down?' he inquired haughtily.

'There's just a chance, you know,' replied Biggles easily, clenching and unclenching his hands in his pockets. 'The English have some good fighters in France, and one may come out here one day. After all, were not Immelmann and Boelcke—'

'Zut! they were foolish,' broke in the Ace, with a movement of his arm that was probably intended to convey regret, but at the same time a suggestion of contempt, as if they were not in the same category as Kurt Hess.

Just where the matter would have ended it is impossible to say, but fortunately at that moment the Count, accompanied by von Stalhein, came into the room. One glance at their faces told Biggles all that he wanted to know about the Arab attack. That it had failed was certain, for the Count looked worried, while von Stalhein was pale under his tan and wore a bandage on his left hand.

The Count turned to speak to Hess while von Stalhein beckoned to Biggles, who walked over quickly to where the German was waiting for him.

'Count von Faubourg has just told me about the business of Mayer,' began von Stalhein abruptly. 'From what I gather, you put up a remarkably fine performance. Can you remember exactly where Mayer's machine crashed?'

'I think I can mark the position to within a mile or two, but Mayer was flying, not me, so I couldn't guarantee to be absolutely correct,' replied Biggles, wondering what was coming.

'Do you think you could find the crash?'

'Oh yes, there should be no difficulty about that.'

'Good! Then I want you to fly over and drop an incendiary bomb on the wreck. You must set it on fire with a direct hit, otherwise there is no point in going. The machine must be utterly destroyed. Do you think you could manage it?'

'I'm quite sure of it,' returned Biggles quickly, looking out of the window so that the other could not see the satisfaction in his eyes for the mission presented an opportunity for which he was anxiously waiting.

'Very well. Then get off at once; and will you please take a camera with you? To satisfy myself I should like to see a photograph—'

'Do you doubt my word, sir?' asked Biggles with an air of injured innocence.

'No, but important matters are at stake, and the only

way to be quite sure of a thing is to see it with one's own eyes.'

'I understand,' replied Biggles. 'I'll take a Pfalz and go over immediately.' He bowed and left the room and, collecting his overalls and flying kit from his room, made his way to the tarmac. As he walked along to the hangars of the Pfalz Squadron he stopped for a moment to look at a new scarlet and white Pfalz D. III Scout, around which a number of mechanics were standing, lost in admiration, for it was the latest product of the famous Pfalz works and far and away the best thing they had ever turned out. There was no aircraft in the Middle East to touch it for speed and climb, and to Biggles, who knew something of the value of these qualities in a fighting aeroplane, the chief reason for the successes of the German Ace was made clear—for he had no doubt to whom the Pfalz belonged.

There was a strange, ruminating look in his eyes as he walked on to the Pfalz Squadron, and asked if he could have a machine for a special mission. On being answered in the affirmative, he requested that four twenty-pound incendiary bombs be fitted to the bomb racks, and in a few minutes, with these in place, he taxied out and took off in the direction of his previous day's adventure.

II

He found plenty to occupy his mind as he cruised watchfully towards the place where the remains of the unfortunate Halberstadt were piled up, but the two chief matters that exercised his thoughts were von Stalhein's anxiety to secure the destruction of the machine, and the possibility of having a word with Algy.

As far as the crashed machine was concerned, it seemed certain that it contained something of importance, something that von Stalhein did not want to leave lying about, possibly a document of some sort. 'Obviously, I shall have to try to find out what it is before I start the bonfire,' he decided. 'I'd better attend to that first, and then go on to Abba Sud afterwards to see if Algy is still hanging about.'

He found the crash without difficulty, and after circling round for a few minutes looking for the best landing place, finally selected a patch free from rocks and camel-thorn, about half a mile away; it was the nearest place where he could get down without taking risks that he preferred to avoid. Leaving the propeller ticking over, he hastened to the well-remembered scene, and began a systematic search of the wreckage. At first he concentrated on the battered pilot's cockpit, going through all the pockets in turn; but they yielded nothing. For half an hour he hunted, and then, just as he was about to abandon the quest, thinking that perhaps after all von Stalhein was simply concerned with the destruction of the machine, he came upon an article so incongruous that he regarded it in stupefied amazement. He found it in what had evidently been a secret stowage place between the two cockpits, but the cavity had been burst open by the crash, revealing what lay within. It was a British officer's field service cap. There was nothing to show to whom it belonged, but the maker's name was that of a well-known London outfitter.

'Well, I don't know what I expected to find, but if I'd been given a thousand guesses I should never have guessed *that*,' thought Biggles, as he turned the cap over and over in his hands. 'But all the same, that must be the thing that friend Erich was scared about; or is it simply a souvenir? It's no use burning a good hat, so I'll take it with me. And I might as well make sure of setting the crash alight, in case I miss it with my bombs,' he went on, as he took out a box of matches, struck one and held it to the sun-dried fabric. When it was well alight he ran back to his machine, took off, and dropped his bombs on the conflagration. Then he took two or three photographs of the fire with the oblique camera that he had brought for the purpose; still not entirely satisfied, he waited for a few minutes until the destruction of the machine was clearly revealed, when he took another photograph, and then raced off in the direction of the oasis of Abba Sud.

He saw Algy afar off long before he reached the oasis, a tiny speck in the sky that circled round and round the dark belt of trees, and presently resolved itself into an aeroplane of unorthodox design. The straight top plane, and lower ones set at a pronounced angle, could not belong to any other machine than a Sopwith Camel. At first Biggles could hardly believe his eyes as it came towards him, and he stared at it wonderingly. He fired a red Very light, the prearranged signal, to ensure that there should be no mistake, and his first words, as he jumped from his cockpit and ran towards the other machine that had landed near him, were, 'Algy! where did you get that kite?'

'Never mind about that; where the dickens have you been all this time?' growled Algy. 'I've been frizzling here like a herring in a pan for the last two blinking days. I was just beginning to think that the Huns must have shot you.'

'I've been busy,' retorted Biggles. 'Do you think I've nothing to do but chase to and fro between Zabala and here? I repeat, where did you get that Camel?'

'It's a special one that's been sent up for headquarters use. Fellows were beginning to grouse because a Hun—Hess, we hear his name is—is playing Old Harry up and down the lines with one of the Pfalz D. III's, and we've nothing to get near him in.'

'So I believe. I was talking to Hess this morning. The Huns think he's a prize piece of furniture, but, as a matter of fact, he's the prince of all swine.'

'Well, we got a Camel up from Heliopolis, and it's been handed over to me *pro tem.*,' went on Algy. 'I shot down a Halberstadt yesterday.'

Biggles started and his eyes narrowed. 'Where?' he asked coldly.

'About twenty miles to the north-east of where we are now. It hit the floor a dickens of a crack and went to pieces.'

'You needn't tell me: I was in it,' Biggles told him, grimly.

'You were—Oh, great Scott! Well, I wasn't to know that, was I? Why didn't you fire a red light?'

'A fat lot of chance you gave me. I didn't even see you until you started pumping out lead.'

'Of course; I didn't think of that. My word! I might have killed you.'

'Might! You thundering nearly did.'

'Well, I wasn't to know. I saw a Hun and I went for him. It didn't occur to me that you might be in it, because I thought you were wandering about behind the British lines.'

Biggles looked perplexed. 'How the deuce did you know that?' he demanded.

'Because sometime about midnight young Fraser, the lad who is in charge of Number Five post, rang up headquarters to say that he had collected a Hun prisoner named Brunow from a bunch of Arabs and wanted to know what he was to do with him. Headquarters

130

told him to hang on to him until the morning and then send him along. Then they sent out the usual chit to Intelligence people asking if they wanted to interrogate him. Poor old Raymond nearly threw a fit when he heard it was you. He sent for me in a hurry, and at the first crack of dawn I went up with special instructions to fly you down to Kantara, but when I got there I found you'd already left in charge of a party of Major Sterne's Arabs who—'

'*Whose* Arabs?' Biggles fired the question like a pistol shot.

'Sterne's—why, what's wrong?'

Biggles looked at him oddly. 'Was Sterne up there when you got there?' he asked quietly.

'No, he'd just gone; pushed off out into the desert on one of his trips.'

Biggles stared and said nothing for a moment. 'Go on,' he murmured at last.

'Well, I went back to report what had happened, and in the afternoon the Arabs rolled up with a tale of how you'd escaped,' continued Algy.

'How had I escaped?'

'By jumping on the best horse while you were all resting, and leaping a terrific chasm over which it was impossible to follow you. They fired at you but missed, and then you disappeared behind some rocks and were never found again.'

'So, that's what they told you, is it?' mused Biggles. 'My gosh! what a tale. Makes those yarns about the Arabian Nights sound tame. I expect you got quite a kick out of it.'

'Why, didn't you bolt?'

'Bolt, my foot. But I haven't time to tell you the whole story now. Mayer, one of our Huns at Zabala, picked me up, and we were on our way back when you

131

butted in and shot us down. Mayer got a crack on the side of the nut from one of your bullets, but he wasn't dead, so I dragged him to an oasis where I saw a big bunch of Arabs collecting. I'd got a machine there— don't ask me how or why—so I flew down to Kantara to let you know what was going on. Did you get my message?'

'We certainly did. The telephone wires were red hot for a bit, I can tell you, and a whole lot of troops, mostly Australian cavalry, lost their beauty sleep. When the Sheikhs rolled up they were waiting for them, and they gave them such a plastering that they're not likely to forget in a hurry. Some got killed and some got away, but a lot were taken prisoners, and they're bleating for the blood of the man who led them into the trap, for that's what they swear happened. When—'

'I see. That clears things up a bit,' interrupted Biggles. 'I begin to see daylight. By the way, did you see the waterworks blow up when you were over Zabala the other night?'

Algy laughed. 'Too true I did,' he cried. 'What a wizard it was! I hooted like a coot in spite of the archie.'

'You reported it when you got back?'

'Of course. Our people were tickled to death, although they still don't know who did it, or how it was done. Raymond is as dumb as a church mouse.'

'I'm glad he is,' declared Biggles. 'And what about that news you had for me—the news you mentioned in the message you dropped?'

'Oh yes! I've been waiting to tell you about that. Raymond got a direct dispatch, in code, from London,. The Air Board told him that if possible he was to warn you to beware of Brunow.'

'Brunow! What the dickens has he got to do with it? He's in London.'

'No, he isn't. Something must have happened in London, and although our people were watching him like a cat watching a mouse, he disappeared suddenly as if he'd got the wind up, and they fancy it was something to do with you. They traced him as far as Hull, and then lost track of him, but they think he departed for Germany hot foot, via Holland. They thought you ought to be warned, in case he turned up here.'

'Why should he?'

'Don't ask me; I don't know.'

'I see.'

'Look! There's one last thing,' went on Algy. 'We've laid out a dummy aerodrome, twelve miles south-east of Kantara. It looks fine from the air. If you want to please the Huns and at the same time would like to see them waste some bombs, you can tell them where it is. It's all ready, fairly aching to be bombed,' he concluded with a broad grin.

'That's fine,' Biggles walked over and took the officer's cap that he had found in Mayer's cockpit from the back seat of his machine and handed it to Algy. 'Hang on to that,' he said. 'Take it back to Raymond when you go and tell him to hide it—bury it if he likes. He can do what he likes with it, but on no account must any one see it. Got that?'

'Yes. That's quite clear.'

'Good! Now lend me that Camel for half an hour. You can wait here for me; I'll bring it back.'

Algy's jaw dropped. 'Lend you the Camel?' he gasped.

'That's what I said,' returned Biggles. 'What are you gaping at; is it an unnatural request?'

'Er—no. But what do you want it for?'

133

'Because I've a strong urge to be myself for a few minutes.'

'Be yourself? What are you talking about? Have you got a touch of sun or something?'

'My goodness! You are dense this morning. I just have a feeling that I'd like to forget that I'm Brunow for a little while and be what I am—a junior officer in the R.F.C.'

'But what for?'

Biggles looked exasperated. 'All right, if you *must* know,' he said slowly and deliberately. 'There's a fellow floating about the atmosphere in a red and white Pfalz D. III who thinks he's cock of the roost. He's promised to fry his twenty-seventh Englishman to-day—the conceited ass—and when I saw your Camel it struck me that it wouldn't be a bad scheme if I took a hand in this frying business.'

'You mean Hess.'

'Yes rhymes with Hess, and so does mess, which is as it should be,' observed Biggles, 'because I'm going to do my best to get Mr. Hess in the biggest mess he was ever in. Are these guns O.K.?'

'Perfectly O.K.'

'Then give me a swing.'

Algy ran to the propeller. The engine sprang into life, and the Camel sped across the desert like a blunt-nosed bullet with the slipstream hurling a cloud of sand high into the air behind it.

Chapter 13
Vickers Versus Spandaus

In his heart Biggles knew that from the first moment he saw the swaggering German Ace the greatest ambition of his life was to see him given the lesson he so richly deserved, the lesson which would inevitably be administered sooner or later by somebody; and he had resolved to set about the task that morning in the Pup he assumed Algy would be flying. That his partner was, in fact, flying a Sopwith Camel was better luck than he could have imagined, for it evened things up.

Previously, in a Pfalz D.III, Hess could choose his own battle-field and select his opponent, for in the event of his catching a foeman who turned out to be a tartar, he could break off the combat and escape by virtue of his superior speed. This advantage of superior equipment was the dominating factor that enabled many German Aces to pile up big scores during certain periods of 1916 and 1917, a lamentable state of affairs that came to a sudden end with the arrival at the front of the Camel and the S.E.5, as the appalling death roll of German Aces towards the end of 1917 reveals.

Sopwith Camels had been in France, where the fighting was most intense, for some time, but none had reached the outlying theatres of war; consequently, a German pilot arriving in one of the distant battle-fields with the latest German fighting machine, finding himself opposed to aeroplanes of obsolete type, had every opportunity of acquiring a reputation that was often proved to be false when he encountered opponents on level terms.

But with these matters Biggles was not concerned as he sped towards the German side of the battlefield, which he knew would be the most likely place to find the German Ace lying in wait for a British two-seater; and he was jubilant at once more finding himself in the cockpit of a Camel for two reasons. In the first place he was thoroughly at home, and secondly he would be able to force the German to fight, provided he found him, for the simple reason that he would not be able to run away, as the two machines were about equal in performance.

He might, of course, have shot the German down from his own Pfalz, but the thought did not occur to him, for it would have been little short of murder; he felt that in a regular British aircraft he was perfectly justified in fighting Hess. He would forget for the moment that he had ever existed as Brunow, and behave precisely as if he had been posted to the Middle East as an ordinary pilot of a fighter squadron. In those circumstances the combat, if it occurred, would be perfectly fair.

He reached the lines but could see no signs of aerial activity, so climbing steadily for height, he began a systematic search of the whole sector. Once he saw a Halberstadt in the distance but he ignored it, for it was not the object of his quest, and he continued on his way, eyes probing the skies above and below for the red and white fuselage of the Pfalz. A little later he passed close to an antiquated B.E.2 C* and exchanged

---

* Designed in 1912 for observation and artillery co-operation this two-seater biplane whose top speed of 72 mph was just half that of the fastest fighters, was clearly obsolete by 1918.

greetings with its crew, at the same time admiring their courage for taking the air in a conveyance so hopelessly out of date. 'That's the sort of kite Hess is hoping to meet, I'll bet; and if he could poke in a burst of fire without being seen he'd be tickled to death; probably go back to Zabala and tell the boys how easy it is to shoot down Englishmen,' he mused. 'Pah! Well, we'll see.'

He had flown on for some little distance and was scanning the sky ahead when something—possibly the instinct which experienced air fighters seemed to develop—made him look back long and searchingly at the B.E., now a speck in the eastern sky. Was it his imagination, or was there a tiny speck moving far above it? He closed his eyes for a moment and then looked again, forcing them to focus in spite of the glare; then he caught his breath sharply and swung the Camel round in the lightning right-hand turn that was one of its most famous characteristics. He had not been mistaken. Far above the plodding B.E. a minute spark of light had flashed for a brief instant. No one but an old hand would have seen it or known what it portended; but Biggles knew that it was the sun's rays catching the wings of a banking aeroplane.

A minute or two later he could see it clearly as it stalked its quarry from the cover of the sun's blinding glare; he could see from its shape that it was a Pfalz, but it was still too far off for him to make out its colours. 'No matter,' he thought; 'I shall have to give those two boys in the B.E. the tip, whether it's Hess or not, or else it looks like being their unlucky day.'

He was flying rather higher than the German scout, which in turn was some distance above the slow two-seater, and his advantage of height gave him the extra speed necessary to come up with them. While he was

137

still half a mile away his lips parted in the grim smile he always wore when he was fighting as he picked out the colours of the Pfalz. They were red and white. It had placed itself in an ideal position for attack, and its nose was already going down to deliver the thrust that would send the British two-seater to its doom.

Biggles shoved his joystick forward savagely, and the needle of his air speed indicator swung upwards to the one hundred and eighty miles an hour mark; but he did not see it, for his eyes were glued on the now diving scout. He snatched a glance downwards and saw the gunner of the B.E. leaning over the side of his cockpit, looking down at the ground and making notes in a writing-pad, unconscious of the hand of death that was falling on him from the skies.

Biggles was afraid he was going to be too late, so he took the only course open to him; his hand closed over the firing lever of his guns and he fired a long deflexion* shot in the direction of the Hun, more with the object of calling attention to himself than in any real hope of hitting it. Hess apparently did not hear the shots, for he continued his swoop, but the British pilot did, and acted with admirable presence of mind. He glanced up, not at the Pfalz but in the direction from which the rattle of guns had come, and saw the Camel. Whether he suspected that the British pilot had mistaken him for a Hun, or whether he felt the presence of some unseen danger, Biggles never knew, but he turned sharply, so sharply that his gunner fell back into his seat with alarm as he reached for his gun.

The action was quite enough to disconcert the Pfalz pilot, who may have suspected a trap, for he swerved

* The amount a gunner or pilot must aim ahead of a fast moving aircraft, passing at right angles, in order to hit it.

wildly and careered round in a wide circle, looking over his shoulder for the cause of the B.E. pilot's manœuvre. It was a foolish move, and at once betrayed the man's lack of real ability, for Biggles swept down on him and could have fired a burst which might well have ended the combat there and had he been so inclined. But this was not his intention. Moved by some impulse altogether foreign to his nature and his usual methods of fighting, he roared down alongside Pfalz, passing it so closely that their wing tips almost touched. As he passed he tore off his helmet and goggles, flung them on the floor of the cockpit, and stared with smouldering eyes into the face of the German. There was no smile on his own face now, but a burning hatred of the man who shot down machines of inferior performance and then boasted of his prowess. He saw the look of recognition spring into the German's eyes, and the fear that followed it. 'Not so sure of yourself now, are you?' snarled Biggles. 'Come on, you skunk—fight!'

With a savage exaltation that he had never known before, he whirled round, and nearly collided with the B.E. which, with the best intentions, had decided to take a hand. For a moment he saw red. 'Get out of my way, you fool,' he raged, uselessly as he tilted his wing, and missing the B.E. by inches, gave its pilot the shock of his life.

The moves had lost him two seconds of time, and before he was on even keel again the Pfalz had got a lead of a quarter of a mile, and was racing, nose down, for home. 'Not so fast, my cock,' growled Biggles, as he stood on the rudder and shoved the stick forward. What happened to the B.E. after that he did not know, for he never saw it again. He sent a stream of tracer down the slipstream of the red and white machine, and sneered as the pilot swerved away from it, regardless of the fact that at such a range the odds were a thousand to one against a hit.

'You cold-footed rabbit; what about the frying you were so anxious about this morning?' muttered Biggles, as he closed the gap that separated them and sewed a line of leaden stitches down the red and white fuselage. The German swung round with the desperate courage born of despair and sprayed a triple* line of bullets at his relentless pursuer; but Biggles touched his rudder-bar lightly and side-slipped away, whereupon Hess, acknowledging his master, cut his engine and began to slip towards the ground.

'You're not getting away with that, you rat,' grated Biggles, blazing up with fury at such a craven display. 'If you want to go down, then go, and I'll help you on your way,' he snarled, as he roared down on the tail of the falling Ace. He held his fire until his propeller was a few feet from the blackcrossed rudder, and then pressed the gun lever. A double line of orange flame leapt from his engine cowling. To Biggles' atonishment, the German made no effort to defend himself. For a fraction of a second he looked back over his shoulder and read his fate in the spouting muzzles of the twin Vickers guns; then he slumped forward in his cockpit. A tiny tongue of flame curled aft from the scarlet petrol tank; it grew larger and larger until it was a devouring furnace that dropped through the air like a stone.

Biggles pulled out of his dive and turned away feeling suddenly sick, as he often did when he sent down an enemy machine in flames; when he looked back a great cloud of black smoke, towards which tiny figures were running, marked the funeral pyre of the man who had

* Some models of the Pfalz DIII were fitted with three Spandau machine guns, synchronised to fire through the propeller.

sworn to fry an Englishman as his own birthday present.

'I might as well get back,' he thought, glancing round the sky. The B.E. had disappeared, and there were no other machines in sight, so he set a course for the oasis, feeling tired and irritable now that his anger had burned itself out.

He found Algy examining the Pfalz with professional interest when he got back to Abba Sud.

'Any luck?' queried Algy, expectantly, as he walked towards him.

'You can call it luck if you like,' replied Biggles, simply, 'but Hess won't worry our fellows any more. Make out a combat report when you get back and put in a claim for a red and white Pfalz that fell in flames three miles north of Jebel Tire at 10.51 a.m. Our forward observation posts must have seen the show and will confirm it.

'I shall do nothing of the sort,' cried Algy indignantly; 'he was your meat.'

'I don't want the Huns to know that, do I, you ass?' snapped Biggles. 'You do what you're told. And remember, you don't know it's Hess. Our people will get that information from the other side in due course. That's all, laddie,' he went on with a change of tone. 'I must be getting back now.' He looked suddenly old and tired.

'O.K., Skipper,' replied Algy, looking at him under his lashes, and noting the symptoms of frayed nerves. 'When am I going to see you again?'

'I don't know,' muttered Biggles, 'but pretty soon, I hope. Tell Raymond that I'm running on a hot scent,' he went on wistfully, 'and I hope to be back in 266 Squadron again before the end of the month—or else—'

'Or else?' questioned Algy.

'Nothing.' Biggles looked Algy squarely in the eyes. 'Thank God it will soon be over one way or the other,' he said quietly. 'I wasn't made for this game, and I've had about enough. But I've got to go on—to the end— you see that, don't you, old lad?'

'Of course,' replied Algy, swallowing something in his throat.

'I thought you would. Well, cheerio, old boy.'

'Cheerio, old son.'

Their hands met in a firm grip, the only time during the whole war that either of them allowed their real feelings to get uppermost.

Algy stood beside the Camel and watched the Pfalz until it disappeared from sight. 'Those soulless hounds at the Air Board need boiling in oil for sending a fellow like Biggles on a job like this,' he muttered huskily. 'Still, I suppose it's what they call war,' he added, as he climbed slowly into his cockpit.

Chapter 14
Biggles Flies a Bomber

Biggles arrived back at Zabala just as the station was closing down work for lunch. He handed his camera to the photographic sergeant with instructions to be particularly careful with the negatives, and to bring him a print of each as quickly as possible, and he was walking down to the headquarters offices when he saw von Stalhein and the Count, who had evidently heard him land, waiting for him.

'Did you manage it all right?' inquired von Stalhein, with his eyes on Biggles' face.

'I burnt the machine and took the photographs, but naturally I can't say what they're like until I've seen them.'

'Did you land?' Von Stalhein asked the question sharply, almost as if his intention was to catch Biggles off his guard.

'Land!' replied Biggles with a puzzled frown. 'Why should I risk a landing in the desert when I had incendiary bombs with me?'

'Oh, I merely wondered if you had—just as a matter of interest,' retorted von Stalhein. 'You've been a long time, haven't you?'

'As a matter of fact, I have,' admitted Biggles. 'I intended going straight there and back, but I saw something that intrigued me and I thought it was worth while following it up.'

'Indeed! and what was it?' asked the Count, interestedly.

'A new type of British machine, sir,' answered Biggles. 'I didn't think they had any of them on this front; maybe they have only just arrived.'

'What sort of machine was it?'

'A very fast machine with no dihedral on the top plane; they call it the Camel, I think, and it's made at the Sopwith works.'

The Count grimaced. 'I've heard of them in France,' he said quickly. 'What did you do?'

'I took up a position in the sun and watched it, thinking it might possibly lead to the aerodrome of a new squadron.'

'Splendid! What then?'

'The machine crossed the British lines and began to glide down, so I climbed as high as my machine would take me and saw it land at what looks like a new aerodrome about twelve miles south-east of Kantara. I'm not sure about it being a new aerodrome because I haven't had time to verify it in the map-room; it may have been there a long time, but I've never noticed it before.'

'I've never heard of an aerodrome there,' declared the Count, while von Stalhein looked puzzled.

'It wasn't there a few days ago,' he said slowly.

Biggles wondered how he knew that, but said nothing.

'Very well, go in and get some lunch,' went on the Count. 'Our Brunow is becoming quite useful, eh, Erich?'

Von Stalhein smiled a curious smile that always gave Biggles a tingling feeling down the spine, but whatever his thoughts were he did not disclose them, so Biggles saluted and departed in the direction of the Mess.

He had just finished lunch when an orderly arrived with a message that he was wanted at headquarters, so he tossed his napkin on the table, swallowed the last drop of coffee in his cup, and with an easy mind made his way to the Count's office.

'Ah, Brunow, there you are,' began von Faubourg, who was sitting at his desk while von Stalhein leaned in his usual position against the side, blowing clouds of cigarette smoke into the air. 'We've been talking about this report of yours concerning the new aerodrome,' continued the Count, 'and we have decided that there is a strong probability that the British have brought out a new squadron, in which case it would be a good plan to let it know what to expect. If we can put some of the machines out of action so much the better, otherwise we're likely to have some casualties. I suppose you've heard that Hess hasn't come back from his morning patrol? We don't take the matter seriously, but I've rung up the other squadrons who say that they have seen nothing of him, so it rather looks as if he had forced landed somewhere.'

Biggles nodded. 'That must be the case, sir. One can hardly imagine him coming to any harm,' he said seriously.

'No, the thought is preposterous. But about this projected bomb raid. You marked down the exact position of the aerodrome, did you not?'

'I did, sir.'

'I thought I understood you to say that. I've detailed six machines to go over this afternoon and strike while the iron is hot, so to speak, and in order that there should be no mistake I want you to fly the leading one.'

Biggles started. 'You want me to lead the bombers, sir?' he ejaculated.

'Why not? It is a trifle irregular, I know, and Oberleutnant* Kranz, who is commanding the *Staffel* in Mayer's absence, may feel hurt about it, but as you know where the place is you will be able to go straight to it. Kranz can still be in command, but you could show the way and take charge of the operation just while you were over the British lines. Is that quite clear?'

'Quite, sir,' replied Biggles, whose head was in a whirl at this fresh complication. The idea that he might have to accompany a raid, much less lead one, had not occurred to him.

'Each machine will carry two heavy bombs,' continued the Count, 'and one machine will, of course, take a camera so that we can study the layout of the aerodrome at our leisure as well as see if the bombs do any damage.'

'I'll take the camera if you like, sir,' volunteered Biggles, who thought he might as well be hung for a sheep as a lamb.

'That would be excellent. Then I'll leave it to you to fix up the details with Kranz. Good luck!'

Biggles saluted and withdrew with mixed feelings, for the fact that the dummy aerodrome lure had worked out well was rather overshadowed by the part that he had been detailed to play, and he realized that during the next two hours there was a strong possibility that he would be shot down by his own countrymen; and he did not overlook the fact that in the event of his formation being attacked, he might find it difficult not to put up some sort of fight, or pretence of fighting, yet he had no desire to be responsible for the death of a British pilot.

'I shall have to hope for the best, that's all there is

* Flying Officer in the German Air Force

to it,' he thought as he walked along to the hangars where the bustle indicated that preparations for the raid were going forward.

Half an hour later the six machines left the ground in V-formation with Biggles flying at the spear-head, and climbed steeply for altitude. For nearly an hour they roared upwards on a broad zigzag course before heading straight for the lines. They crossed over through a thin and futile archie barrage, and then raced on full throttle towards the now visible aerodrome.

Biggles, who, of course, had not seen it before, was completely amused at the realism of the bait. It was complete in every detail, even to some machines standing on the tarmac. There was no wind so it was unneccesary to turn in order to deliver the attack, and the first six bombs sailed down. But to Biggles' disgust they nearly all went wide; one only fell on the aerodrome and none touched any of the buildings. He had hoped to take a really thrilling photograph back to the Count, showing at least one hangar in flames.

The six machines turned slowly in a wide circle in order not to lose formation, and then returning from the opposite direction, laid their remaining eggs, that is, all except Biggles, who was determined to score a hit, for now that he was actually engaged in the task, the idea of bombing a British aerodrome amused him.

This time the aim was better. Two bombs fell on the aerodrome, and one in the end hangar, but still he was not satisfied, so he dived out of formation, losing height as quickly as possible, and turning again towards the aerodrome, took the centre buildings in his bomb-sight and pulled the toggle. For a few seconds the bomb diminished in size in a remarkable manner as it plunged earthwards, and then a pillar of smoke and flame leapt high into the air. It was a direct hit. He had his camera over the side in an instant, but the movement might almost have been a signal, for he had only taken two photographs when such a tornado of archie burst around him that he dropped the instrument quickly on to the floor of the cockpit and pulled up his nose to rejoin the formation.

The other five machines were in no better case, and it seemed to him as he raced through a sea of smoke and flame that every anti-aircraft gun on the British front had been concentrated on the spot.

'Of course they have: what a fool I am,' he swore. 'Raymond would know that I'd give the Huns the position of the aerodrome, in which case it would be certain that sooner or later a formation of Boche bombers would come over. He could easily get the guns together without disclosing anything about my part of the business. My gosh! I ought to have thought of that.' He flinched as a piece of metal tore through his wing and made the machine vibrate from nose to rudder. A shell burst under his tail, and his observer, a youth named Bronveld, made desperate signals to him to get out of the vicinity as soon as possible.

He needed no urging. His one idea at that moment was to remove himself with the utmost possible speed from the hornets' nest he had stirred up, and all the time he was wondering what the other pilots would say, and more important still, what the Count would say when they got back—if they did—for the whole exploit bore a suspicious likeness to a well-laid trap. 'No,' he reasoned, as he side-slipped away from a well-placed bracket* that blossomed out in front of him, 'they can't blame me very well, for after all, I'm in the show myself, and no one is fool enough to step into a

* Bursting shells on both sides of a target

trap they have themselves set. In fact, it begins to look almost as if it were a good thing that I came on the show, otherwise—'

His high speed soliloquy was cut short by an explosion under his wing tip that nearly turned him upside down. He tried the controls with frantic haste, and breathed a prayer of thankfulness when he found that they were still functioning, but a long strip of fabric that trailed aft from his lower starboard plane made him feel uneasy. One of the other machines suddenly dipped its nose and began gliding down; he noted that its propeller had stopped, but thought it might just manage to reach the German lines that now loomed up ahead of them.

The formation, which had become badly scattered in the barrage, now began to re-form, and he had just taken his place in the lead when, glancing forward through the centre-section, he saw something that set his finger-tips tingling. Cutting across their front on a course that would effectually cut them off from the German lines were two squadrons of aeroplanes that needed no second look to identify them. One squadron, approaching from the west, was composed of eight Sopwith Pups with a solitary Camel hanging on its flank; the other, which was coming up from the east, comprised six Bristol Fighters.

Biggles eyed the Camel with a strange expression on his face, for the circumstances were so—well, he didn't know quite what to call them, for never before had he seen comedy and imminent tragedy so hopelessly intermingled. 'I'd bet a month's pay to a piastre that Algy has a smack at me first; he always does like taking on the leader,' he muttered. 'And I'd have won,' he went on bitterly, as the Camel pulled up in a steep zoom, half-rolled, and then whirled round for the attack with its nose pointing down at Biggles' Halberstadt.

For once Biggles was nonplussed and a thousand ideas flashed through his brain, only to be abandoned instantly as he realized their uselessness. He glanced back over his shoulder and saw Bronveld crouching over his gun, waiting for the Camel to come within range. The lad's face was grim and set, but his hands were steady, and Biggles felt a thrill of apprehension. 'That kid's going to put up a good fight,' he thought anxiously. 'And from the way Algy is handling that Camel it looks to me as if the young fool stands a good chance of stopping a packet of Spandau bullets. He must be crazy to come down on top of us like that, straight over our rear gun.'

Then something like panic seized him as he visualized the unthinkable picture of his gunner killing Algy, or conversely, Algy's feelings when he found he had shot down his best friend. Whatever else happened, that must be avoided at all costs. Better to betray himself and be shot by the Huns than that should happen. 'At least I can let him know it's me,' he thought as, white-faced, he reached for his signal pistol, slipped in a red cartridge, and sent a streak of scarlet fire blazing across the nose of the diving Camel. But to his horror the pilot paid no attention to it, although, as if actuated by a common motive, the four remaining Halberstadts banked hard to the right and closed in on him. More with the object of avoiding a collision, he swung round in a fairly steep bank, and the other machines fell in line behind him.

The movement disconcerted the British pilots, who now found themselves facing an ever-circling ring from which guns spat every time they tried to approach, and while they were still milling round them in indecision,

Biggles darted out of the circle at a tangent and raced, nose down, for home. By the time the Pups and Bristols realized what had happened the other Halberstadts had followed on his tail and had established a clear lead, which they were able to keep until they were well inside their own territory. The danger was averted.

Biggles brushed his hand across his forehead. 'Phew! that was quite enough of that,' he muttered, as he looked back over his shoulder, and then stiffened with horror at the sight that met his eyes. The British machines, with the exception of one, had turned back, but the Camel, by reason of its superior speed, had continued the chase and had caught them. What was worse, its pilot was evidently still determined to strike at the leader of the Hun formation, and was roaring down in a final effort. As it came within range jets of orange flame darted from the muzzles of the guns on its engine cowling, and at the same moment, Bronveld, who was alive to the danger and crouching low behind his Parabellum gun, pulled the trigger. His aim was true. Biggles saw the tracer leap across the intervening space in a straight line that ended at the whirling engine of the British machine. Something stung his shoulder but he hardly felt it, for his eyes were fixed on the Camel in a kind of fascinated horror. Its nose had jerked up in a vertical zoom; for a moment it hung in space with its propeller threshing the air uselessly; then it turned slowly over on to its back and plunged earthward.

In a state of mental paralysis Biggles watched it hurtling through space. He couldn't think. He couldn't act. He could only stare ashen-faced at the spinning machine. He saw a wing break off, and the fuselage with its human cargo drop like a cannon-ball; then he turned away. He shifted his gaze to Bronveld, who was clapping his hands jubilantly. As their eyes met the German showed his teeth in a victorious smile and turned his thumbs upwards, a signal that means the same thing the world over. Biggles could not find it in his heart to blame him, for it was the boy's first victory, and once, long ago, he had behaved in exactly the same way; only that time the spinning machine had black crosses on its wings, not red, white, and blue circles.

He turned back to his own cockpit feeling as if he had turned into a block of stone. Something seemed to have died inside him, leaving in its place only a bitter hatred of the war and everything connected with it. He ground his teeth under the emotion that shook him like a leaf, while in his mind hammered a single thought, 'Algy has gone west . . . Algy has gone west.' The wind seemed to howl it in the wires, and the deep-throated Mercedes engine purred it in a monotonous vibrating drone.

Through a shimmering atmosphere of unreality he saw the aerodrome at Zabala loom up, and automatically throttled back to land. His actions were purely instinctive as he flattened out and taxied slowly up to the hangars. The Count, von Stalhein, and several other officers were standing on the tarmac waiting, but none of them meant anything to him now. He no longer feared von Stalhein. He no longer cared a fig if he was suspected, arrested, or even shot.

He switched off, climbed stiffly to the ground, and walked slowly towards the spot upon which the others were converging. He could hear a babel of voices around him, German voices, and a wave of hatred swept over him. What was happening? He hardly knew. He became aware that Bronveld was tapping him on the back while he spoke rapidly to Faubourg. They were all laughing, talking over the battle, and a strange feeling swept over Biggles that he had seen it all before. Where had he seen the same thing? Suddenly he knew. The scene was precisely that which occurred on any British aerodrome after a raid; only the uniforms and the machines with the sinister Maltese crosses were different. As in a dream he heard the Count speaking.

'Splendid,' he was saying, 'splendid. Kranz is full of praise for the way you handled a nasty situation. Your firing of the red signal to form circle when you did, he says, saved the whole formation. And that last bomb of yours, and the way you left the formation to make sure of a hit, was brilliant. Your recommendation for the Iron Cross shall go off to-day. And Bronveld has shot down a Camel. We knew that before you got home; it fell in our lines and the artillery rang up to say they are sending the body here for burial. We will see that it is done properly, as we always do, because we know the British do the same for us. But what's this? Why! you're wounded, man.' He pointed to Biggles' shoulder, where a nasty-looking red stain was slowly spreading round a jagged tear in his overalls.

'Oh, that.' Biggles laughed, a hard, unpleasant sound. 'That's nothing. I hardly noticed it. The Camel fired the shot,' he added, wishing that it had gone through his head instead of his shoulder.

'While you were holding your machine steady so that Bronveld could shoot,' observed the Count. 'That is the sort of courage that will serve the *Vaterland.** But go and get your shoulder attended to and make out your reports, all of you. I am looking forward to seeing the photographs.'

Biggles removed his flying cap and goggles and walked towards the Medical Officer's tent. He was

* The Fatherland: Germany

153

conscious that von Stalhein was watching him with the same puzzled expression that he had worn after the Mayer exploit. 'He doesn't know what to make of me,' he thought. 'Well, a fat lot I care what he thinks. I'll fly over to Raymond to-morrow, and throw my hand in; in future I'm flying in my own uniform, in France, or not at all. I've had enough of this dirty game and I never want to see a palm tree again.'

The wound, which was little more than a graze, was washed and bandaged by the elderly, good-natured German doctor, after which he went to his room and threw himself on his bed. The sun was sinking like a fiery orange ball in a crimson sky that merged into purple overhead, and threw a lurid glow on the hangars and the sentinel-like palms. It flooded into his room and bathed his bed, his uniform, and his tired face in a blood-red sheen.

For a long time he lay quite still, trying to think, trying to adjust himself to the new state of things, but in vain. His most poignant thought, the thing that worried him most, was the fact that he had been responsible for Algy's death in the first place by causing him to be posted from France to the land of the Israelites. That Algy might have been killed if he had remained in France did not occur to him. 'But there, what does it matter? What does anything matter? The lad's gone topsides, and that's the end of it,' he thought, as he rose wearily. He washed, and was drying his face, when an unusual sound took him to the window. A tender had stopped and half a dozen grey-coated soldiers in the uniform of the German Field Artillery, under the supervision of a Flying Corps officer, were unloading something. It was a long slim object shrouded in a dark blanket.

He watched with an expressionless face, for he was

past feeling anything. It was all a part of the scheme, the moving of the relentless finger of Fate that had lain over Palestine like a blight for nearly two thousand years and left a trail of death in its wake. He watched the soldiers carry the body into the tent that had been set aside as a temporary mortuary. He saw them come out, close the flap behind them, salute, and return to the tender, which, with a grinding of gears, moved slowly across the sand and disappeared from sight. It was like watching a scene in a play.

Then, moved by some impulse, he picked up his cap, left the room, and strode firmly towards the tent. 'I might as well say good-bye to the lad,' he thought, with his nostrils quivering. He threw aside the flap, entered, and stood in dumb misery at the end of the camp bed on which the pitiful object rested. Slowly and with a hand that shook, he lifted the end of the blanket—and looked.

How long he stood there he never knew. Time seemed to stand still. The deathly hush that falls over the desert at the approach of twilight had fallen; some-where in the desert a sand-cricket was chirping. That was all. And still he stared—and stared.

At last, with a movement that was almost convulsive, he replaced the blanket, stepped back, and leaned against the tent-pole while he fought back an hysterical desire to laugh aloud—for the face was not Algy's. It was that of a middle-aged man in the uniform of an infantry regiment, with pilot's wings sewn on his tunic above the white and violet ribbon of the Military Cross. It was quite peaceful. A tiny blue hole above the left eyebrow showed where life had fled, leaving a faint smile of surprise on the countenance, so suddenly had the end come.

Biggles pulled himself together with a stupendous

effort and walked reverently from the presence of Death. With his teeth clenched, he hurried back to his room and flung himself face downwards on his bed, laughing and sobbing in turn. He did not hear the door open quietly to admit an orderly with tea on a tray, who, when his startled eyes fell on his superior officer, withdrew quickly and returned to the camp kitchen.

'Karl,' he called to the cook, 'Brunow's finished— nerve's gone to bits. Funny how all these flyers go the same in the end. Well, I don't care as long as they'll let me keep *my* feet on the ground.'

Chapter 15
Ordeal by Night

The German orderly, although he had good reason for thinking that 'Brunow's nerves had gone to bits', was far from right. Biggles' nerves were unimpaired, although it must be admitted that he had been badly shaken by the belief that Algy had been killed, but after the first reaction had spent itself the knowledge that the whole thing had been nothing more than a bad dream was such a relief that he prepared to resume his work with a greater determination than before. Lying propped up on his pillow, he reviewed the events of the day which, taking things all round, might have panned out a good deal worse. Hess had gone west, and he had no regrets on that score. 'Yes, taking it all round I've been pretty lucky to-day,' he mused, which was not strictly true, for such successes as he had achieved had been due more to clear thinking and ability than to good fortune. His only stroke of what could be regarded as luck was the firing of the red signal light which had saved the formation, thereby putting up his reputation with the *Staffel*, for when he had fired it he had not the remotest idea that it was the German signal to 'form circle', a fact that he could only assume was the case from what followed.

By dinner-time he was normal again but eager to see the end of his masquerade in order that he might return to normal duties. So deep-rooted was this longing that he was prepared to take almost any chance, regardless of risks, in order to expedite the conclusion of the affair.

Certain vital facts he had already grasped; of others, a shrewd suspicion was rapidly forming in his mind, and he only needed confirmation of them to send him to British headquarters and place his knowledge at the disposal of those who would know best how to act upon it.

It was with a determination born of these thoughts that he decided during dinner to pursue his quest in a manner which inwardly appalled him, but which, he thought, if successful could hardly fail to produce results. The idea came to him on the spur of the moment when he heard a machine taxi out across the aerodrome. Subconsciously he waited, expecting to hear it take off, but when it did not he knew—guessed would perhaps be a better word—that it was standing on the far side of the aerodrome waiting for a passenger about whose identity there was no doubt in his mind. And when a few minutes later von Stalhein left his chair, and after a whispered conversation with the Count, went out of the room, he fancied that he knew what was about to take place.

He would have liked to follow at once in order to watch von Stanhein, but that was out of the question, for it was a matter of etiquette that until the Count rose and led the way to the ante-room, no one could leave his place without asking his permission, and then a very good excuse would be demanded.

So he sat where he was, sipping his coffee, but listening for the sound that would denote von Stalhein's departure for the British lines; and he had not long to wait. Within a few minutes there came the distant roar of an aero engine; it swelled to a deep crescendo and then died away in the distance. 'There he goes,' he thought. 'If I could only be at the other end when he lands I might learn something.'

Now that his mind was made up on a course of action he fidgeted with impatience for the meal to end, and when at length the Count got up, the signal for a general move, he followed the others through to the ante-room with a light-heartedness which sprang, not from anticipation of the self-imposed undertaking before him, but from relief of knowing that the time had come to begin. He hung about conspicuously for a little while, turning over the pages of a magazine, and then satisfied that everyone was settling down for a quiet evening, he left the room and walked unhurriedly to his quarters, where he changed his regulation boots for a pair of the canvas shoes that most of the officers wore when off duty, and slipped an electric torch into his pocket. This done, he strolled towards the tarmac. He did not go as far as the front of the hangars, but turned to the left behind them and moved along in the direction of the fort. The building was in darkness, but knowing that a sentry would be on door duty, he kept to the rear, and then worked his way down the side until he stood under the window where, a few nights before, he had seen von Stalhein writing.

With his heart thumping in spite of his outward calm, he took a swift glance around to make sure that he was not being watched, and then, reaching for the window-sill, drew himself up until he could throw a leg across the wooden frame. The other followed, and he slipped quietly inside.

After the bright starlight outside he could see nothing at first, but by waiting a minute or two for his eyes to become accustomed to the darkness, he could just make out the general outlines of the furniture. He crossed swiftly to the door, and tried it, but as he expected, it was locked, so he went over to the writing-desk upon which a number of documents were lying, but they were, of course, written in German, so he did not touch them. In any case he was not particularly concerned with them. Working swiftly but quietly, he made a complete inspection of the room, and then turned to the tall wardrobe which stood against the far wall. He opened it, and shielding the torch with his cupped hands, he flashed it on the interior, when he heard a sound that brought him round with a start although not particularly alarmed, for it came from the direction of the window. It seemed to be a soft scraping noise, a rustling, as if a large bird had settled on the ledge.

Bending forward, he could just make out two dark objects that moved along the window-sill with a kind of groping movement. For a moment he could not make out what they were, and then he understood. They were hands. Some one was coming in through the window.

Now even in the flash of time that remained for him to think, he knew there were only two courses open to him. One was to step forward and confront the marauder, who, by his clandestine method of entry, obviously had no more right in the room than he had, and the other was to hide. Of the two the latter found more favour, for the very last thing he wanted was the hullabaloo that might conceivably take place if he allowed himself to be seen. So he stepped back, squeezed himself into the wardrobe, and pulled the door nearly shut behind him just as a man's head appeared in the square of star-spangled deep blue that marked the position of the window. Even in the uncertain light a single glance was sufficient to show that it was not a European, for the dark-bearded face was surmounted by a turban. As silent as a shadow, the Arab swung his legs and body over the sill with the feline grace of a panther, and stood in a tense attitude, listening, precisely as Biggles had done a few minutes before. Then, still without making a sound, he glided forward into the room.

For one ghastly moment Biggles thought he was coming straight to the wardrobe, and he had already braced himself for the shock of meeting when the man stepped aside and disappeared from his limited line of vision. For a moment he wondered if he had gone to the electric light switch with the object of turning it on, but the half-expected click did not come. Nor did the man reappear. Nothing happened. All was as silent as the grave. A minute passed, and another, and still nothing happened.

Then began a period of time which to Biggles' keyed-up nerves seemed like eternity; but still nothing happened. Where was the man? What was he doing? Was he still in the room? Could it be possible that he had slipped out of the window again without being noticed? No, that was quite impossible. Had he in some way opened the door and gone out into the corridor? Definitely no; in such an aching silence, for any one to attempt to turn the handle, much less the lock, without being heard, was manifestly absurd. What, then, was happening?

Such were Biggles' thoughts as he stood in his stuffy hiding-place fighting to steady his palpitating heart. Another ten minutes passed slowly and he began to wonder if there had been a man at all. Could the whole thing have been a vision conjured up by his already overtaxed nerves? The tension became electric in its intensity, and he knew he could not stand the strain much longer. Could he rush to the window, throw himself through, and bolt before the man in the room had recovered from the shock of discovering that he was not alone? He thought he could, but it was a desperate expedient that he preferred not to undertake until it became vitally necessary.

Then at last the silence was broken, broken by a sound which, as it reached his ears, seemed to turn his blood to ice. He had heard it many times before, and it never failed to fill him with a vague dread, but in his present position it literally paralysed him. It was the slow dragging gait of a lame man, and it was coming down the corridor. Then it stopped and there was a faint tap, tap, and Biggles knew that von Stalhein was propping his stick against the wall while he felt for his keys. In his agitated imagination he could see him, follow his every action, and the grinding of the key in the lock sounded like the first laborious move of a piece of badly oiled machinery. Slowly the door creaked open on its hinges. There was a sharp click, a blaze of blinding light, and von Stalhein stepped into the room.

At that moment the Arab sprang. Biggles saw him streak across the room with a brown arm upraised, and caught the flash of steel. But if the Arab hoped to catch the German unaware, he was doomed to disappointment.

Never in his life before had Biggles seen anything quite so swift as that which followed. With a lithe movement that would have been miraculous even for an athlete, von Stalhein dived forward with a galvanic jerk; the top part of his body twisted, and the curved blade that was aimed at his throat missed his shoulder by what must have been literally a hair's breadth. His sticks crashed to the floor. All the force of the Arab's arm must have been behind the blow, for his lunge carried him beyond the German, who was round in a flash. His hand darted to his hip pocket, but before he could draw the weapon he obviously kept there the

Arab was on him again, and he was compelled to use both hands to fight off his attack.

Again the Arab sprang, and as his right arm flashed down von Stalhein caught it with his left, while his right groped through the folds of his flowing burnous for the brown throat. In that position they remained while Biggles could have counted ten, looking for all the world like a piece of magnificent statuary. Neither of them spoke; only the swift intake of breath revealed the quivering energy that was being expended by each of them to hold the other off. Then the tableau snapped into lightning-like activity.

Biggles couldn't see just what happened. All he knew was that the knife crashed to the floor; at the same moment the Arab tore himself free and flung himself at the window. He went through it like a greyhound, but, even so, the German was faster. His right hand flashed down and came up gripping a squat automatic, and at the precise moment that the Arab disappeared from sight a spurt of yellow flame streaked across the room. Von Stalhein was at the window before the crash of the report had died away; with the agility of an eel he threw his legs across the sill and sprang downward out of sight.

Biggles seized his opportunity; he stepped out of the wardrobe, closed it behind him, darted to the door and sped down the corridor. He hesitated as he reached the main entrance, eyes seeking the sentry, but no one was in sight, so he ran out and took refuge behind the nearest hangar. At that stage he would have asked nothing more than to be allowed to return to his room, but he saw figures hurrying towards the fort from the Mess, so he turned about and ran back as if he had heard the report of the shot and was anxious to know the cause. Doors were banging inside and voices were calling; he paid no attention to them but ran round the side of the building, and then pulled up with a jerk as he almost collided with von Stalhein and the door sentry, who were bending over a recumbent figure on the ground. He saw that it was the Arab.

'Good gracious, von Stalhein,' he exclaimed, 'what's happened? What was that shot?'

'Nothing very much,' replied the German coolly. 'Fellow tried to knife me, that's all. One of the sheikhs who was on the raid the other night; the poor fools are blaming me because the thing went wrong. By the way, where have you just sprung from?'

It was on the tip of Biggles' tongue to say 'from my room', but something warned him to be careful. Instead, 'I was admiring the night from the tarmac,' he smiled; 'I can't sit indoors this weather. Why?'

'Because I looked into your room just now to have a word with you, and you weren't there,' was the casual reply.

Biggles caught his breath as he realized how nearly he had made a blunder. 'What did you want me for?' he inquired.

'Oh, merely a job the Count had in mind, but don't worry about it now; I'll see you in the morning. I shall have to stay and see this mess cleared up, confound it.' Von Stalhein touched the Arab with the toe of his patent leather shoe.

'All right. Then I think I'll get to bed,' returned Biggles, as several officers and mechanics joined the party.

Safely out of sight round the corner of a hangar he mopped his face with a handkerchief. 'My gosh,' he muttered, 'this business is nothing but one shock after another. "Where have you just sprung from?" he asked. I felt like saying, "And where the dickens have *you*

164

come from?" He couldn't have been in that machine that took off, after all; I'm beginning to take too much for granted, which doesn't pay, evidently, at this game. And so he's got a job for me in the morning, eh? Well, with any luck I shan't be taking on many more jobs in this part of the world, I hope.'

Chapter 16
Checked

The next morning he was awakened by his batman*
bringing early morning tea. He got out of bed, lit a
cigarette, and sat by the open window while he con-
sidered the results of his investigations. How far had
he progressed? How much had he learned about El
Shereef, the German super-spy? Had he arrived at a
stage when, figuratively speaking, he could lay his cards
on Major Raymond's desk and ask to be posted back
to his old squadron, leaving the Intelligence people to
do the rest? No, he decided regretfully, he had not. He
had learned something, enough perhaps to end von
Stalhein's activities, but that was not enough, for while
the British Intelligence Staff might agree that he had
concluded his task, something inside told him that it
was still incomplete; that something more, the unmask-
ing of a deeper plot than either he or British headquarters at first suspected, remained to be done. Just
what that was he did not know, but he had a vague
suspicion, and at the moment he felt he was standing
on the threshold of discoveries that might alter the
whole course of the war in that part of the world.
Moreover, it was unlikely that another British agent
would ever again be in such a sound position to bring
about the exposure; so it was up to him to hang on
whatever the cost to himself.

* An attendant serving an officer. A position discontinued in today's
Royal Air Force.

That von Stalhein was the super-spy, El Shereef, he no longer doubted, for it was hardly possible that there could be two German spies masquerading as Arabs behind the British lines, and that von Stalhein did adopt Arab disguise was certain; the incident at the oasis was sufficient proof of that. If further proof were needed there was the business of the feigned limp, which he felt was all part of a clever pose to throw possible investigators off the scent. The limp was so pronounced, and he played the part of a lame man to such perfection, that the very act of abandoning it would have been a disguise in itself. No one could even think of von Stalhein without the infirmity. For what purpose other than espionage, or disguise, should he pretend to be incapacitated when he was not?

He knew now that von Stalhein was as active as any normal man. The way he had behaved when attacked by the Arab in his room revealed that, for he had dropped his sticks and dashed to the window with a speed that would have done credit to a professional runner. If he were not El Shereef, why the pose? As Erich von Stalhein he made his headquarters at Zabala; at night he changed, and under the pseudonym of El Shereef, worked behind the British lines, coming and going by means of a special detailed aeroplane. And the more Biggles thought about it the more he was convinced that he was right.

'The pilot flies him over, lands him well behind the lines—at the oasis for instance—and then comes home. Later, at a pre-arranged time and place, he goes over and picks him up,' he mused. 'That's what Mayer was doing the day he picked me up. Mayer landed for von Stalhein, but when he found me there instead he knew he had to bring me back. If only I could catch von Stalhein in the act of landing, there would be an end to it, but I'll bet he never again uses the place where *I* was picked up; he'd be too cunning for that; he doesn't trust me a yard, in spite of the fact that he has no foundation for his suspicions. He must have an instinct for danger like a cat. The only other way to nab him would be to find out the Arab name he adopts when he is over there, hanging about our troops picking up information. The thing I can't get over is that shadow on the tent, and but for the fact that he must have been somewhere around in order to learn that I was a prisoner, and then effect my rescue, I should feel inclined to think that I'd been mistaken. It's rather funny he has never mentioned a thing to me, taken credit for getting me out of the mess. No, perhaps it isn't funny. Oh, dash it, I don't know . . . unless . . .'

He stared thoughtfully at the desert for some time, drumming on the window-sill with his fingers. 'Well, I'd better go and see what the Count wants, I suppose,' he concluded, as he finished his toilet and went down to the Mess to breakfast, after which he walked along to the fort. He found von Stalhein in the headquarters office, but the Count had not yet arrived.

'Good morning, Brunow,' greeted the German affably. 'Quite a good photo—look.' He passed the last photograph Biggles had taken of Mayer's burning Halberstadt.

'Good morning, von Stalhein,' replied Biggles, taking it and looking at it closely, aware that that the German's eyes were on him. He finished his scrutiny and passed it back, wondering if von Stalhein had overlooked something in the photograph which he had spotted instantly. The photograph had been taken from a very low altitude and from an oblique angle, which showed not only the charred, smoking wreck but the desert beyond. Across the soft sand where he had landed ran a line of wheel tracks; they began some distance from the crash and ran off the top right-hand corner of the photograph. He looked up to see von Stalhein looking at him; his eyes were smiling mockingly, but there was no smile about his thin lips.

'I may be mistaken, but I understood you to say that you didn't land,' observed the German, in a low careless voice that nevertheless held a hard, steely quality.

Biggles raised his eyebrows. 'No, you were not mistaken,' he replied; 'why did you say that?'

'I was wondering how the wheel marks got there, that's all.'

Biggles laughed. 'Oh, those,' he said. 'Those were the marks made by my home-made trailer, I expect— have a cigarette?'

He offered his case as if his explanation of such a trivial point was sufficient—as indeed it was.

'Of course,' said von Stalhein, slowly—very slowly. 'Funny, I didn't think of that.'

'One cannot always expect to think of everything,' rejoined Biggles simply. 'What does the Count want— do you know?'

'Here he is, so he'll tell you himself,' answered von Stalhein shortly.

Biggles sprang to attention. 'Good morning, sir,' he said.

'Good morning, Brunow— morning, Erich. Going to be hot again,' observed the Count, dropping into his chair behind the desk. And then, glancing up at Biggles, he asked, 'Has Hauptmann von Stalhein told you what we were discussing last night?'

'No, sir.'

'I see.' The Count unfastened his stiff upright collar. 'Well, the position is this,' he went on. 'As you are no doubt aware, the chief reason why you were sent here was because of your knowledge of the English and their language. It was thought that you might be able to undertake duties that would be impossible for a—one of our own people. You have a British R.F.C. uniform, and we have British aeroplanes, yet neither have been fully exploited. In fact, you are rapidly becoming an ordinary flying officer engaged on routine duties, and in that capacity you have done remarkably well; in fact, if it goes on one of the *Staffels* will be putting in a request for you to be posted to them. I think it's time we did something about it, don't you?'

'As you wish, sir. I have thought about it myself, but I didn't mention it because I thought you'd give me orders for special duty when you were ready.'

'Quite so.' The Count turned to von Stalhein. 'We shall make a good German officer of him yet, Erich,' he observed dryly, in German.

'Thank you, sir,' put in Biggles absent-mindedly, in the same language.

'Ah-ha, so you are progressing with your German, too,' asserted the Count, raising his eyebrows.

Biggles flushed slightly, for the words had slipped out unthinkingly. 'I'm doing my best, and what with my book and conversations in the Mess, I am picking it up slowly,' he explained.

'Capital. But let us come to this business we are here for,' continued the Count. He lit a long black cigar and studied the glowing end closely before he went on. 'Last night I was merely concerned with the idea of sending you over to the British lines for a day or two to pick up any odd scraps of information that might be useful, paying particular regard to the preparations the British are making for the attack we know is soon to be launched near Gaza—at least, everything points to the battle being fought there. Since then, however, a blow has fallen the importance of which cannot be exaggerated. It is, in fact, the most serious set-back we have had for a long time. Fortunately it does not affect us personally, but I hear that General Headquarters in Jerusalem is in a fever about it; if we could recover what we have lost, it would be a feather in our caps.'

'In your cap, you mean,' thought Biggles, but he said nothing.

'Tell me, Brunow'—the Count dropped his voice to little more than a whisper—'have you ever heard of one who is called El Shereef?'

Had he pulled out a revolver and fired point blank he could hardly have given Biggles a bigger shock. How he kept his face immobile he never knew, for the words set every nerve in his body jangling. He pretended to think for a moment before he replied. 'I seem to recall it, sir, but in what connexion I cannot think—yes, I have it. You remember the first day I came here I landed at Kantara. I heard some of the officers in the Mess using the name quite a lot, but I didn't pay much attention to it.'

'Then I will tell you. El Shereef was a—an agent, a German agent. Not only was he the cleverest agent in Palestine, but in the world.'

'Was . . . ?'

'He has been caught at last.'

Biggles felt the room rocking about him, but he continued staring straight at the Count, struggling to prevent his face from betraying what he was thinking. 'What a pity,' he said at last. For the life of him he couldn't think of anything else to say.

'Pity! it's a tragedy—an overwhelming misfortune. He was taken yesterday in a cunningly set trap by Major Sterne, who as you may know is one of the cleverest men on the British side.'

'By Major Sterne,' repeated Biggles foolishly.

The Count nodded. 'So we understand. The British have made no announcement about it—nor do we expect them to—yet. But General Headquarters, by means known only to themselves, got the news through late last night.'

Von Stalhein was lighting a fresh cigarette as if the matter hardly interested him.

Biggles tried to think, but could not. His mind seemed to have collapsed in complete chaos as all his so-called facts, conjectures, and suppositions crashed to the ground. He could hardly follow what the Count was saying when he continued.

'Well, there it is. The British will give him a trial—of sorts—of course, but we shall know only one thing more for certain—and that soon—and that is that El Shereef has faced a firing party. If you are to do anything it will have to be done at once.'

'Do anything, sir,' ejaculated Biggles. 'Me! What can I do?'

'You can get into the British lines. I was hoping that you might try to effect a rescue.'

Biggles nearly laughed aloud, for he felt that he was going insane. Was the Count seriously asking him to rescue El Shereef, when . . . ? The thing was too utterly ridiculous. He saw the Count was waiting for his answer. 'I'll do anything I can, sir,' he offered. 'If you could give me any further information that might be useful I should be grateful.'

The Count shook his head. 'All I can tell you is that El Shereef will probably be sent under special escort to British General Headquarters for interrogation.'

'Then I'd better go over and do what I can,' said Biggles thoughtfully; and then added in a flash of inspiration, 'Can you give me any idea of what he looks like, so that I shall be able to recognize him when I see him?'

'Yes, I can do that,' agreed the Count. 'He is, as you no doubt imagine, really a German, although he will of course be dressed as an Arab. He has lived with the Arabs for so long that he is nearly one of them—looks Arab—thinks Arab—speaks Arabic. Tall, brown—really brown, not merely grease paint—drooping black moustache. Dark eyes, and rather a big nose, like the beak of a hawk. Not much of a description, but it's the best I can give you. If you can get near him, show your ring and he'll understand. He will still have his hidden about him if the British didn't take it away when they searched him.'

'Very good, sir; I'll get off right away.' Biggles did not so much as glance at von Stalhein as he saluted, turned on his heel and departed to his room.

When he reached it he slumped down wearily on his bed and gave expression to his disappointment and mortification, for his feelings at that moment were not unlike those of a very tired man who, in the act of sitting down, realizes that some one has pulled the chair away from under him. After a period of deadly risk and anxiety he thought he had the situation well summed up, and all he needed to do to win was to play his trump cards carefully. The knowledge that his cards were useless was a disappointment not easily overcome, and it was followed by an almost overwhelming sense of depression, for if what the Count had told him was true, he had been running on a false scent all along. The only redeeming thing about the new development was that, if the British had really caught El Shereef, then this work was finished, and there was no longer any reason why he should stay at Zabala. Officially, his retirement from the scene would now be permiss-

173

ible, even though he had failed, but he knew he could not conscientiously do so while in his heart he was still certain that von Stalhein was engaged in some sinister scheme about which the British authorities knew nothing. Suppose the story were not true? Suppose the whole thing was pure fabrication, a story invented by the Count and von Stalhein to draw a red herring across the trail of British agents whom they suspected — or knew — to be engaged in counter-espionage behind their lines. Conversely, might it not be a gigantic piece of bluff devised by the British Intelligence Staff to mislead the Germans, or cause them to make a move which might betray the very man whom they claimed to have caught? Both theories were possible.

Thinking the new situation over, Biggles felt like a man who, faced with the task of unravelling a tangled ball of string, sees a dozen ends sticking out, but does not know which is the right one. 'I've had a few boneshakers since I started this job, but this one certainly is a bazouka,' he mused. 'Well, I suppose I'd better do something about it, and the best thing I can do is to push off through the atmosphere to Kantara to find out how much truth there is in it.'

He changed into his R.F.C. uniform, pulled his overalls on over it, went down to the tarmac, ordered out the Bristol Fighter, and landed at Kantara exactly thirty-five minutes later. He taxied up to the hangars, and telling the duty N.C.O. to leave his machine where it was in case he needed it urgently, went straight to Major Raymond's tent.

He found the Major working at his desk.

'Good morning, Bigglesworth —'

But Biggles was too impatient to indulge in conventional greetings. 'Is this tale true about your catching El Shereef, sir,' he asked abruptly.

174

'Quite true.'

Biggles stared. 'Well, I'll be shot for the son of a gun,' he muttered. 'You're quite sure—I mean, you're not just spinning a yarn?'

'Good gracious, no. But how did you know about it?'

'Von Faubourg told me this morning.'

'He wasn't long getting the news then.'

'So it seems. How did you work it?'

'Sterne did it. He's been on the trail for some time, working in his own way. He managed to pick up a clue and laid a pretty trap, and El Shereef, cunning as he is, walked straight into it.'

'That's what the Huns told me,' nodded Biggles. 'It begins to look as if it's true.'

'Of course it's true—we've got him here.'

'What! at Kantara?'

'Well, at Jebel Zaloud, the village just behind. General Headquarters are there. They've had El Shereef there trying to get some information out of him, but it's no use. He won't speak. He won't do anything else if it comes to that—won't eat or drink. He's an Arab, you know.'

'Arab? You mean he's disguised as an Arab?'

'If it's a disguise, then it's a thundering good one.'

'It would be. He's lived amongst the Arabs half his life, until he is one, or as near as makes no difference. The Count told me so himself.'

'I don't know about that, but it's no wonder things went wrong over here. He is—or rather, was—one of our most trusted Sheikhs. He's a fellow with a big following, too.'

'How do you know it's El Shereef?'

'Sterne was sure of it before he collared him. When we took him he was wearing one of those same rings

175

that you've got—the German Secret Service ring. I've got it here: here it is. He had also got some very interesting documents on him—plans of British positions, and so on.'

Biggles picked up the ring that the Major had tossed on to the table and looked at it with interest. 'I should like to see this cove,' he said quietly.

'I think it could be arranged, although I can't see much point in it. You'll have to make haste, though.'

'Why?'

'He was tried by a specially convened Field General Court Martial this morning and sentenced to death.'

'Good God! When is sentence to be carried out?'

'To-day, some time. He's too tricky a customer to keep hanging about. He'll certainly be shot before sundown.'

Biggles jaw set grimly. 'That's awkward,' he said.

'Why?'

'Because I've been sent over here to rescue him.'

It was the Major's turn to look startled. 'Are you serious?' he asked incredulously.

'Too true I am.'

'What are you going to do about it?'

'Nothing—now. I'm through. If you've got the fellow, then that's the end of the story as far as I'm concerned.'

'That's what I thought; in fact, that's why I sent Lacey over to let you know.'

'You did what?'

'Sent Lacey over. I couldn't do less. There was no point in your going on risking your neck at Zabala.'

'Where's Algy now?'

'He's gone. He took off just before you landed. He's going to do the message-dropping stunt in the olive grove. It's a pity he went, but naturally I didn't expect the Huns would tell you about our catching El Shereef.'

Biggles nodded sagely. 'Which, to my mind, is a perfectly good reason why you might have guessed they'd do it,' he declared. 'In my experience, it's the very last thing that you'd expect that always happens at this game. My word! dog-fighting* is child's play to it.'

'Well, what are you going to do? I'm busy over this affair, as you may imagine.'

'Just as a matter of curiosity I'd like to have a dekko at this nimble chap who is called El Shereef.'

'Very well; after what you've done we can hardly refuse such a natural request. I'll see if it can be arranged.' The Major reached for his telephone.

* An aerial battle rather than a hit and run attack.

Chapter 17
Hare and Hounds

Two hours later Biggles again sat in Major Raymond's tent with his face buried in his hands; the Major was busy writing on a pad. 'How's this?' he said, passing two sheets of paper. 'The first is an official notification of the execution that will appear in to-night's confidential orders; the other is the notice that will be issued to the press. Naturally, we make as much of a thing like this as we can; it's good propaganda, and it bucks up the public at home to know that we are as quick-witted as the Huns.'

Biggles read the notices. 'They seem to be O.K., sir,' he said, passing them back. 'I'll be going now,' he added, rising and picking up his cap.

'You still insist in going back to Zabala?'

'I don't want to go, sir, don't think that, but I think it's up to me to try to get the truth about von Stalhein's game while I can come and go. I know I said I wouldn't go back, but I've been thinking it over. I shan't be long, anyway. If I find things are getting too hot I'll pack up and report here.'

'As you wish,' agreed the Major.

Biggles walked towards the door. 'Cheerio for the present, then, sir,' he said. 'You might remember me to Algy when he comes back.'

'He's probably back by now; can't you stay and have a word with him?'

'No, I haven't time now; besides, I've nothing particular to talk about,' decided Biggles. Lost in thought,

178

he walked slowly back to where he had left his Bristol, climbed into the cockpit, and took off. Still in a brown study, he hardly bothered to watch the sky, for while he was over the British side of the lines he had nothing to fear, and over the German side the white bar on his wings made him safe from attack from German aeroplanes.

Once he caught sight of a large formation of Pfalz Scouts, but he paid no attention to them; he did not even watch them but continued on a straight course for Zabala, still turning over in his mind the knotty problems that beset him.

It was, therefore, with a start of surprise and annoyance that he was aroused from his reverie by the distant clatter of a machine-gun, and while he was in the act of looking back for the source of the noise he was galvanized into activity by a staccato burst which he knew from experience was well inside effective range. Cursing himself for his carelessness, he half-rolled desperately, but not before he had felt the vicious thud of bullets ripping through his machine. 'What the dickens do the fools think they're playing at?' he snarled, as he levelled out and saw that he was in the middle of a swarm of Pfalz. 'They must be blind,' he went on furiously, as he threw the Bristol into a steep bank in order to display the white bar on his top plane. But either the Germans did not see it or they deliberately ignored it, for two or three of them darted in, guns going, obviously with the intention of shooting him down.

Biggles knew that something had gone wrong, but the present was no time to wonder what it was. He must act quickly if he was to escape the fate that he had often meted out to others, but he was at once faced with a difficult problem. At the back of his mind still lingered the conviction that the Pfalz pilots had forgotten all about his distinguishing mark, and would presently see and remember it, but whether that was so or not, the only thing that really counted at the moment was that they were doing their best to kill him. And by reason of their numbers they were likely to succeed. In the ordinary way, had he been flying a real British machine, the matter would not have worried him unduly; he would simply have fought the best fight he could as long as his machine held together and remained in the air. He had, in fact, fought against even greater odds and escaped, but then he had been able to give as good as he got. 'If I shoot any of these fellows down it puts the tin hat on my ever going back to Zabala, even if I do get away with it,' he thought desperately, as he turned round and round, kicking on right and left rudder alternately to avoid the streams of lead that were being poured at him from all directions.

He knew that the only thing he could do was to attempt to escape, either by trying to get back to the British lines, or by making a dash for Zabala, which was nearer. He would have spun down and landed had it been possible to land, but it was not, for the country below was a vast tract of broken rock and camel-thorn bushes. Nevertheless, he threw the Bristol into a spin with the object of getting as near to the ground as possible, and 'hedge-hopping'—or rather, rock-hopping—home. Looking back over his shoulder he saw the Pfalz spinning down behind him. He pulled out at a hundred feet above the ground, but still eased the stick forward until his wheels were literally skimming the rocks; and swerving from side to side to throw the gunners off their mark, raced for Zabala. Behind him screamed the Pfalz, like a pack of hounds after the hare.

Occasionally the sound of guns reached his ears, and once in a while a bullet bit into the machine, but the chance of being hit by a stray shot was the risk he had to take. By flying low he had made shooting difficult for the Boche pilots, who dare not dive as steeply as they would have liked to have done, and could have done higher up. Their difficulty was that of a diver who knows that the water into which he is about to plunge is shallow; to dive deep would mean hitting the bottom. In the case of the Pfalz, they dare not risk over shooting* their target for fear of crashing into the ground. So, unable to dive, they could only hang behind and take long shots. Their task was not made any easier by the fact that the Bristol did not fly on the same course for more than two or three seconds at a time; it turned and twisted from side to side like a snipe when it hears the sportsmen's guns.

This sort of flying needs a cool head and steady nerves, and Biggles possessed both; his many battles in France had given him those desirable qualities. He had to have eyes in the back of his head, as the saying goes, for it was necessary to keep a sharp look-out in front for possible obstacles, and at the same time keep watch behind for the more daring pilots who sometimes took a chance and came in close, whereupon he would turn at right angles and dash off on a new course, thereby upsetting their aim.

In spite of his precarious position, he smiled as the chase roared over the heads of a squadron of cavalry, sending the horses stampeding in all directions. On another occasion a German Staff car that was racing along the road down which he was then roaring in the opposite direction, pulled up so quickly that he was

* To fly past another aeroplane when following through an attack.

181

given the never-to-be-forgotten spectacle of a German general in full uniform, with his head through the windscreen.

As he approached Zabala the German scouts doubled their efforts to stop him, evidently under the impression that the British two-seater intended to bomb their aerodrome, and the consequence was that Biggles, who by this time was not in the least particular as to how or where he got down, made a landing that was as spectacular as it was unusual. He throttled back, side-slipped off his last few feet of height, flattened out and hurtled down-wind across the sun-baked sandy aerodrome. His wheels touched, but he did not stop. The hangars seemed to rush towards him, and he braced himself for the collision that seemed inevitable.

Leaning over the side of his cockpit to get a clear view round his windscreen, he saw German mechanics hauling a Halberstadt out of his path with frantic haste; others were unashamedly sprinting for cover. But the machine was beginning to lose speed, and fifty yards from the tarmac Biggles risked applying a little rudder and aileron, although he clenched his teeth as he did so, fully expecting to hear the undercarriage collapse under the strain. A grinding jar proclaimed the Bristol's protest, but the wheels stood up to the terrific strain, and slowly the machine swung round until it was tearing straight along the tarmac in a cloud of dust.

The Count himself, and von Stalhein, who had heard the shouting and had dashed out to see what was happening, just had time to throw themselves aside as the Bristol ran to a standstill in front of the fort, leaving a line of staring mechanics and swirling sand to mark it tempestuous course.

'What the devil do you think you're doing?' roared the Count, white with anger.

Biggles climbed out and pushed up his goggles before he replied. 'With all respect to you, sir,' he said bitterly, 'I think that is a question that might well be put to the pilots of the Pfalz *Staffel*.'

'What do you mean?' asked the Count, glancing up at the scouts, some of which were already landing, while others circled round awaiting their turn.

Biggles glared at von Stalhein as a new suspicion flashed into his mind. 'They've done their best to shoot me down, sir,' he told the Count. 'Look at my machine,' he added, nearly choking with rage as he thought he saw the solution of the whole thing. Von Stalhein still mistrusted him, and had deliberately set the Pfalz on to him as the easiest way to removing him without awkward questions or the formality of a court martial.

The Count looked in surprise at the bullet holes in the wings and tail of the Bristol. 'I don't understand this,' he said with a puzzled expression. 'Do you, Erich?' He turned to von Stalhein, who shook his head.

'I suppose there must be an explanation,' he said calmly. 'Here come the Pfalz pilots: perhaps they can tell us what it is.'

The scout pilots who now arrived on the scene pulled up short when thcy saw the pilot of the Bristol Fighter; they seemed to have difficulty in finding words. For a few moments nobody spoke. The Count looked from one to the other. Von Stalhein waited, with a faint inscrutable smile on his face. Biggles glared at all of them in turn. 'Well, he said at last, 'what about it?'

One of the German pilots said something quickly and half apologetically to the Count; Biggles caught the words, 'mark and wings'.

Von Faubourg started and turned to Biggles. 'He says you've no markings on your wings,' he cried.

'No markings,' exclaimed Biggles incredulously.

'Impossible!' He swung up and stood on the side of the fuselage from where he could see the whole of the top plane. From end to end it was painted the standard dull biscuit colour; there was not a speck of white on it anywhere. He stared as if it were some strange new creature that he had never seen before, while his brain struggled to absorb this miracle, for it seemed no less. He jumped down, eyes seeking the maker's number on the tail; and then he understood. It was not the number of his original machine. For some reason as incomprehensible as it was unbelievable, the machine he had flown over to Kantara that morning had been removed while it was standing on the tarmac, and another substituted in its place. It must have been done during the three hours he was with Major Raymond or away from the aerodrome.

He pulled himself together with an effort and turned to the Count. 'He's quite right, sir,' he said, 'there is no white mark. But do not ask me to explain it, because I cannot. The only suggestion that I can offer is that a change of machines took place while I was at Kantara.'

The Count was obviously unconvinced, but as he could offer no better explanation he dismissed the matter with a wave of his hand. 'Come along to my office, Brunow, I want you,' he said, and with von Stalhein at his side, disappeared into the porch of the fort.

Biggles turned to follow, but before he went in he turned to one of the Pfalz pilots who he knew spoke a little English and said, 'How was it you happened to be where you were—when I came along?'

'Well, we are usually somewhere about there,' replied the German, 'but as we were taking off von Stalhein told us that we should probably find some British machines there this morning.'

'I see,' said Biggles, 'thanks.' Then he followed the Count into his office.

'What happened over the other side?' was the curt question that greeted him as he stepped into the room.

'I'm sorry, sir, but I was too late to do anything,' answered Biggles simply.

'Too late?'

'Sheikh Haroun Ibn Said, better known as El Shereef, of the German Intelligence Staff, was tried by Field General Court Martial this morning and sentenced to death for espionage,' said Biggles in a low voice. 'The sentence was carried out within an hour on the grounds of the undesirability of keeping such a dangerous man in captivity. I'm not sure, but I believe the British are making an official announcement about it to-night.'

The Count sat down slowly in his chair and looked at von Stalhein. Biggles also looked at him, and thought he detected a faint gleam of triumph in the unflinching eyes. There was silence for a few minutes broken only by the Count tapping on his teeth with a lead pencil. 'Ah, well,' he said at last with a shrug of his massive shoulders, 'we have failed, but we did our best. Did you learn anything else while you were over there?'

'Only that there seems to be a good deal of activity going on, sir.'

'We are already aware of that. Anything else?'

'No, sir.'

'What excuse did you give to account for your presence at Kantara?'

'The same as before. I said I was a delivery pilot; they are always coming and going and nobody questioned it.'

'I see. That's all for the present.'

Biggles saluted and marched out of the room into

the blazing sunshine, but he did not go straight to his room, which, as events showed, was a fortunate thing. Instead, he walked along to the hangar where the two British machines were kept, with the object of testing a theory he had formed during his interview with the Count. Several mechanics were at work on the damaged Bristol, covering the bullet holes with small slips of fabric, but he went past them to where the Pup was standing in a corner and put his hand on the engine. One touch told him all he needed to know. The engine was still warm.

'I'm right,' he thought. 'That's how it was done.'

Chapter 18
An Unwelcome Visitor

'Yes, that's how he did it, the cunning beggar,' he mused again, as he walked back slowly to his room and changed into his German uniform. 'One false move now, and he'll be on me like a ton of—hello! what's going on over there, I wonder?' He broke off his soliloquy to watch with casual interest a little scene that was being enacted at the entrance gate of the camp, which was quite close to his quarters, and which he could just see by leaning out of the window. The sound of what seemed to be an argument reached him, and looking out to see what it was all about, he noticed that a service tender had drawn up to discharge a single passenger who was now engaged in a heated discussion with the N.C.O. in charge of the guard.

From his actions it was clear that he was trying to obtain admission to the station, but he was in civilian clothes, and the attitude of the N.C.O. suggested that he was not satisfied with his credentials. The man's suitcase had been stood on the ground, and as Biggles automatically read the name that was painted on its side in black letters he drew in his breath sharply, while his fingers gripped the window-sill until his knuckles showed white through the tan. The name on the suitcase was L. Brunow.

For a moment he came near to panic, and it was all he could do to prevent himself from dashing down to the tarmac, jumping into the first aeroplane he came to, and placing himself behind the British lines in the shortest possible space of time. He knew that he was in the tightest corner of his life, but he did not lose his head. He slipped his German Mauser revolver into his pocket and hurried round to the gate.

'What is the matter?' he asked the N.C.O. in German—one of the phrases he had learnt by heart.

The N.C.O. saluted and said something too quickly for him to catch, so Biggles resorted to the friend that had so often before helped him in difficult situations—bluff. He waved the N.C.O. aside, and indicated by his manner that the newcomer was known to him, and that he would accept responsibility for him. At the same time he picked up the suitcase and held it close to his side so that the name could not be read.

The real Brunow—for Biggles was in no doubt whatever as to the identity of the new arrival—wiped the perspiration from his face with a handkerchief. 'Can you speak English by any chance?' he said apologetically; 'I'm afraid my German isn't very good.'

'A leedle,' replied Biggles awkwardly. 'I understand better than I speak perhaps—yes?'

'Thank goodness. Then will you show me Count von Faubourg's office; I have an important message for him.'

'Yes, I will show you,' replied Biggles, but the thought that flashed through his mind was, 'Yes, I'll bet you have'. 'Der Count has just gone away,' he went on aloud. 'You must have the thirst, after your journey in der sun. I go to my room for a drink now—perhaps you come—no?'

'Thanks, I will,' replied Brunow with alacrity. 'I can't stand this heat.'

'It vas derrible,' agreed Biggles, as he led the way to his room, wondering what he was going to do with the man when he got there.

188

Brunow threw himself into a chair while Biggles took from the cupboard two glasses, a siphon of soda-water, and a bottle of brandy that he kept for visitors. The amount of brandy that he poured into Brunow's glass nearly made him blush, but Brunow did not seem to notice it, so he added a little soda-water and passed it over. His own glass he filled from the siphon, at the same time regretfully observing that he had had a touch of dysentery, and was forbidden alcohol by doctor's orders. He half smiled as Brunow drank deeply like a thirsty man—as he probably was—and decided in his mind that whatever happened Brunow must not be allowed to leave the room, for if ever he reached the Count's office his own hours were numbered.

'How long is the Count going to be, do you think?' inquired Brunow, setting down his empty glass, which Biggles casually refilled.

'He may be gone some time,' he answered in his best pseudo-German accent. 'Why, is it something impor-tant—yes?'

Brunow took another drink. 'I should say it is,' he retorted, settling himself down more comfortably in the chair. 'Too important to be put in a dispatch,' he added, rather boastfully, as an afterthought.

Biggles whistled softly, and made up his mind that his best chance of getting into the man's confidence was through his vanity. 'So! and they send you,' he exclaimed.

'That's right,' declared Brunow. 'They've sent me all the way from Berlin rather than trust the telegraph or the post-bag.' He leaned forward confidentially and looked up into Biggles' face. 'Perhaps I shouldn't tell you—keep this to yourself—but there's going to be a fine old row when I see the Count.'

Biggles laughed and refilled the glasses. 'That will

be not new,' he said. 'We of the staff have plenty of those.'

'But this one will be something to remember,' Brunow told him with a leer.

Biggles looked sceptical, which seemed to annoy Brunow.

'What would you say if I told you there was a spy here—here—here at Zabala?' he asked bellicosely.

Biggles shrugged his shoulders. 'It would be a funny place where there were no rumours about spies,' he said inconsequentially.

The combined effects of the heat and the brandy were becoming apparent in Brunow's manner. He put his feet up on the table and frowned at Biggles through half-closed eyes. 'Are you suggesting that I don't know what I'm talking about?' he inquired coldly. 'You'll be telling me next that I'm drunk,' he added with the aggressive indignation of a man who is well on his way to intoxication.

'I should hope not,' replied Biggles, in well simulated surprise. 'We are all two-bottle men here. Have another drink?' Without waiting for a reply, he filled the glasses again, inwardly disgusted that a man on special duty could behave in a manner so utterly foolish and irresponsible. 'Well,' he thought, 'it's either him or me for it, so it's no time to be squeamish.'

'Funny thing, you know,' went on Brunow confidingly; 'I'm not really German, but I went to Germany to offer my services. When I got there and told them my name, what do you think they did?'

'I'm no good at riddles,' admitted Biggles.

'They threw me in clink,' declared the other, picking up his glass.

'Clink?'

'In quod—you know, prison.

190

'*Donner blitz**,*' muttered Biggles, looking shocked.

'They did,' went on Brunow reflectively, sinking a little lower in his chair. 'Had the brass face to tell me that I was already serving in the Secret Service. What would you say if any one told you that, eh?'

'Biggles shook his head. 'Impossible!' he exclaimed, for want of something better to say.

'That's what I told them,' swore Brunow, waxing eloquent. 'The funny thing is, though, they were right. Can you beat that, eh?'

'It vas not possible.'

'Wasn't it! Ha! that's all that you know about it. I kicked up a proper stink and showed them my papers; when they saw those they smelt a rat and got busy. Quick wasn't the word. To make a long story short, they found that some skunk had got in under the canvas and was pretending to be me—*me*! What do you know about that?'

Biggles knew quite a lot about it but he did not say so. 'Too bad,' he murmured sympathetically.

'Too bad!' exploded Brunow, starting up. 'Is that all you've got to say about it? Don't you realize that this other fellow is a *spy*? Well, I've got it in for him,' he declared venomously, as he sank back. 'They believe it's a fellow named Bigglesworth, who's disappeared from France, though it beats me how they found that out. But whoever he is, he's here at Zabala.'

Biggles poured out more brandy with a hand that shook slightly, for Brunow had raised his voice. Twilight was falling over the desert, and in the hush the sound of voices carried far.

'So you've come here to put an end to his little game,

* By thunder!

191

eh?' he said quietly. 'Good! Still, there's no need to get excited about it.'

'Who are you, telling me not to get excited about it?' fumed Brunow. 'These cursed British chucked—' He pulled up as if he realized that he was saying too much. 'I want to see them shoot this skunk Bigglesworth, and I want to see him twitch when he gets a neck full of lead. That's what I want to see,' he snarled.

'Well, maybe you will,' Biggles told him.

'That's what I've come here for. The people in Berlin were going to send a telegram; then they thought they'd send a dispatch, but in the end they decided to send a special messenger. They chose me, and here I am,' stated Brunow. 'Pretty good, eh?'

'How about another drink?' smiled Biggles, and the instant he said it he knew he had gone too far. A look of suspicion darted into Brunow's bloodshot eyes, and the corners of his mouth came down ominously. 'Say! what's the big idea?' he growled. 'Are you trying to get me tanked?'

'Tanked?' Biggles tried to look as if he did not understand.

'Yes—blotto . . . sewn up. You sit there swilling that gut-rot, lacing me with brandy, and letting me do the talking. Do you know this skate Bigglesworth? You must have met him if you're stationed here. That's it. Is he a pal of yours, or—'

Biggles could almost see Brunow's bemused brain wrestling with the problem. The half-drunken man knew he had said too much, and was trying to recall just how much he had said. Then into his eyes came suddenly a new look; it was as if a dreadful possibility had struck him. Quickly, as he stared into Biggles face, doubt changed to certainty, and with certainty came hate and fear. He sprang to his feet, and grabbing the brandy bottle by the neck, swung it upwards; the table went over with a crash. 'Curse you,' he screamed. 'You're—'

Biggles dodged the bottle that would have brained him if it had reached its mark, and grabbed him by the throat. So sudden had been the attack that he was nearly caught off his guard, but once he realized that Brunow, in a flash of drunken inspiration, had recognized him, he acted with the speed of light, knowing that at all costs he must prevent him from shouting. One call for help and he was lost.

As his right hand found Brunow's throat and choked off the cry that rose to his lips, his left hand gripped the wrist that still held the bottle and a wave of fighting fury swept over him. It was the first time in his life that he had actually made physical contact with one of the enemy, and his reaction to it was shattering in its intensity; it aroused a latent instinct to destroy that he had never suspected was in him, and the knowledge that the man was not only an enemy but a traitor fanned the red-heat of his rage to a searing white-hot flame. 'Yes,' he ground out through his clenched teeth, 'I'm Bigglesworth—you dirty traitorous rat.'

But Brunow was no weakling. He was a trifle older than Biggles, and more heavily built, but what he gained from this advantage was lost by being out of condition, although he fought with the fear of death on him.

Locked in an unyielding embrace, they lost their balance and toppled over on to the bed. For a moment they lay on it panting, and then with a sudden wrench, Brunow tore himself free; but Biggles clung to his wrist and they both crashed to the floor. The shock broke his hold and they both sprang up simultaneously.

Brunow had lost too much breath to shout; he aimed

a murderous blow with the bottle, but he was a fraction of a second too slow. Biggles sprang sideways like a cat and then darted in behind the other arm, while as he moved his right hand flashed down and up, bringing the Mauser with it. The force Brunow had put behind his blow almost over-balanced him, and before he could recover Biggles brought the butt of his gun down on the back of his head.

Brunow swayed for a moment with a look of startled surprise on his face, and then pitched forward over the table.

Biggles stood rigid, listening, wondering fearfully if the noise of the struggle had been heard, and his lips closed in a thin straight line as his worst fears were realized. Slowly dragging footsteps were coming down the corridor, accompanied by the tap, tap, of walking-sticks.

He literally flung Brunow under the bed and kicked his suitcase after him. He set the table on its legs, replaced the siphon and the bottle which had fallen from Brunow's hand, and put one of the tumblers beside it. The other had been broken and there was no time to pick up the pieces. Then he pushed the Mauser under his pillow, and flung himself down on the disarranged bed in an attitude of sleep.

With every nerve tingling, he heard the footsteps stop outside; the door was opened quietly and he knew that von Stalhein was standing looking into the room.

How long the German stood there he did not know. He did not hear him go, and for some time he dare not risk opening his eyes; but when at length he risked a peep through his lashes the door was closed again. Still, he took no chances. He got up like a man rising from a deep sleep, but seeing that the room was really empty he glided to the window and looked out. In the twilight he could just see von Stalhein limping towards the fort. 'Thought I'd been drinking, I suppose,' mused Biggles, as he began to act on the plan he had formed while lying on the bed.

Brunow must be disposed of, that was vital. How long it would be before the people in Berlin became aware of his non-arrival he did not know; nor did he care particularly. The first thing must be to put Brunow where he could do no harm. But how—where? To murder a man in cold blood was unthinkable; to keep him hidden in his room for any length of time was impossible; yet every moment he remained would be alive with deadly danger. 'Somehow or other I've got to get him into that Bristol and fly him over the lines; that's the only possible solution,' he thought swiftly, although he was by no means clear as to how he was going to get him from his room to the aeroplane. 'If I can get the machine out I'll manage it somehow or other, but I shall have to leave him here while I go down to see about it,' were the thoughts that raced through his mind.

His first action was to retrieve the revolver and slip it into his pocket. Next, he pulled the still unconscious man from under the bed, tied his hands and feet securely with a strip of towel and gagged him with a piece of the same material. Then he pushed him back far under the bed and hurried down to the tarmac, feeling that time was everything. It was nearly dark, and it could only be under cover of darkness that he could hope to get Brunow to the machine. What the mechanics would think about getting the Bristol out at such an hour he hardly knew, but there was no help for it. They could think what they liked providing they raised no objection. He found them just knocking off work, and the sergeant in charge looked at him in

195

surprise when he asked that the two-seater be stood out on the tarmac in readiness for a flight. 'I understand I am to do some night flying soon,' Biggles told him carelessly, 'and I want some practice. Just stand her outside; there is no need for you to wait, and it may be some time before I take off. I shall be able to manage by myself.' He spoke of course in German and hoped that the N.C.O. understood what he said, but he was no means sure of it.

He breathed a sigh of relief as the mechanics obeyed his orders unquestioningly, and then disappeared in the direction of their quarters. 'All I've got to do now is to get the body there and think of a good excuse to account for my flip when I get back—if I decide to come back. Confound the fellow; what the dickens did he want to roll up here for just at this time,' he thought angrily.

He started off back towards his room, but before he reached it he saw von Stalhein hurrying along the tarmac to intercept him. 'Now what the dickens does he want, I wonder?' he muttered savagely, as the German hailed him.

'Ah, there you are,' cried von Stalhein as he came up. 'I've been looking for you. I came up to your room, but you seemed to be—well, I thought it best not to disturb you,' he smiled.

Biggles nodded. 'I had a drink or two and I must have dropped off to sleep,' he admitted.

'That's all right, but I've got a little job I want you to do for me if you will.'

'Certainly,' replied Biggles, outwardly calm but inwardly raging. 'What is it?'

'We've just had a prisoner brought in and he's as close as an oyster,' answered von Stalhein. 'He won't say a word—just sulks. We want to try the old trick on him to see if he knows anything worth knowing. Will you slip on your British uniform and we'll march you in as if you were another prisoner—you know the idea? He'll probably unloosen a bit if you start talking to him.'

'All right,' agreed Biggles, wishing that the unfortunate prisoner had chosen some other time to fall into the hands of the enemy. The trick referred to by von Stalhein was common enough. When a prisoner refused to speak, as duty demanded, and his captors thought he might be in possession of information of importance, it was customary to turn another so-called prisoner in with him, dressed in the same uniform, in the hope that confidences would be exchanged.

To Biggles this interruption of his plans at such a crucial moment was unnerving, but he could not demur, so he went to his room, and after ascertaining that Brunow was still in the position in which he had left him, he changed quickly and went along to the fort, where he found von Stalhein waiting for him with an escort of two soldiers armed with rifles and fixed bayonets.

'Where is he?' he asked.

'In the pen,' replied von Stalhein, nodding to the barbed-wire cage beside the fort in which a number of wooden huts had been erected to provide sleeping quarters.

Biggles took his place between the escort, who marched him ceremoniously to the gate of the detention camp, where another sentry was on duty. At a word of command the gate was thrown open and Biggles was marched inside. He was escorted to a room in which a light was burning. The door was unlocked; he was pushed roughly inside and the door closed behind him. But he remained standing staring unbelievably at a

British officer who sat dejectedly on a wooden stool near the far side of the room. It was Algy.

Chapter 19
Biggles Gets Busy

I

It would be hard to say who of the two was more shaken, Biggles or Algy. For a good ten seconds they simply stared at each other in utter amazement, and then they both moved together. Algy sprang up and opened his mouth to speak, but Biggles laid a warning finger on his lips, at the same time shaking his head violently. He covered the intervening distance in a stride. 'Be careful—there may be dictaphones*,' he hissed. Then aloud he exclaimed in a normal voice for the benefit of possible listeners. 'Hello, it looks as if we were both in the same boat. How long have you been here?'

'They got me this afternoon,' said Algy aloud in a disgruntled voice, but he nodded to indicate that he grasped the reason of Biggles' warning.

'Well, it looks as if the war's over as far as we're concerned,' continued Biggles.

'Looks like it,' agreed Algy.

Then began an amazing double-sided conversation, one carried on in a natural way, and consisting of such condolences and explanations as one would expect between two British officers who found they were brothers in misfortune. The other consisted of a whis-

---

*During the war both sides used hidden microphones, in prisoner of war camps, to overhear the prisoners' conversation. These conversations would be recorded on a dictaphone.

pered dialogue of why's and wherefore's, in which Biggles learnt that Algy's engine had failed and let him down in enemy country while he was flying over to Zabala with the message about the capture of El Shereef.

This went on for about half an hour, during which time Biggles racked his brains for a means of overcoming the difficulties and dangers that seemed to be closing in on him. All his original plans went by the board in the face of this new complication; first and foremost now was the pressing obsession that whatever else he did, or did not do, he must free Algy from the ghastly ordeal of spending the rest of the war in a German prison camp. What with Algy being a prisoner, Brunow tied up in his room, and von Stalhein already suspicious and waiting to spring, it can hardly be wondered at that he was appalled by the immediate prospect. One thing was certain; he must make the most of his time with Algy if ways and means of escape were to be discussed.

'I can't tell you all about it now,' he breathed, 'but things are fairly buzzing here. I don't know what's going to happen next, but I'm going to try to get you out before I do anything else; I can't tell you how exactly because I don't know myself, but I shall think of something presently. When the time comes you'll have to take your cue from me and do what you think is the right thing. For heaven's sake don't make a slip and say anything—or do anything—that will lead them to think that we know each other. I expect they'll come back in a minute to fetch me in order that I can make my report on what you've been saying, unless, of course, they've got the conversation taken down in shorthand from a dictaphone. After I've gone, stand by for anything. You come first now; I've got to get you away, and I can't worry any more about von Stalhein and his rotten schemes until that's done. In fact, this looks to me like the end of the whole business, and believe me, I shan't burst into tears if it is. I've had about enough of it. Be careful, here they come,' he went on quickly as heavy footsteps and a word of command were heard outside. 'Don't worry; I shan't be far away.'

Taking up the role he was playing, he looked over his shoulder as the door opened and the escort entered.

'Come—you,' said the N.C.O. in the harsh German military manner. He beckoned to Biggles.

Biggles rose obediently. 'Cheerio, old fellow, I may see you later perhaps,' he said casually to Algy as he left the room.

As soon as he was outside all pretence was abandoned, as of course the guards knew him, and knew quite well what was going on. The N.C.O. saluted, as did the sentry on gate duty as he left the *gefangenenlager**
and walked briskly towards the fort, thinking with the speed and clarity that is so often the result of continual flying.

Just before he reached the porch he heard an aero-engine start up and a machine begin to taxi from the Halberstadt sheds towards the far side of the aerodrome. He had a nasty moment, for at first he thought that it might be some one moving the Bristol, but he breathed again as he recognized the unmistakable purr of a Mercedes engine. He paused in his stride and a queer look came into his eyes as he peered through the darkness in the direction of the sound. 'That's the same Halberstadt going out to wait on the far side of the aerodrome, which means that friend Erich is going off

* German: prison camp.

on one of his jaunts,' he thought swiftly. For another moment or two he lingered, still thinking hard, and then he turned and walked boldly through the main porch of the fort. A light showed under the Count's door, and another under von Stalhein's, but he passed them both and went on to the far end of the corridor to what had originally been the back door of the building. He tried it and found that it was unlocked, so he went through and closed the door quietly behind him. For a moment he stood listening, and then made his way swiftly to his room where, after satisfying himself that Brunow was still unconscious, he changed into his German uniform and then hurried back to the fort. He went in by the way he had come out and emerged again through the front porch for the benefit of the sentry on duty. He did not stop but went on straight to the prison camp. 'Well, it's neck or nothing now,' he mused as he beckoned to the N.C.O. in charge of the guard. 'Bring the officer-prisoner,' he said curtly; 'Hauptmann von Stalhein wishes to speak with him.'

The N.C.O. obeyed with the blind obedience of the German soldier; he called the escort to attention, marched them to Algy's door and called him out. Biggles did not so much as glance at him as he walked back towards the main entrance of the fort with the prisoner and his escort following.

'Wait,' he told the guards shortly, and signalling to Algy to follow, he led the way into the corridor. But he did not stop at von Stalhein's door, nor at the Count's, but went straight on to the back of the building. Little beads of perspiration were on his forehead as he opened the door and they both went outside, for he knew that if either the Count or von Stalhein had come out during the few moments they were walking through the corridor all would have been lost.

As they stepped quietly outside he looked swiftly to left and right, but no one was in sight as far as he could see, which was not very far for the moon had not yet risen. 'Come on,' he said tersely, and set off at a quick trot towards his room with Algy following close behind.

Their footfalls made no sound on the soft sand as they sprinted along the back of the hangars to the side of the building in which Biggles' room was situated. 'I daren't risk taking you in through the door in case we meet some one coming out,' he said softly, leading the way to the window. 'I had to take you through the fort to get rid of the guards,' he explained, 'but if either von Stalhein or the Count go out and see them standing there they may smell a rat, so we've no time to lose. Here we are; give me a leg up.' A jump and a heave and he was on the window-sill, reaching down for Algy, and a second later they were both standing inside the room breathing heavily from their exertion.

'Now listen,' said Biggles quietly. 'I've got a Bristol standing on the tarmac. You're going to fly it back; but you've got to take a passenger.'

'You mean—you?'

'No.'

'Who?'

'Brunow, the real Brunow. He turned up to-day.'

Algy's eyes opened wide. 'My gosh!' he breathed, 'where is he now?'

'Here.' Biggles stooped down and dragged the still unconscious man from under the bed. 'I'm afraid I socked him on the head rather hard,' he observed, 'but he asked for it. Get him to the M.O.* as soon as you can when you get back; don't for goodness' sake let him escape. Now do exactly what I tell you to,' he

* Medical Officer.

went on as he ripped off his German tunic. 'Slip this on—make haste, never mind your own tunic. If we meet any one look as much like a Hun as you can. Don't speak. I'm going to put on my overalls, but I shall be recognized so it doesn't matter much about me. Got that clear?'

'Absolutely.'

'Come on then, bear a hand; we've got to get Brunow down to the Bristol. If we are spotted I'll try to bluff that there has been an accident, but if there is an alarm follow me. I shall leave Brunow and make a dash for the machine. I'll take the pilot's seat; you get to the prop and swing it. When she starts get in as fast as you can; it would be our only chance. Are you ready?'

'Quite.'

'Then off we go. Steady—don't drop the blighter through the window, we don't want to break his neck.' Biggles looked outside, but all was silent, so between them they got the limp figure to the ground and set off at a clumsy trot towards the hangar where the British machines were housed. They reached it without seeing a soul, and to Biggles' infinite relief he saw that the Bristol was still standing as he had left it. 'We're going to have a job to get him into the cockpit,' he muttered. 'Just a minute—let me get up first.' He climbed up into the back seat, and reaching down, took Brunow by the shoulders. 'It's a good thing you got shot down to-day after all,' he panted. 'I should never have managed this job alone. He's heavier than I thought—go on—push.

Between them they got the unconscious man into the back seat and fastened the safety-belt tightly round him. 'That's fine,' muttered Biggles with satisfaction. 'If he happens to come round while you're in the air, he'll think he's dead and on the way to the place where he ought to be,' he grinned. 'Go on—in you get.'

Algy climbed into the pilot's seat while Biggles ran round to the propeller.

'Hold hard, what are you going to do?' cried Algy in sudden alarm.

'That's all right, off you go.'

'And leave you here? Not on your life.'

'Don't sit there arguing, you fool; some one will come along presently. Do as you're told.'

'Not me—not until you tell me how you're going to get back.'

'I shall probably follow you in the Pup.'

'Where is it?'

'In the hangar.'

'Can you start it alone?'

'Yes, I shall probably take straight off out of the hangar.'

'Why not get it started while I'm here?'

'I'll give you a thick ear if you don't push off,' snarled Biggles. 'I shall be all right, I tell you.'

Algy looked doubtful. 'I don't like leaving you; why not dump Brunow and let's fly back together?' he suggested.

'Because when I start on a job I like to finish it,' snapped Biggles.

'What do you mean?'

'Von Stalhein—now will you go?'

'But why—?'

'I'll shoot you if you don't start that blooming engine,' grated Biggles.

Algy saw that Biggles was in no mood to be trifled with. 'All right,' he said shortly. 'Switches off!'

'Switch off!'

'Suck in!'

'Suck in.'

Biggles pulled the big propeller round several times and then balanced it on contact. 'Contact!' he called.

'Contact!' Biggles balanced himself on the ball of his right foot and swung the blade of the propeller down. With a roar that sounded like the end of the world, the Rolls Royce engine came to life and shattered the silence with its powerful bellow.

For a minute or two Algy sat waiting for it to warm up and then looked round to wave good-bye; but Biggles had disappeared. Slowly he pushed the throttle open and the Bristol began to move over the darkened aerodrome, slowly at first but with ever increasing speed. Its tail lifted and it roared upwards into the night sky.

II

Biggles watched the Bristol take off from the inside of the hangar into which he had run for cover when the engine started. He knew that by allowing Algy to take the Bristol he had burnt his boats behind him as far as staying at Zabala was concerned, for when the prisoner was missed, and the N.C.O. in charge of the guard explained—as he was bound to—how the Engländer had been taken by Leutnant 'Brunow' to Hauptmann von Stalhein for interview, the fat would be in the fire with a vengeance. No, Zabala was finished for ever, and he knew it; all that remained for him to do was to follow the Bristol as quickly as possible into the security of the British lines.

Two methods of achieving this presented themselves, and the first was—or appeared to be—comparatively simple. It was merely to pull out the Pup, now standing in the hangar, start it up, and take off. The other made a far greater appeal to him, but it was audacious in its conception and would require nerve to bring off. Curiously enough, it was while he was still weighing up the pros and cons that his mind was made up for him in no uncertain manner. It began when he walked to the back of the hangar and struck a match to see if the Pup was still in its usual position. It was, but he was staggered to see that its engine had been taken out, presumably for overhaul, and while he had not made up his mind to use the machine except in case of emergency, it gave him a shock to discover that his only safe method of escape from Zabala was effectually barred. He could have kicked himself for not finding it out earlier, for he might have based his plans on the understanding that the Pup would be airworthy. 'My word! I should have been in a bonny mess if I'd wanted it in a hurry,' he thought, and then dodged behind the wide canvas door-flap as he heard soft footsteps on the sand near at hand.

Peeping out, he saw the station *Vize-feldwebel**, who acted in the capacity of Adjutant**, standing on the tarmac looking about with a puzzled air. From his manner it was clear that he had heard the British machine take off and had hurried down to see what was going on, and Biggles blamed himself for leaving things so late, for the arrival of the *Feldwebel* was something that he had not bargained for; and he had still greater cause to regret the delay when a minute or two later the Adjutant was joined by von Stalhein. He was in a state of undress with a dressing-gown thrown over his shoulders; he, too, had evidently heard the Bristol take off and had hurried along to ascertain the cause.

* German: Sergeant Major.
** An officer specially appointed to assist the commanding officer.

207

He said something that Biggles did not catch to the *Feldwebel*, who went off at the double and presently returned with the Sergeant of the Flight responsible for the upkeep of the British machines—the same man to whom Biggles had given instructions regarding the preparation of the Bristol. A crisp conversation ensued, but it was carried on too quickly for Biggles to follow it, although by the mention of his name more than once, and the sergeant's actions, he guessed that the N.C.O. was explaining the reason why Leutnant Brunow was flying.

To Biggles' horror they all came into the hangar. The light was switched on, but they did not stay very long, for after von Stalhein had satisfied himself that the Bristol had actually gone, he went off and the others followed soon afterwards.

Biggles lingered no longer; the discovery of the dismantled Pup left him no choice of action, and he knew that he was faced with one of the most desperate adventures of his career, one that would either see him successful in his quest, or—but he preferred not to think of the alternative.

He was curiously calm as he stepped out of his hiding-place and set off in long swinging strides towards the far side of the aerodrome. As he walked he hummed the tune *Deutschland Über Alles* which he had often heard sung in the Mess, for the desert was forbidding in its deathly silence, and the very atmosphere seemed to be peopled by the spirits of a long-forgotten past. 'Gosh! This place gives me the creeps,' he muttered once as he stopped to get his bearings from the distant lights of Zabala, to make sure he was keeping in the right direction. 'Give me France every time.' He was far too much of a realist to be impressed by the historical associations of the ground over which he walked, land which had once been trodden by Xenophon, at the head of his gallant ten thousand, Alexander the Great, Roman generals, and Crusaders at the head of their armed hosts, but he was conscious of the vague depression that is so often the result of contact with remote antiquity. 'I don't wonder that people who get lost in the desert go dotty,' he said quietly to himself, as he quickened his pace.

He passed the bush behind which he had lain hidden on the night when he had first seen von Stalhein disguised as an Arab, and gave a little muttered exclamation of satisfaction when he saw a Halberstadt standing just where he expected to find it. Its pilot had not seen him, for he had his back towards him as he turned the propeller in the act of starting the engine. Biggles waited till the engine was ticking over and the pilot had taken his place in the front seat; then he walked up quickly, put his foot in the fuselage stirrup, swung himself up beside the pilot and tapped him on the shoulder. 'The Count wants you urgently,' he said in his best German.

'What?' exclaimed the startled pilot.

'The Count wants you,' repeated Biggles. 'There is a change of plans. I have been sent out to relieve you. Hurry up.'

'But I have been—'

'I know,' interrupted Biggles desperately, for he was afraid that von Stalhein might turn up at any moment. 'You are to go back at once. I am to fly to-night.'

To his unutterable relief the man, a rather surly fellow named Greichbach, whom he had spoken to once or twice in the Mess, made no further demur, but climbed out of his seat and stood beside the self-appointed pilot.

'What is the course to-night?' asked Biggles carelessly. 'They told me, but I had no time to write it down; I think I remember but I'd like to confirm it.'

'Jebel Hind—Galada—Wadi Baroud—Pauta,' replied the other without hesitation.

'Where do you usually land?'

'You may not have to land, but you will know in the air about that.'

'Thanks. You'd better get back now. Don't go straight across the aerodrome, though, in case I run into you taking off; go round by the boundary,' Biggles told him, and a grim smile played about the corners of his mouth as he watched the German set off in the desired direction. At the same time he released his grip on the butt of his Mauser, for the moment had been an anxious one. If was fortunate for Greichbach that he had not questioned the instructions, for Biggles had determined to have the Halberstadt even if he had to take it by force. He saw the figure of the German disappear into the darkness, still taking the course he had suggested, for the last thing he wanted to happen was for Greichbach to meet von Stalhein on the way out.

He buckled on his flying cap, pulled his goggles low over his face, removed the spare joystick from the back seat, took his place in the front cockpit, and waited. The seconds ticked by. Minutes passed and he began to feel uncomfortable, worried by the fear that Greichbach might get back to the station before von Stalhein left; but his muscles tightened with a jerk as a tall figure in Arab costume suddenly loomed up in the darkness close at hand, and without saying a word swung up into the rear cockpit.

Biggles felt a light tap on the shoulder; the word 'Go' came faintly to his ears above the noise of the engine. With a curious smile on his set face he eased the throttle open and held the stick forward. The Mercedes engine roared; the Halberstadt skimmed lightly over the sand and then soared upwards in a steep climbing turn.

Biggles saw the lights of the camp below him, and knew that whatever happened he was looking at them for the last time. Then he turned in a wide circle and, climbing slowly for height, headed for the lines.

Chapter 20
The Night Riders

I

For twenty minutes he flew on a straight course for Jebel Hind, the first landmark mentioned by Greichbach, crouching well forward in the cockpit and taking care not to turn his head to left or right, which might give von Stalhein a view of his profile. At first he could not dismiss from his mind the fear that the German would speak to him or make some move that would require an explanation, in which case exposure would be inevitable, and he wondered vaguely what von Stalhein would do about it.

As usual in two-seater aeroplanes, the pilot occupied the front seat and the observer the back one, and in this case the two cockpits were not more than a couple of feet apart. Biggles would have felt happier if the German had been in the front seat, for then he could have watched him; it was unnerving to know that an enemy whom he could not see was sitting within a couple of feet of him; but, on the other hand, he realized that if von Stalhein had been in the front seat and had happened to turn round, he would have seen him at once and discovered that a change of pilots had taken place.

'Suppose he does discover who I am, what can he do about it?' thought Biggles. 'Nothing, as far as I can see. If he hits me over the back of the head, the machine will fall and we shall both go west together, for he couldn't possibly get into my seat and take over the controls without first throwing me out; and he wouldn't have time to do that before we crashed. He'd be crazy to start a free fight in an aeroplane, anyway. The next thing is, what am *I* going to do? If he tells me to go down and land I should be able to handle the situation all right provided there isn't a party of Huns or Hun-minded Arabs waiting for him. But suppose he says nothing about landing? He'll want to know what's up if I try to land on my own account. It's no use pretending that the engine has failed, because as soon as I throttle back he'll know it by the movement of his own throttle lever. If I cut the switch and lose the engine altogether, we should probably crash trying to land, in which case I stand a better chance than he does of getting hurt. Well, we shall see.'

The lifeless rocky country around Jebel Hind loomed up ahead, and the machine bumped once or twice as the change in the terrain affected the atmosphere. The mountains of rock, heated nearly to furnace heat by the sun during the day, were not yet cool, and were throwing up columns of hot air. Cooler air from the desert was rushing in to fill the partial vacuum thus caused, and the result was vertical currents of considerable velocity.

Overcoming an almost irresistible desire to look back and see what von Stalhein was doing, he concentrated on correcting the bumps, which now became more frequent as the country below grew more rugged. A solitary searchlight stabbed a tapering finger of white light into the starry sky some little distance ahead, and he knew he was approaching the British lines. Jagged flashes of orange and crimson flame began to appear around him, showing that the anti-aircraft batteries were aware of his presence; but the searchlight had failed to pick him up and the shooting was poor, so he roared on through the night until he reached the village of Galada, when he turned sharply to the right and continued on a course that would bring him to the Wadi Baroud, which, according to Greichbach, was the next landmark.

They were flying over desert country again now, a flat expanse of wilderness surrounded on all sides by hills on which twinkled the many camp fires of troops who were being concentrated in preparation for the coming battle. 'A sort of place he might ask me to land,' thought Biggles, correcting an unusually bad bump, but the expected tap on the shoulder did not come and he roared on through the star-lit sky.

He seemed to have been flying for a long time; the cockpit was warm and cosy and his fear of the man in the back seat began to give way to lassitude. 'It's about time he was doing something,' he thought drowsily, wondering what the outcome of the whole thing would be. Strange thoughts began to drift into his mind. 'Winged chariots! Some one on the ground down there had said something about winged chariots three thousand years ago. Or was it later?' He couldn't remember, so he dismissed the matter as of no consequence, and then pulled himself up with a jerk, for he realized with a shock that he had been on the point of dozing.

The edge of the moon crept up above the rim of the desert; from his elevated position he could see it, but he knew that it was still invisible to people on the ground, which remained a vast well of mysterious darkness, broken only by vague, still darker shadows which marked the position of hills and valleys. Still he flew on, heading towards Pauta, his next landmark, which still lay some distance to the west.

Then, far ahead over his port wing appeared a little

214

cluster of yellow lights that he knew was the British aerodrome of Kantara; he thought for a moment, and then eased the nose of the machine a trifle towards it. Would von Stalhein notice the move and call attention to it? No, apparently not, for nothing happened. Again he touched the rudder-bar lightly and brought his nose in a straight line with the aerodrome, and almost started as a new thought flashed into his mind. 'What could he do if I decided to land there,' he mused, quivering at the idea. 'Nothing. I don't see that he could do a thing; at least, not until we were actually on the ground. Then he'd probably try to pull a gun on me, jump into the pilot's seat and escape. Well, I can act as quickly as he can,' he thought. The more he toyed with the plan the more it appealed to him. It would end the whole business one way or the other right away. To march the German up to Major Raymond's tent would be a fitting end to his adventures. Von Stalhein's plans, whatever they were, would not—could not—materialize then. But whatever he did would have to be done quickly. 'The moment I start to glide down he'll know something's wrong, and he'll be on his feet in a jiffy,' he thought. 'And then anything can happen. No! When I go down I'll go so fast that he won't be able to speak, move, or do anything else except hang on. Maybe he'll think that something has broken and we're falling out of control; so much the better if he does.'

Tingling with excitement, he held on to his course, watching the aerodrome lights creeping slowly nearer. They were nearly under the leading edge of his port wing now—still nearer they crept—nearer. Suddenly they disappeared from sight and he knew he was over the middle of the aerodrome. A glance at the luminous altimeter showed the needle resting on the five-thousand-feet mark. It was now or never. 'Well, come on,' he muttered aloud, and did several things simultaneously. With his left hand he cut the throttle; his left foot kicked the rudder-bar, while with his right hand he flung the joystick over to the left and then dragged it back into his right thigh.

To any one in the back seat, experienced or otherwise, the result would have been terrifying—as indeed he intended it to be. The machine lurched drunkenly as it quivered in a stall; its nose flopped over heavily, swung down, and then plunged earthward in a vicious spin. With his eyes glued on the whirling cluster of lights below, Biggles counted the revolutions dispassionately. When he reached number five he shoved the stick forward, kicked on top rudder, and then spun in the opposite direction. At what he judged to be trifle less than a thousand feet he pulled out of the spin, and then pushed his left wing down in a vertical side-slip. A blast of air struck him on the side of the face, while struts and wires howled in protest—but still the machine dropped like a stone.

Only at the last moment did he level out, make a swift S turn and glide in to a fast wheel landing. As his wheels touched the ground he flicked off the ignition switch with a sharp movement of his left hand while with his right he felt for the Mauser. The tail-skid dropped, dragged a few yards, and the machine stopped. Biggles made a flying leap at the ground, revolver in hand.

'Stick up your hands, von Stalhein,' he snapped.

There was no reply.

'Come on, stick 'em up; I've got you covered. One false move and it's your last—I mean it.'

Still no reply.

Biggles stooped low so that he could see the silhouette of the cockpit against the sky, but he could not see the German. 'Come on, look lively,' he snarled. 'It's no use crouching down there on the floor. In five seconds I shall start shooting.'

Still no reply.

Biggles felt a thrill of doubt run through him. Had von Stalhein jumped out, too? He dodged round to the far side of the machine and looked around; he could see a hundred yards in all directions, but there was no one in sight. With his revolver ready, he put his foot in the fuselage stirrup and stood up so that he could see inside the back cockpit. One glance was enough. It was empty.

He put the gun back into his pocket and leaned weakly against the trailing edge of the lower wing. 'I'm mad,' he muttered, 'daft—dreaming. I've got sunstroke—that's what it is.' He closed his eyes, shook his head violently, and then opened them again. 'No, it isn't a dream,' he went on, as he saw mechanics racing towards the spot. The reaction after the terrific strain of the last few minutes, when every nerve had been keyed up to breaking-point, was almost overwhelming. The unexpected anti-climax nearly upset his mental balance. He threw back his head and laughed aloud.

'Hands up, there, Jerry!' yelled the leading mechanic as he ran up.

'What are you getting excited about?' snarled Biggles.

The shock to the unfortunate ack emma* when he heard a normal English voice was nearly as great as Biggles' had been a few moments before. He stared at the pilot, then at the machine, and then back at Biggles.

A flight-sergeant pushed his way to the front of the

* Slang: Aircraft Mechanic.

217

rapidly forming group of spectators. 'What's all this?' he growled.

'It's all right; I've brought you a souvenir, flight-sergeant,' grinned Biggles, indicating the machine with a nod. 'You can take it, you can keep it, and you can jolly well stick it up your tunic as far as I'm concerned. And I hope it bites you,' he added bitterly, as he realized that his well-laid plans, carried out at frightful risk, had come to naught.

'Any one else in that machine?' asked the flight-sergeant suspiciously.

'Take a look and see,' invited Biggles. 'As a matter of fact there is, but I can't find him. Just see if you can do any better.'

The flight-sergeant made a swift examination of the Halberstadt. 'No, sir, there's nobody here,' he said.

'That's what I thought,' murmured Biggles slowly.

The flight-sergeant eyed him oddly, and then looked relieved when a number of officers, who had heard the machine land, ran up and relieved him of any further responsibility in the matter. Major Raymond was amongst them, and Biggles took him gently by the arm. 'Better get the machine in a hangar out of the way, sir,' he said. 'If people start asking questions I shall tell them that I'm a delivery pilot taking a captured machine down to the repair depot, but I lost my way and had to make a night landing. I'll wait for you in your tent. Is Algy back?'

'Yes; he was in the Mess having his dinner when I came out. He said something about not letting stray Huns interfere with his meals.'

'He wouldn't,' replied Biggles bitterly. 'Has he told you—'

'Yes, he's told me all about it.'

'And Brunow?'

218

The Major nodded. 'Yes, we've got him where he can do no harm. You'd better trot along to the Mess and get something to eat, and then come and see me in my tent.'

'Right you are, sir.' Biggles started off in the direction of the distant Officers' Mess.

II

An hour later he reclined in a long cane chair in Major Raymond's tent. The Major sat at his desk with his chin resting in the palms of his hands; Algy sat on the other side of him, listening.

'Well, there it is,' Biggles was saying. 'I think it was, without exception, the biggest shock I have ever had in my life—and I've had some, as you know. It was also the biggest disappointment. I'll tell you straight, sir. I could have burst into tears when I landed and found he wasn't there. I couldn't believe it, and that's a fact. When I think of all the trouble I went to, and risks I took—but there, what's the use of moaning about it? I only hope he broke his blinking neck on a perishing boulder when he hit the floor.'

'How do you mean?'

'Well, there's no doubt about what he did. When he was over the place where he wanted to get to he just stepped over the side with a parachute; there's no other solution that I can think of—unless, of course, he suddenly got tired of life and took a running jump into space. Or he may have decided to go for a stroll, forgetting where he was, but knowing von Stalhein pretty well I should say that's hardly likely. No! the cunning blighter stepped over with a brolley, and I can guess where it happened. I remember an extra bad bump. And for all I know he's been getting into our lines like

219

that all the time. After all, it's no more risky than landing in an aeroplane in a rough country like this. The point is he's still alive and kicking, and from my point of view, the sooner he makes his last kick the better. He's not a man; he's a rattlesnake. He's somewhere over this side of the lines floating about in his Ali Baba outfit, How are we going to find him?—that's what I want to know. By the way, Algy, how did you get on with Brunow?'

'Right as rain, no trouble at all. I flew straight back and landed here. I dumped him in my room with a sentry on guard, slipped an overcoat over my Hun uniform, and reported to the Major. Brunow came round just as I got back and took off my coat. He started bleating a prayer of thanksgiving when he saw my uniform, and then told me in no uncertain terms just what sort of swine the British were and what he thought of you in particular. He asked me if you'd been arrested yet, and if so, when were you to be shot.'

'Go on,' put in Biggles interestedly. 'What did you tell him?'

'I just broke the news gently, and told him he'd got things all wrong. He wouldn't believe it at first, and I had to explain that since the last time he was awake he'd been on a long, long journey, and was now nicely settled in the hands of the British swines.'

'What did he say to that?'

'He didn't say anything; he just went all to pieces. Now he's trying to pretend that he didn't mean it.'

'Where is he now?'

'In the Kantara prison camp, in solitary confinement,' put in the Major.

'What are you going to do with him, sir?'

'He'll be tried by General Court Martial, of course.

But what about this fellow von Stalhein? That's far more important.'

'I was coming to that,' answered Biggles slowly. 'I think we can lay him by the heels, but I shall want some help.'

'What sort of help?'

'Personal assistance from somebody who knows the country well—and the Arabs; Major Sterne for instance.'

Major Raymond looked serious. 'He's a difficult fellow to get hold of,' he said. 'He's all over the place, and we seldom know just where he is. Won't any one else do?'

'I'd prefer Sterne. It's only right that as he caught El Shereef, he should have a hand in the affair. Surely if you sent out an SOS amongst the Arabs it would reach his ears and he'd come in.'

'He might. He doesn't like being interfered with when he's on a job, but if the matter was exceptionally serious he might take it the right way. Just what do you suggest?'

'I suggest that a message be sent out that his presence is urgently required at General Headquarters in connexion with plans for the British advance, so will he please report as quickly as possible. That should bring him in.'

'But good gracious, man, the General would never consent to that.'

'Why not? He more than any one else should be glad to lay a dangerous fellow like von Stalhein by the heels.'

'And suppose I can arrange it: where would you like to see Sterne?'

'At General Headquarters, if possible; it would save him coming here. If you'll get the message out I'll go

221

to headquarters with Lacey and wait until he comes. Perhaps you'd like to come along too?'

'The General isn't going to be pleased if you waste his time.'

'I shan't be pleased if I waste my own, if it comes to that,' observed Biggles coolly. 'I've been risking my neck, so he can hardly object to giving up a few minutes of his time. All right, sir, let's start moving.'

Chapter 21
Sterne Takes a Hand

The pearly glow of a new day spread slowly over the eastern sky; it threw a cold grey light over the inhospitable wilderness, and intensified the whiteness of a house that stood on the outskirts of the village of Jebel Zaloud, a house that once had been the residence of the merchant Ali Ben Sadoum, but was now the air Headquarters of the British Expeditionary Force in Palestine.

A wan beam crept through the unglazed window of a room on the ground floor, and awoke two officers who were sleeping uncomfortably in deck chairs. Biggles started, blinked, and then sprang to his feet as he observed the daylight. 'Looks as if he isn't coming, Algy,' he said crisply. 'It's getting light.'

Algy rubbed his eyes, yawned, and stood up, stretching. 'You're right,' he said. 'In which case we shall have to try to find the wily Erich ourselves, I suppose.'

'Yes; it's a pity though,' muttered Biggles thoughtfully, rubbing his chin. 'I hoped we should save ourselves a lot of trouble.' He yawned. 'We must have dropped off to sleep soon after midnight. Well, well, it can't be helped, but I expect the General will be peeved if he's been waiting about all night.'

'He wasn't going to bed anyway,' Algy told him. 'I heard the Brigade-Major say that the General would be up most of the night working on important dispatches. Where is Raymond do you suppose?'

'Up in the General's room, I imagine—he was last night.'

'Gosh! he'll be sick if we let the General down.'

'I expect he will; as I said before, it's a pity, but it can't be helped. I've acted as I thought best.'

There was a tap on the door and an orderly appeared. 'The General wishes to see you in his room immediately,' he said.

Biggles grimaced. 'This is where we get our ears twisted,' he muttered ruefully, as he followed the orderly to a large apartment on the first floor.

The General looked up wearily from his desk as they entered. Several Staff officers and Major Raymond were there, and they regarded the two airmen with disapproval plainly written on their faces.

'Which of you is Bigglesworth?' began the General.

Biggles stepped forward. 'I am, sir,' he said.

'Will you have the goodness to explain what all this means? Major Raymond has told me of the excellent work you have done since you have been in Palestine, and in view of that I am prepared to take a broad view, but I am very tired, and this business all seems very pointless.'

Biggles looked uncomfortable. 'I agree, sir, it does,' he admitted; 'but I had hoped to prove that my unusual request was justified.'

'I believe it was on your intervention that stay of execution was granted in the death sentence promulgated in connexion with Sheikh Haroun Ibn Said, otherwise the spy, El Shereef. Frankly, Bigglesworth, we are prepared to give officers sent out here on special detached duty from the Air Board a lot of rope, but there is a limit as to how far we can allow them to interfere with ordinary service routine.'

'Quite, sir. I hope to repay you for your consideration.'

'How?'

'By saving you from the mental discomfort you would surely have suffered when you discovered that you had shot an innocent man, sir.'

'Innocent man! What are you talking about?'

'The Sheikh Haroun Ibn Said is not El Shereef, sir.' Biggles spoke quietly but firmly.

'Good heavens, man, what do you mean?'

'What I say, sir. The whole thing was a frame-up — if I may use an American expression. Sheikh Haroun is what he has always claimed to be — a good friend of the British. By causing him to be arrested and — as they hoped — shot as a spy, the German agent who handled the job hoped to achieve two ends. To remove a powerful Sheikh who was sincerely loyal to British arms, and at the same time lull you into a sense of false security by leading you to believe that you had at last put an end to the notorious activities of the spy, El Shereef. Sheikh Haroun Ibn Said, in his ignorance of western matters, was easily induced to wear a German Secret Service ring, and carry on his person incriminating documents without having the slightest idea of what they meant. In short, he was induced to adopt the personality of El Shereef.'

The General's face was grim. 'By whom?' he snapped.

'By El Shereef, sir,' said Biggles simply.

The General started and a look of understanding dawned in his eyes. Silence fell on the room. What Biggles had just told him might not have occurred to him, but its dreadful possibilities were now only too apparent. 'Good God!' he breathed. 'Are you sure of this?'

225

'I am, sir.'

'So El Shereef is still at large.'

'He is, sir.'

'Who is the man whom you flew into the British lines last night—Major Raymond has told me about it—this Hauptmann Erich von Stalhein. Has he any connexion with El Shereef?'

'He has, sir.'

'What is it?'

'He's the same man, sir—El Shereef.'

Another silence fell. The General sat staring like a man hypnotized, and so did his staff for that matter, although one or two of them looked incredulous.

'Why did you not tell me this before?' asked the General harshly. There was reproach and anger in his voice.

'Because there was a thing that I valued above all others at stake, sir,' replied Biggles firmly. 'For that reason I told nobody what I had discovered.'

'And what was that?'

'My life, sir. I do not mean to be disrespectful, but German agents have ears in the very highest places— even in your headquarters, sir.'

The General frowned. 'I find it hard to believe that,' he said. 'Still, this story of yours puts a very different complexion on things. Von Stalhein, alias El Shereef, is still at large, and you want Sterne to help you run him to earth—is that it?'

'That is correct, sir.'

'I see. I sent out a general call for him last night, but it begins to look as if he isn't coming. If he does come, I'll let you know.'

There was a sharp rap on the door, and the duty Staff sergeant entered. 'Major Sterne is here, sir,' he said.

'Ask him to come up here at once,' ordered the General. 'I'll speak to him first and tell him what is proposed,' he added quickly, turning to Biggles.

'Thank you, sir.' Biggles, after a nod to Algy, stepped back against the far wall.

The next moment he was watching with a kind of fascinated interest a man who had swept into the room, for he knew he was looking at one of the most talked-of men in the Middle East, a man whose knowledge of native law was proverbial and who could disguise himself to deceive even the Arabs themselves. Even now he was dressed in flowing Arab robes, but he clicked his heels and raised his hand in the military salute.

'Hello, Sterne, here you are then,' began the General, as he reached over his desk and shook hands. 'You got my message?'

'Yes, sir,' replied the other briskly. 'I was anxious to know what it was about.'

'It's about this confounded fellow, El Shereef,' continued the General. 'It seems that there has been some mistake; the fellow you brought in was not El Shereef at all.'

Biggles stepped forward quietly.

'Not El Shereef!' cried Sterne. 'What nonsense! If *he* isn't El Shereef, then who is?'

'You are, I think,' said Biggles quietly. 'Don't move—von Stalhein.'

The man who had been known as Major Sterne spun round on his heel and looked into the muzzle of Biggles' revolver. He lifted eyes that were glittering with hate to Biggles' face. 'Ah,' he said softly, and then again, 'Ah. So I was right.'

'You were,' said Biggles shortly, 'and so was I.'

Von Stalhein slowly raised his hands. As they drew level with the top of his burnous, he tore the garment off with a swift movement and hurled it straight into Biggles' face. At the same time he leapt for the door. Algy barred his way, but he turned like a hare and sprang at the window with Algy at his heels. For a second pandemonium reigned.

Biggles dared not risk shooting for fear of hitting Algy or the Staff officers who tried to intercept the German; but they were too late. Biggles saw a flash of white as von Stalhein went through the window like a bird. He did not attempt to follow, but dashed through the door, shouting for the headquarter's guard. 'Outside, outside,' he shouted furiously, as they came running up the stairs. He dashed past them, raced to the door, and looked out. An Arab, bent double over a magnificent horse, was streaking through the village street. Before Biggles could raise his weapon horse and rider had disappeared round the corner of the road that led to Kantara.

'Get my car, get my car,' roared the General. 'Baines! Baines! Where the devil are you? Confound the man, he's never here when he's wanted.'

'Here, sir.' The chauffeur, very red about the ears, for he had been snatching a surreptitious cup of tea with the cook, started the big Crossley tourer and took his place at the wheel.

The General jumped in beside him, and the others squeezed into the back seats. There was not room for Algy, but determined not to be left behind, he flung himself on the running board.

'Faster, man, faster,' cried the General, as they tore through the village with Arabs, mangy dogs, scraggy fowls, and stray donkeys missing death by inches. The car, swaying under its heavy load, dry-skidded round the corner where von Stalhein had last been seen, and the open road lay before them.

228

A mile away the tents of Kantara gleamed pink and gold in the rays of the rising sun; two hundred yards this side of them von Stalhein was flogging his horse unmercifully, as, crouching low in the saddle, he sped like an arrow towards the hangars.

'He'll beat us,' fumed the General. 'He'll take one of those machines just starting up.'

It was apparent that such was von Stalhein's intention. Several machines of different types were standing on the tarmac; the propeller of one of them, a Bristol Fighter, was flashing in the sunlight, warming up the engine while its pilot and observer finished their cigarettes outside the Mess some thirty or forty yards away.

Von Stalhein swerved like a greyhound towards the machine. The pilot and observer watched his unusual actions in astonishment; they made no attempt to stop him.

At a distance of ten yards von Stalhein pulled up with a jerk that threw the horse on to its haunches; in a twinkling of an eye he had pulled away the chocks from under the wheels and had taken a flying leap into the cockpit. The engine roared and the Bristol began to move over the ground.

'We've lost him,' cried the General. Then, as an afterthought, he added, 'Stop at the archie battery, Baines.'

The usual protective anti-aircraft battery was only a hundred yards down the road, the muzzles of its four guns pointing into the air like chimneys set awry as the crews sleepily sipped their early morning tea. But the arrival of the General's car brought them to their feet with a rush. A startled subaltern ran forward and saluted.

'Get that machine,' snapped the General, pointing at the Bristol that was now a thousand feet in the air and climbing swiftly towards the German lines. 'Get it and I'll promote you to Captain in to-night's orders.'

The lieutenant asked no questions; he shouted an order and dashed to the range-finder. Mess tins were flung aside as the gunners leapt to their stations, and within five seconds the first gun had roared its brass-coated shell at the British machine. It went wide. The officer corrected the aim, and a second shot was nearer. Another correction, and a shell burst fifty yards in front of the two-seater. Another word of command, and the four guns began firing salvoes as fast as the gunners could feed them.

Tiny sparks of yellow flame, followed by mushrooming clouds of white smoke, appeared round the Bristol, the pilot of which began to swerve from side to side as he realized his danger.

Biggles was torn between desire to watch the frantic but methodical activity of the gunners—for he had seldom stood at the starting end of archie—and the machine, but he could not tear his eyes away from the swerving two-seater; knowing from bitter experience just what von Stalhein was going through, he felt almost sorry for him. A shell burst almost under the fuselage and the machine rocked.

'He's hit,' cried the General excitedly.

'No, sir, it was only the bump of the explosion, I think,' declared Biggles.

Another shell burst almost between the wings of the Bristol, and its nose jerked up spasmodically.

'He's hit now, sir,' yelled Biggles, clutching Algy's arm.

A silence fell on the little group of watchers; the roar of the guns and the distant sullen *whoof—whoof—whoof* of the bursting shells died away as the Bristol lurched, recovered, lurched again, and then fell off on its wing into a dizzy earthward plunge. Twice it tried to come out, as if the pilot was still alive and making desperate efforts to right his machine; then it disappeared behind a distant hill.

A hush of tense expectancy fell as every man held his breath and strained his ears for the sound that he knew would come.

It came. Clear-cut through the still morning air, far away over the German side of the lines, came the sound as if some one had jumped on a flimsy wooden box, crushing it flat: the sinister but unmistakable sound of an aeroplane hitting the ground.

Biggles drew a deep breath. 'Well,' he said slowly, 'that's that.'

Chapter 22
Biggles Explains

That evening a little party dined quietly in the Head-quarters Mess; it consisted of the General, his Aide-de-Camp, Major Raymond, Algy, and Biggles, who, over coffee, at the General's request, ran over the whole story.

'And so you see, sir,' he concluded, 'the unravelling of the skein was not so difficult as one might imagine.'

'But when did you first suspect that von Stalhein and El Shereef were one and the same?' asked the General.

'It's rather hard to say, sir,' replied Biggles slowly. 'I fancy the idea was at the back of my mind before I was really aware of it—if I can put it that way,' he continued. 'I felt from the very beginning that von Stalhein was more than he appeared to be on the surface.'

'Why did you think that?'

'Because he was so obviously suspicious—not only where I was concerned but with any stranger that came to the camp. "Why should he be?" I asked myself, and the only answer I could find was, because he had more to lose than any one else on the station. After all, a man is only suspicious when he has something to be suspicious about. Something was going on behind the scenes. What was it? When I saw him dressed as an Arab—well, that seemed to be the answer to the question.

'He never appeared in that garb in daylight, and I

am convinced that only a few people at Zabala knew what he was doing; he didn't want them to know; that's why he used to send the aeroplane to the far side of the aerodrome and slip out after dark when no one was about. The Count knew all about it, of course; he had to, and if you ask my opinion I should say that he wasn't too pleased about it—hence his attitude towards me.'

'But why should he feel like that?'

'Because he was secretly jealous of von Stalhein. He wanted all the kudos. Von Faubourg was vain and inefficient and it annoyed him to know that a subordinate had ten times the amount of brain that he had; he had sense enough to recognize that, you may be sure. And von Stalhein knew it too. He knew that nothing would please the Count more than to see him take down a peg. I will go as far as to say that I believe the Count was actually pleased when von Stalhein's plans went wrong. Take the business of the Australian troops, for example. Von Stalhein put that over to try to trap me; he merely wanted to see what I would do in such a case. When I got back and reported that the Australians were at Sidi Arish the Count was tickled to death because von Stalhein's scheme had failed; I could tell it by his manner. He was so pleased that he came round to my room to congratulate me. That showed me how things were between them, and I knew that I had a friend in the Count as long as I didn't tread on his toes; the more I upset von Stalhein—to a point—the better he was pleased.

'Take the business of when I dropped my ring near the waterworks. That was a careless blunder that might have cost me my life; even the Count couldn't overlook that, but he was quite pleased when I cleared myself for no other reason than that von Stalhein had told him that he had got me stone cold. If the Count had made the discovery it would have been quite a different matter. Von Stalhein sent Leffens out to watch me. Leffens was, I think, the one man he really trusted; he used to fly him over the lines until I killed him, and after that he used Mayer. He never knew what happened to Leffens, but he thought he did when he found one of his bullets in my machine. I've got a feeling that he tipped Leffens off to shoot me down if he got a chance, and that was why he daren't make much of a song when he found the bullet.

'I had already thought a lot about Sterne, who as far as I could make out was playing pretty much the same game for the British, and there were two things that put me on the right track there. First, the shadow on the tent, and secondly, the fact that some one—obviously in sympathy with the Germans—arranged my escape. Who could it be? Who had access to British posts? Mind you, sir, at that stage the association was nothing more than a bare possibility. I could hardly bring myself to believe that it might be remotely possible, but once the germ was in my mind it stayed there, and I was always on the look-out for a clue that might confirm it. That's why I went to von Stalhein's room. I hardly admitted it to myself but I knew I was hoping to find a British uniform—or something of the sort. As a matter of fact I did see a Sam Browne belt in the wardrobe, but I could hardly regard that as proof; it might easily have been nothing more than a souvenir. But then there was the British hat in Mayer's machine! It may sound easy to put two and two together now but it wasn't so easy then. Would you have believed me, sir, if I had come to you and said that Major Sterne was von Stalhein? I doubt it.

'Von Stalhein's scheme for the capture of El Shereef

was a clever piece of work, there's no denying that; it shook me to the marrow. At first it took me in, and I'll admit it. But he overreached himself. He made one little slip—took one risk, would perhaps be nearer the truth—and it gave the game away. Then I saw how simple the whole thing really was.'

'Do you mean when you went and saw Sheikh Haroun?' put in the Major.

'No, I got nothing out of him,' declared Biggles. 'He behaved just as one would expect a well-bred Arab to behave in such circumstances. He closed up like an oyster at the bare thought of the British suspecting him to be a traitor, and he would have died with his mouth shut if I hadn't butted in. No, it was what I saw in your tent that gave the game away.'

'What was it?'

'The ring. Those rings are few and far between. They daren't leave spare ones lying about: it would be too dangerous. Yet they knew that one of those rings found on the Sheikh would be sufficient evidence to hang him. There was only one available; it was Leffens', and I recognized it—as, indeed, I had every reason to. That set me thinking, and I reconstructed the crime—as the police say. Yet I had to act warily. One word and we shouldn't have seen von Stalhein—El Shereef—call him what you like—for dust and small pebbles.'

'But he sent you over to try to rescue El Shereef,' exclaimed the General. 'What was his idea in doing that?'

'It was simply another try-on; he wanted me to confirm that El Shereef had been arrested, and at the same time he hoped I'd make a boob. He had nothing to lose. Suppose I had managed to "rescue" El Shereef— or rather, Sheikh Haroun. The Huns would have asked for nothing more than to have had him in their hands.'

235

'Yes, of course, I quite see that. And by reporting that he had been shot you led him to think that we had been completely taken in.'

'Exactly, sir. I went on playing my own game, and as it happened it came off, although he made a clever move to get rid of me. He never trusted me; he was no fool; he was the only one of the lot of them who spotted that things started going wrong from the moment I arrived. It might have been coincidence, but von Stalhein didn't think so.'

'How do you mean?'

'Well, first of all the waterworks were blown up; then Leffens failed to return; then the Arab raid went wrong; then Hess got killed! Mayer crashes and gets his leg smashed—oh, no, sir, he wasn't going to believe this was just a run of bad luck. Something was radically wrong somewhere and he knew it. Whether it was anything to do with me or not, he would have felt happier if he could have got me out of the way. That's why he tried to get me pushed into the ground.'

'When?'

'The day I came over here to confirm that you had captured El Shereef.'

'What did he do?'

'He followed me over in the Pup—dressed as Major Sterne. He simply walked along the tarmac, told the flight-sergeant to put my machine in the shed and put another in its place—one which, of course, had no distinguishing mark on the top plane.'

'You assume he did that?'

'I assumed it at the time; I know it now.'

'How?'

'I've asked the flight-sergeant about it and he told me just what happened; he obeyed the Major's orders unquestioningly, as he was bound to. Then von Stalhein went back and sent out the Pfalz crowd to intercept me on the way home. It was clever, that, because if I had been shot no one would have been the wiser. I should just have disappeared, and that was all he wanted. But I knew things were rapidly coming to a head, and that's why I played a big stake to end it one way or the other; but all the same, I thought I'd bungled things badly when I landed here and found he wasn't in the back seat of that Halberstadt. I never even thought of his going over the side by parachute. After that there was one chance left, for if once a hue and cry had started we should never have seen him again, you may be sure of that. Von Stalhein had set plenty of traps, so I thought it was about time I set one, with what result you know.'

'And what do you propose to do now?' asked the General.

'I am going to submit an application to you, sir, to post me back to my old unit, number 266 Squadron in France, and I hope you will put it through, sir.'

The General looked hurt. 'I hoped you would stay out here,' he said. 'I could have found you a place on Headquarters Staff—both of you.'

'I'm sorry, sir—it's very kind of you—but—well, somehow I don't feel at home here. I would prefer to go back to France if you have no objection.'

'Very well, so be it. I can't refuse, and I need hardly say how grateful I am for what you have done during your tour of duty in the Middle East. The success of the British Army in Palestine may have rested on you alone. Naturally, I am forwarding a report on your work to the Air Board, and doubtless they will ask you to do the same. And now I must get back to my work—pray that you are never a General, Bigglesworth.'

'I should think that's the last thing I'm ever likely

237

to be, sir,' smiled Biggles. 'A Camel, blue skies, and plenty of Huns is the height of my ambition, and I hope to find them all in France. Good-bye, sir.'

'Good-bye—and good luck.' The General watched them go and then turned to his Aide-de-Camp. 'If we had a few more officers of that type the war would have been over long ago,' he observed.

BIGGLES
FLIES WEST

The moon is up, the stars are bright,
*   The wind is fresh and free;*
We're out to seek for gold to-night
*   Across the silver sea.*
The world was growing grey and old;
*   Break out the sails again!*
We're out to seek a realm of gold
*   Beyond the Spanish Main.*

ALFRED NOYES: *Drake*

Prologue

I. *Murder on the Main*

There was a soft creaking of blocks and tackle as the two ships, *Rose of Bristol* and *Santa Anna*, stirred uneasily on the gently heaving ocean. The ropes of the grappling irons that held them in a fast embrace grew taut, slackened, and grew taut again; it was almost as if the *Rose* shrank from the contact and strove to escape. But the steel hooks in her gunwales held her fast.

Overhead, from horizon to horizon, the sky was the deep azure blue of the tropics, unbroken except in the distant west, where, high above the misty peaks of Hispaniola,* a fleecy cloud was sailing slowly eastward. Nearer, a snow-white albatross swung low on rigid wings, its shadow sweeping the limpid surface of the sea, clear aquamarine, with little purple shadows here and there between the ripples that lapped gently at the *Santa*'s stern, or broke when a school of dolphins hurried by.

This scene of grace and colour was well matched by the splendour of the Spanish ship, a stately galleon, her counter red and silver, her towering poop all gold-encrusted, her sails, now loosely furled, rich cream and crimson, bright pennants streaming from her mastheads to the coats of arms that lined her sides above the bristling guns.

Only the *Rose*, belying her name, looked out of place, as out of place as a tramp on the threshold of a palace. Her sea-stained canvas, torn and shot-holed, lay in piles about the

* Now Haiti.

foot of her broken and splintered mainmast, or trailed with twisted skeins of cordage over her sides. From her bluff, Bristol-built bows to her sweeping stern she was painted black, a fitting colour, for about her well-scrubbed decks, in a welter of fast congealing blood, lay her crew, their glazing eyes upturned to the grim emblem of piracy that hung limply from the galleon's peak – a sable flag with a white device: the dreaded skull and crossbones.

The scene was all too common in the days when Charles the Second was king. The *Rose of Bristol*, a barque of two hundred and fifty tons, homeward bound from the Spanish Main, had fallen in with the *Santa Anna*, lately captured by the most notorious pirate on the coast: Louis Dakeyne, leader of the Brethren, half French, half Dutch, half man, half devil, whose name was execrated wherever sailors met between the Old World and the New; for he spared neither man nor maid, or old or young of any nationality. His latest exploit, so it was rumoured, had been the capture, off Cartagena, of the galleon *Santa Anna*, to which, after subjecting her captain to unspeakable tortures, he had transferred his cut-throat crew. So when at dawn the foretop of the Spaniard had appeared above the clear horizon, John Chandler, Master of the *Rose*, had clapped on sail and fled, knowing that, outmanned and outgunned, he stood no chance against the monster with its heavy metal and swarming crowd of villains. And for a time it seemed as if he would escape, for the barque was the better sailer of the two; but then the breeze that could have saved him passed him by, and while he had lain becalmed the bigger vessel with its enormous spread of canvas had crept slowly nearer, and with sinking heart the English captain knew his hour had come. With steady voice he had called his crew to prayer, then bade them die like men.

He had fought to the end, refusing to strike his colours,

firing his one small piece of ordnance until the pirates poured aboard. Then, with his loyal crew around him, he had made his last stand near the mainmast, neither asking nor giving quarter. Cutlass in hand, the name of his God on his lips, he had done all that one man could do while his gallant hands were beaten down and slain, and only he remained, to fall at length under a foul blow from behind.

But not to die at once. Sorely wounded, he was dragged aboard the galleon while his ship was looted. This done, he was questioned by Dakeyne about other ships in harbour, soon to sail for England; but he set his lips in an obstinate line and not a word came from them. At that they flogged him until he swooned, but they could not make him speak. And now, the pirate's patience soon exhausted, he stood upon the fatal plank, looking death in the face, with his hands tied behind his back.

A sudden silence fell, a hush broken only by the plaintive cry of the seabird, now circling very near, and the gentle murmur of the water far below.

Well might it have been for Louis Dakeyne, Louis le Grande, self-styled, or Louis the Exterminator, as many called him, had he dispatched his prisoner there and then, for the English mariner had still one card to play, and he played it with such deadly calm that those who heard his words turned pale, knowing that one on the point of death must speak the truth.

Turning from the end of the plank that hung far over the limpid sea so that he faced his ship, he regarded the grinning mob, his captors, with steadfast eyes that held not fear, nor hate, but scorn and triumph. For a moment he stood thus while a bead of blood crept down his ashen brow, crossing a cut so that a cross of red was formed.

The omen did not pass unseen, and a low mutter, like breakers on a distant beach, ran through the mob. It died away to silence as the stricken captain spoke.

'Harken unto me, black hounds of hell,' he cried, in a clear, ringing voice. 'Harken at these my words, for they will be in the ears of each and all of you when your hour comes, as it will, before another moon shall wax and wane.'

A howl of derision rose into the sun-soaked air.

'Shoot him,' screamed one.

'*Perro! Vamos a ver,**' snarled a renegade Spaniard.

'Swing him by the heels,' roared a one-eyed monster.

'Woodle him,**' bawled another.

'Silence!' At the pirate captain's sharp command the imprecations ceased. He was watching the doomed man with a peculiar expression, not far removed from fear, upon his face.

'Amongst the gold that you have taken from my ship and put with yours,' went on the English captain dispassionately, 'there is one coin, a gold doubloon, that carries all your fates, for it is cursed. When Joseph Bawn, a red-haired thief whom some of you may know, was brought to the scaffold at Port Royal this day last week, that coin was in his pocket. And there, within the shadow of the gallows, he spat upon it thrice. And as he spat he cursed the God who made him, and everyone into whose hands the gold should fall.'

A shudder, like the sound of the wind in leafless trees, ran through the superstitious audience.

'That piece was put upon my ship because it was the

---

* Spanish: 'Dog! We'll see about that.'
** 'Woodling' was a barbarous form of torture favoured by buccaneers to induce prisoners to divulge the hiding places of their valuables. (Naturally, in the sacking of a ship, or town, those who possessed gold or jewels hid them in the hope that they would not be found.) Woodling, the process employed to make them speak, consisted of tying a piece of cord round the prisoner's brows, and then screwing it up with a piece of wood, like a tourniquet. WEJ

king's and had to go to England,' continued the captain relentlessly. 'Mark well my fate, and see how true the curse is working; then contemplate your own that soon must follow. For you can not escape. The piece is in your hoard, and to disown it you must throw your treasure overboard, which you have not the heart to do.'

There was no more laughing. Upon the faces of the pirates were frowns and scowls; upon their lips were oaths, but in their hearts cold fear.

John Chandler lifted his blue eyes to the blue sky. 'With my last breath I beseech my God to strengthen now that curse until—'

He got no farther. Dakeyne's pistol blazed. A stream of flame and sparks leapt from its gaping muzzle and ended at the sailor's breast.

For an instant he remained standing, eyes upturned, lips moving. Then his knees bent; his body sagged limply and plunged down into the void.

At the sound of the splash the pirates rushed to the side of their ship, eyes seeking the corpse. But all they saw was an ever-spreading ring of ripples that circled slowly outwards from a crimson stain. And as they stared aghast an icy slant of wind moaned through the rigging.

'What's that?' muttered Dakeyne, white-faced.

'The bird! It was the albatross!' cried Jamaica Joe, his quartermaster.

The pirate's eyes flashed round the sky. 'The bird has gone!' he gasped. 'Look!'

There was a sudden hush as all eyes followed his quivering forefinger.

Far to the west, from north to south, across the sky, an indigo belt was racing low towards them, blotting out the blue.

The pirate's voice scarce rose above the hubbub. 'All

hands aloft,' he croaked through lips that were suddenly dry.

II. *The Curse*

In setting down the disasters that befell the *Santa Anna* following immediately after the murder of Captain John Chandler, it is not suggested that these were caused directly by the sacrilegious words of a drunken buccaneer on the scaffold at Port Royal, but that they were the indirect cause is certain.

There is no question about the incident happening. We know from the famous chronicles of Exquemelin, the surgeon who served under the most notorious pirate captains, including the celebrated Morgan, and who afterwards wrote an account of his adventures, that Joseph Bawn was a pirate of the most villainous type. We know that he was turned off* at Port Royal in January 1689, for the foul murder of a comrade whose rations he had tried to steal, and Sir John Modyford, Governor of Jamaica at that time, refers to the condemned pirate's frightful curse in a letter to Lord Arlington, Secretary of State to Charles II's 'Cabal' Cabinet. But to presume that the last wish of a red-handed murderer was fulfilled by his Maker would be going too far. As far as the *Santa Anna* was concerned, the truth is probably to be found in four perfectly natural causes.

In the first place there was the incident itself, which distracted the attention of every soul on board, including the watch, so that the hurricane caught them unprepared. Secondly, there was the ship. Like all Spanish ships of the period she was unseaworthy; the high poop and short keel were so opposed to all natural laws that one marvels that

* ie hanged.

they sailed at all. Thirdly, the firmly ingrained superstitions of the crew – notwithstanding their professed godlessness – must be taken into account. And lastly, but by no means least, their lack of discipline or control.

From the years 1680 to 1720, when piracy was in its heyday, it would be no exaggeration to say that the Brethren of the Coast – as they called themselves – were virtually in command of the West Indies and the Spanish Mainland. Morgan was probably more powerful in Jamaica than the Governor; he certainly had more men at his beck and call. That he was superior to the Spanish colonists is proved by his exploits, which included the taking and sacking of such cities as Panama, Porto Bello, and Maracaibo; Panama was the most strongly fortified city on the Main. At Tortuga, the Brethren had practically established a colony of their own, and that they did not, in fact, do so, was due to the weakness already referred to – lack of discipline.

Their commanders were appointed by themselves and held their posts only by the goodwill of the crews. Such orders as they gave, except in the heat of battle, were, in fact, only suggestions, for if they did not meet with the approval of the ship's companies they were not carried out. If the captain dared to insist, more often than not he was deposed, sometimes by the simple expedient of being thrown overboard. Admittedly, in times of success, orders were, on the whole, obeyed, but when things started going wrong the officers had to look to the priming of their pistols. It is on record that one pirate ship had no less than thirteen captains in a few months. Bartholomew Roberts, who maintained his command for four years, probably held the record for duration of office – popular fiction notwithstanding.

At the time of the capture of the *Rose of Bristol* the popularity of Louis Dakeyne ran high, for a very good reason. The *Santa Anna*, which he had waylaid, had proved to be a veritable treasure ship, laden with such minted coins as doubloons, golden moidores, pieces of eight, and cross money, to say nothing of plate, silks, lace, and other rare fabrics that would fetch good money at Port Royal, where unscrupulous traders were making fortunes. In their minds, Dakeyne's *matelots** – as the pirates sometimes called themselves – were already spending their ill-gotten gains in the iniquitous and pestilential drinking booths that lined the waterfront, so it may be safely assumed that the bare possibility of this depraved ambition being frustrated soon set them grumbling.

When the hurricane struck the galleon she heeled over until the grapnels tore the side clean out of the English ship. The foresail, carelessly stowed, burst like a paper bag, flinging overboard two men, who soon disappeared astern in the smother of foam whipped up from the surface of the sea. By an odd coincidence they were two of the very men who had clamoured for the English captain's instant death as he stood on the plank, a fact that was not overlooked by the rest of the crew, who saw in the disaster the direct hand of God. Meanwhile the *Santa Anna* heeled away before a wind of such violence as no man on board had ever before experienced. It beat up terrific seas that poured over the poop and splashed half way up the mainmast.

For seven days the tempest raged, and in that time nine men were killed. The rest were so exhausted that they could hardly stand, much less keep the ship clear of water.

On the fifth day a deputation, headed by the quartermaster, had staggered to the captain, imploring him to throw all the gold overboard that their lives might be spared. Dakeyne refused peremptorily to jettison what had cost so much blood and toil to get. The men grumbled, the

* French: sailors.

quartermaster louder than the rest, and Dakeyne, seeing in him as the only other navigator a likely rival, had pistolled him on the spot.

On the eighth day the wind died away, and the galleon lay becalmed on a sea that was as flat as a sheet of glass. She was short of water and short of provisions. What little water she had left was foul, and the food, badly cured *boucan*,* was rotten and full of maggots, due to the damp heat. The muttering grew ominous.

By nightfall the crew had split into two parties, those who wished to jettison the treasure and those who sided with the captain. The latter were in the minority. Fighting broke out more than once, and several men were killed. Their bodies, after the custom of the pirates, were flung overboard. And all the time the ship lay like a log on the glassy sea while sharks gathered round to enjoy a grisly feast.

When the calm had lasted for six days Dakeyne lived up to the reputation that had earned for him his sinister nickname of Exterminator. While the larger party were together in the fo'castle, plotting, no doubt, Dakeyne and his adherents crept upon them with loaded muskets and delivered such a volley that half of them fell dead or dying. The rest were easily dispatched. More bodies were flung overboard, and the number of sharks increased. Eleven men only remained alive, not counting the captain. Having no water, they drank rum, and, rolling drunk, consoled themselves by roaring Morgan's famous slogan, coined after the dreadful sacking of Porto Bello:

> If there be few amongst us
> Our hearts are very great;
> And each will have more plunder,
> And each will have more plate.

* Salted beef.

Their hearts were not very great on the morrow. Louis the Exterminator whistled for a wind. He whistled in vain.

A blood-red sun was sinking into a blood-red sea the following evening when the pirate captain, a scarlet bandanna tied about his head, called to one of the men who were lounging listlessly aft to bring him a drink of rum. His throat, he declared, was parched – as well it might be after the quantity of liquor he had already drunk that day. The man fetched the rum bottle and passed it to the captain. But he did not watch him drink it. His eyes were on the back of the captain's hand as it rested on the rail, and had Dakeyne been sober he might have remarked the seaman's expression. But he did not. It is doubtful even if he had noticed what the sailor had seen – a round patch of what looked like white dust on the back of his hand.

The sailor, a Frenchman who had sailed with L'Ollonois, returned swiftly to the others. With ashen face and staring eyes he told them what he had seen. 'It is the plague,' he muttered hoarsely.

Lorton, a one-armed gunner who had sailed many seas, sprang to his feet, an oath on his lips, hand groping for his knife; but the Frenchman restrained him, casting furtive glances over his shoulder in case the captain should be watching.

That night, while Dakeyne was heavy in drunken sleep, the remnant of the crew launched the one boat that had escaped damage by the storm, and stole away across a moonlit sea, not knowing that the sun had warped the planks and opened up the seams. For three days of purgatory they kept the boat afloat by constant bailing before they were picked up by a Spanish ship, whose commander, being a humane man, hanged them out of hand instead of subjecting them to the usual tortures.

Dakeyne awoke to find himself alone and all the rum

gone. All that day he moped about; but during the night came another storm, as furious as the last. For a time he tried to work the ship alone, but at length his strength gave out and he staggered to his cabin to rest.

When he awoke he was surprised to find that the rolling had ceased, and going up on deck, saw that a remarkable thing had happened, so remarkable that he could scarcely believe his good fortune. The ship was aground on an island the size of which he could not judge; more than that, she was high and dry where the tide had left her. What was still more surprising, she appeared to be in a land-locked harbour, an inlet so small that at first he could not understand how she had got there. Presently, exploring, the apparent miracle was explained.

The galleon had drifted into a narrow channel between grey rocks about the same height as herself, which opened out at the inner end into a sort of miniature lagoon. He could not see the sea, but he could hear it, a short distance away. The rocks on either side were so close that he could jump ashore, which presently he did, to make certain that no Indians were hidden in the jungle that crowded nearly to the water's edge. From a comfortable seat on a rock he regarded the ship and her position with considerable satisfaction. Never were Morgan's words more appropriate, he reflected, for now there was only one to share the treasure, and it was he. If the ship had come in it could be got out, he opined, not unreasonably. There was bound to be food and water on the island. He would fill the casks and lay in a store of provisions, and then sail the ship to a proper harbour. By thunder, so he would! He'd show them what one man could do. Dakeyne was no coward or he would not have been the captain of a pirate crew.

It would not take him long to work out his position, he thought, and he was about to put this plan into execution when he remembered something that caused a cold shiver to run down his spine. Bawn's doubloon! The curse, the potency of which he could no longer ignore. It would be the act of a madman to set off on such a voyage as the one he proposed with that dreadful piece of gold on board. No matter. There was an easy way of getting over that difficulty. He would put the doubloons ashore, every jack one of 'em; hide 'em until such time as he could come back with a stout ship and a stout-hearted crew to retrieve them.

He set to work with commendable method and determination, but he had neither the time nor inclination to dig a hole; instead, he selected a depression in the rocks, a hole large enough to take perhaps two or three casks lying one on top of another, and into this he began to pour the coins. He did not like the idea of handling the gold, and he looked at the minted pieces suspiciously as he scooped them into the piece of canvas he was using as a carrier; but his heart grew lighter with each load he carried, hoping that the treacherous piece was already in the hole.

It took him a long time to transfer them all, for the gold was heavy and the sun was hot; but at last the job was done. Then, too wise to trust his memory, he sat down at the Spanish captain's desk and began to make a note of the exact position of the hole in which the treasure lay, the note taking the form of a rough map to which bearings and measurements could afterwards be added.

While thus engaged it struck him suddenly that all was strangely quiet, unnaturally quiet; also, for no apparent reason, the temperature had dropped several degrees, causing the sweat on his face to turn cold and clammy. It sent a shiver running through him, leaving as an aftermath an apprehension of danger. But as we have already observed, Louis the Exterminator was no coward. His jaw set at an ugly angle as he primed and cocked his pistol; then, with a faint sneer curling the corners of his loose mouth, he crept quietly up the companion and looked around.

Not a soul was in sight. Not a movement could he see. Not a sound could he hear but the sullen murmur of the sea against the rocks outside the little inlet. Satisfied that all was well, he returned to the cabin, but before he could resume his task a sudden cry outside brought him round with a nervous start. Pistol in hand, he strode swiftly to one of the poop lights.

His face paled as a snow-white albatross sailed slowly past his field of vision. There seemed to be something familiar about it. Was it imagination or was it the same bird that had hovered round the ill-fated *Rose of Bristol?* He could not be sure, but a superstitious conscience tugged his heart-strings and the presentiment of an unseen danger still persisted. For a moment or two he waited, pistol at the ready, hoping that the bird would come within range. Whether the ball struck it or not, he would derive some satisfaction from having alarmed it, he thought savagely. But no such opportunity presented itself. It was almost as if the great bird understood what was passing in his mind, for it banked slowly to and fro just out of range, turning its head all the while to watch him in a curiously human manner, from time to time uttering its mournful cry.

The Exterminator spat contemptuously, but he could not deceive himself. For the first time in his life he was afraid, afraid of he knew not what. He hurried back to the desk, propped the pistol against a heavy church candlestick that stood within easy reach, and picked up the quill to finish marking out his map. As he did so, something dropped heavily out of the gathered-in part of his silken doublet. Idly, he looked to see what it was. But as his eyes came to rest on the object he caught his breath sharply; the pupils of his eyes dilated and his face set in lines of unspeakable horror. The object was a gold doubloon.

For a few moments he continued to stare at it unbelievingly. Then, with an oath, he sprang to his feet. His eyes did not leave the coin. It seemed to fascinate him. He knew what it was. He did not know how he knew, but he *knew*. Knew that the one coin that had slipped out of the canvas carrier was THE coin. The doubloon to which still clung the dying pirate's curse. Somehow it had dropped into one of the many pleats of his doublet. To what purpose?

Had he been less enthralled by the crudely cut piece of gold he might have seen. He might have noticed that his trembling hand was resting on the desk, and the slight vibration was causing the muzzle of the pistol to slip. At first it moved very slowly, hesitatingly, but as it passed the point of balance it dropped sharply, with a thud. The weapon roared. A tongue of blood-red flame spurted from the gaping muzzle. For a fleeting instant it seemed to lick the pirate's silken doublet Then it was gone. Silence fell. A sickly smell of scorching mingled with the acrid reek of powder-smoke.

For perhaps three seconds after his first convulsive spasm of agony the pirate did not move. Then, his staring eyes still fixed on the coin, his right hand crept down until it rested on the dreadful hole made by the pistol ball. Slowly, as if he feared what he might see, he looked down, and saw his life-blood pumping through his grimy fingers. At the sight, the horror on his ashen face gave way to hopeless resignation. He sank down in the chair and covered his face with his hands. No sound broke the silence except a sinister drip – drip – drip. A little crimson pool began to form at his feet.

Slowly, so slowly that the movement was hardly perceptible, his body began to sag forward until at length it lay asprawl the desk. A fly settled on the pallid, red-streaked face, but the pirate did not move. Others joined it. Still he did not move.

There was a flash of white as the albatross swept past the open port. Louis le Grande did not see it; nor did he hear the cry that seemed to swell to a note of triumph as it soared into the sun-drenched blue of heaven.

Inside the cabin settled the hush that comes with the presence of Death. A hush that was to remain unbroken for just two hundred and fifty years.

III. *Time Marches On*

The years rolled by, and with their passing, nature triumphed. Came sun and rain and wind and calm, but no man came to the island where Louis, once le Grande, kept lonely vigil with his fate.

Before a year was out the gruesome stains upon the galleon's deck were hidden beneath a mantle of fallen leaves that died and rotted where they lay, and made a sure foundation for the ever-questing moss.

When James the Second ruled in England there came a storm that undermined the rocks which lay about the harbour's narrow mouth, so that they fell, and falling, made a wall against the waves; and year by year the tireless sea cemented them with sand.

The years rolled on, each year contributing its little to the shrouding of the dying ship. While Queen Anne wore the crown came briers and vines to seek a foothold in the moss that blanketed the rotting timbers. In the reign of George the First the masts collapsed and struck a futile blow at the all-devouring jungle; but the briers and vines and weeds embraced them, and dragged them down to oblivion and decay.

The years rolled on. In the reign of George the Second a ship came watering at the island, and although the thirsty sailors came ashore they did not learn its secret. When George the Third was king came several ships, but a hundred years had passed and no sign remained to reveal what they could not suspect, and so they sailed away.

The years rolled on. When George the Fourth sat on the throne a shipwrecked mariner was cast away upon the island, and although he stayed there for a year, often in his lonely wanderings passing within a score of paces of the green-girt wreck, he did not find it. And so he went away in the next ship that called, and in due course died a pauper's death, not knowing that once he had made a frugal meal within a yard of enough doubloons to pay a prince's ransom.

The years rolled on. William the Fourth, Victoria, King Edward – the seventh of the name – King George the Fifth, the eighth King Edward, all ruled in turn, but still the island kept its secret.

And then one day, when George the Sixth upheld the British Empire, a man came running on the rocks, a sailor, judging by his clothes. And as he ran he gasped for breath, and looked behind as one who runs in fear. Reaching the rock on which Dakeyne once stood, he turned towards the briers and vines as if to seek a hiding place. A little dell of green moss beckoned, and bracing himself, he jumped. He landed fair and square, but stumbled as the rotting timbers which the moss concealed collapsed beneath his weight. A scream of mortal fear broke from his lips as he clutched at the air for support. But the effort was in vain, and he plunged headlong into the void.

Thus was the silence broken.

Chapter 1
An Ugly Customer

Through the fog-frosted glass of his attic window Dick Denver stared with unseeing eyes at the muddy water of the River Thames as it surged sullenly through the grey November murk towards the sea. Only fifteen years of life lay behind him; how many lay ahead he did not know, nor did he care, and the despondency of his mood was reflected in his thin, pale face.

In the years that were gone he had known at least a few happy hours, the all-too-brief spells when his sailor father had come home from the deep seas, but now there would be no more. A horror that had haunted him ever since he was old enough to know that ships were sometimes wrecked had come to pass. The *Seadream* had made her last voyage and his father would come home no more. There would be no more counting the days until his return; no more scanning the shipping columns of the papers he sold for a living, seeking the name of his father's ship, and its position; no more watching for the *Seadream*'s blunt, rust-encrusted bows to come ploughing up the river; no more cheering at the wharf; no more long, after-supper talks about strange, foreign parts of the world. No more. Those days had gone, gone for good, and with them had gone the only thing that had made his life worth living – his father.

His mother he had never known. A hard-faced, bad-tempered woman had looked after him during his father's long absences at sea until he was thirteen; then she, too, had died, and thereafter he had fended for himself, maintaining a tiny attic in Wapping, overlooking the river, which his father shared when he was home.

But the struggle for existence had been a hard one, and although his short fair hair was neatly brushed, and his clear blue eyes alert, his cheeks were pale and pinched from under-nourishment. His clothes were, as might be expected, threadbare, and did little either to protect his body, or improve his down-and-out appearance. Dick was, in fact, down – down in the depths of despondency; but he was far from out.

He had first read of the wreck of the *Seadream* in one of the papers he had been selling, and the memory of that dreadful moment still kept him awake at night. Then, weeks afterwards, had come the joyful news that his father had been one of the two or three survivors and was in hospital at Boston, in America. This had been followed by more weeks of silence and suspense that had only an hour before been ended by the arrival at his dingy room of an unknown sailor who had broken the terrible news that his father, exhausted by privations as a castaway after the wreck, had died. At least, that was the official story, but the sailor, whose name Dick had forgotten to ask, had told a different tale.

That it was true Dick had no reason to doubt, for the sailor had brought him a letter from his father, which now lay on the deal table in front of him. He had – so the sailor had said – handed it to him on his deathbed, charging him to give it to his son when he returned to London. These instructions the sailor had obeyed faithfully, as a service from one sailor to another, and thereafter departed, Dick knew not whither.

The circumstances of his father's death were as painful as they were mysterious, for he had died, not in hospital as might have been supposed, but in a low dive on the

258

waterfront. The sailor had told him how he also had spent the night in the dive while looking for a ship, but in the early hours of the morning he had been awakened by low moans coming from the next room. Upon investigation he had found a British sailor named Jack Denver, Dick's father, bleeding to death from a knife thrust in the back; but before he had died he had handed him the letter, asking him as a favour to deliver it into the hands of his son, at Number 1, Bride's Alley, Wapping, on his return to the Port of London. The sailor, who had left Boston on the next tide, true to his word, had delivered the letter, which still lay unopened on the table.

Why he had not opened it Dick did not know. Possibly it was because he felt that once the letter was opened, it would be the end. While it remained sealed there would still be a final message to look forward to from the only human being he had ever loved. So he had hesitated, trying to prolong the pleasure that was really agony.

For the hundredth time he picked up the envelope, turning it over and over in his hands. It was bulky, and heavy, with the name and address written faintly in lead pencil. He recognized his father's handwriting, but he knew that he must have been very weak when he had written it, for normally his writing was bold and decisive.

The hoarse hoot of a ship's siren made him glance through the window again, and he saw the bulk of a deep-sea tramp steamer, huge and distorted in the gloom, creeping out on the tide. The picture would have been a dismal one at any time, but now it was depressing in the extreme. The mist, which was really a fine drizzle, hung low, like dirty yellow smoke, saturating everything with its clammy moisture. The water dripped slowly from the eaves, splashed monotonously from the leaky spouting and ran in tiny rivulets down the window panes. Far away on

259

the other side of the river a line of dim, yellow sparks showed where the street lamps were being lighted.

From the contemplation of this miserable scene Dick was suddenly interrupted by a sound that brought a perplexed frown to his forehead, for it was a noise that he seldom heard. Heavy footsteps were coming up the stairs; loud, clumsy footsteps, as if the feet were unaccustomed to thick boots or narrow stairs. That they were coming to his room was certain, for the staircase was a cul-de-sac that ended in the attic. Who could it be? His heart gave a lurch and his hands began to tremble, as the deliberate tread on the bare boards struck a chord in his memory. It reminded him of his father.

Dropping the letter among some unsold papers that lay scattered on the far side of the table, he walked quickly to the door and threw it open just as a stranger arrived at the head of the stairs, and there was something so sinister in his manner and appearance that, prompted by an acute instinct of self-preservation, Dick recoiled backward into the room. The man followed until his bulk filled the narrow doorway, from where he regarded Dick with cold, questioning eyes, that slanted upwards at the ends in a manner that suggested remote oriental ancestry.

In stature he was short, but broad, and obviously of great physical strength, an impression that was emphasized by arms that hung nearly down to his knees, like those of a gorilla. Indeed, he was not unlike a great ape, for the backs of his hands, now slowly opening and closing, were covered with downy red hair. His face, like his body, was short and broad, with a wide, thin-lipped mouth that was not improved by a large, semicircular scar, like a crescent moon, at one corner. His eyebrows, the same colour as the hair on his hands, were straight, shaggy, and hung far over his little restless eyes. A greasy blue jersey covered his powerful torso and suggested that he was a seafaring man.

For a moment or two they regarded each other speculatively, and then the stranger spoke.

'What's your name, pup?' he asked slowly, in a low, expressionless voice.

'Dick – Dick Denver,' replied Dick a trifle nervously, for although he was no coward there was something in the other's manner that alarmed him.

'Jack Denver's brat, eh?'

'Jack Denver was my father.'

'Him as was on the *Seadream*?'

'Yes – that's right.'

'Joe Dawkin 'as been 'ere to see you, ain't he?'

Dick shook his head. 'I've never heard of Joe Dawkin,' he answered truthfully.

'Well, you've had a sailor man 'ere?'

'Yes.'

'Brought you a letter from your old man?'

'Yes, he did.'

'Where is it?' The stranger fired out the words like pistol shots.

'Why, what's that got to do—'

'Never mind what that's got to do with me. Where is it?' The stranger seemed to force the words through his teeth, slowly, in a manner that was distinctly threatening.

'What do you want with it?'

'*Give it to me!*'

Dick's eyes flashed suddenly, and he set his teeth. 'No,' he said obstinately.

With horrible deliberation the other drew a heavy clasp knife from his pocket. A long, pointed blade jerked open with a click. 'So you won't, eh?' he said in the same monotonous undertone that he had first employed.

The wicked-looking blade seemed to fascinate Dick; he could not tear his eyes away from it. He was still staring at it when the sailor began to edge very slowly into the room, his body bent forward, jaw out-thrust, his thin lips curled back in an animal snarl revealing two rows of broken, discoloured teeth.

For one dreadful moment Dick retreated before him, but when his groping hands touched the wall behind him and he knew he could go no farther he nearly fell into a panic. Picking up the one rickety chair the room possessed, he swung it with all his force against the window, and before the crash of falling glass had died away he had rushed to the spot. 'Help! Help!' he screamed.

He heard the sailor coming and leapt aside just in time. A whirling arm missed him by inches. But the sailor's quick rush had left the doorway open, and before he could prevent it Dick had ducked like lightning under the table and was streaking for the stairs like a rabbit going into its burrow. Nor did he stop when he reached them. Down he went, taking them four and five at a time at imminent risk of breaking his neck. Nor did he stop even when he reached the hall at the bottom. The front door stood wide open. Through it he dashed into the street, and turning sharply to the right, ran down the shining pavement in search of a policeman.

He had not gone a dozen yards, however, when his progress was cut short by a collision that knocked most of the breath out of him. Three figures emerged suddenly from the gloom as they walked briskly along the pavement; he tried to avoid them, but his feet slipped on the greasy stone, and almost before he knew what was happening he found himself being tightly held in a pair of strong arms.

'Hi, hi! Not so fast, my lad. What's all the hurry about?' said a quiet voice reproachfully, yet not without a twinge of humour.

Dick knew by the softly modulated tones that his captor was a gentleman, and he gave a gasp of relief. 'There's a man up in my room, sir,' he gasped desperately.

The other laughed softly. 'Well, I don't suppose he'll eat you,' he said cheerfully.

'He tried to kill me, though,' declared Dick bitterly.

'Tried to kill you?'

'Yes, sir.'

'How?'

'With a knife.'

'What made him try to do that?'

'He came to rob me.'

'Rob you?' There was incredulity in the question.

One of the others laughed. 'Of what?'

'A letter, sir. A letter I've just had from my father. Don't let him take it, sir,' pleaded Dick passionately.

'We'd better look into this, Algy,' muttered the man who held him, as he relaxed his grip. 'Where do you live, son?'

'Up here, sir, on the top floor.' Dick led the way to the sombre hall.

'Mind how you go, Biggles. It doesn't look too healthy in there to me,' said the youngest of the three strangers, who, Dick now saw, was not much older than himself.

'Fiddlesticks! We're in London, not Port Said,' was the curt reply. 'Come on.'

Dick followed his helpers to the top of the stairs. The landing was in darkness, but a narrow bar of light below the closed door suggested that someone was inside.

The one whom the others had called Biggles, a slim, clean-shaven man with a keen, thoughtful face, tried the door. It was locked. He struck a match and looked at Dick. 'Could he get away through a window?' he asked in a low voice.

'No, sir. It's a forty foot drop down to the street.'

'Good.' Biggles knocked sharply on a flimsy panel. 'Open this door,' he called loudly.

There was no reply.

'This is your room, you're sure of that?' Biggles asked Dick suspiciously.

'Yes, sir.'

'I mean – you rent it?'

'Yes, sir.'

'You're telling me the truth?'

'On my oath, sir.'

'All right! Stand back.' There was a splintering crash as Biggles hurled his weight against the door. It flew open and the scene within was revealed.

The stranger was standing by the table, with the letter, which presumably he had just found, in his left hand. The knife lay open on the table, and as his slanting eyes rested malevolently on the newcomers his right hand began to creep towards it.

'What are you doing in this lad's room?' asked Biggles sharply.

'That's no business of yourn,' growled the other, scowling.

'I'm sorry to disappoint you, my friend, but I happen to have made it my business,' rapped out Biggles coldly. 'Put that letter down.'

'I should say so.'

'There's no need for you to say so; I've already said it.'

'Are you looking fer trouble, Mr Nosey Parker?'

'If anyone is doing that, it's you. Come along, put the letter down and clear out. I don't want to make this a police court job any more than you do.'

An ugly sneer curled the sailor's lips. He picked up the knife. 'So that's your tune, is it?' he snarled.

'It's the only tune I've got for you.'

'Then let's see how you like this one,' grated the other, gripping the knife firmly and taking a pace forward.

Biggles did not move. 'Ginger, run down and fetch a policeman, will you?' he said quietly. 'And now, my man,' he resumed, as Ginger ran noisily down the wooden stairs, 'I'm going to give you a last chance. Put that letter on the table and the knife in your pocket, and you are free to go. Refuse, and I'll see to it that you are clapped somewhere where you won't be able to make a nuisance of yourself for a long time to come. We don't stand for robbery with violence in this country, as you'll soon learn to your cost. Now then, make up your mind. Which is it going to be?'

The sailor hesitated, looking from one to the other of the three figures framed in the doorway. Possibly he realized that even if he succeeded in passing them he might encounter a policeman before he reached the street. A moment later heavy footsteps on the stairs helped him to decide, for with a foul oath he flung the letter on the table and thrust the knife through his belt, under his jacket. 'I'll remember you the next time I see you, my cock,' he gritted vindictively. 'Maybe you won't chirp so loud then.'

'We'll talk about chirping when that time comes,' replied Biggles coolly.

'What's going on here?' demanded a fresh voice from the background. A policeman pushed his way to the front.

'It's all right, officer; I thought we were going to have a little trouble, but our seafaring friend here has thought better of it,' said Biggles quietly.

'Don't you want to charge him, sir?' There was genuine regret in the policeman's tone as he eyed the intruder with disfavour.

'No, he can go as far as I'm concerned.'

If looks could kill, Biggles would have been struck dead on the spot as the sailor passed between him and the constable and disappeared down the stairs.

Biggles put his hand in his pocket and slipped something into the policeman's palm. 'Sorry I had to trouble you,' he said softly. 'Much obliged for your assistance, but every-thing is all right now, I think.'

'Thank you, sir. Glad I could be of service,' replied the constable. 'If you don't mind, I'll slip along and keep an eye on that customer. I don't like the look of him,' he added quickly, as he followed the sailor down the stairs.

Biggles picked up the letter and handed it to Dick. 'Well, my lad, there's your letter,' he said. 'What was all the trouble about, anyway?'

'I don't know, sir, and that's a fact,' confessed Dick frankly.

'But why should a man risk putting his head into a noose in order to get what one can only suppose to be a purely personal message from your father to you?'

'That's more than I can say, sir,' replied Dick. 'You see, sir, my father is dead. A sailor brought the letter to me today; I haven't read it yet.'

'I see,' nodded Biggles. 'Well, maybe the thing will explain itself when you do read it. But we shall have to be getting along.' He turned towards the stairs when another thought seemed to strike him. 'What are you going to do, laddie?' he asked, looking back at Dick.

'I dunno, sir. I daren't stop here in case that sailor comes back and does me in.'

'Haven't you any friends or relatives where you can stay?'

'No, sir.'

'Any money?'

'No, sir.'

'None at all?'

'Only tuppence.'

'Humph! That won't see you very far, I'm afraid,' murmured Biggles.

'That's all right, sir. I'll doss down on the allotments,' declared Dick.

'*Where?*'

'In one of the gardening huts on the allotments. I'll go

round until I find one of 'em open. I've had to do it many a time before.'

Biggles made a grimace. 'Bless my heart and soul! I've slept rough myself on occasion, but this is no night for picnicking,' he declared. 'I tell you what. It must be about tea-time. Let's find a restaurant where we can talk things over while we have a bite of food. By the way, what's your name?'

'Dick, sir. Dick Denver.'

'Good! That's easy to remember,' smiled Biggles. 'We don't know our way very well in this part of the world, so perhaps you can guide us to a place where we can tear a plate of crumpets to pieces.'

Dick nodded, grinning broadly. 'I know 'em all, sir,' he declared promptly. 'There's Old Kate's at the corner. That's where I usually go because you can get sausage and mash there for fivepence a go. Bread a ha'penny extra. Or there's the "Jolly Shipmates" coffee tavern, but they charge a bob there and a penny for bread.'

Biggles smiled faintly. 'It sounds like the "Jolly Shipmates" to me,' he decided. 'I think we shall be able to raise a shilling apiece between us,' he added seriously. 'Come on.'

Chapter 2

The Doubloon

Dick led the way jubilantly, for it was not often that he was treated to a free meal, and in a few minutes they were all seated round a marble-topped table with their feet on a newly sawdusted floor. The place was fairly full, sailors and watermen forming the bulk of the customers, and the air was blue with tobacco smoke, but no-one paid any attention to them as they took their places in a quiet corner.

A pale-faced youth in a white apron waited on them.

'Sausage and mash for four, a pot of tea and plenty of bread,' ordered Biggles.

'While we are waiting, just to satisfy my curiosity, you might cast your eye over your father's letter,' suggested Algy to Dick. 'I've got an idea that that ugly-looking swab of a sailor had a reason for wanting to get hold of it – in fact, he must have had, and a very good one, too, or he wouldn't have gone to such lengths to get it.'

'All the same, my dad never had any money, so I don't see how it could be anything worth pinching,' replied Dick, taking the letter from his pocket. 'I dunno, though, it feels a bit heavy,' he went on quickly, with a sudden flash of interest. 'I believe there's something in it besides paper.'

As he spoke he slit the top of the envelope, rather carelessly. Instantly there was a yellow gleam as something fell out and rang musically on the marble top of the table.

In a flash Biggles's hand had shot out and covered it, just as the waiter hurried up with the four plates. Not until he had departed did Biggles lift his hand, disclosing what lay underneath. A low whistle left his lips. 'Oh-ho! Oh-ho!' he ejaculated quickly, and then cast a swift glance around. 'You'd better put that in your pocket, Dick,' he said in a low voice. 'This is no place to throw that sort of stuff about.'

'What sort of stuff?' asked Dick, agape, eyes on a roughly circular disk that lay on the table.

'Gold,' breathed Biggles.

Dick caught his breath. 'Gold!' he cried incredulously.

'Ssh, not so loud. There's no need to tell the world about it.'

'Go on, you're kidding,' muttered Dick unbelievingly.

Biggles shook his head. 'There's no kidding about that particular metal,' he murmured.

'But that isn't a sovereign, is it?' whispered Dick. 'I never saw one but once,' he added, by way of explanation.

'No, it isn't a sovereign,' agreed Biggles, 'but it's worth a good deal more. I fancy any numismatist would give you several sovereigns for it.'

'Numis – thingamajig – who's he?'

'A man who buys and sells old coins.'

'That's enough of the highbrow stuff. What is it, anyway?' demanded Algy shortly.

'I've only seen one once before, and that was in a museum, but I believe I am right in saying that it is a doubloon,' answered Biggles quietly.

Ginger leaned forward, eyes sparkling. 'Great Scott! Those are the things the pirates used to collect, aren't they?'

Biggles nodded. 'The reason being that doubloons were Spanish currency in the days when buccaneers and pirates sailed the seas. Put it in your pocket, Dick – and the letter. I've got an idea that your father's message is going to prove more interesting than you imagined – a lot more. And, to be quite honest, I'd like to have a look at it myself,' he added, as Dick put the coin, and the letter, out of sight.

'Read it, sir, by all means,' invited Dick.

'Not here. Our seafaring friend might be hanging about. We'll go to my rooms, if it's all the same to you.'

'It's all the same to me – better, in fact,' declared Dick. 'But for you I shouldn't have had it.'

'Well, let's finish our sausages and go home,' suggested Ginger. 'I'm fairly aching to see that letter. All my life I've wanted to find a bag of doubloons.'

'A lot of people feel that way,' murmured Biggles.

'Just now you said buccaneers *and* pirates,' ventured Dick, as they resumed their meal with renewed interest. 'What was the difference – was there any?'

'Yes, and no,' answered Biggles. 'The buccaneers came first. When there were more sailors than could find employment, some of them took to a life ashore in the West Indies, where they made a living by killing the animals that had been left behind by the Spaniards on such islands as Hispaniola – the place we now call Haiti. You see, when gold was discovered on the mainland, in Mexico and Peru, the Spaniards who had settled on the island sailed away to see if they could get hold of some of it, and having no means of transporting them, they left their domestic animals behind – cows, pigs, and the like. These ran wild and soon increased in numbers. The out-of-work English and French sailors hunted them, killed them, dried the meat and sold it to the ships that called. They called the stuff *boucan*, which was really the French word for cured beef. So they became known as *boucaniers*, or, in our language, buccaneers, and buccaneers they would have stayed if the Spaniards had had any sense. But they objected to anyone else trading in the New World, and tried to drive the buccaneers, who at that time were perfectly harmless people, out of Hispaniola. They did, in fact, kill a lot of them. Naturally, the buccaneers resented this treatment, to say the least of it; they fought back, and there were some nasty goings-on. In

270

the end the Spaniards won – or it looked that way to them at the time. The buccaneers were driven out, but they didn't go far. They pulled up at a rocky island not far away called Tortuga, where they started thinking about revenge. Not only thinking. They built boats and began making raids against the Spaniards. From that they went to attacking Spanish ships at sea. They fought like fury, and taking the guns from the ships they captured, soon made Tortuga a pretty impregnable fortress. They also constructed forts at other points about the islands.

'What happened after that was a pretty natural consequence,' continued Biggles. 'Rumours of the great quantities of gold being captured from the Spanish galleons got abroad, and the toughest toughs in the world headed for Tortuga to join in the fun. Another colony sprang up at Port Royal, in Jamaica, which must have been a pretty hot spot. The Spaniards now began to get what they'd asked for. The old buccaneering business was forgotten and the one-time buccaneers became pirates pure and simple. They attacked anything and everything anywhere and anyhow. Knowing that if the Spanish caught them they'd be burned, and if the English caught them they'd be hanged, they fought like devils, neither giving nor asking quarter. The Spanish government couldn't shift them, and neither, for that matter, could the British. In the end they were strong enough to take and sack even the largest Spanish cities on the Main. Morgan had eighteen hundred men behind him when he went to Panama.'

'What happened to them at the finish?' asked Dick breathlessly.

'The English government did the only thing it could do. It offered them all a free pardon if they'd turn from their wicked ways. Most of them accepted and either settled down or joined the navy. Morgan, probably the biggest cutthroat of the lot, was knighted by the king and made governor of Jamaica. Knowing all the tricks of the trade, he rounded up and hanged all his old pals who had not accepted the free pardon, so in the course of time the business of piracy fizzled out. The coming of steamships finally put the tin hat on it.'

'Pity,' murmured Dick, with genuine regret.

Biggles smiled. 'So you'd like to be a pirate, you bloodthirsty young rascal, would you?'

'There must have been a lot more fun in it than selling papers at three-ha'pence a dozen.'

'Yes, perhaps you're right,' agreed Biggles, 'although there was nothing funny in swinging on a yard-arm or a gibbet. But if everyone has finished we might as well get along.'

He paid the bill and they passed out into the dreary, lamp-lit street.

Dick opened his mouth to speak, and stepped into the gutter to get beside Biggles just as a heavy lorry swung round the corner.

Algy saw his danger and dragged him aside just in time. The lorry whirled past, missing him by inches.

Biggles eyed Dick seriously. 'My goodness! That was a close squeak,' he breathed. 'You ought to know better than to wander in the road like that.'

Dick turned up a startled face. 'Yes,' he said, thoroughly shaken. 'I can't think what came over me; I never did a thing like that before in my life.'

'Well, don't do it again, or your doubloon won't bring you much luck,' admonished Biggles as, reaching a broad street, he beckoned a cruising taxi.

They got in, and the driver, possibly because he had a long journey before him, set off at high speed. From his position in the rear seat of the cab Biggles regarded the back of the driver's head with strong disapproval. 'This fellow is either mad or drunk,' he declared. 'He has no business to go at this rate; we shall bump into something in a minute, the silly ass.'

'That would be a shame, just as I've come into some money,' protested Dick.

'As far as I can make out, you're going to be lucky if you live long enough to spend it,' muttered Biggles angrily as the taxi skidded round the corner, narrowly missing a stationary dray. 'Open the window, Algy, and tell that fool at the wheel that we didn't ask him to set up a record.'

Algy did as he was asked, but the driver merely laughed as though the whole thing was a joke.

Biggles muttered savagely, and regarded the oncoming traffic with increasing anxiety.

The end came suddenly, at the corner of Mount Street, not far from Biggles's rooms, where the driver swerved to miss a private car that was creeping out of a side street. There was a scream of brakes, and an instant later a sickening crash as the cab struck a traffic signal. Fortunately, it did not turn over.

Biggles was white with anger as he extricated himself from the others on the floor and kicked open the buckled door. 'Anybody hurt?' he asked quickly.

Receiving assurances that no-one was injured, he turned to the driver who, looking thoroughly frightened and ashamed, was wiping the blood from a cut on his forehead with his handkerchief. But before he could speak a policeman appeared, notebook in hand, thrusting his way through the rapidly forming crowd. 'Who did this?' he asked menacingly, pointing to the smashed traffic light.

Biggles nodded in the direction of the driver. 'He did. He drove like a lunatic. He must be drunk,' declared Biggles bitterly.

The driver denied the charge indignantly. 'That ain't

273

true, sir. I ain't 'ad a drink all day, and that's the 'onest truth, strike me dead if it ain't. You smell my breath if you don't believe me.'

Biggles shook his head. 'No, I don't think I'll do that, thank you. The constable might like to,' he added. There was something in the man's attitude that led him to think that the driver was speaking the truth. 'What on earth made you drive as you did?' he asked.

'I don't know, s'welp me,' declared the wretched man, regarding the ruins of his cab. 'It just seemed as if I couldn't 'elp meself. The funny thing was, I knew I was going too fast, yet I didn't seem able to stop. It was almost as if some one was sitting on the seat beside me saying, "Go on, put your foot down and let her rip." I—'

'All right, that'll do,' put in the constable heavily. 'You come along with me; I'll get the doctor to have a look at you.'

Still protesting volubly, the driver was led away. The others were left standing on the pavement.

'Come on,' muttered Biggles disgustedly. 'We might as well walk the rest of the way. And we'd better insure our lives before we do anything else, I think. That's two narrow escapes inside half an hour. If this sort of thing goes on I shall soon begin to think you're a hoodoo, Dick.'

However, they reached Biggles's flat without further incident, beyond the fact that they all got wet, for it was now raining steadily. They changed their jackets, Ginger lending Dick one of his, and then settled round the fire. Biggles lit a cigarette 'Go ahead, Dick,' he invited. 'Let's hear what your father has to say about the doubloon.'

'I'd rather you read the letter yourself, sir,' suggested Dick nervously. 'My dad didn't write much of a hand, and it always took me a long time to make out the words.'

'All right.' Biggles took the proffered letter. 'I'll read it aloud,' he said, 'then we shall all hear what there is to hear at the same time.' He unfolded several sheets of flimsy paper and smoothed them out on his knee. 'Now then, pay attention, everybody,' he said. 'I'm going to start.'

Chapter 3

The Letter

Dear Dick,

I don't suppose you'll ever get this, but if you do I want you to read it very carefully, and likewise take care of it, because one day it may help you to find a fortune. Yes, a fortune. But don't say nothing to nobody, see, or belike you'll get your throat cut afore you can get yer hands on the dibs. Now then; I'll start at the beginning.

As you know, a finer ship's company you couldn't find than we had in the old *Seadream*, bless her rusty sides. She was a good 'un if ever there was one, and now gone to Davy Jones with most of the good shipmates on her because of that drunken villain Dooch, or Deutch, however he spells his name. A nasty looking man with a round scar at the end of his mouth what don't make him no prettier. But I can't talk about him now because I must get on, having a lot to say.

On this last trip I knew we was in for trouble the minute I clapped eyes on Deutch, who was our new first mate in place of poor Sam Hankin, who was as fine a sailor as ever handled a rope, and knew us all down in the fo'castle like we were his own boys. Sam was sick and Deutch took his place. That was the way of it. And we hadn't sighted the Nab Light when I knew we was in for a dirty trip. Bound for Rio, we was, in ballast, and rolling in a middling north-west gale, we runs down a ketch, making close reefed for port. All because Deutch, who was on the bridge, wouldn't give way, like he ought to have done, us being a steamer. What was worse, we didn't stop. And why? I'll tell you. Deutch was drunk. I needn't say no more about that, but I can tell you there was some funny talk in the fo'castle, as you might guess. In the morning someone tells the skipper, and then the fat was in the fire. Deutch had it in for the lot of us. That was the start.

I needn't tell you about the next fortnight. Deutch made all our lives a hell, and I began to see that if we got to Rio without bloodshed we should be lucky. To make matters worse, the Old Man* slips down the fore companion and lays himself out by knocking his head on a block. And that was how things was when the big blow hits us. Skipper sick, mate drunk, hands grumbling and nothing shipshape. And this, Dick, is where the story really begins.

It ain't no manner of use me trying to tell you just where we was when the hurricane struck us. It ain't for the likes of me to know. But the blow come from the south-east'ard and it tore up such waves as I never see in my life afore. The seas turned into hollow breakers which made the *Seadream* stick her nose into the air, and we began to ship water faster than we could pump it out. The water doused the fires and the mainmast went by the board, taking with it a lot of gear including the wireless, and before long we was drifting as helpless as an old barrel.

For four days we drifted without sighting a ship, and all the time we was leaking like a sieve and getting lower and lower in the water. I tell you, son, me and my shipmates was a pretty miserable lot, what with not having no sleep and exhausted working the hand pumps and knowing as how we couldn't keep afloat much longer.

Presently it was clear that the old *Seadream* would founder any minute, and we see about getting the boats out. None of

* Sailor's slang for the Captain of a ship.

277

us would go without the skipper, so we carries him up and puts him in the first boat. Pity Deutch hadn't been in her, too. There was still a big sea running, and the boat, swinging on the davits as we lurched, smashed to bits, and every soul in her fell into the water and was drowned. Deutch was hanging on a rope just getting into the boat when it happened, but he managed to hold on and claw his way back on deck. There was five of us left all told; me, Deutch, Tom Allen from Pompey, Joe Stevens, the cook, and Charlie Bender, the same Charlie as come 'ome with me once. You remember Charlie, a little fellow with a fair moustache? He come from Gillingham.

Now it ain't no use wasting time telling you about our voyage in the last boat. About a fortnight it was before we sighted land, and how we kept alive, only the Almighty knows. I can't make it out nohow. No, nor how we got to where we did, for our first landfall was an island called Providence in the Caribbean Sea. Deutch and me both knew it by the funny shaped hill at the end, both of us having watered there in the old sailing days. A caution it was how we got there. But before we could set foot on shore a current carried us out to sea again on a new course to the south-west. We hadn't no strength left to pull on the oars, so we had to put up with it. A bitter sight it was to see the land disappearing again, I can tell you, after all we had been through, and us half dead with hunger and thirst. I forgot to tell you that Tom Allen was already dead. Poor Joe died that night. But at last the current took us to another island; and when me, Charlie, and Deutch lands on it, it looks like our troubles was about over, for there was coconuts to eat and milk to drink. I don't know the name of this island. I wish I did, as you will see. But my worst troubles was yet to come.

Deutch's temper now that he couldn't get liquor was awful, and while we was waiting for a boat to pick us up I used to go off by myself looking for grub or watching for a ship. Our island wasn't by any means a little place. As some islands go it might be, but I reckon it was best part of ten miles long by five wide at the widest part, narrowing down at the ends like a new moon. And now there comes a surprise that will sound like a story in a book, but it's true, as you will see from what I enclose in this letter.

One morning, after we had been on the island about a month, Deutch wakes up and curses me for not having water handy. I like a fool ups and tells him that I ain't no lackey, whereupon he comes at me with his knife, and I, not having nothing to defend myself with, runs off with him after me. Soon I comes to a place what I'd seen afore, a sort of dip, or dell-hole, a mossy place filled with bushes and creepers and things, and thinking as how it would make a good hiding place, I jumps into it. I jumped into more than I bargained for, by a long shot, for the ground seemed to open and swallow me up, as they say, and I lands slap in another world. When I opens my eyes I sees as I'm in the saloon of an old fashioned ship like they've got models of in the Museum at Greenwich. I thought for a minute I was dead, or knocked unconscious, with my spirit wandering about in some other place. You see, son, I couldn't make sense of it nohow, because here I was some way from the shore, and how could a ship get there? A ship can't sail over land. So, as I say, I thought as how I'd got knocked silly, and I just lay there waiting to see what was going to happen next. After a time, when nothing does happen, I gets up and begins to wonder if I'm dreaming after all. The things all seemed solid enough, but so quiet you could hear a pin drop. Well, I thinks, this is a rum go, and starts to have a look round. Then I see the hole in the roof where I'd tumbled in, and that sort of gave me an idea of what was what. And now I'll tell you what I saw.

The first thing I claps eyes on give me a rare fright, I can tell you. It was a dead man, although I see at a glance that he'd been dead a long time. It wasn't so much a corpse as a skellington, with the old-fashioned clothes still hanging on the bones, and it fair gave me the creeps to see him sitting there at a big desk grinning out of empty eye-holes at something what lay in front of him.

Presently I plucks up courage to go closer and look at what he was grinning at. There was several things on the desk, and I reckon they are still there, because I didn't touch nothing except what — p'raps you can guess. But I'm going too fast. On the desk there was a big candlestick what looks as if might be silver. Beside it there was an old-fashioned pistol like those you see decorating the walls at the Tower of London. Likewise there was a bit of paper and an old feather sharpened to a point, what I believe the dead man had been using as a pen to write with, because there was writing on the paper, which is the yellow piece I am putting in this letter. But what the pore dead feller seemed to be grinning at was a queer sort of foreign-looking medal. By the weight of it I thinks it's gold. Anyway, thinking as how it might be handy, I slips it in my pocket. Likewise I am sending it to you with the paper, which I can't make head nor tail of, but it struck me it might be a sort of chart marking where there is some money, being as how I couldn't find none, which seemed a bit funny considering the other things I found when I looked round.

I ain't got time to tell you everything I seen in this ramshackle old hulk, but I can tell you I was fair amazed, as you will be if ever you claps eyes on it. There was all sorts of things stored in chests: clothes and silks and satins. Maybe this is what the pore feller was going to hide when he died. As I say, I couldn't work it out nohow, but it's a fair knockout.

When I comes to go I find as I'm in a rare mess, because I couldn't get back up to the hole I'd fell in. You'll laugh when I tell you how I got out. I stove a hole through the bows of the hulk. Rotten they was, like sawdust, but I got out, and had a good look round so as I'd know the place again. And now I'll tell you how to find it if ever you go looking for it, although my bit of a chart what I've made to put in this letter ought to give you the general direction.

The place seems like at some time or other it had been a narrow channel, running up from the sea about a hundred yards from the shore. How the ship got in I can't make out, because there certainly ain't no way out. And when you're out you can't see the ship because she's all overgrown with weeds and things. But there she is, as large as life, with rocks on each side of her. Anyway, I thinks to myself, Deutch shan't know anything about this, I'll share it with Charlie, so I covers up the hole I'd fallen in with some bits of palm so that it couldn't be seen by no one outside, which I reckoned was pretty smart. And then, thinking that Deutch might have quieted down by now, back I goes to the place where we lived, under a piece of overhanging rock by a little lagoon.

Deutch was sitting there as quiet as a lamb, but he gives me a dirty look when I comes up and says I'd better see about the water in future, which I promises to do. And just as I was going to sit down, would you believe it, the golden medal I'd picked up in the ship slips through a hole in my pocket what I'd forgot, and there it lays on the sand as plain as daylight for Deutch to see. 'Where the blazes did you get that?' he cries out, with his eyes fairly popping out of his head, in a manner of speaking. 'That's my business,' I sez boldly, as Charlie picks up the medal to have a look at it. At this Deutch changes his tune. 'Come on, old shipmate,' he sez in a weedling voice. 'We've shared everything up to now. Let bygones be bygones and share and share alike, like good companions everyone.' 'No, Mr Deutch,' I sez. 'Findings keepings. You ain't never shared anything with me, and I ain't parting.' 'Ho, ain't you, you old fool,' he snarls, and before I knew what he was going to be at he comes at me with his knife, which he always kept handy. Charlie, like a good shipmate, jumps in to stop him, and the blade catches him fair in the throat. There he stood, still holding the medal in his hand, making a horrible gurgling noise, with the blood spurting out on the sand. Made me feel fair sick, it did. Then he gives a loud cry, lets go the medal and drops down dead. Like lightning I snatches up the medal and backs away from Deutch, who goes all white and frightened when he sees the dreadful thing he's done. 'That's murder, Mr Deutch,' I hollers, hardly knowing what I was saying. 'I'll report this to the owners when we get back.'

Deutch didn't wait for no more, no more did I. After me he comes and off we go, him cursing, which don't do no man any good. Any fool can curse, but it takes a still tongue to make a wise head, as an old captain of mine used to say. But I was telling you. Somehow I managed to get away, and hid in the woods, where I stayed for the rest of the time I was on the island. Many a time I saw Deutch hunting for the place where I'd found the gold piece, but he never found it and he never found me. And that's how things were when one day the *Portsdown*, an American schooner, puts in for water. I sees her first and went running down to the beach, and then Deutch comes too, only he daren't do anything to me in case the sailors were looking. So when the *Portsdown* sailed we went with her. What a trip it was, too. Everything going wrong all the time. We lost our rudder and a spar fell, killing two men. I haven't time to tell you all about the things that happened on the *Portsdown* while we were aboard her, but at last we comes to Boston where I am now, in fear of my life from Deutch, who told me on the *Portsdown* that unless I told him where I'd found the gold he'd knife me. I shan't tell him, you may be sure.

I'm hoping I shall be lucky enough to work a passage home, so tonight when I leave the hospital I'm going down to the docks. If I can't find a ship I shall give this letter to a sailor homeward bound; then no matter what happens Deutch won't get the gold.

In case anything should happen to me, you try and find the island when you get old enough because I think there is a lot of money hidden there. If not, the things in the old ship should be worth a fair bit. Steer a course for Providence, then swing to the south-west for maybe forty or fifty miles. You can tell the island by high rocky hills on the east side. You'll find the wreck I've marked on the map at the north end, near an islet, which is as near as I can fix it.

You can't tell how much I am looking forward to seeing you again after all this time. Trusting this finds you in better health than I am.

Your affectionate Father

Chapter 4

Biggles Makes a Proposition

There was a full minute's silence after Biggles stopped reading, a silence broken only by the faint rustle as he unfolded a little yellowish slip of paper that had been enclosed in the letter. He gazed at it for some seconds without speaking; then, looking up, he smiled faintly at the intent expressions on the faces of the others. 'Well, so now we know,' he observed quietly.

'You mean — why that sailor was after my letter?' said Dick, quickly.

'Of course.'

'Because he knew that piece of gold was in it?'

Biggles shook his head. 'No, I don't think *that* was what he was after. What *he* wanted to know was where your father found it.'

'So that he could go and get the rest, if there was any?'

'That's more like it.'

'What do you make of it, sir? Do you think that my father really did stumble on to one of these old treasures?'

'I don't think there is any doubt about it. Your father wasn't the sort of man to sit down and make up a tale like that, was he?'

'No, he wasn't, and that's a fact,' declared Dick emphatically. 'He wouldn't do a thing like that.'

'That's what I thought. There is a tone about this letter that makes every word ring true, and there's the coin to prove it.'

'And what's your opinion of it all, sir?' inquired Dick eagerly.

'There's no need to keep calling me "sir",' Biggles told him quietly. 'It looks to me, Dick, as if your father discovered one of the several secret hoards that undoubtedly exist in that part of the world where the pirates did their hunting. There were no banks available, and they had either to carry their ill-gotten gains about with them, or hide them. Inevitably, their ships were often wrecked and all hands drowned, so their secrets died with them – either that, or the money went to the bottom of the sea when their ship foundered. I should say that your father found an old wreck which, through the centuries, has become covered with vegetation; the jungle grows very quickly in the tropics, you know. Wait a minute.' Biggles walked over to the bookcase and took down a heavy encyclopedia. 'Listen to this,' he went on, after he had run quickly through the pages.

'For those who may be sceptical about the vast wealth carried by galleons of this period, the following well-authenticated instance is given. In 1680, a sailor in this country told of a Spanish galleon he had seen lying wrecked on the north-east coast of Hispaniola. Lord Albemarle persuaded Charles the Second to lend him a frigate and he financed an expedition to recover the treasure. It failed. Five years later, another sailor, this time in Jamaica, reported that he had found the wreck with gold and silver lying all around her. Lord Albemarle formed a company and sent out another expedition under a Captain Phips. It returned laden with as much gold as it could carry. Some silver had perforce been left behind. The King received ten per cent of the treasure trove, the value of which exceeded £300,000. Lord Albemarle received £90,000 for his share, and investors of one hundred pounds in the company received £8,000 each.'

'That will give you an idea of the sort of money-boxes that used to float about the high seas in the old days,' observed Biggles. 'When Deutch spotted that doubloon he was cute enough to guess what it might lead to, but your father was too clever for him. Or maybe he wasn't so clever after all, since he did not manage to get back to England, whereas Deutch did.'

Dick started. 'What makes you think that Deutch got back?'

'I imagine it was Mr Deutch who called upon you this afternoon, and with whom we afterwards had a few sharp words. Your father describes just such a scar as was worn by your unpleasant visitor. Surely that can't be coincidence?'

There was another short silence.

'You think he might have killed my dad?' said Dick in a low voice.

'I think it is highly probable. We saw for ourselves how handy he was with his knife, and with such an incentive to murder as treasure, he wouldn't make any bones about using it. I'm sorry, laddie, but it's no use shutting our eyes to the facts, and that's how they look to me.'

'My father was dying in a low dive from a knife wound, so the sailor who brought the letter told me,' muttered Dick chokingly.

Biggles shrugged his shoulders. 'Which all goes to confirm our deductions. Deutch thought probably your father had a map, or something of the sort, and he hoped to get it. To a great extent he was right, because quite apart from the fact that your father may have already drawn the map of the island which he sent home, there was the piece of paper found on the desk on the old ship. But either Deutch was too late, or your father had it too well hidden. Perhaps he had already given it to the sailor to bring home.' A puzzled look came suddenly into Biggles's eyes, and he glanced again at the letter. '*When* did you say the sailor brought the letter to you?' he asked sharply.

'This afternoon.'

'Then he was the dickens of a long time delivering it. This letter is dated nearly three months ago. I wonder why he was so long.'

'He told me about that,' answered Dick quickly. 'They had an awful voyage. At first they ran into gales, then they cast a propeller blade, and then, to finish up with, they had a collision with a trawler coming up the Channel and had to go into a French port for repairs.'

Biggles whistled softly. 'I *shall* begin to think there is something fishy about this business if these tales of trouble go on,' he said half jokingly. 'Well, there it is, Dick. I'm afraid you'll never learn the details of what happened in America after your father wrote this letter. The point is, it has reached you. What are you going to do about it?'

'Hadn't I better go to the police?'

'With what object?'

'To get Deutch run in for murdering my dad.'

'What evidence have you got for making such an accusation? My dear boy, it's one thing to suspect somebody of committing a crime, but quite another matter to prove it. Besides, the affair happened in America.'

'What can I do about it, then?'

Biggles stared thoughtfully into the fire. 'It's a bit hard to know what to advise,' he said slowly. 'Far from looking for Deutch, you'd better keep out of his way. He's far more likely to hurt you than you him. He's still on the trail of the treasure. Somehow, we don't know how, he knows about you. Your father may have mentioned you to him before the trouble started. He might even have discovered that your father wrote a letter to you, in which case he might have sent you the secret. Indeed, I think his actions rather go to prove that. But it is really guesswork. Let us stick to facts. What we do know is this. First, somewhere in the West Indies there is an old hulk, with articles of value, possibly treasure, on board; secondly, there is a nasty piece of work named Deutch prowling about who also knows it; thirdly, he knows you've had a letter because he has held it in his hand; and lastly, but by no means least, he has shown you that he is going to leave no stone unturned to get hold of it. That's all, but it should be enough to convince you that it isn't safe for you to wander about the East End of London by yourself. If you do, as sure as fate Deutch will get hold of that letter and you will come to a sticky end trying to defend it.'

Dick moved uneasily. 'What the dickens can I do?' he asked. 'It looks to me as if I'm in a nice fix. For two pins I'd burn the blessed thing, and tell Deutch what I'd done if he came after me.'

'You don't suppose he'd believe that, do you?'

Dick made a gesture of helplessness. 'No, I don't suppose he would, now I come to think about it. I don't want a knife in my ribs.'

'You haven't said anything about trying to find the treasure,' pointed out Biggles helpfully.

'It wouldn't be much use, would it?' muttered Dick despondently. 'I mean, tuppence wouldn't get me much further than Gillingham, even on a workman's ticket,* much less the West Indies.'

Biggles turned to the others. 'Do you think we might help him?' he suggested.

'Help me!' Dick sprang to his feet, face radiant. 'You mean—'

'We might all go on this treasure hunt.'

---

* A special cheap ticket for people travelling before a certain hour in the morning by bus or train.

Dick turned pale with excitement. 'Gosh! That would be grand,' he cried. 'When could we start?'

Biggles laughed softly. 'Wait a minute! Wait a minute!' he said lightly. 'You can't just put on your hat and coat and dash off on a trip of this sort. There are a lot of things to be thought of. We've done a bit of travelling in our time, and we know. First of all, there is the question of money; we should need rather a lot.'

'Ah! I was afraid of that!' exclaimed Dick miserably.

'I didn't say that we hadn't got enough,' went on Biggles quickly. 'Look here, Dick. Here's a proposition. Suppose I found the money for this show and we all went with you to collect the doubloons; would you agree to divide the profits into two, you taking one half and we the other, after deducting the cost of the expedition, whatever it may be? That sounds fair to me.'

'It sounds more than fair,' declared Dick promptly. 'I reckon the treasure is as much yours as it is mine. But for you I should have lost the letter and known nothing about it.'

'All right. That's fine. I can see that we shan't fall out over the division of the doubloons – if there are any – in which case all that remains is to make the necessary arrangements for getting hold of them as soon as possible, before Mr Deutch starts any monkey business. But we've got to go to work carefully. Well begun is half done on a job like this. First of all, we've got to locate the island, which may not be as easy as it sounds.'

'What about the map?' put in Algy quickly.

'It only gives the general configuration of the island,' answered Biggles. 'It doesn't give its position. All we know about it is what Dick's father says in his letter, that it is about fifty miles south-west of Providence. There may be several islands. In fact, there are pretty certain to be, because the Caribbean fairly bristles with islands, large and small.'

'What about the paper Dick's father found in the cabin – the one that was lying in front of the skeleton?' put in Algy.

Biggles pursed his lips. 'I'm afraid that isn't going to be much use,' he answered dubiously. 'It looks more like a jigsaw puzzle than a map, although it may take on some sort of meaning when we get to the actual spot. What we've got to do for a start is to find the island; after that, the chart will give us the approximate position of the galleon. I say approximate because I've had some experience of sketch-maps. When the thing that is drawn on this sheet of paper—' Biggles touched the map drawn by Dick's father '—becomes a mass of rock and undergrowth, perhaps a mile or two square, it becomes a different proposition. Take the case of Cocos Island, in the Pacific. It is known for certain that there is at least one treasure there. It isn't a very big island, yet any number of men have searched for years without finding anything more interesting than sand and pebbles. One fellow, a German, lived on the spot for, I think, eighteen years, during which time he dug enough trenches to make a fair-sized battlefield, but all he got for his pains were calloused palms and malaria. But that's by the way. Let's concentrate on getting to the island; we can start looking for the bullion bags when we get there.'

'That suits me,' agreed Dick, optimistically.

'Then we'll have a look at the big atlas in a minute,' resumed Biggles. 'The obvious course seems to be to choose a base as near as possible to the general locality, and then see about getting an aircraft out to it.'

'Did you say *aircraft*?' asked Dick breathlessly.

'I did,' answered Biggles. 'I suppose you were thinking about a ship?'

'Of course; I didn't think of anything else,' admitted Dick.

'I think we can do better than that,' returned Biggles.

'You see, Dick, we all happen to be pilots, so, naturally, when we go anywhere, we fly.'

'That makes it all the better,' cried Dick enthusiastically. 'I've never been in an aeroplane in my life, but I've always wanted to fly.'

'You'll have plenty of flying by the time this business is over, if I know anything about it,' smiled Biggles. 'Get down the atlas, Ginger, and let's have a look at the Caribbean.'

In a moment or two the heavy tome was on the table, open at a double page entitled 'The West Indies and the Caribbean Sea'.

'Now then! Here we are,' murmured Biggles, drawing a rough oval on the map with a lead pencil. 'Here is Providence, the island Dick's father and Deutch saw when they were in the open boat, but on which they could not effect a landing. Instead, they drifted away to the south-west, like this—' Biggles followed a south-westerly course with his pencil '—and here we come to a whole lot of little islands. As you can see, most of them are such mere specks that they wouldn't be shown on an ordinary atlas. Some of them are probably nothing more than cays, which are really only glorified sandbanks. On the other hand, some of them will probably turn out to be a good deal larger than you might suspect from looking at the map. Don't forget that an island of twenty or thirty square miles can only be shown as a dot on a map of this size. But that's by the way. This is the area we have got to explore. I don't think it's any use thinking of trying to make a base among the islands themselves because it would not be possible to get petrol there, or stores. Kingston, Jamaica, is too far away; so is Port of Spain.* But we needn't worry about that. The

* On the island of Trinidad.

nearest island isn't more than a couple of hundred miles from the mainland, a matter of two hour's flight at the very outside, so there should be no particular hardship in flying to and fro. So what we've got to do is choose a town on the mainland where we can get fuel and food.'

'How about Marabina?' suggested Algy.

'I was just looking at it; it ought to suit us admirably; in fact, I don't think we could do better,' replied Biggles.

'Marabina? That's a new one on me,' declared Ginger.

'I've never heard of the place, either,' confessed Dick, who, with the others, was leaning over Biggles's shoulder looking at the atlas.

'It's the capital of one of those funny little countries in Central America, tucked in between Costa Rica and Honduras,' Biggles told him as he closed the book. 'It's on the Pan-American air route to South America, so we ought to have no difficulty in getting petrol there. I expect it's a marine airport; most of them are along that stretch, which means that we shall need a marine aircraft.'

'You mean a seaplane?' asked Dick.

'A flying-boat, probably, or possibly an amphibian,' returned Biggles. 'An amphibian can come down on either land or water. It would be useful to be able to land on a beach, should we find it necessary,' he went on. 'We'll see what we can pick up in America. I've no intention of trying to fly the Atlantic, and I don't think there is any point in going to the expense of shipping a machine across from England. But there, we can settle these details later on. We'll spend the day tomorrow going into the whole thing. Meanwhile, I think it would be a sound scheme if we went out and had a bite of dinner.'

'I was just thinking the same thing,' agreed Algy.

They all got up as Mrs Symes, Biggles's old housekeeper, appeared in the doorway. She turned a reproachful eye on the party. 'How many times have I got to tell you boys to wipe your feet on the front door mat when you come in?' she scolded, half jokingly, half angrily.

Biggles looked up in surprise. 'But we did, Mrs Symes,' he protested. 'I certainly did. We've been in a couple of hours or more, anyway.'

'Well, there now. I wonder who could have made such a mess,' went on the housekeeper. 'One of those young rascals of errand boys, I'll warrant.'

A suspicious look came suddenly into Biggles's eyes. Getting up rather quickly, he walked over to where she was standing and stared down at a number of muddy footmarks on the landing close to the door. In one place there was quite a pool of water. 'It's still raining, isn't it?' he said quietly.

'It's coming down cats and dogs,' declared the house-keeper.

'Humph! That's queer.' Biggles lit a cigarette and then looked back at the floor. 'Sorry we made this mess, Mrs Symes,' he said slowly. 'You'd better clean it up. I'll try not to let it happen again.'

Algy looked at him askance as Mrs Symes went through to her kitchen. 'What's on your mind?' he inquired shrewdly.

'Somebody has been standing outside this door – for some time, too, by the look of it,' murmured Biggles. 'Why do people stand outside doors when other people are inside, talking? Anyone know?'

'To listen to what's being said,' declared Dick promptly.

Biggles nodded sagely. 'That's the answer, Dick. Further, I rather fancy that whoever stood here was wearing oilskins. An ordinary woollen overcoat absorbs water; the outside garment our eavesdropping friend was wearing shot it off on the floor, as you can see. What sort of people wear oilskins besides policemen and postmen, neither of whom are given to keyhole-peeping – not on honest citizens, anyway?'

'Sailors.'

'Right again,' murmured Biggles approvingly.

Dick started as he understood what Biggles was driving at. 'You mean – you think – Deutch followed us here?'

Biggles tapped the ash off his cigarette. 'Come to think of it, there was no reason why he couldn't, if he decided to, was there?' he said quietly. 'You'd better keep close to us, Dick, or we may lose you, and London is a mighty big place to start looking for a small boy with a doubloon in his pocket.'

Chapter 5

Unexpected Difficulties

From five thousand feet Biggles looked down through his windscreen over rolling leagues of sapphire sea, unmarked by a ripple except at the edge, where, in a long line of creamy turquoise, tiny waves lapped idly at the coral strand that meandered mile after mile ahead until at last it lost itself in the purple distance. Beyond it, to the right as the aeroplane flew, stretched the jungle, a vague, monotonous blanket of sombre green that rolled away, fold after fold, to the mysterious shadows of the far horizon.

Beside him, in the second pilot's seat, sat Algy, also gazing ahead, while behind, side by side in the cabin, Ginger and Dick regarded the unchanging scene with the bored disinterest that comes from familiarity.

Nearly a month had elapsed since the discussion in Biggles's rooms. For Dick it had been a period of eager anticipation and delight; for the others, hard work and preparation. It had taken them a fortnight to clear up their affairs and make the necessary arrangements in London, which had included the acquisition of the necessary passports, visas, and carnets.*

---

* A private aeroplane cannot just travel about the world from country to country as some people suppose. Before flying over a foreign country a pilot must first obtain permission in writing from the Government of that country. It will be understood, therefore, that when several countries are involved, the preparations for a long-distance flight are often a tedious and tiresome process, although the aero clubs of the countries concerned do their best to expedite permits and provide facilities. WEJ

Nearly a week had been spent crossing the Atlantic, and then several more days of bustle and anxiety in the United States while Biggles sought an aircraft suitable for their purpose.

In the end he had selected a Sikorsky amphibian, four-seater, twin-engined monoplane with a large luggage compartment, and with this he professed himself satisfied. And so far his opinion had been justified, for the machine had not given them a moment's anxiety since they had taken off, four days previously, on their long run southward, progress being facilitated by the officials of Pan-American Airways – the Imperial Airways of America – whose far-flung system they had obtained permission to use. The only piece of additional equipment they had acquired was a collapsible rubber boat, which Biggles had insisted on taking in case of an emergency landing.

As far as Dick was concerned, four long days in the air had removed all novelty from that mode of travel, and he was looking forward to the time when he would be able to stretch his legs in a sandy cove similar to those they had so often passed, and bathe in the warm, limpid waters of the tropic sea. He knew that according to Biggles's calculations they might reach their objective at any time now, so he was not surprised when presently the roar of the engine died away and the nose of the machine tilted downward. By craning his neck he could just see a large cluster of white, flat-roofed houses, which he knew from the shape of the harbour they skirted was their destination. He caught Ginger's eye and grinned. 'We're there!' he called cheerfully.

Ginger smiled back, nodding. 'Looks like Marabina,' he said, for after some discussion they had finally settled on their original choice as a base from which to work.

'I wonder what sort of a place it is?'

Ginger shrugged his shoulders. 'Much like the other places we've stopped at, except that it is smaller. It's nearer the Equator, so it will certainly be hotter,' he concluded, as the boat-like hull of the amphibian cut a white line of foam across the placid surface of the bay that formed the harbour.

The machine came to rest, rocking gently on an invisible swell. Biggles stood up and folded back the glass cockpit cover. 'That must be Pan-American's moorings, over there,' he said, pointing to a slipway and a wide-mouthed hangar at the water's edge, near which a flying-boat was riding at anchor. 'They told me in New York that this was one of the depots where they keep a spare machine for emergencies. We'll go over there, I think, and tie up by the slipway.'

He was about to sit down again in order to put the plan into execution when a small motor-boat put off from the quay farther down and came chugging towards them; an official in a gaudy but sadly dilapidated uniform stood in the bows, holding up his right hand.

'I think that chap is signalling to us, isn't he?' said Algy dubiously, with his eyes on the boat.

'I believe he is,' replied Biggles standing up again. 'Yes; it's us he's after. I suppose he's coming to have a look at our papers. What's all the hurry, I wonder?'

The boat pulled up alongside the amphibian, the official, a pompous-looking little man, making dramatic signals to the airmen, at the same time firing out a stream of words.

'*No comprendo*,*' said Biggles, who knew a little Spanish, but not enough to keep pace with the present situation.

'I think he means that we are to go with him,' ventured Algy, who was trying to follow the signals.

* Spanish: I don't understand.

297

Biggles pointed towards the tumble-down landing-stage from whence the boat had appeared, at the same time raising his eyebrows questioningly.

'*Si, si,**' called the official peremptorily.

'That's it,' observed Biggles quietly. 'Pity about that. I'd rather have gone over to the Pan-American people, but apparently we shall have to leave that until later. We had better go with this fellow or we may get into trouble. The smaller the place the bigger idea the officials have of their importance; at least, that's my experience.'

While they had been speaking Biggles had opened the throttle slightly, and had followed the boat to the landing-place where the usual small crowd of loungers were watching the proceedings from behind half a dozen rifle-armed policeman, or soldiers; they might have been either.

'Something tells me that I am not going to like this place,' observed Biggles drily, as he switched off the engine and threw a quick glance at the policemen.

'Why not?' asked Algy sharply, as he made the amphibian fast by the bows.

'I don't know, but there is something in the attitude of those fellows with the rifles that warns me that we shall have to be careful,' answered Biggles. 'I can feel a sort of hostility in the air.'

'Our papers are all in order, so I don't see that we have anything to worry about,' put in Ginger carelessly.

'You might, if you knew as much about these people as I do,' Biggles told him shortly. 'The predatory instincts of their forefathers, the Brethren of the Coast, still breaks out at the slightest excuse. But there, we shall see,' he concluded moodily as he collected all the papers they would be likely to require and prepared to step ashore.

* Spanish: Yes, yes.

'Hadn't somebody better stay here to look after the boat?' inquired Ginger. 'We don't want to get our stuff pinched.'

'They'll want us all ashore for Customs regulations and passport examination,' replied Biggles. 'Come on; you have to take chances and hope for the best in this part of the world. The gentleman in the natty uniform is getting impatient.'

Slowly, for the sun was blazing down fiercely on the exposed wharf, they followed the officer up a flight of ramshackle stairs, and then across a badly kept road to a flight of steps that led upwards towards a stone building standing on a knoll overlooking the harbour.

'Where the dickins is he taking us, I wonder?' muttered Biggles anxiously, eyeing the building towards which they were advancing with disfavour.

'It looks to me more like a prison than anything else,' suggested Algy.

'I was thinking the same thing,' declared Biggles. 'Customs offices are usually on the waterfront, for obvious reasons.'

Still, the official in whose charge they were, approached the building, so they could do nothing but follow, and in a few minutes they were guided through a beautifully carved doorway, evidently a relic of the old colonial days, into a well-furnished office, where a swarthy, cadaverous-looking man, with two armed policemen in attendance, awaited them.

Biggles raised his solar topee courteously. '*Buenos diaz, señor,**' he greeted pleasantly.

The other returned the greeting, rather coldly, and held out a dirty hand for the documents Biggles tendered. He gave the four travellers a long, searching scrutiny, and then, with irritating slowness, turned over the pages of their passports.

* Spanish: Good day, Sir.

299

'Do you speak English?' Biggles asked him, quite nicely. The man at the desk took no notice.

Biggles glanced at the others. 'In a case like this the great thing is to keep one's temper,' he said, *sotto voce*. 'I have an increasing suspicion that this fellow is going to be awkward.'

Slowly the minutes ticked by. Algy yawned. Ginger began to fidget. Biggles stood quite still, waiting, knowing only too well the folly of trying to hurry matters.

At last the man at the desk looked up and said something sharply in Spanish.

'What did he say?' asked Algy.

'I'm not sure, but I believe he's telling us that there is something wrong with our papers,' answered Biggles, walking nearer to the desk.

Thereafter followed a long conversation, the official, regardless of Biggles's halting Spanish, pouring out a stream of words every time he spoke. At length Biggles shrugged his shoulders helplessly and turned to the others. 'As far as I can make out, he says there should be another paper which we haven't got.'

'What are we going to do about it?' asked Algy.

The question was soon answered. The official said something to Biggles, and then gave an order to the two policemen, who turned towards the door.

'He says it will be quite all right, but we shall have to wait,' explained Biggles. 'Meanwhile we're to go with these fellows. Come on, it's no use kicking; resistance will only make matters worse.'

They all trooped out behind the policemen and followed them up a flight of stairs to a white-washed room, unfurnished except for three or four wooden forms that stood against the walls. The door was closed; a key grated in the lock and they found themselves alone.

Algy looked at Biggles questioningly. 'What's the big idea, do you think?'

'I don't know,' replied Biggles slowly. 'I can't quite make out what's going on. I'm prepared to swear that our papers are in order, and that the hatchet-faced gentleman downstairs knows it, but he's got some reason for holding us up. I can tell it by his manner. Maybe he's just looking for an excuse to charge us with some technical offence as a ready means of making us pay a fine which will probably go into his pocket. If that's the case, the sooner he says so the better. It's usually a matter of money. Half these fellows live on graft – not that one can altogether blame them, because it's their only source of income.'

'I'd see him to the dickens before I'd stand for being blackmailed,' protested Ginger indignantly.

Biggles smiled sadly. 'In these little tinpot states, particularly in Central and South America, the best policy is to pay up and look pleasant,' he said evenly. 'Otherwise it only costs you more in the end, to say nothing of the delay. Still, I must say I don't like the idea of being locked in, or of that window over there being barred.'

They all sat down to pass the time as well as they could. The room was like an oven in spite of the open, iron-barred window, overlooking the harbour, from which they could clearly see the amphibian, less than a quarter of a mile away.

'What about asking to see the British Consul?' suggested Algy. 'There should be one here, I imagine.'

'There will be a Vice-Consul, anyway,' replied Biggles, 'but I don't think it would be wise to mention him at this stage. We don't want to put their backs up. If the worst comes to the worst we shall have to do that, of course.'

An hour passed slowly, another, and another. The sun began to sink behind the jungle-clad hills. A little cloud of mosquitoes appeared and circled slowly in the centre of the room.

Algy suddenly jumped up from the form on which he had

been lying. 'Dash this for a joke,' he snorted wrathfully. 'I've had about as much as I'm going to stand. Anyone would think that we were a bunch of crooks instead of bona-fide travellers. Come on, Biggles, let's raise a stink.'

Biggles got slowly to his feet. 'Yes, I've had about enough of it myself,' he admitted, strolling over to the window. As he looked out the others saw his manner change. His body stiffened. 'What the devil's going on down there?' he cried, pointing towards the amphibian, about which a number of police were standing. One had just emerged from the cabin carrying a bundle. 'Of course, it may only be the Customs people doing their job,' he went on, 'but I don't like the idea of people prowling about our machine when we're not there. I'm going to demand an explanation.'

He walked quickly towards the door, but before he reached it, it was opened from the far side, and no fewer than six policemen entered. With them were the two officials, the one who had met them in the boat, and the other who had examined their passports.

'What is the meaning of all this?' demanded Biggles harshly.

A policeman laid his hand on Algy's arm, but he shook it off angrily.

'All right, take it easy, Algy,' Biggles told him quickly. 'It's no use starting a rough house; we shall only come off worse in the end.'

The passport officer came forward. His manner when he spoke to Biggles was polite, almost obsequious.

'What's going on?' asked Algy, controlling his temper by an effort.

Biggles shook his head helplessly. 'This fellow says that an American aeroplane has been stolen, and as we may have taken it we must submit to being searched.'

'I'll see them frizzling in Hades first,' choked Algy

302

passionately. 'I've never heard of such a thing in my life. Why don't you demand to see the Consul?'

'I have.'

'What did they say?'

'He isn't here. He has had the fever, and has gone up to the mountains for a change of air.'

Algy swallowed hard. 'I believe the whole thing is a racket,' he grated through set teeth.

Biggles smiled wanly. 'Of course it is,' he agreed. 'The point is, what can we do about it? We can kick up a row when we get back home, but that doesn't help us now, does it? I hate the idea of being searched as much as you do, but, frankly, I don't see that we are in any condition to prevent it. If once we give them an excuse to clap us into jail, we might languish here for months.'

'We made a pretty smart choice of a base, didn't we?' sneered Algy sarcastically.

'I agree, but it's a bit late to think about changing it. Regrets won't get us anywhere. We'd better submit. Luckily, most of my money is in letters of credit and travellers' cheques, so they won't be able to rob us of much.'

After that they submitted to the indignity of being searched, a proceeding that was carried out very thoroughly. Everything was taken from their pockets, including the map of the island and Dick's doubloon. The things were put in a bag and taken away, and again the airmen found themselves alone.

Biggles and Dick alone retained their equanimity. Algy was livid with rage, while Ginger sat on a form and made threats that he was quite powerless to carry out. 'Did you ask that lean-faced swine what his stiffs were doing in our machine?' he challenged Biggles.

'What was the use?' replied Biggles coolly. 'My dear boy, it's no use going off at the deep end. Ill-advisedly, not that we were to know better, we have put ourselves in the clutches of these sharks, and all we can do is sit tight until we get out. Don't think that I am going to let them get away with it. I'm not. But this is neither the time nor place to start threatening.'

'What about my doubloon – and the map?' asked Dick anxiously.

'What about them?' returned Biggles. 'One can only hope that they do not realize their significance. Your doubloon might simply be a souvenir. The map may mean anything. After all, as aeroplane pilots, there is nothing surprising about our being in possession of a map. I've usually got one of some sort on me. In any case, we couldn't have stopped them from taking them with the rest of our things; to have protested would only have called attention to them and aroused suspicion. Don't think I wasn't sorry to see them go out of our possession, but by saying nothing I hoped that they wouldn't attach any particular importance to them.'

'But suppose they *were* sharp enough to connect the doubloon and the map?' insisted Dick plaintively.

But Biggles did not answer. He was standing by the window gazing down at the road that wound round to the harbour. Slowly, an expression of utter incredulity crept over his face.

'What is it?' asked Algy sharply, sensing disaster.

'The answer, I fancy, to the circumstances of our peculiar reception here,' replied Biggles tersely. 'Take a look and see who's walking down the path with our officious friend of the cadaverous face.'

Algy ran to the window. As he looked in the direction indicated his eyes grew round with wonder. 'Heavens!' he breathed. 'It's Deutch!'

Biggles laughed bitterly. 'Astonishing though it may appear, I'm afraid you're right,' he said quietly. 'So now we know. That makes everything as clear as daylight.'

'But how in the name of goodness did *he* get here?' asked Ginger.

Biggles thrust his hands deep into his trousers pockets and bit his lower lip thoughtfully. 'I must admit that such a possibility as his arrival here did not for one instant cross my mind,' he confessed.

'But how did he know we were coming here?' argued Algy.

'You haven't by any chance forgotten the puddle outside our door in London, have you?' inquired Biggles. 'We suspected an eavesdropper, you remember. We even suspected that it was Deutch. He must have heard us decide on this place as a base and got here before us, which accounts for the fact that we saw no more of him in London, a circumstance which struck me at the time as odd. Very clever of him. It looks as if we have made the old and often fatal mistake of underestimating the calibre of our man. We shall know better in future. He got here ahead of us and has apparently managed to get on the right side of the not-too-particular people who run the place. As a sailor, he has probably been here before. Goodness knows what he has told them about us, but whatever it is you may be sure that it's no good. In short, Mr Blessed Deutch has rather upset our carefully loaded applecart.'

'But what about the map and the letter?' cried Algy aghast. 'I'll warrant he's got them by now.'

'He hasn't got the letter because, having committed to memory the rather meagre sailing directions, I left it where, in the event of our non-return, it will be handed over to Colonel Raymond at Scotland Yard, who might one day use it as evidence against friend Deutch.'

'But the map?' cried Algy again.

'A fat lot of use that will be to him.'

'What do you mean?'

Biggles permitted a slow smile to spread over his face. 'I

think you will agree that an incorrect map is worse than no map at all, since it leads one in the wrong direction. You see,' he explained, 'once I suspected that the astute Mr Deutch had followed us home in London, and always taking into consideration the possibility of his getting hold of the map – which, obviously, was what he wanted – I took the precaution of making certain alterations which, while of a minor nature, not only destroys its value, but makes it definitely misleading. Mr Deutch has been clever, but not quite clever enough. He thinks he's won the first round. Has he? We shall see.'

'And in the meantime, what are we going to do about it?' inquired Algy.

'Bar breaking out of this place, which seems to be a rather formidable proposition besides being of questionable wisdom, I don't see that we can do anything except sit here and wait for the next move,' murmured Biggles.

'What! Do you think they'll keep us here all night?' inquired Ginger angrily.

'I shouldn't be surprised,' replied Biggles calmly. 'Now that Mr Deutch has got what he wanted, they will probably keep us here until he gets a good start and then let us go.'

In which supposition Biggles was nearer the truth than he imagined, but not for one instant did he suspect how Deutch's good start was to be achieved.

Little more was said. As the sun sank behind the jungle the sky turned swiftly from azure to egg-shell blue, and then to ever-darkening purple. Night came, and with it the heavy silence of the tropics. Wondering what the morning would bring, the prisoners settled themselves down to pass the night in the least uncomfortable positions they could find.

Chapter 6
Tragic Events

Fluted bars of soft mother-of-pearl light were filtering through the window when Biggles awoke with a start. He was on his feet in an instant. 'Hark!' he cried, as the others sat up in various degrees of wakefulness.

Vibrant on the still air came the roar of aero engines.

'It's only the Pan-American machine getting ready to take off,' declared Algy, settling back again with a yawn.

Biggles darted to the window. 'Pan-American my foot!' he cried. 'It's our machine!'

The others rushed to the window and stared down at the Sikorsky, which was taxi-ing slowly towards the mouth of the harbour, leaving two ever-widening ripples in its wake.

'What the dickens are they going to do with her?' muttered Ginger.

'Perhaps they are just getting the Pan-American people to move her across to the other side out of the way, to make room for a ship, or something,' suggested Algy optimistically.

'Don't you believe it,' snapped Biggles. 'That machine is being taken out of the harbour.' His face was pale as he strode to the door and began beating a rapid tattoo on it with his fists.

Somewhat to his surprise, it was opened almost at once, by a policeman who was evidently just coming in with their breakfasts, for he carried a tray on which was a jug, some cups, a loaf of bread and some fruit. Biggles brushed him aside, as he did two others who tried to stop him, and dashed out of the building and down the road that led to the wharf. But by the time he got there the machine was in the air, so after watching it impotently for a moment or two, he turned about, and with the others close behind, made for the Pan-American hangar, outside which two or three white-clad figures were standing watching the amphibian. The Americans turned to face the airmen as they ran up.

'Did you fellows see who was in that machine?' cried Biggles, waiving formalities.

'Sure,' answered one, a cheerful looking youth, evidently one of the company's mechanics, for the well-known 'flying wing' trademark was embroidered on the breast of his overalls. 'That's your ship, isn't it?' he added.

'It is,' returned Biggles tersely.

'That's what I told my buddy here,' went on the mechanic. 'I watched you bring her in yesterday. I saw you go ashore. Why didn't you come down here to re-fuel, instead of carrying the gas all the way to the wharf?'

Biggles stared. 'Carry the gas?' he echoed in tones of astonishment. 'What do you mean? We haven't had a chance to refuel yet.'

'Your ship was filled up last night by a bunch of guys who carried the stuff from our depot to the wharf.'

Biggles breathed heavily. 'They took our papers and held us on a trumped-up charge of irregularity,' he said bitterly. 'It looks as if we've been swindled out of our machine.'

The other nodded sympathetically. 'Yeah! I guess you've been framed.'

Another of the Americans laughed, but there was no humour on his face. 'These skunks'd frame a mosquito for its hide,' he drawled. 'Looks like you're in a jam.'

'We are,' agreed Biggles crisply. 'I was prepared to be robbed, but I didn't think they'd dare to go so far as to steal an aeroplane. Who took her, boys?'

'Feller named Deutch and his partner. Anyway, Deutch was one of 'em. I saw him get in.'

Biggles caught his breath. 'But he's not a pilot,' he said wonderingly.

'No, but there's a guy with him who is, according to what he says, although I ain't seen his ticket. Deutch blew in here about a week ago with a guy named Harvey, asking about a machine. Harvey claimed that he could fly, and it looks like he told the truth.'

Biggles moistened his lips. 'What have they been doing since they came here?'

'Search me. They rolled up here together asking about hiring a ship, but when the boss asked to see the colour of their money they sheered off. I've seen them once or twice in the town with Mallichore, which was all I needed to put me wise that they were crooks.'

'Who's Mallichore?'

'The Chief of Police. That's his official title. He's the big cheese here, runs the whole burg.'

'Do you mean a cadaverous looking fellow with a yellow skin?'

'That's the boy. You wanna keep clear o' him. He's bad medicine.'

'I'd have kept clear of him had I known what sort of a shark he was, you can bet your life on that,' returned Biggles with bitter emphasis. 'Did anyone see how many people got into my machine?'

'Yeah,' chipped in another mechanic who had appeared from the direction of the wharf while Biggles was speaking. 'There was Deutch, his boozy looking pal Harvey, 'Frisco Jack and Martinez.'

Biggles stared. ''Frisco Jack – Martinez! Who the dickens are they?' he jerked out.

'Good company for the other two,' declared the mechanic who had just spoken. ''Frisco Jack was one of Slick

309

Ferrara's boys in New York. He bolted here when the cops put him on the spot for plugging one of them. There ain't no extradition here, so he can sit pretty. He runs a dive on the waterfront; he still packs a gun under his armpit, and he knows how to use it, so you'd be a sucker to start anything against him unless you had a machine-gun trained on him first.'

'And the other fellow – Martinez?'

'Pedro Martinez! He's a black guy, besides which I guess he's just about the slimiest thug who walks on two legs. He's Mallichore's bumper-off – does all his dirty work for him. The folks around here say he carries a razor in each pocket, and I guess they oughta know. A guy up on the hill told me he's cut more throats than there are fish in the sea, and if ever you catch sight of him you won't find it hard to believe that. Everyone here's scared stiff of him. If he's in your ship you can bet that Mallichore is in on the deal, whatever it may be.'

'Sounds a nice little party,' observed Biggles in a hard voice.

'As nice as you'd find between Rio and l'il old New York.'

Biggles thought swiftly. Out of the corner of his eyes he could see several armed police running down the hill, and he was in no doubt as to their mission. 'Is your boss about?' he asked.

'Sure. Here he comes now. This is the Superintendent. The name's Timms. You can bet on him for a square deal.'

Biggles turned quickly to meet a broad, cheerful-looking, thick-set man in spotless white ducks* who was coming towards them. 'Good morning,' he said. 'I've just had my ship stolen.'

The Superintendent made a grimace. 'Well, say!' he

* White clothes worn in the tropics.

ejaculated. 'I saw her take off. Got me guessing when I saw you standing here.'

Biggles nodded. 'I'm not letting them get away with it,' he said grimly. 'Have you got radio equipment here?'

'Sure.'

'Good,' went on Biggles quickly. 'Then just listen to this, because I can see a bunch of trouble coming down the hill. My name's Bigglesworth. You can check up on it. We're a private party cruising the Islands, and the ship you just saw take off is mine. I bought it off your people at Floyd Bennet Field last week. They'll confirm that. There are fifty thousand dollars standing to my credit in the bank on which I drew the cheque. My letters of credit and cheque book have been taken off me, but I'm going to fetch them in a minute. I want another machine. What about the one you've got here? I'm open to buy it outright, or take it on charter, whichever way you prefer.'

The American looked serious. 'I daren't let you have this one,' he said slowly. 'She's our reserve ship.'

'Yes, I know that. How far away is the next one?'

'Maracibo.'

'They could fly it down here in a day, if you needed a spare.'

'Mebbe.'

'Will you get in touch with your people right away and see what you can do? I'm going up to get my things now, then I'll be back. If your people say I can have the ship, fill up the tanks and start her up. I may be in a hurry. I'll bring the cheque with me.'

'OK. I'll do my best.'

'And as we haven't had anything to eat for about twenty-four hours, if you could get a bit of grub aboard—'

The Superintendent waved his hand. 'Leave it to me,' he cried. 'Watch how you go.'

'Thanks!' Biggles turned to face the party of police, or

311

soldiers, who had now arrived on the scene. With them was the man in the tawdry uniform who had met them in the motor-boat, and he indicated in no uncertain manner that they were to return with him forthwith. Biggles needed no second invitation. His mouth was set in a hard line as, with the others behind him, he set off up the hill. Reaching the stone building, without stopping he strode straight through to the inner office.

Mallichore was sitting at his desk, but he started up as the airmen burst in, with the police at their heels. 'Listen, you,' snapped Biggles harshly, in English. 'I've stood for about as much as I'm going to stand from you. My friends below are already sending a radio message through to the British Foreign Office for me. Get that? The British Foreign Office! I want my things – where are they?'

Mallichore evidently understood, or gathered from Biggles's manner what he meant, for he pointed to the desk on which were piled the things that had been taken from their pockets. He spoke quickly in Spanish, shrugging his shoulders and waving his hands melodramatically.

'What does he say?' asked Ginger.

'Just what I expected he would. He's full of apologies now. Says he's very sorry indeed about the delay, but it is the usual procedure here.'

'Ask him if it's usual for people to have their ships stolen,' growled Algy.

'That won't bring ours back, will it? Pah! What's the use of arguing with the swine? He knows what's happened as well as we do, and he knows we know, but it won't do any good to talk about it. Let's get out. If we can have the Pan-American machine we'll find another base, if we have to go as far as the Bermudas.'

As he spoke, Biggles began picking up the things from the desk and handing them to their respective owners. At last nothing was left. 'Anyone lost anything?' he asked.

'My doubloon,' replied Dick. 'The dirty hound has pinched my doubloon.'

'I thought the sight of a piece of gold would be too much for him,' muttered Biggles. 'I've got everything except the map, not counting a hundred dollar bill that has been taken out of my notecase. I don't think it's any use fighting about it. The sooner we are out of this the better.'

He had half turned towards the door when Dick caught him by the arm. 'Look!' he said. 'There's my doubloon, under the glass.'

Biggles followed the direction of his eyes and saw the coin lying as Dick had described it. It was as if Mallichore had been in the act of examining it when the others had made their abrupt entry, and he had pushed it hurriedly out of sight – as he thought.

Vicious irritation surged through Biggles at the paltry theft. With his eyes on the coin, he took a quick pace forward and stretched out his hand to pick it up, but Mallichore was too quick.

'Why, you dirty crook!' snarled Biggles. Losing his temper and clenching his fists, he took a flying leap over the desk to get at the thief.

'Look out!' Algy yelled the warning.

Biggles snatched a quick glance over his shoulder and saw the muzzle of a rifle pointing at him. He leapt aside just in time. With a deafening roar, intensified by the enclosed area, the weapon exploded. The reek of cordite flooded the room.

In the silence that followed the distant lapping of the waves against the wharf could be heard distinctly. But no-one noticed it. All eyes were on Mallichore. His face was ashen. For perhaps two seconds he stood erect, hand pressed to his breast, while a scarlet blot widened beyond his fingers. Then he fell headlong, with a crash that shook the room. The coin flew from his fingers and spun, a gleaming streak of gold, across the desk. Biggles whipped it up just as it was going to fall to the floor. 'Come on,' he snapped. 'They'll blame us for this.'

As they all made for the door the officer tried to stop them, but Algy hurled him aside. The policeman who had fired the fatal shot was too horrified to move, but another threw up his weapon. Before he could fire it Biggles's fist had caught him on the point of the jaw and sent him spinning into a corner. 'Don't stop for anything,' he snapped, as he slammed the door behind him and took the steps three at a time.

The run down the hill was something none of them will forget. The sun was now high in the sky and the heat was terrific. Occasional pedestrians stared at them, and one or two, apparently connecting them with the uproar that had broken out at police head-quarters, moved as if to stop them, but their courage failed when it came to facing the determined onslaught of the airmen.

'Look!' yelled Biggles exultantly, and the others, following the direction of his outstretched finger, saw the propellers of the flying-boat flashing as they ticked over in the bright sunlight.

They arrived panting. The Americans were grinning. 'Good work, boys,' cried the Superintendent approvingly.

'What about the machine?' gasped Biggles. 'We're in a hurry.'

'Yeah, I noticed it. She's an old ship, so the firm say you can have her for ten thousand-bucks, or you can take her on charter at two hundred and fifty a day, you're to pay insurance and leave five thousand deposit.'

Biggles barely heard the end of the sentence. He was writing out a cheque with his fountain-pen faster than he had ever written before, for a full score of police were pelting down the hill.

'OK,' said the Superintendent, glancing at the cheque.

Biggles ran to the machine. The others were already aboard. 'What range have I got?' he called to the chief mechanic.

'A thousand miles.'

Biggles dropped into the pilot's seat as a bullet whistled through the plane. There was a peculiar smile on his face as he groped for the throttle. The engines roared. The nose swung round in a smother of milky foam. The machine surged forward, cutting a clean V-shaped ripple in the water. He jerked the stick back; the keel unstuck, and the flying-boat rose gracefully into the air. 'Phew!' he breathed, with a sidelong glance at Algy. 'I'm glad to be out of that hole.'

'Same here,' agreed Algy. 'I don't think we had better come back this way.'

'We shan't, not if I can prevent it,' declared Biggles grimly.

Chapter 7

The Hurricane

The new aircraft was a pure flying-boat; that is to say, it was not fitted with a land undercarriage. It was larger than their own machine, having accommodation for eight passengers, but being designed for commercial work, the pilot's compartment was separated from the cabin by a bulkhead, although communication could be established by means of a small doorway, the door itself having a glass panel in it through which passengers could, if they wished, see into the cockpit. All of which was, of course, orthodox design in that class of aircraft. It was not the machine Biggles would have chosen in the ordinary way, but he had had no choice, and in the circumstances he accounted himself extremely fortunate in being able to acquire an aircraft of any sort.

He set the machine on a course for the approximate position of the island, and then told Algy to take over control. 'Keep her as she goes,' he ordered. 'We'll put her down at the first decent anchorage we see and have a council of war. Keep your eyes open for the other machine. Deutch must know pretty well where the island is, although he doesn't know the position of the wreck, so if we see our machine on the water near an island it will be fairly safe to assume that it's the one we're looking for.'

'Suppose we spot it, what then?' inquired Algy. 'Are we going down to tackle them?'

'We will go down, but without weapons we're in no case to tackle anybody. I'm hoping the island will be large enough for us to choose a mooring of our own, without our being seen. Even if they see us – or what is more likely, see the machine – there is no reason why they should assume we are in it. I think they will be more likely to take the machine for what it really is, a Pan-American airliner, on routine service.'

'True enough,' agreed Algy. 'We're doing a hundred and forty, so in about an hour or a little more we should make a landfall at the group of islands we looked at in the atlas.'

'That's right. I'd take her up a bit higher, I think; the higher we are the farther we shall be able to see. Level her out at around eight thousand.'

'OK,' acknowledged Algy. 'What are you going to do?'

'I'm going through to the cabin to have a look round. I asked Timms to try to get some food aboard; I hope he managed it, because if I don't soon have something to eat I shall pass out.'

Biggles opened the bulkhead door and went through into the cabin where Ginger and Dick smiled a welcome. But he was not so interested in them as he was at what rested on the table between them. The American had not overlooked his request for food, although there was nothing particularly outstanding about it. A loaf of bread, a piece of cheese, a pot of jam, and a large bunch of bananas made up the total, and although in their hungry condition they might have wished for more, it was enough to satisfy their immediate cravings.

'Take a banana or two out to Algy,' Biggles told Ginger. 'He can eat them as he flies. I'll go and relieve him as soon as I've had a bite.' He broke a piece off the loaf, cut a slice off the cheese with his penknife, and sat down in an empty seat.

'I'm glad you managed to save my doubloon,' said Dick, helping himself to another banana.

'I'd forgotten all about it,' declared Biggles, feeling in his pocket. 'Here you are, you'd better have it.' He took the coin from his pocket and passed it over.

317

As Dick stretched out his hand to take it a remarkable thing happened. The aircraft soared high, as if it had encountered a colossal up-current, and then dropped like a stone for a good two hundred feet. So violent was the bump when they struck solid air again that Biggles was thrown out of his seat, the bread going in one direction and the cheese in another. Ginger, who was just coming back into the cabin, hurtled inside as if he had been thrown in, and came to rest in a sitting position on the floor with a comical expression of surprise on his face.

'What the dickens was that?' he gasped.

Dick clasped his stomach. 'Crikey!' he breathed. 'Another bump like that and I shall be sick. I feel as if I've left my inside up in the air somewhere.'

Biggles had hurried through to the cockpit. 'Everything all right?' he asked Algy, who threw him a mystified glance.

'Everything's all right as far as I can see.'

'What caused that bump?'

'I don't know. There was absolutely nothing to account for it, not even a cloud. I wasn't ready for it, and it nearly threw me out of my seat. I came to the conclusion that you were up to something in the cabin and had accidentally fouled the controls.'

'No; I was just passing Dick's doubloon over to him,' asserted Biggles. A puzzled expression suddenly crossed his face, but it gave way just as quickly to a smile of derision.

'What's the joke?' asked Algy.

'Nothing much. It just struck me that Dick's doubloon seems to be a hoodoo.'

'Hoodoo?'

'Well, it hasn't been exactly lucky for the people who have owned it, has it? Every time the confounded thing comes to light something seems to happen, like that bump just now.'

'You're not going to ask me to believe that an old coin can have any effect on natural causes, are you?'

'Of course not. It does seem funny, though, doesn't it? First of all there was the ship in which it was found. Something unpleasant happened to that, or it wouldn't be where it is. Something unpleasant also happened to the chap in the cabin, the skeleton Dick's father talked about in his letter. Apparently he died with his boots on. Then there was Charlie, who was with Dick's father and Deutch on the island. He died a sudden death. Dick's father had the coin next, and it didn't do *him* much good, either. Then look at the things that happened to the ship that brought the coin to England. It cast a propeller-blade and was involved in a collision. Before the coin had been in Dick's possession for a day he nearly shared his father's fate, and might have done so had we not appeared on the scene. Half an hour later, with the coin in his pocket, he was nearly run over. On the way home our taxi crashes – a thing that has never happened to us before. Mallichore steals the coin from us, and gets plugged before the day is out! Call it coincidence, call it what you like, but you can't get away from the fact that no less than four men, to our certain knowledge, who have touched the coin have all died sudden deaths. I'm not superstitious, but there is no denying that there have been cases where a sort of evil luck, or fate, has clung to certain objects, and this confounded coin seems to be one of them. Frankly, I don't mind telling you that I shouldn't shed any tears if we lost it. For two pins I'd make Dick throw the thing overboard; there's no sense in taking unnecessary risks. Hang on for a bit; I'll go back and finish my lunch and then relieve you while you have a bite yourself.' Biggles returned to the cabin where he found Ginger and Dick regarding a pile of banana skins with considerable satisfaction. 'Have you finished your lunch, Ginger?' he asked.

'I think I've had my share,' admitted Ginger.

'Then you might go through and relieve Algy for a few minutes while he comes in for his,' Biggles said, as he prepared to resume his interrupted meal.

Ginger disappeared through the doorway, but came back almost immediately. 'Land-ho!' he called.

'Good,' replied Biggles. 'Is Algy coming?'

'He's looking at something ahead; he can't make out what it is, and I think he's getting a bit worried. It looks to me like a storm of some sort. Maybe you'd better go and have a dekko.'

Biggles finished his bread-and-cheese quickly, tore a banana from the reduced bunch, and went back to the cockpit. 'What's the matter?' he asked Algy, who was staring forward through the windscreen.

'What do you make of that?'

Biggles took one long piercing look forward and put the banana in his pocket. 'I don't know, but I don't like the look of it,' he answered shortly. 'We're in the hurricane belt here, don't forget, and when it does decide to blow, things happen. You'd better let me take over. Go and snatch a mouthful of food while you can – and you'd better tell the others to get ready to hang on to something. That's dirty weather coming if I know anything about it.' Biggles slipped into the seat Algy had vacated and fixed his eyes ahead on what was an impressive if rather alarming spectacle.

Some twenty miles away, from out of a motionless sea that resembled nothing so much as a floor of polished steel, rose a large, crescent-shaped island that towered up to a jagged peak in the centre. Beyond it, and on either side, misty blue with distance, were others, their bases merging so softly with the sea that they appeared to float in space. But it was not this impression of dreamlike tranquillity that caused Biggles's lips to come together in a hard line. It was a dark, indigo ridge that was rising with incredible speed above the horizon, almost as if an unseen hand was drawing a giant curtain across the blue dome overhead.

For a moment he hesitated, uncertain whether it would be better to try to get above the storm, or race for the big island in the hope of finding a sheltered anchorage in which to ride it out. Making up his mind to adopt the latter plan, he opened the master throttle to its fullest extent, and thrust the joystick forward for all the speed he could get.

Algy reappeared almost immediately. 'What are you doing?' he asked.

'We're in for a snorter,' muttered Biggles grimly. 'We should use up all our petrol if we ran away from it, or tried to get round it, so I am hoping to reach the island before it hits us. If we can find a cove on the leeward side we ought to be able to weather anything in a craft of this size.'

Algy nodded, satisfied with Biggles's judgement, but a worried frown that deepened quickly to real apprehension settled on his face as he watched the ominous mass sweeping towards them. 'I never saw anything quite like that in my life,' he muttered. 'Looks terrifying, doesn't it?'

'That stuff is travelling at a hundred miles an hour, if it's moving an inch,' replied Biggles tersely. 'We shall go up in the air like a feather if it hits us. Tell the boys to stow everything and lie on the floor.'

'Can we make the island, do you think?'

'I'm hoping so, but it's going to be a close thing.'

They were down to a thousand feet now, roaring over an ocean that was just beginning to stir uneasily, like a sleeping giant who senses danger.

'The water is calm, anyway,' observed Algy optimistically.

'It won't be in a minute,' retorted Biggles grimly. 'The wind that's coming will blow up such a sea as I've no desire to be on. It's going to be touch and go. We—'

'Look out! Mind you don't hit that bird,' interrupted Algy.

Biggles altered his course slightly to keep clear of a great white albatross that came swerving across their bows, outspread wings vibrating, like those of a rook trying to reach a cornfield in the teeth of a gale.

'Look out!' Algy's warning cry rose to a shrill crescendo.

Biggles did not really need the warning. He could see the bird clearly enough. Watching it, he saw it swerve again and come tearing towards them like a piece of tissue paper in a high wind. He did his best to avoid it but it almost seemed as if the bird deliberately charged the aircraft. At the last second Algy flung up an arm to protect his face. Biggles flinched.

There was a splintering crash as the bird struck the machine. Algy, when he had seen that a collision was unavoidable, had ducked below the level of the windscreen. At the crash of the impact he turned a white, startled face upwards. The roar of the engines ceased abruptly.

'It flew slap into the port prop! Smashed it to pieces!' yelled Biggles, wiping a spatter of blood from his face. 'Look!'

Algy got up and saw that only the boss remained on the shaft of the port engine. Of the propeller itself there was no sign, but a nasty red mess of blood and feathers jammed against the splintered windscreen told its own story. 'Good heavens!' he muttered through dry lips, as the starboard engine came to life again when Biggles opened the throttle. 'Can we hold our height on one engine?'

Biggles, who had cut both engines in his anxiety, looked at the island through the fast approaching murk. The sun had disappeared and the black curtain was almost overhead. The sea was glassy. 'We might,' he said simply. 'We can only try.'

As he spoke, a white ruffle shimmered across the water

322

beneath them, and the flying-boat soared like a ship riding a big roller. 'Here she comes,' he said grimly, and took a fresh grip of the joystick. The island, now white-fringed with breakers, was not more than two miles away.

The ruffle on the sea died away, but Biggles was not deceived. He knew that the lull would not last for more than a few seconds, after which the full force of the hurricane would strike them. 'Hang on,' he said crisply. 'She'll buck like a wild horse when we hit the next lot. Look at the island.'

Algy was already looking at it, and his lips parted with anxiety at what he saw. The jungle with which it was covered was writhing until the whole island seemed to shake like a jelly. Palm fronds and debris whirled high into the air and sped away before the wind like smoke.

Biggles jammed the stick still further forward as he spied a little sheltered cove, protected on the seaward side by a coral reef, now half buried under a smother of foam.

At that moment the hurricane struck them.

The flying-boat rocketed like a wounded pheasant, and half turned over, but Biggles fought it back to even keel, and then put the nose down in a dive that was not far short of vertical. Quivering, twisting, and vibrating like a live thing, the machine crept slowly nearer to the lagoon. The needle of the air-speed indicator rested on the one hundred and forty mark, but the speed at which they approached their objective could not have been more than thirty or forty miles an hour, which meant a wind velocity of a hundred miles an hour. Still, they continued to make way towards the reef, now a swirling, seething, churning line of milk-white foam and spray less than a hundred feet below.

'We shall do it,' shouted Algy exultantly, and at that moment their remaining engine cut out dead.

Apart from a tightening of his jaw muscles, Biggles's expression did not change. He slammed the joystick forward viciously and held it with both hands, his one idea now being to reach dry land regardless of what happened to the machine. He knew only too well that if they were forced down on the water the seas that would follow the wind would swamp them within five minutes. He threw a fleeting glance at Algy. 'Get ready to swim!' he yelled. 'I'm going to try to reach those rocks over there, but I don't think we shall quite manage it. It will have to be every one for himself when she strikes. Tell the boys to get their clothes off and jump for it if we get close enough.'

'But what about the machine?' shouted Algy aghast.

'Let it go hang. If we can save our lives we shall be lucky,' answered Biggles desperately.

Yard by yard the flying-boat crept nearer to the rocks which Biggles had now made his objective, but for every yard it gained it lost three feet of height. It was nearly on the water. Subconsciously, Biggles was aware of the others crowding behind him, throwing off their clothes. The noise of the waves and the scream of the wind in the wires made normal speech futile. 'Get ready!' he roared.

Dick clutched the edge of the cockpit as the machine hovered for an instant on the edge of the rocks.

'The wing!' yelled Biggles. 'The wing! Slide down the wing!'

Dick saw instantly what he meant. The port wing was actually hanging over the rocks. In a flash he was on it, but before he could find a handhold, a terrific gust had caught the machine and whirled it round, so that instead of being over the rocks he was now over the churning water. For one dreadful moment he clawed frantically at the smooth fabric, seeking in vain for a handhold, sliding all the time nearer to the trailing edge. Another gust shook the machine; the wing seemed to drop like a lift under him and he was flung clean into space. For a fleeting instant he seemed to hang in the air, with the foam-capped waves leaping up to meet him, then he was struggling in a deep blue world with unseen monsters that dragged him this way and that, choking the life out of him as they did so. The blue world began to grow darker, with little flecks of white light flashing in it. Dick knew that he was drowning. And just as he knew that whatever else happened he must open his mouth to breathe, the blueness exploded into white daylight. He gave a great gasp. Air poured into his lungs, but before he could see where he was, or even think of swimming, he was down in the blue world again, fighting a hopeless battle against the unseen clutching hands. He knew that he could not fight much longer. His strength was nearly gone. It would be easier not to fight, but to allow the hands to drag him where they would. They were pushing him up again now – up – up – up.

Again he burst into daylight. Again he breathed. Weakly, he looked around for something to which he might cling, but all he could see through a smother of foam was a white line of breakers over which tall, graceful palms were tossing their wind-torn crowns. Feebly he struck out towards them, but before he had taken three strokes he was down in the blue world again, turning over and over as he was borne along, as lightly as a feather, in the heart of a wave. A sound like distant thunder, growing ever louder, reached his ears. It seemed to swell in volume until it was all around him, pulverizing him with sound. Then, just as he thought he could bear it no longer, he struck something solid, and clutched at it wildly. But it seemed to slip between his fingers, ever eluding his frenzied grip. Then miraculously the blue world faded away; the noise abated suddenly, and he found himself kneeling on a bank of sand and shingle that was sliding swiftly back towards the churning waves. In his hands were the rolling stones on which he had striven to obtain a grip. Panting, eyes wide with horror, he saw another white-crested wave rushing towards him, its top, flecked with green, curling ominously. Weakly he struggled to his feet and began fighting his way up the shelving beach.

He knew that the wave would catch him. He could hear it as it hissed along; he could feel it overtaking him, towering high above him. Knowing that he could not escape, he dropped to his knees and dug his hands deeply into the loose stones, at the same time trying to get a grip on them with his feet and knees. He just had time to snatch a last deep breath when the wave, with a roar like an express train, overwhelmed him. In a flash he was whipped up from his unstable handhold and the blue demons had him in their clutches again. Swiftly the blue deepened to indigo, then slowly to black, across which darted flashes of vivid lightning. In his ears was the beating of a thousand drums and the clanging of bells, but the noise grew fainter and fainter as he slipped over an invisible precipice and plunged downwards into a bottomless void.

He seemed to be falling for a long time. It was not an unpleasant sensation, but he wished it would end. He could see the earth now, in the distance, a vague, misty plain coming up to meet him. Down – down – down he plunged, towards a world of silence, leaving the thunder far behind. The earth leapt upwards. As he struck it, it seemed to explode in a great blaze of crimson flame.

Chapter 8

Wrecked

Out of the corner of his eyes Biggles saw Dick go overboard and disappear under the foam, but he could do nothing to help him. Indeed, as he fought to keep the flying-boat under control, it seemed certain that during the next minute or two the others must join him. Ashen, he looked at Algy. 'Jump when she hits!' he cried, in a shrill, strangled voice, and dived deliberately at the rocks.

He did not quite reach them. The machine struck the sea a few yards short, but the result of the impact was almost the same as if she had struck solid earth. There was a rending crash as the wings tore off at the roots, and the bows crumpled like a crushed eggshell.

Ginger jumped. He landed on a rock, but it was wet and slippery with seaweed, and he slid back into the water, only to be thrown up again by the next wave. Algy followed him. He landed short but, providentially, the next wave carried him in so that he could grasp the hand that Ginger, with great presence of mind, held out to him. Gasping, he flung himself flat on the rock and took a grip on the slippery weed.

All this had taken place in a second of time, and before Biggles could get clear of the cockpit the shattered aircraft had been blown a good twenty yards from the land, where it rolled in a boiling maelstrom. To jump now, he saw, would be suicidal, so he threw off his clothes and clung to the top of the hull, ready to make a leap for the shore should an opportunity present itself. But, unhappily, although the force of the storm seemed to have abated suddenly, the wind was still strong enough to blow the aircraft farther and farther from the rock on which the others crouched, and Biggles could only hang on and watch helplessly as the shore receded and the big seas began to batter the flying-boat to pieces.

Algy and Ginger, safe ashore although not a little bruised, clambered along the rocks waiting for the end that now seemed inevitable. It was apparent that the aircraft could not survive the punishment it was receiving for many more minutes; already it was sinking fast. They followed it as far as they could, but presently a great mass of rock, round which the aircraft was drifting, barred their way. Frantically they sought a way over it, but in vain, and the last they saw of him, as the machine was blown beyond the point, Biggles was still clinging to the half-submerged hull. With horror-stricken eyes they watched the machine out of sight beyond the rock.

'Come on! We must do something!' cried Ginger, in a voice shrill with anxiety. He was naked except for a pair of elastic topped trunks. His wet hair was plastered down over his face, while blood from a cut in his shoulder, where it had struck the rock, mingled with the water that poured down his body so that it formed little pink rivulets.

Algy started up, limping, vaguely conscious of a pain in his right ankle; but such was his state of mind that he did not even look to see what had caused it. 'He's being carried out to sea,' he cried in a choking voice. 'We must get to the other side of this rock.'

'We can't get over it; we shall have to find a way round,' muttered Ginger.

'What about Dick?'

'I'm afraid he's gone. We can't do anything about him, anyway. Let's try to see what happens to Biggles.'

They started off in a direction at right angles to the one taken by the flying-boat with the object of forcing a passage through the jungle that overhung the inland side of the rock barring their passage.

'We shall never get through this stuff,' declared Algy in something like a panic.

'We've got to!'

They did their best, but the task, almost naked as they were, was practically impossible. A direct course was out of the question, but by following the most open places in the luxuriant vegetation they were able to make some progress up the side of the fairly steep hill that flanked the mass of rock they were so anxious to get round. Thorns pricked their feet, briers and trailing lianas clutched at their legs and bodies, but they pushed on, hardly feeling the pain.

Ginger was first to reach the top, where he pulled up suddenly, staring out to sea. His face, already pale, turned as white as a sheet. 'Look!' he muttered hoarsely.

Algy, following the direction of his trembling forefinger, said nothing. There was no need to say anything. The end of the tragedy was there before their eyes. Nearly a mile away the hull of the wrecked aeroplane was still wallowing in the waves, but of Biggles there was no sign.

For several minutes, during which neither of them spoke, they stared at the storm-churned water between the wreck and the shore. Then Algy drew a deep breath. 'He's gone,' he said simply.

Ginger bit his lip. 'Yes, he's gone,' he said in a dull voice. Sitting down, he buried his face in his hands.

For two or three minutes they remained thus, Algy staring out across the white-capped waves, loath to abandon hope. 'I'm afraid it's no use standing here,' he said at last, in tones of utter misery. 'Let's go back to see if we can find Dick.'

Slowly they retraced their steps, or rather, they tried to, but it was soon clear to both of them that they had lost their original path. Not that they cared particularly. One way seemed as good as another. They knew that by going downhill sooner or later they would come to the seashore, which they did, striking it at a long, sandy beach. Two things caught their eyes at once. One was an elevator that had been torn off the ill-fated aircraft, and the other, a dark object that was being rocked gently to and fro at the extremity of the surging waves. They hurried towards it.

'It's Dick's jacket,' said Algy unnecessarily, for there was no mistaking the water-soaked garment that he dragged from the edge of the sea. He picked it up and stood staring at it, not knowing what to do with it, yet unwilling to cast it aside. Holding it thus, something fell from a pocket and dropped flat on the white coral sand. It was the doubloon.

Slowly Ginger stooped and picked it up, and gazed at it pensively as it lay in the palm of his hand. 'I think Biggles was about right,' he said heavily. 'One way or another, this piece of metal seems to have caused a good deal of trouble.'

Algy nodded. 'Yes,' he agreed. 'I think I've seen about as much of that coin as I want to.'

'Then the sooner it goes where it can't do any more harm, the better,' declared Ginger viciously, and throwing back his arm, was about to hurl the doubloon far out to sea when he was arrested in the act by the sound of a distant rifle shot.

'What the deuce!' muttered Algy, staring in the direction whence the sound had come, which appeared to be just beyond the end of the strand on which they stood.

'It couldn't be Biggles because he couldn't possibly have got there in the time, and he hadn't a rifle, anyway,' muttered Ginger. 'This island must be inhabited. Perhaps there is a town or a village a little farther along.'

'Maybe it's a trading-station, or something,' murmured Algy vaguely. 'You had better hang on to the doubloon; after all, it's gold, and it may enable us to buy food or clothes. Let's go and have a look.'

They set off at a brisk pace, Algy limping on his injured

ankle, which a swelling suggested had been wrenched. But with the aid of a piece of driftwood, which he used as a walking stick, he was able to make fairly good progress.

It was farther to the end of the beach than they thought; in fact, it must have been a good two miles, for they were more than half an hour reaching it, by which time it was beginning to get dark.

Facing them, at the end of the gently curving bay round which they had walked, a mass of boulders lay like a great wall athwart the beach, high on the landward side, but sloping steeply down into the sea, evidently an old landslide from the hills that towered up in the centre of the island. From it sprang a small but graceful group of coconut palms.

'If we can get to the top of that pile we ought to be able to see who fired the shot, if he's still there,' observed Algy.

With a quickening sense of expectancy they scrambled up over the boulders, and arriving at the crest near the palms, stood rooted to the ground in astonishment at what they saw.

In a small lagoon, made perfect by a coral breakwater that lay across the entrance, rode an aeroplane. One glance was sufficient to reveal that it was the amphibian that had been stolen from them in Marabina. Like a giant sea-bird, it sat lightly on the water, rocking gently in the swell coming in through the opening that gave access to the sea. It was some thirty or forty yards from the shore, on which lay the collapsible canoe that had formed part of its equipment, and about the same distance from another landslide that formed the farther side of the natural harbour.

After one swift, incredulous glance, Algy's eyes had switched to the beach and the jungle behind it, seeking the men he fully expected to see. But to his blank surprise there was no sign of them. He turned to Ginger. 'Well, what do you make of that?' he said tersely.

'Deutch and his crowd must be here.'

'Without any shadow of doubt.'

'Then—' a sudden, almost unbelievable possibility rushed into Ginger's mind '—then this must be *the* island,' he whispered, almost breathlessly.

Algy stared at him. Curiously enough, that possibility had not occurred to him. 'What an amazing chance,' he said.

'What can we do about it?'

'What *can* we do?'

'We can get our machine.'

Algy looked at the sea, still flecked with white, and shook his head. 'How?' he asked. 'There isn't room to take off in the lagoon; she'd be swamped in five seconds in the open sea, and the beach is nothing like big enough for a land take-off. We can't lift the machine over these rocks to the beach on the other side. Besides, it's nearly dark. It seems a pity, but I'm afraid there is nothing we can do about it except hide up and wait for another opportunity. It's something to know the machine is here, anyway.' He spoke without enthusiasm, for the dreadful uncertainty of Biggles's fate – for he still hoped, although in his heart he feared the worst – left him careless of the future. 'Let's get away from here in case Deutch happens to come back. No doubt he is treasure hunting,' he concluded.

By mutual consent, they walked quickly along the ridge on which they stood in order to reach the woods, but if they thought their adventures were over for the day they were soon to be disillusioned. They were among the slim boles of the coconut palms, looking for the easiest way down, when they almost collided with a slight, pale faced man, coming in the opposite direction. He was a stranger to them, but his first words, and the manner in which he instantly covered them with the rifle he carried, left them in no doubt as to his identity.

'Waal, waal,' he drawled. 'Say now, ain't that jest too

dandy. Come right along. Deutch was hopin' you'd drop in sometime!'

Algy eyed the speaker dispassionately. He felt no fear. His only sensation was one of cold anger. 'You're 'Frisco Jack, I suppose?'

'Sure! Come on, let's go, or we may slip on these stones in the dark.'

Algy and Ginger were quite helpless, and they had the sense to realize it. Without speaking, they accompanied their captor to the far side of the lagoon where, in a small open space that had previously been hidden from their sight by an outcrop of rock, three men were seated. Deutch was one; a tall man with a slight cast in his deep set eyes, was another; the third was an enormous black man wearing a uniform so elaborate that in different circumstances he might have cut a comical figure. But there was nothing funny about the way he sprang to his feet when the small party appeared, and stood glowering, his mouth half open with surprise and the fingers of his hands slowly opening and closing.

'So you've got here, hey?' began Deutch, addressing Algy, after the first buzz of astonishment had died away.

'It looks like it, doesn't it?' answered Algy evenly.

'You keep a civil tongue in your head, my cock, or I'll make you sing a different tune,' snarled Deutch. 'Where's your smart partner – the tall feller?'

'I wish I knew,' replied Algy briefly.

'Come on; no lies. Where is he?'

Algy was in no mood for lying. In fact, he was so utterly sick that he didn't care much what happened. 'To the best of my knowledge he was drowned about an hour ago,' he said curtly. 'Our ship was smashed to pieces in the hurricane. It fell into the sea. As far as I know we are the only survivors. Now you know the whole story.'

Silence fell for a moment or two. There was something so

333

convincing in the way in which Algy had spoken that they could not do other than believe him.

'That comes o' bein' too clever,' sneered Deutch. He turned to the others. 'What shall we do with 'em, boys?'

The black man grinned broadly. In an instant he had whipped out a razor which he began to whet in a horrible manner on the palm of his hand.

'Put that thing away,' growled the cross-eyed man. 'If there's any bumpin' off to be done, let's have it clean. Why not turn 'em loose? They can do no harm.'

'And have 'em slipping off with the machine? These guys can fly, don't forget,' grated the American harshly.

'They might know something about – what we're looking for,' suggested Deutch thoughtfully.

'Sure; so they might,' agreed 'Frisco Jack. 'Why not tie 'em up and ask 'em a few questions in the morning? Maybe they'll feel different then. Anyway, there ain't no sense in doin' nothin' in a hurry.'

'Maybe you're right,' agreed Deutch. 'That's it, tie 'em up. We can allus get rid of 'em when they ain't no more use. Get a bit o' rope, Pedro.'

Pedro found a piece of cord amongst the pile of stores that lay a little to one side, and grabbed Ginger, who was nearest, by the arm. Involuntarily, Ginger's fingers opened under the pressure, and the doubloon, which he was still carrying, fell out of his hand on to the sand.

With a whoop of joy Pedro snatched it up. 'Whar you get this?' he growled, showing it to the others.

Ginger did not reply.

'Where'd you get it?' snapped Deutch.

'It's the original coin we had in London,' replied Ginger, coolly.

'Tha's a lie. Mallichore's got that 'n,' snarled Pedro. 'They know where t'others are.'

'Where did you get it?'

'I tell you it's the same one,' protested Ginger wearily. 'We got it from Mallichore with the rest of our things. Do we look as if we've been treasure hunting?' he concluded sarcastically.

'Pass it over to me, Pedro,' ordered Deutch.

For a moment Pedro hesitated, obviously reluctant to part with the coin, and the thought flashed into Algy's mind that a similar incident had been enacted, not long before, perhaps on that very spot, when Dick's father had refused to give the coin up to Deutch.

'Let me keep it, boss,' pleaded Pedro.

'All right. There'll be plenty more of 'em presently,' agreed Deutch in a surly voice.

With a grin of delight Pedro slipped the doubloon into his pocket; then, taking the cord, he tied Ginger's wrists and ankles and pushed him brutally on to the ground. Fortunately, the sand was soft. He then treated Algy in the same way.

By the time this was done night had fallen, but the moon came up and flooded the lagoon with a silvery radiance.

'Frisco Jack fetched a blanket and spread it out on the sand. The others, including Deutch, did the same. 'We'll attend to you in the morning,' was his parting threat, as he regarded his captives with unpleasant satisfaction.

Chapter 9

What Happened to Dick

Had Algy or Ginger, at the time when they had recovered Dick's jacket from the sea, looked a little more closely to the left, where great heaps of seaweed, torn from the ocean bed by the fury of the hurricane, had been cast up, they might have noticed a little white crumpled heap, half buried under long ribbons of slimy kelp, in which case this story would have had a different ending. For the crumpled heap was Dick's bruised body, pounded into unconsciousness by the weight of the giant rollers which had, at the finish, flung him far up the gently shelving beach.

For a long time after Algy and Ginger had gone the pathetic figure did not move. It might have been a corpse. The sun sank. The tide ebbed. The moon came up, and presently cast a pale, eerie light on Dick's pallid face. A crab marched out of a hole in a rock, a curious crab with high, stilt-like legs, and long waving antennae. With a soft clicking noise it advanced with the characteristic movement of its kind upon the recumbent form. Two yards away it stopped, as if suspecting a trap. Another joined it. Presently came others, until they formed a semicircle on the seaward side of the motionless figure. The quiet of the night was filled with their soft clicking. Slowly the serried ranks advanced.

Slowly, also, the moonbeams moved across Dick's deathlike face until they reached his eyes. He stirred uneasily. Instantly the clicking army receded like a wave.

He moaned weakly. Then, suddenly, he opened his eyes. For a moment or two he stared vacantly at the star-spangled sky. With a rush consciousness returned, and he sat up, resting on his right hand, gazing at the shining sea. For a full minute he remained thus while he strove to separate dreams from reality. Then, knowing the truth at last, he tried to stand up. Instantly he was violently sick, evacuating vast quantities of sea-water. This not only relieved him but restored him to full consciousness, and he managed to get to his feet, stiffly, feeling his bruised body with shaking fingers.

Another spell of nausea passed, and he looked round to see where he was. He did not expect to see the others. Nor did he. Nor could he see any signs of the aircraft. A feeling of terrible loneliness crept over him as he realized that he was alone. It was impossible to believe that the others had all been drowned, but it was equally impossible to believe that they had been saved. A white object lying on the high-water mark some distance away caught his eye, and he walked unsteadily towards it. Before he reached it he saw that it was an elevator, and tears that he could not keep back welled to his eyes as he realized what it portended. Sick with weariness and grief, he sank down on the sand and buried his face in his hands.

A little while later, however, as the spasm of misery expended itself, he got up again and contemplated his own position. Not that he was concerned particularly about it; his distress was far too poignant for that. Nevertheless, he felt an uncomfortable twinge as he regarded the silent jungle that rose up like a towering wall behind him. What terrible beasts did it harbour? What horrors crouched in its sable heart? He did not know, but it was impossible not to feel its hidden menace.

Fighting down his fears by sheer will-power, he turned and looked back at the sea, recognizing at once the scene of the disaster. There were the rocks that he had tried to reach, left high and dry by the receding tide; there, also, was the place where Biggles had tried to crash the flying-boat; the great buttress of rock jutted far out, but the lashing waves were no longer there. Perhaps – the others – were lying there, he thought miserably. What was it his father used to say? The sea always gives up its dead.

Looking to right and left for something he dreaded to find, he began to walk towards the end of the buttress of rock which Algy and Ginger had been unable to surmount; but now, because the tide had ebbed, it was possible to walk right round it. He reached the end and climbed up on the lowest rocks, still looking for what he feared to find – the bodies of his comrades. Satisfied that they were not there, he retraced his steps, and walking up to the dry sand beyond the high-water mark, as near to the forest as he dared go, he sat down to rest and wonder what he should do. Water was his most pressing need; his mouth was parched, but he did not feel like exploring in the moonlight and the grotesque shadows that it cast. So, with his chin cupped in the palm of his right hand, and his eyes fixed unseeingly on the mass of rock, he prepared to wait for dawn.

How far distant it was, he had, of course, no means of knowing, because he had no idea of how long he had been unconscious. Thus he sat for a long time. Never had a night seemed so long. Fortunately the air was warm, or in his nude condition his misery would have been intensified. Slowly the time passed. The moon moved silently on its allotted course; it crept round the bay that lay at his right hand until at last it bathed the rocks on his left in its blue radiance.

He was nearly asleep when he saw one of the rocks move – or thought he saw it move. He had, in fact, sunk into that condition midway between sleep and wakefulness when one hesitates to believe what one sees. But he was wide awake instantly, holding his breath, every nerve taut. Slowly the rock took shape; it became a human figure, and as he stared with wide, affrighted eyes he knew that he was dreaming. Either that, or he was seeing something at which he had always scoffed. A ghost. For the figure was not that of an ordinary man. Around its head was tied a spotted handkerchief, the corners hanging down over the nape of the neck. A vest, woven in a pattern of wide, alternate bars, covered the chest, the lower part ending in crimson, pleated pantaloons, which were tucked into wide-topped boots with silver buckles, on which the moon shone brightly. In its hand it carried an enormous cutlass, the point of which rested on the rock.

With parted lips, his heart palpitating wildly, Dick could only stare, while the figure slowly turned, and raising its hand to shield its eyes, gazed long and steadily down the coral strand. Then, as mysteriously as it had appeared, it had gone.

In Dick's mind there was no longer any doubt. It was the ghost of a long-dead buccaneer. A spirit walking in death the path it had trodden in life. He waited for no more. With a convulsive gasp he sprang to his feet and set off along the sand as fast as his legs could carry him. And not until another pile of rocks appeared ahead did he begin to slow down, looking back fearfully over his shoulder. Seeing nothing of the apparition, however, he paused to recover his breath. Relieved, he set off again, making for a clump of coconut palms that rose up from the rocks, for he recognized them for what they were and hoped to find a fallen nut from which he might be able to quench his thirst.

Reaching his objective, he was casting about on the ground when something just beyond the rocks caught his eye, an object that shone white in the moonlight. For a moment he stared unbelievingly. He rubbed his eyes and stared again. But there was no mistake. The gleam that had caught his eye was the moonlight playing on the white wings of an aeroplane that rode lightly on the still water of a small lagoon. Naturally, it did not occur to him that it was any other than the machine in which he had arrived – or rather, from which he had fallen – and he was half way towards it when he saw his mistake. He pulled up dead, choking back the cry of joy that rose to his lips and struggling to understand the full significance of what he saw. Was he dreaming again, or was it the Sikorsky? It looked like it. Could it be possible, he asked himself? He soon realized that it could, and what its presence meant. But where was the crew – Deutch and the others? If the aircraft was here, it meant that they were here, too. They could not be far away. Standing quite still, he surveyed the shore of the lagoon, foot by foot, yard by yard. But still he could not see them. He had just made up his mind to approach nearer when he heard a sound that sent the blood racing through his veins. It was unmistakable. Someone, not far away, had snored.

He moistened his lips, wondering how to take advantage of the situation. There was the machine, but he could not fly it. He did not even know how to start the engines. But there, lying on its side on the beach, was the canoe, and that was something he did understand. But of what use was that to him? At that moment he could not see how it could help him, unless he took it right away and hid it, when at some future date it might enable him to reach another island or the mainland. Yes, he decided, that was what he would do. He would take the canoe. But first of all he would try to find out what Deutch and the others were doing. Raising his eyes, he saw that the sky was paling and knew that the dawn could not be far off. Soon it would be light, so whatever he proposed doing would have to be done quickly.

Swiftly, but making no sound and keeping well in the

dense black shade of the jungle, he crept towards the place from which the snore had come. Again he heard the sound, and although it made his skin turn to gooseflesh, he kept on. With his heart seeming to beat in his throat, but making no more noise than a shadow, he crept nearer to the rocks, and at last peeped over them. He was down again instantly. Six figures were lying on the sand, four dressed and two undressed. Why six? The Americans had said that there were only four people on board the machine when it was stolen. He risked another peep, a longer one this time. As he did so, one of the nearest figures, one of the undressed ones, moaned slightly and turned towards him. Instinctively his eyes went to his face, and he recognized Algy.

The shock of this discovery was so terrific that he was only just able to stifle a cry. As it was, it left him weak and trembling. Hardly able to breathe, he looked again, and saw, as he already half suspected, that the other undressed figure was Ginger. He also saw from their positions that their hands and wrists were tied.

He almost panicked as he realized his helplessness to assist them. Never in his life had he wanted anything so much as he wanted a knife at that moment. Could he untie the knots? He could not do less than try, he decided. He glanced again at the sky, and groaned inwardly as he saw that the once-longed-for dawn was now approaching all too quickly. At any moment the others might awake. It was now or never.

Steeling himself, he crept swiftly round the rocks and approached Algy, who was the nearer. He saw that his eyes were wide open and saw the look of wonderment that leapt into them, but he did not stop. In a moment he was down beside him, working at his fettered ankles. His heart sank as he saw how tightly the knots were drawn, and realized that it would take some time to undo them.

He started as Algy struggled into a sitting position, but

then saw that he was trying to tell him something. 'The razor,' he breathed.

Dick, following the direction of his eyes, saw what he meant. A few yards away a large black man in a blue coat lay stretched out on the sand; beside him, half open, lay a razor. With a little gasp of relief, he moved towards it. His hand went out, fingers outspread. At that moment the man awoke.

For one ghastly moment they stared into each other's eyes. Then, with an oath, the man sprang to his feet.

'Run for it, Dick.' It was Algy's voice, clear and sharp.

It galvanized Dick into violent activity. In a sort of dreadful nightmare, he leapt aside just as the man snatched up the razor and aimed such a slash at him that had the weapon reached its mark it would have taken his head from his shoulders. With an involuntary cry of horror, he darted up the rocks with the alacrity of a mountain goat, and then, taking the far side in a dozen bounds, he set off up the beach as if a pack of demons was at his heels. In the grip of stark panic, he dared not risk a glance behind until he had covered a good hundred yards; when he did, his worst fears were realized. The man was leaping down the rocks in hot pursuit, something in his hand reflecting brightly the rays of the sun, the rim of which was now showing above the horizon.

A shot rang out. Sand spurted from under Dick's feet and urged him to even more frenzied efforts, but he had the good sense to swerve, which may have been as well, for another bullet, with a vicious *zip*, tore a long furrow in the sand. On he raced, his feet flying over the pounded coral, and not until he was within striking distance of the rocky *massif* on which he had seen the ghost of the buccaneer did he snatch another fleeting glance over his shoulder. For a moment his knees seemed to sag as he saw that the other man was not only racing along in his footsteps but had halved the distance between them. Seeing that he could not climb the rock that lay across his path, he swerved wildly towards the seaward end round which the incoming tide was now flowing. He nearly fell under his own impetus as the water dragged at his shins, but with an effort he recovered his balance and rounded the point. In front of him lay another stretch of beach, terminating in more rocks, and, slightly out to sea, a rocky islet.

Again he set off at full pelt, glancing often at the tangle of jungle on his left hand in case an avenue of escape should offer itself in that direction. But it appeared to be impenetrable, and he dare not risk a halt to explore in case that should, in fact, prove to be the case.

His strength was nearly gone and he was catching his breath in great gasps by the time he reached the next barrier of rocks. He knew that he could not run much farther. As it was, only the dreadful fear inspired by the heavy footsteps behind him kept him going. Actually, he was running over the same ground that his father had run a few months previously, when he had fled from Deutch, but, of course, he did not know that. He chose the same way up the rocks, and then, at the top, faltered, appalled by what he saw. Before him, as far as he could see, lay a wilderness of broken rock; on the right a headland jutted out towards the islet, but between him and it lay a jungle-filled ravine, through which, naked as he was, he could not hope to force a way. Yet he knew that barefoot on the sharp rocks the man would soon overtake him. With eyes round with despair, he looked for a hiding-place. There were several holes in the rock, some large, some small, and choosing one of them near the edge of the ravine, he jumped into it and lay flat on the bottom.

Motionless, with his hand over his mouth in an attempt to quiet his gasping breath, he heard the man arrive on the rocks, run forward a few paces, and then stop, obviously at

343

a loss to know what had become of him. Then he heard him move forward again. To his unspeakable horror, the footsteps approached his hiding-place. Again they stopped. He breathed again as they began to recede. But it was only for a moment. Slowly, with frequent halts, they came nearer again, and Dick knew that the man, the cut-throat the American had called Pedro, was examining the holes one by one.

Dick knew that if he persisted in this, discovery was inevitable, for the hole in which he lay was not more than five or six feet deep; yet his only chance now was to remain in it.

Slowly, but with dreadful deliberation, the padding steps came nearer. He could hear the heavy breathing of the searcher now. Nearer and nearer they came. Then, very close, they stopped, and in the dreadful silence his heart seemed to stop beating and he had to bite his lip to prevent himself from crying out. At last came the sound he dreaded to hear: a low, horrible chuckle. With a convulsive start he looked up. The man was standing on the lip of his hiding-place, grinning broadly as he whetted his razor on the palm of his hand. Then, dropping flat, he reached downward, and his fingers closed in Dick's hair.

A scream of stark terror that he could no longer repress broke from Dick's lips as he was hauled out, squirming, like a fish from a pool. The man took him in his left hand while his right swept back for the blow.

Instinctively, Dick threw up his arm to protect his throat. He closed his eyes, and kept them shut while an eternity seemed to pass. Then came a crashing report in his ears and he felt himself fall.

At that moment he thought that he was dead. He thought that the fatal blow had been struck. Curiously, he opened his eyes, and was surprised to find that he could still see. No startling alteration had taken place in the scene. The man was still standing there, although the expression on his face had changed. He was no longer smiling. The horrible grin had given way to an expression of comical surprise, and he swayed slowly to and fro like a big tree in a wind. A black hand jerked open and the razor fell, tinkling musically on the hard rock. The hand came up, groping at the breast of the blue coat. For three or four seconds Pedro stood thus; then his legs collapsed suddenly and he pitched forward on to his face.

Instantly, it seemed, his place was taken by another figure, a figure that confirmed Dick's conviction that he was no longer in the world of the living. It was the buccaneer, the ends of his red bandana flapping in the breeze. In his left hand he still carried the cutlass; in his right was a smoking pistol.

Dick stared at the face, speechless, his reeling brain trying to fit together the confusing pieces of a dreamlike jigsaw puzzle. 'Biggles!' he cried weakly.

Chapter 10

What Happened to Biggles

When Biggles, on the sinking aircraft, had been driven beyond the point of rock that hid him from the others' gaze, his position was not quite so desperate as it undoubtedly appeared to them. In the first place, the half empty tanks, and the air filled wings that still trailed behind the hull, gave it a certain degree of buoyancy. Secondly – and this, of course, they could not see – the wreck was being driven towards a small islet, little more than a big mound of rock, that rose out of the water some distance farther along, perhaps two hundred yards from the main island. It appeared to be a piece broken off the end of the island, the very tip of the crescent which in shape it resembled. Beyond it lay the open sea.

Biggles, watching with a degree of anxiety that can be better imagined than described, saw at once that if the wreck went ashore at the islet he might be able to climb up the face of the rock beyond the reach of the waves, from where, when the sea calmed down, he could swim to the island. On the other hand, if it was blown beyond the point, it would certainly be carried out to sea where it would quickly founder.

It was a close thing. At one time he thought he would strike the islet fairly in the centre, but at the last moment a contrary current, or a back-blast of wind, slewed the wreck sideways, so that it became obvious that it would miss it. Observing this, he took a desperate risk, although it was his only possible chance of salvation. He waited for a

346

momentary lull between the waves, and then jumped. He fell short, as he knew he would, but half a dozen desperate strokes took him to an out-jutting crag, to which he clung with the strength of despair. The next wave struck him before he could pull himself up, but he was prepared for it, and although what little breath he had left was beaten out of him by the force of the blow, and the backwash nearly tore his arms out of his body, he managed to drag himself above the water line, where, still drenched by spray, he sank down, utterly exhausted.

For some minutes he remained still, his face buried in his hands, elbows on his knees, while he recovered his strength; then, seeing that he was on the seaward side of the rock, he started climbing to the top, from where he hoped to obtain a view of the island and thus let Algy and Ginger know that he was at least temporarily safe.

Before he reached the actual peak, however, a surprise was in store for him. With a mild shock he realized that the stones over which he was climbing were artificial; that they were hand-hewn in great blocks, forming a sort of ramp, or bastion. It took him some time to find a way over them, but when he did, he saw to his astonishment that he stood in what, in the remote past, had been a fort. A low, castellated wall circumscribed the top of the knoll, which had been levelled and paved with flat stones. Placed at intervals, some pointing landward and some seaward, were six old-fashioned iron cannon on rotting wooden carriages. Small heaps of cannon-balls lay beside them.

Biggles stared about him blankly, realizing that he was standing in one of the many forts that had been established by the navigators and settlers in the great days of discovery.* At one corner a flight of stone steps led downward

* Such forts, with their old cannon still in place, still exist on many of the West Indian islands, and on the Main itself. WEJ

347

into the heart of the living rock, but with Dick's fate weighing heavily upon him, he was in no mood for exploration. Remembering the others, and the anxiety he knew they must be suffering, he walked over to the landward side, and leaning over the battlements, looked long and steadily at the island, hoping to see them. They were not in sight, however, so as the sea was still in such a state that it would have been suicidal to attempt to swim the channel, he sat down to await their arrival.

For once he was utterly sick at heart. Dick's fate, which he did not for one moment doubt, depressed him to the point of complete dejection. He had grown fond of the lad with his ever-ready cockney wit. The other things, bad as they were, did not really matter. The expedition had gone to pieces. They had lost two machines and all their belongings. They were stranded on an unknown island, without food, without clothes, without weapons – in fact, without anything. Never in all their adventures had they been in such a plight. Meanwhile, Deutch and his companions were no doubt on Treasure Island, using their machine, living on their stores, and perhaps unearthing the doubloons. The memory of the way he had been tricked made him writhe.

In this melancholy mood he could only sit and wait. Where were the others? Why didn't they come? Already the sun was far down; soon it would be dark. The sea was abating rapidly, but it would still be some time before he dare risk the swim. Pensively, he gazed at the rocks nearest to the islet, those on which he would have to land – the 'Land's End' of the island, now softly purple in the glow of the setting sun. Where were Algy and Ginger? Doubts began to assail him. Could it be possible that they had been washed back into the sea after all? Miserable, he could only stand and stare. If he could get to the island he might be able to do something. Looking down, he saw that the face of the rock below him was almost sheer, so he began to walk round the ramparts looking for the easiest way down when the time should come for him to go.

He was not greatly surprised when, on the side opposite to the one up which he had climbed, he saw a number of rough steps cut in the rock, evidently the path used by the builders, and afterwards by the garrison, when a ship called with stores. It struck him suddenly that there ought to be some sort of reservoir in or under the rock, possibly a tank for the collection of rain-water; otherwise the garrison could not have survived a siege; so, as the salt water had parched his mouth, he turned towards the flight of steps that went down apparently into the very heart of the islet. The passage was pitch dark, and it was with a feeling of expectant curiosity that he groped his way downward.

Before he reached the bottom he could see that light was coming in from somewhere, and presently he saw that it entered through cunningly cut apertures in the rock, which admitted just enough twilight for him to make out the details of the chamber in which he shortly found himself. A strange sensation that he was living in the past swept over him as he gazed around.

The interior of the fort was one large room some forty feet square, cut out of the living rock. It gave the appearance of having been hurriedly evacuated. A pile of old clothes lay in one corner, while others were thrown carelessly over an old brass swivel-gun that leaned against a loophole. Propped against the rear wall, curled up in positions which suggested a violent death, were two skeletons. Near the bony fingers of one lay a cutlass, pitted with the rust of centuries, while scattered about the floor were several flintlock muskets and pistols. The only other articles of note were six large barrels. Investigation showed that four of them had probably contained food, either salt pork or *boucan*, for some mouldering bones still remained in three of them, while the fourth was still half full of musty flour. The last two had been used for gunpowder, a little of which remained. In a corner, under a thick coating of dust, was a little pile of objects that looked like marbles. Biggles picked up a handful, but dropped them again at once; he knew by their weight that they were either musket balls, or grape-shot for the swivel gun. There was no sign of a water cistern.

For a little while he stood silent in the gathering gloom obsessed by a morbid depression as he pondered over the frailty of humanity. Who were these men who had left their bones so far from home? What grim tragedy had been enacted here? He could never know. No one would ever know. With a sigh he turned his back on the dismal scene, preferring to wait in the fresh air above, but at the foot of the steps a thought occurred to him, and he strode back to the pile of clothes. He might as well go clad, he thought, if only as a protection against the briers and the mosquitoes which he suspected would soon appear.

He selected three garments: a shirt woven in a pattern of broad horizontal bands, a pair of reddish-coloured breeches, and a spotted handkerchief to tie about his head. They smelt stale, musty, but he did not mind that, for the morrow's sun would, he knew, purify them. Hunting about, he found a pair of old boots that fitted him, also a piece of tarpaulin, and this he took in order to keep the other things dry during his proposed swim to the island. At the last minute, with a curious smile playing about his mouth, he added a brace of pistols, some bullets and a flask of powder. The flask, once soft leather, was as hard as iron, but it still served its purpose. Satisfied that there was nothing more worth taking, he put the things he had selected on the tarpaulin, tied the ends together, and thrusting the cutlass under the knots as a means of carrying the bundle more easily, he returned to the battlements.

He saw at once that the sea had gone down as swiftly as it had got up, and, moreover, the tide had ebbed considerably, lessening the distance of the swim; so, throwing his leg over the low wall, he made his way down the outside steps to the water. Another minute and he had slid gently into it. Then, by swimming on his back and holding his burden clear of the water, he was able to reach the rocks opposite without the contents getting wet.

Finding a convenient place, he shook as much water off himself as possible, after which he donned the old-fashioned garments. This done, he looked about him. The moon had risen; and everything was very still. What dangers lurked, if any? He did not know, but having brought the pistols, he thought he might as well load them, so this he did, and leaving the hammers down for safety, he stuck them in the top of his pantaloons as the easiest way of carrying them. Then, cutlass in hand, he set off along the beach towards the spot where Dick had fallen, and where he had last seen Algy and Ginger on the weed-covered rocks. It still struck him as extraordinary that they had not appeared.

Reaching the spot, he searched the foreshore carefully, but all he found was Dick's jacket, which was lying where Ginger had dropped it when he had heard the distant shot. Slowly he walked on, still searching, dreading to find what he sought, until further progress was interrupted by another barrier of rock. He looked at it for some minutes, and then, deciding that there was no point in going on, he returned to the place where he had landed on the island. On the high-water mark he found some coconuts that had been brought down by the recent hurricane. These he collected, and breaking them with his cutlass, drank the milk with

351

relish. Then, utterly worn out by the day's fatigues, he lay down to rest until the morning.

For a long time he could not sleep. The fate of the others haunted him, but at last, towards dawn, he must have dropped off, for it was broad daylight when a piercing scream of fear brought him staggering to his feet. For a second or two he stood blinking, fighting for complete consciousness, wondering where he was, and if the scream had been part of the nightmare that had disturbed his rest. But then he saw a movement, and knew that it was no dream. Fifty yards away an enormous black man was kneeling, reaching down for something he could not see. Wonderingly, he began to walk towards him, watching with interest as he got to his feet, dragging something up with him. Unbelievingly, he saw that it was Dick. The whole thing was fantastic, but too vivid to be anything but reality. He saw the man's arm go up, and caught the flash of steel. Whipping out a pistol, he dashed forward. At ten yards, seeing that he would be too late if he did not act, he took swift aim and fired. The pistol roared. The man twitched convulsively. Dick slumped to the ground. A razor tinkled on the rock.

Biggles ran forward again just as the man pitched headlong.

Chapter 11

The Rescue

Biggles stooped, caught Dick by the arm and helped him to his feet. 'You're all right now, laddie,' he said kindly. 'I was just about in time, wasn't I?' he added gravely.

Dick nodded. He was too far gone to speak. The sky seemed to be turning purple. His strength seemed to be running out of his feet.

'Here! Hold up!' cried Biggles sharply. 'We don't allow fainting.'

Dick forced a sickly grin. 'Sorry,' he said, wiping beads of perspiration from his forehead with the back of his hand. 'I thought I was a goner that time.'

'Yes,' agreed Biggles. 'It was touch and go.' As he spoke his eyes focused suddenly on a point just beyond where they were standing. 'Take a look at that,' he said in a low voice, indicating something that lay on the ground. 'It should give you something to think about.'

Dick's eyes followed the point of the rusty blade. He saw Pedro, lying face downwards. On the water-worn rock a few inches from his outflung right hand was a little yellow disk. It was the doubloon.

'As I have remarked before, that coin doesn't seem to bring its owner much luck, does it?' remarked Biggles suspiciously. 'Don't touch it,' he went on sharply, as Dick moved towards it with the obvious intention of picking it up.

'Are you going to leave it lying there?'

Biggles shook his head, the corners of his mouth turned

353

down. 'I think the sooner it's out of sight the better,' he said grimly. 'I've seen enough of the confounded thing, anyway,' he added almost viciously, as he walked over to the coin. Then abruptly, with the sole of his boot, he kicked it sideways into the hole in which Dick had sought refuge. 'That's that,' he muttered, as it disappeared from sight. 'Now then, my lad, we've got a lot to talk about. I don't mind telling you that you're the last person I expected to meet here. Have you seen anything of Algy or Ginger?'

'I jolly well have!' declared Dick emphatically. 'I was trying to get them away when this devil woke up and chased me.'

'Get them away? Then they're alive! Thank God for that.' Biggles's fervent tone of voice revealed the depth of his relief.

'They're prisoners,' explained Dick quickly.

Biggles stared. 'Prisoners!' he ejaculated.

Briefly Dick described his adventures which had led to the present situation.

When he had finished Biggles drew a deep breath. 'We must get them out of the clutches of these thugs right away,' he declared.

Dick glanced at the figure lying on the ground. 'What about – him?' he asked.

'I can't stop to attend to him now,' answered Biggles coldly. 'His pals will have to do that.' As he spoke, Biggles reloaded the pistol he had fired. 'Bring that razor along,' he ordered. 'If Algy and Ginger are still tied up it will be useful.'

'Where the dickens did you get these things you're wearing?' asked Dick curiously. 'Great Scott! It must have been you I saw last night,' he went on quickly, remembering his moonlight adventure. 'I took you for the ghost of a buccaneer.'

'They were in an old fort I found over there on that islet,' replied Biggles. 'I haven't time to tell you all about it now. I'm worried about the others. Come on, let's march.'

'Are you going to attack the whole gang?' inquired Dick as they walked along the beach in the direction of the lagoon.

'I don't know. We'll spy out the land first, and make our plans afterwards,' replied Biggles. 'I wouldn't hesitate to attack except for one thing, and that's this fellow the American told us about, 'Frisco Jack. Apparently he's by way of being an expert with a revolver, so it would be asking for trouble to get within range of his guns. These pistols I've got are better than nothing, but I wouldn't bet on their accuracy outside a dozen yards. Anyway, I should be sorry to take on 'Frisco Jack with a revolver — Hark! What's that?' He broke off sharply as a loud hail rang out not far away. It appeared to come from the far side of the first barrier of rocks over which they were about to climb, so he crept quietly to the top and peeped over. He was down again in an instant, and grabbed Dick by the arm. 'Quick!' he whispered. 'Into the bushes.'

Dick followed him to the edge of the jungle, and by keeping close behind as he forced a passage, was able to follow without scratching himself very badly. 'Who is it?' he breathed.

''Frisco Jack, I suspect, and he's coming this way. He's probably looking for his friend, or else he's wondering who fired the shot. Not a word; this may be a bit of luck for us.'

From their place of concealment they were able to watch the ex-gangster's movements. He appeared on the top of the barrier, and from this point of vantage gazed along the shore. 'Hi! Pedro!' he hailed. Then, suddenly, he saw the man lying on the rocks where he had fallen, and with a terse oath ran towards him.

'Come on, this is our chance,' breathed Biggles, and began to force a passage to the beach, making for the far side of the rocks, a position in which the American would not be able to see them. Thrusting the bushes aside with as little noise as possible, they soon reached their objective.

'Now then, where is the place you last saw Algy and Ginger?' asked Biggles crisply.

Dick pointed to the next barrier of rocks, the landslide on which grew the clump of coconut palms. 'Just over the other side of that,' he answered.

'Then let's run for it, and try to get there before 'Frisco Jack comes back,' announced Biggles, and suiting the action to the word, he set off at a steady run, glancing round occasionally to see if 'Frisco Jack had reappeared.

To his intense satisfaction there was still no sign of him when they slowed down near the landslide. 'Now then, Dick,' he said quietly. 'This is where you will have to show your mettle. If we don't rescue Algy and Ginger now we may never get another chance. It's no time for half-measures. We shall have to go the whole hog. I don't go about the world shooting at people for the sake of stirring up strife, but, by thunder, when other people start the row I do my best to make things hot for them. We haven't more than two people to tackle, Deutch and the fellow who stole our ship – what's his name? – Harvey. When I stick 'em up at the point of the pistol, you run down and cut the others free. Keep your head down, because if they start any rough stuff I shall let fly. With luck, we ought to be able to rescue Algy and Ginger and get our machine back at the same time. Anyway, that's what I'm aiming to do. But whatever happens, once we've shown ourselves, you must get on with your job, which is to get the others free. Is that clear?'

'Absolutely.'

'Good! Then let's get at 'em.'

With pistol in one hand and cutlass in the other, Biggles ran quickly to the top of the rock. Dick, the razor open and gripped firmly, followed. From the ridge they looked down into the lagoon, and although they could see the aircraft, now close to the gap that led to the open sea, and the canoe lying on the sand, there was no sign of the men they sought.

'They're behind the rocks, over there,' said Dick tensely, pointing with the razor. 'That's where they've made their camp.'

Their feet making no noise on the soft sand, they crept forward and peeped round the outcrop of rock that hid the enemy camp from view. Not more than six paces away sat Deutch, cross-legged, eating something out of a tin. Ginger and Algy were still lying on the ground. Harvey was not there.

Biggles levelled his pistol. 'Hands up, Mr Deutch – and keep them up,' he ordered harshly. 'Any argument from you and I'll blow you in halves. And if you have any doubt about that, just try it,' he added vindictively. 'Go ahead, Dick.'

The expression on Deutch's face was almost comical in its astonishment, but he dropped the tin and raised his hands. Biggles walked over to him and clapped the muzzle of the pistol to his head. 'Keep quite still, please,' he murmured as his eyes darted this way and that, seeking the other man he expected to find. Satisfied that he was not there, he looked towards the spot where Dick was helping the others. Ginger was trying to get on his feet. Algy, his face twisted with pain, was massaging his ankles.

Biggles's lips set in a hard line as he realized what had happened, that the tightness of the cords had temporarily crippled them. 'Dick!' he called. 'Come here.'

Dick ran to him as an obedient dog answers its master.

'Take hold of the handle of this pistol,' ordered Biggles. 'If you feel the muzzle move, don't speak – just pull the trigger.' He relinquished the weapon and went swiftly through Deutch's pockets. Among other things he found a revolver, which he transferred to his left hand, and the maps that had been taken from them at Marabina. He did not particularly want them, but he kept them. This done, he went quickly to Algy and Ginger. One glance, and he saw that it would be some minutes before they would be in a fit state to travel, for their wrists and ankles were badly swollen. 'All right,' he said quietly, 'take your time. Keep rubbing them. Let me know when you think you can hobble as far as the canoe.'

'You're going to take the machine, then, are you?' asked Algy quickly, as he understood what Biggles meant.

'You bet your life I am,' returned Biggles promptly. 'I — what the—'

He spun round as a musical whirr reached his ears. He knew instantly what it was. Someone was operating the self-starter in the amphibian, but before he could do anything – indeed, almost before he was able to move – the engines had sprung to life and the machine was taxiing through the breach in the coral reef out on to the open sea. He dashed forward, although he knew it was useless from the start. Before he had taken a dozen steps the amphibian was racing over the water, leaving a creamy trail to mark its passage. With bitter chagrin on his face he returned to the others. 'It must be Harvey,' he said angrily. 'I expected to find him here, and I looked for him, but for some reason or other I did not think of the machine. Well, there he goes; he's one less to contend with, anyway.'

Deutch's face registered vicious satisfaction as the amphibian soared skyward.

Biggles's eyes narrowed. 'I think perhaps a little of your own medicine wouldn't do you any harm,' he murmured vindictively. 'Ginger, just knot those pieces of cord together and truss him up.'

Ginger smiled as he moved forward to obey. 'OK,' he said cheerfully.

'Dick,' went on Biggles, 'go and take a look over the rock to see if 'Frisco is on his way back yet. Give the pistol to Algy; he can take care of Deutch for a minute or two.'

Dick handed over his charge and ran lightly to the top of the rock. One glance, and he was on his way back, gesticulating urgently. 'Buck up! He's coming!' he cried.

Biggles started. 'How far away is he?'

'Not more than a hundred yards, but he's coming very slowly because he's helping Pedro along.'

Biggles thought swiftly. 'Stand by, everybody,' he ordered crisply. 'We shall have to be going.'

Algy raised his eyebrows. 'Are you going to run away from that cheap American crook?' he snorted angrily.

'I am,' replied Biggles curtly. 'I don't believe in taking unnecessary risks. He may be a cheap crook, but he's also a sharp-shooter. If it comes to a shooting match, sooner or later someone will get in the way of a bullet, and it is more likely to be one of us than him. I'd sooner leave him running loose than one of us should get plugged in a place like this where there's no chance of getting medical attention. Let's get out of his way; there will be plenty of time for sniping before we're off this island, if I know anything about it. Come on, jump to it.'

Algy looked at the mass of rock that cut off their retreat on one side, and the thick jungle behind them. 'Which way are you going?' he questioned.

'That way!' Biggles pointed to the sea. 'Dick – Ginger, get down to the canoe and put her on the water. Algy, give me a hand with some of this stuff. We may as well take as much of our own property with us as we can.' He hurried to the pile of stores which their enemies had taken out of the amphibian and began making a heap of those things which he thought would be of most benefit, chiefly tinned foodstuffs.

Algy helped him to carry the stores down to the boat,

which without further delay was pushed off into deep water. Heavily loaded, the rather flimsy craft had only an inch or two of freeboard, but as the sea was flat calm there was little danger of her swamping.

'You guys think you're pretty smart, but I haven't finished with you yet, not by a long shot,' shouted Deutch furiously. 'You wait!'

'We'll be waiting,' promised Biggles as he picked up the paddle and sent the little craft skimming towards the open sea.

'Hey, 'Frisco!' roared Deutch. 'Help! Quick!'

There was an answering shout from the other side of the rock.

'Keep steady if 'Frisco opens fire, or we may capsize,' ordered Biggles tersely as he put his weight behind the paddle.

The boat was about a hundred and fifty yards from the shore when 'Frisco Jack dashed round the corner.

'He's seen us,' said Algy quietly. 'He's got his gun in his hand, and he's running out on to the rocks to get as near to us as he can.'

'I don't think he'll hit us at this distance,' replied Biggles calmly, as he continued to drive the boat through the water. 'Outside a hundred yards revolver shooting becomes pure chance.'

A moment later 'Frisco's automatic crashed, but the bullet that ricochetted off the water was several feet away.

Biggles continued to paddle. 'Take a shot at him, Algy; it will upset his shooting,' ordered Biggles, knowing from experience that it is much more difficult for a marksman to take careful aim when he himself is under fire than when he knows he is secure.

The pistol roared, and they heard the shrill scream of the bullet as it glanced off a rock.

'Frisco continued to fire, but the range was getting longer

every second, and presently he gave it up, and returned to the beach where Deutch was yelling to be released.

Biggles turned the nose of the canoe to the left and took up a new course, keeping parallel with the shore.

'Where are you making for?' asked Algy.

'Can you see an islet just off the end of the island, about half a mile or so ahead?'

'Yes.'

'I think that's the best place for us. We can watch the shore from there, so there will be no risk of a surprise attack while we do two things that are getting overdue. The first is eat, and the other is talk. It's time we had a council of war and reviewed the position, as they say in books.'

'The thing that intrigues me most is, where the deuce you got that amazing clobber you're wearing,' said Ginger curiously.

'I'll tell you about that presently,' answered Biggles, pausing to wipe the perspiration from his forehead, for the sun was now getting very hot. 'Couldn't you fellows find any place to land without barging into Deutch and his crowd?' he inquired caustically.

'You can bet we didn't join him from choice,' replied Algy sarcastically.

Biggles resumed his task and nothing more was said until they reached their objective. He did not land immediately, as Deutch and 'Frisco Jack were standing out on the rocks watching them; instead he passed straight on until the islet was between them and the lagoon, thus concealing their movements. Then, still keeping out of sight, he backed the canoe slowly to the foot of the steps that gave access to the fort. 'Up you go,' he said, looking for something to which to make the painter fast. 'Take the grub with you.'

'Why, what are *you* going to do?' asked Algy.

'I'm just going to slip across to the island for a few coconuts,' returned Biggles. 'I don't know about you, but I could do with a drink. I'll join you in a minute.' As he spoke, he pushed the now lightened canoe clear, and sent it skimming towards the island.

Chapter 12

A Lucky Fall

When he came back, and, after making the canoe secure, climbed up to the fort, he found the others still marvelling at it. They were agog with enthusiasm and excitement, pardonable in the circumstances, for it was impossible for anyone with imagination to be in such a place without feeling something of its romantic, if tragic, associations.

'How on earth did you come to discover it?' asked Ginger.

'To tell the truth, I didn't exactly discover it,' admitted Biggles. 'It was shoved under my nose, so to speak. In other words, this is where I managed to get ashore. Naturally, I climbed to the top to see if I could see anything of you on the island, and this is what I found.'

'But where did you get those clothes?' asked Algy, for the others had not yet been below.

'Downstairs.'

'Are there any more?'

'Quite a lot – of sorts.'

There was a rush for the stairway while Biggles remained on the roof in order to watch the distant lagoon. From where he stood it was just possible to see it, which he realized at once was a great advantage, since it enabled them to keep an eye on their enemies without going ashore. At that moment Deutch and 'Frisco Jack were bending over a dark object on the ground; he thought it was Pedro, and he was still watching them when a cry from below sent him hurrying down.

363

'Did you know this was here?' asked Algy, pointing to another flight of stairs, leading downwards, which had been exposed by the removal of a stone slab in the centre of which was an iron ring.

'No, I'm dashed if I did,' admitted Biggles. 'I looked for it, too. I suppose I didn't see it because it was buried under those rags.' He pointed to the old clothes that had been turned over and now lay scattered about the floor.

'You looked for it? You mean, you suspected it was there?'

'I thought it was bound to be somewhere.'

'What do you think it is?'

'A water tank, to store the rain water that falls on the roof. How could anyone live here without water? No doubt there is water somewhere on the island, but that wouldn't be much good to a beleaguered garrison. If you go upstairs you can see the hole which drains the roof; the water must run straight through a duct into here. Is there any water in it now, I wonder?'

Biggles picked up one of the bullets from the heap on the floor and tossed it through the yawning hole. A soft splash told him what he wanted to know. 'Draw some up and let's have a look at it,' he said. 'There's the bucket.' He pointed to a black, cylindrical object that lay among the old clothes. Like the powder-flask, it had once been leather, but now, having perished, it was as hard as wood.

Algy picked it up, went down the steps till he reached the water, dipped the utensil in, and returned with it squirting water through several cracks.

Biggles took some up in the palm of his hand and tested it with his lips. 'Seems to be all right,' he said, 'but I'd rather not use it unless I was compelled. I prefer fresh coconut milk. Put the lid back on or someone might tumble in. And let's have a bite to eat; I'm hungry.' Turning away from the reservoir, he smiled broadly as, for the first time, he took in the details of the garments the others had selected. In turning over the old clothes they had all found something to suit themselves.

Algy wore a moth-eaten red shirt with a pair of what had once been white breeches that fitted tightly at the knees. On his head was a chimney-pot hat of the sort commonly worn by sailors during the sixteenth and seventeenth centuries. Ginger had selected a blue and white banded shirt like his own; there was a small hole, with a dark, sinister stain round it, in the breast. Dirty calico trousers covered his lower half. For headgear he had chosen a black, three-cornered hat. Dick, for whom everything had been too large, wore a faded blue silk shirt, which he had tied in round the waist with an old belt, so that the lower part formed a sort of kilt, or skirt. Through the belt he had thrust a large pistol. On his head, pulled down well over his ears, was a crimson night-cap with a tassel on the end.

Biggles looked at him in mock terror. 'By thunder! Israel Hands himself!' he gasped. 'All we need is a Jolly Roger to fly at the peak and we should look as bonny a bunch of pirates as ever boarded a prize or sacked a town.'

The others laughed.

'Israel Hands was one of the pirates in Stevenson's story *Treasure Island*, wasn't he?' asked Ginger. 'I read it once, but that was a long time ago.'

'Stevenson only borrowed the name for his book,' Biggles informed him. 'The original Israel Hands was quarter-master to that shocking ruffian Captain Edward Teach, more often known as Blackbeard, perhaps the most blood-thirsty villain of the whole cut-throat crowd, excepting possibly Louis Dakeyne, sometimes called Louis the Grand, who bestowed upon himself the pleasing nickname The Exterminator. Louis, by the way, claimed to be the originator of "walking the plank" as a handy means of disposing of his victims.'

'What happened to him at the finish?' asked Dick. 'Did he sun-dry at Execution Dock, like most of the others?'

'As a matter of fact, nobody knows what did become of him,' answered Biggles. 'Speaking from memory, I believe he was the fellow who disappeared just after he had captured a whacking great galleon – much to the relief of every honest sailor engaged in the West Indian trade. I expect he was drowned. Most of the pirates died with their boots on. It's funny to think that some of them may have stood on this very spot, isn't it?'

'Talking of treasure and treasure islands, this must be *our* treasure island, surely, or Deutch wouldn't be here?' suggested Algy.

'I don't think there's much doubt about that,' answered Biggles. 'It struck me as soon as Dick told me that Deutch was here, with our machine, that we had at last reached the place we set out for. What's more, according to the map made by Dick's father, we must be within a quarter of a mile of the old ship he talks about in his letter.' Biggles took the map, which he had recovered from Deutch, from his pocket. 'I made some alterations on it, as I told you,' he continued, 'but in its original form, the cross that marked the position of the ship was up here, at the most northerly point of the island, which is the point immediately opposite to us. This islet we are on is the one marked. We'll go over to the island and have a look round as soon as we've had something to eat, providing Deutch and Co. keep out of the way. It won't do to let them see where we are searching or they'll spot what's afoot and want to join in the fun.'

'Come on, then, let's eat,' cried Dick excitedly.

'We'd better bring the food down here,' suggested Biggles. 'It will be blazing hot on top, in the sun, and Deutch won't be able to see us if we keep below. It will be to our advantage if he doesn't know where we are.'

There was a rush up the stairs, and the stores which they had brought in the canoe, as well as the coconuts Biggles had fetched from the island, were carried below. There was nothing to sit on except the floor, but that did not worry them.

'I don't like the idea of these gentlemen watching us as we eat,' protested Algy with a sidelong glance at the two skeletons.

'They won't hurt us. Dead men don't bite,' retorted Biggles lightly.

While the meal was in progress Algy and Ginger described their adventures, which had ended in their falling into the enemy's hands, after which, for their benefit, Dick told his, describing how he had been rescued by Biggles from Pedro. In this way the time passed quickly, and it was well after midday by the time their hunger was satisfied and the stories told.

Biggles made a little pile of the coconut shells, which they had used as cups after eating their contents. 'Taking it generally, the position has become rather peculiar,' he observed thoughtfully. 'We are here, and Deutch is here, and neither side can get away – at least, not until Harvey comes back with the machine. Where has he gone? Why hasn't he returned? When he first took off I thought, naturally, that he had seen what was happening ashore and was simply concerned with saving the aircraft. Yet if that was the case, one would have expected him to hang around waiting for a chance to get back to the others. Instead, he went straight off as if he was going on an errand; and don't overlook the fact that the course he took up would take him to Marabina – or somewhere near it. I can't help thinking that that is where he has gone. Yet what reason could he have for going back there?'

'He may have gone to fetch some more stores,' suggested Ginger.

'They had ours at their disposal. There must have been ample for their present needs.'

'He may have gone to fetch some tools – shovels and things – to dig for the treasure.'

'Possibly, but knowing the sort of job on which they were engaged, one would have thought that they would have brought such things with them. *We* didn't bring any because we happened to know that they were unnecessary – that is, assuming that the treasure is somewhere in the ship.'

'Do you think Harvey might have lost his nerve and bolted, leaving the others to take care of themselves?' ventured Dick.

'There is just a chance of it, but, somehow, I find that difficult to accept,' returned Biggles shaking his head. 'Men of his stamp don't run away while there is a chance of sharing a treasure. But there, it's no use guessing. If he doesn't come back, then, treasure or no treasure, we're in for a pretty thin time. It's bad enough being marooned on a place like this – for make no mistake, we shall soon get sick of the sight of coconuts when our stores are finished – but when, into the bargain, there's a fellow like 'Frisco Jack prowling about taking pot shots at us, the ordeal is likely to become even more trying. We have only enough food for two or three days at the most; after that we shall have to rely on coconuts.'

'Deutch and Co. will have to do the same thing,' Algy pointed out.

'I know all about that,' agreed Biggles, 'but our position is a very different one from theirs. We should hesitate to shoot them in cold blood, even if we had an opportunity, whereas they'll try to bump us off at the first chance they get.'

'Well, thank goodness one of them is out of action,' declared Dick fervently.

'I thought I'd killed him, but apparently I didn't,' murmured Biggles. 'Still, I fancy he must be pretty sick. Let's go on deck and see what they're up to. Incidentally, from now on we had better mount guards, or they may catch us napping one day.'

'Well, I reckon it's all good fun,' observed Dick optimistically. 'When I read *Treasure Island* at school I never thought the day would come when I'd be on one myself.'

Biggles smiled. 'It's funny, isn't it?' he murmured. 'As a matter of fact, now one comes to think about it, the position here is not unlike the critical situation in the story. Deutch and his confederates are Long John Silver and the pirates, and we—' Biggles grinned delightedly '—why, dash it, it works out exactly. Dick here is Jim Hawkins, Algy is Squire Trelawny, Ginger is Doctor Live-say, and I'm—'

'Captain Smollett,' put in Dick promptly.

Biggles sprang to his feet and bowed. 'At your service, gentlemen. With your assistance we shall yet see Long John Silver – I mean Deutch – sun-drying at Execution Dock. Yes, sir, or my name's not Captain Smollett, and you may lay to that. Avast there! All hands on deck, and step lively, please; let us see what the rascals are at.'

Algy struck a pose. 'By my wig, Captain, you're right, as usual. Stand by for the doubloons.'

They all laughed and then filed up to the roof, from where they could see Pedro still lying on the shore of the lagoon, with Deutch and 'Frisco Jack sitting beside him.

'Don't show yourselves,' warned Biggles.

'Are we going ashore?' inquired Dick excitedly.

Biggles nodded. 'Yes, I think it's safe for us to go and have a look round,' he answered. 'But we had better all be armed. For goodness' sake be careful with these old weapons, though, or we shall have an accident. Dick, is that pistol of yours loaded?'

'No.'

'All right; I'll show you how to load it. Algy – Ginger, you'd better take a musket apiece.'

They went below again where they selected their weapons and loaded them. This done, they returned to the roof and then descended the steps to where the canoe was moored. A few minutes later they were on the island, landing on the rocks of the point, where they lifted the boat into a fissure just above the high-water mark. Satisfied that the coast was clear, they made their way to the top of the headland, where Biggles stopped and surveyed the ground ahead. It was nothing but a matted jungle of bushes, huge cacti, and trailing lianas, and after regarding it for some minutes he shook his head.

'I don't see any galleons lying about, do you?' he asked the others generally.

'It doesn't look the sort of place where you'd expect to find one – at least, not to me,' answered Algy. 'If the wreck is somewhere under this tangle of bushes, then we're in for a long job. It would take an army of men weeks to clear them.'

'Well, let's go and have a look,' replied Biggles. 'I didn't expect to find it with the masts still standing and flags flying; in fact, if you remember, I prophesied that finding the ship was likely to be more difficult than the map might lead one to suppose; but, I must say, now that we are here, it is even worse than I expected. Let's go on for a bit.'

For nearly two hours they searched, thrusting their way into the tangle wherever an opening presented itself, staring about, stamping on the ground, and climbing such elevations as commanded a wider view of the lower ground. Slowly, for it was impossible to move quickly on account of the vegetation, they made their way across the depression that could just be distinguished, until at last they stood on the bare rocks at the far side, where Pedro had overtaken Dick.

Biggles sat down on a boulder and mopped his forehead with his sleeve. 'Phew! This is warm work,' he declared. 'We shall soon have to be getting back; the daylight won't last much longer. We'd better start collecting some nuts to eke out our bully beef, and postpone further operations until tomorrow. In fact, I think it would be a good thing to lay in a good store of nuts while we've got the chance; there are only two or three left in the fort. Dick, go and take a peep over the ridge to make sure the beach is clear. Deutch or 'Frisco may come along, and I'd rather not have a clash if it can be avoided.'

Dick ran off to obey the order, while Ginger and Algy walked towards a little colony of coconut palms that fringed the edge of the jungle not far away; but before they had taken a dozen paces their progress was arrested by Dick, who came dashing back with alarm on his face. 'Look out!' he hissed. ''Frisco and Deutch are coming this way!'

Biggles spun round. 'How far away are they?'

'They are just over the other side of the rock – not more than a stone's throw,' whispered Dick tersely. 'They are creeping along in the shadow of the bushes.'

'Confound them!' Biggles looked annoyed. 'They'll see us as we go across if we try to get to the islet. What a nuisance. I think we'd better get down over the front of the headland and wait by the boat until they go back. Come on, I believe we can get through here.'

With the others following close behind, he led the way at a brisk trot towards a place where the network of briers and lianas appeared to be less dense than usual, in order to reach the far side of the depression previously mentioned, which seemed to stretch from the sea to some distance inland. It was, in fact, the same weak place in the undergrowth that Dick's father had selected as a hiding-place when he had been pursued by Deutch a few months

371

previously, so what followed was not really so much a coincidence as a direct example of cause and effect.

They had almost reached the centre of the depression when Biggles stumbled over a long, round, moss-covered object that lay across their path. 'Hello! What's this?' he muttered, stooping down in order to look along the object for its full length, for it struck him suddenly that it was far too straight and symmetrical to be anything but artificial. It was, in fact, the fallen mainmast of the galleon, and a suspicion of this had just flashed into his mind when Algy, in endeavouring to remove a thorn from his foot, fell forward, and clutched at him for support. Unprepared, Biggles lost his balance, and grabbing wildly at a sapling to save himself, he fell, with Algy on top of him. Instantly there was a loud crack and the ground under them began to sag.

'Look out! The ground's caving in!' gasped Biggles in affright as he struggled to get to his feet. He opened his mouth again to speak, but the words never came. With a soft splintering crash, the rotting, moss-covered timbers of the galleon's deck collapsed, and the next moment they were all precipitated through a gaping hole, landing on the floor, some eight or ten feet lower, with varying degrees of shock.

Biggles was first on his feet, breathing heavily. 'Great Scott! What's happened?' he cried, looking quickly about him. His eyes told him the truth, but even so, he could only stare incredulously, while the others, with groans and mutterings, got up.

'What the—' began Algy, but his astonishment was such that he could get no further.

'I think this is what we've been looking for,' observed Biggles, recovering his self-control as he brushed moss and dirt from his clothes. 'We fell into it, as you might say. I — hark!' He broke off, listening intently.

From not far away came the sound of a human voice. It was Deutch's, and the words reached them clearly. 'I tell you I heard 'em somewhere about here, not a minute ago,' he said.

Biggles laid his finger on his lips warningly. 'Don't speak,' he breathed.

Silently Algy stooped and picked up his musket, which had, of course, fallen in with him. Ginger did the same. Then they all gazed upwards at the breach in the deck through which a shaft of greenish light filtered.

'It must have been a pig, or an animal of some sort,' came 'Frisco's voice doubtfully.

'I tell you I heard 'em talking,' declared Deutch emphatically.

'Then they must have bolted when they heard us coming,' asserted 'Frisco Jack. 'Anyway, there ain't no sense in standing here; the big guy's got a gun, and I don't wanna get plugged through the back, like Pedro. There will be plenty of time to attend to them tomorrow. Let's get back.'

Apparently Deutch acquiesced, for the sound of footsteps, slowly receding, reached the ears of the listeners. Biggles waited for some time to make sure that they had gone before he spoke, but at last he turned to the others. 'Good!' he whispered. 'I think they've gone back. Let's do a bit of exploring.'

Chapter 13

Revelations

Biggles and his companions had not fallen into the galleon in the same place as Dick's father, who had crashed through into the saloon, which, in accordance with the usual practice of the period in which the ship was built, was situated in the poop. They were, as Biggles pointed out, in the fo'castle, which they saw at once was precisely as it had been abandoned, except that what had once been blankets were now mouldering heaps of mildew from which sprouted unhealthy-looking growths of green fungus. Indeed, from them and the few odd articles of clothing that lay about rose an unwholesome stench of corruption and decay. There was little else there of interest except a few weapons, corroded with rust, that had been discarded by the last of the pirates when they had abandoned the ship. Anything of value had been taken with them.

'I don't think we shall find any treasure here,' said Biggles, speaking in an awed whisper, for even he found it impossible not to be affected by the mournful atmosphere of things long dead.

Slowly, almost reverently, they made their way through the waist of the ship, past long-silent cannon, their muzzles half buried in the silt of ages, cannon-balls, powder barrels – some still full – grappling irons – the same that had held the ill-fated *Rose of Bristol* – ropes, blocks, and tackle, all of which they could just see in the eerie light that crept through the cracks in the warping timbers.

'Quite apart from any treasure, this ship ought to be put

into a museum just as it is,' said Biggles quietly. 'I doubt very much if there is another in the same state of preservation in the world, and a lot of people would like to see just how a vessel of this period and class was equipped. I wouldn't have missed it for anything. Unless I am mistaken, we have made a discovery that will cause a sensation at home when it becomes known, particularly among sailors and people interested in the sea.'

Slowly they walked on, staring about them like tourists in the cloisters of an old cathedral. Biggles pointed to a stone jar with a narrow neck, on the bulging sides of which were stamped, in large, black letters, BEST OLD JAMAICA. 'Yo ho ho, and a bottle of rum,' he quoted, singing Stevenson's famous lines with a morbid sort of humour.

Algy nodded thoughtfully as he regarded the old rum puncheon. 'It certainly looks as if "Drink and the devil have done for the rest",' he observed.

They wandered on until at last they came to a companionway leading upwards. They tested the timbers and, finding them sound, went up. From the top they could see a shaft of pale light falling obliquely across a large room a short distance in front of them. Wonderingly, they made their way towards it, and a moment later they were standing in the captain's saloon, which took up most of the high stern.

Biggles pointed to a jagged hole in the upper deck. Immediately below it lay a quantity of debris, dead moss and the like. 'That, Dick, is where your father must have fallen through,' he said in a low voice.

Dick looked up, fighting to keep back the tears that dimmed his eyes. The fact that his father had stood on the very spot on which he was now standing brought his memory back very clearly. But his grief was short-lived, for there were other things to think of.

'Great heavens above! Look at this!' whispered Biggles, in an awe-stricken voice, shaking his head slowly like a man who finds it hard to believe what he sees. The others, looking about them, were too deeply moved for words.

The room was sumptuously furnished. Around the walls, in panels between the gilded lights, were painted pictures of saints and other holy scenes. The whole floor was covered by a magnificent eastern carpet, woven in rich shades of blue and crimson; on it, placed end to end around the outskirts, were several iron-bound chests, with huge, elaborate locks. Most of them were open. Set against the forward bulkhead was a magnificent walnut desk, exquisitely carved, but it was towards a gruesome figure that leaned over it from a high-backed, brass-studded chair, padded with scarlet velvet, that all eyes were irresistibly drawn. It was a skeleton, to which the clothes still clung with dreadful realism.

Biggles, war-hardened, went up to it. A trifle pale, he glanced at the grinning mouth and empty sockets, and then ran his eyes over the details of the clothes. 'This was a Spanish ship,' he said, his voice sounding strangely loud in the eerie silence. 'But this man was no Spaniard; his clothes are more suggestive of a pirate. He must have been the last survivor of some ill-fated crew. What evil fate overtook him, I wonder? What tale of tragedy could he tell if he could speak? It was on this desk that Dick's father found the gold doubloon.' He picked up the silver-mounted pistol, still lying where it had fallen so long ago, and examined it – the first hand to touch it since the pirate's fatal day. 'It has been discharged,' he went on quietly, as if to himself. 'I wonder ... I wonder ...' He moved the figure slightly. 'Look!' he said, in a hard, strained voice.

The others came closer to see what had attracted his attention, and this is what they saw. The bony fingers of the skeleton's right hand were pressed to the faded material that still covered the place where the stomach had once been. Under them was a round hole with scorched edges, and a tell-tale stain. Biggles looked down at the floor and caught his breath. His face turned a shade paler. 'Holy smoke!' he breathed, moistening his lips. 'He died by his own pistol. Look!' The others looked down. On the carpet, around the booted feet of the long-dead pirate, was the black, sinister mark that had been made by his drying blood.

'Pretty grim, isn't it?' went on Biggles, recovering some of his self-possession, and moving the skeleton back to its original position. As he did so, something fell heavily to the floor. Almost with repugnance he stooped and picked it up, and holding it between finger and thumb, looked at the others with a curious expression on his face. 'The bullet,' he said. 'The ball that destroyed him. It must have lodged somewhere inside him, and the first movement has shaken it out. Want a souvenir, Dick?'

Dick backed away, an expression of disgust on his face. 'No, thank you,' he said emphatically.

The others laughed, and the spell that had held them in its grip since first they entered the ship was broken.

Biggles stuck the pistol through his belt and pointed to the silver candlestick. 'I should say that's worth a hundred pounds at least,' he observed. 'I wonder if there is anything in these drawers.' He opened the top drawer of the desk. 'Hello! What's this,' he cried, as he took out a leather-bound book. Gently he lifted the cover, and with his eyes turned down inquiringly he studied the first page.

The others saw him start, staring incredulously, lean forward, and stare again. His eyes went round with wonder, and the fingers that held the open page began to tremble slightly. Then, looking up at the faces that were watching him, 'Gentlemen,' he said, in a queer, husky voice, 'allow me to introduce you to the most blood-thirsty member of a bloodthirsty race; the man I spoke about only a short while ago; the self-appointed head of the Brethren of the Coast; cut-throat and murderer – Louis Dakeyne, Louis le Grande, The Exterminator – himself exterminated.'

Dead silence fell, such a silence as had haunted the death-chamber for two hundred and fifty years.

Biggles drew a deep breath. He was finding the experience rather unnerving. 'This is his log,' he said. 'It should make interesting reading. What tales of death, and worse, will it reveal, I wonder? What stories of heroism, until now untold, of lonely mariners fighting their last fight against overwhelming odds led by this fiend in human form? Let us see if we can solve the mystery of his death.' He turned quickly to the last entry in the log, and began to read aloud:

'Rum all out, mutiny aboard, and everything in confusion. Bawn's cursed doubloon the cause, blister him. Put the doubloons overboard, they say. Not me. May the devil seize them first.

'Wind rising again and no-one to take in sail. Murder, mutiny, storm, calm, and out of drink, and now the wind again. The devil himself must be aboard us, and all through Bawn's doubloon, may he rot in his chains at Port Royal. Blast him for a false rogue. The rest have gone to Davy Jones, some by the plank, some by the knife, but I'll ...'

Biggles broke off breathlessly.

'Is that all?' asked Algy.

'That's all.'

'What was he going to do, I wonder?'

'I'm afraid that is something we will never know. But mark well what he says about Bawn's doubloon. Bawn's *cursed* doubloon. It brought confusion upon them – at least, so he declares. Who Bawn was we do not know, although we may one day find out from the old records that are still kept in Jamaica, but I'll warrant that it was Bawn's doubloon that lay on this desk—'

378

'The doubloon my father took,' interrupted Dick. '*My* doubloon.'

'That's it. I'm not superstitious, but I've felt all along that there was something funny about that coin. It has left a trail of death and disaster behind it. We had no luck while we had it. The only normal luck we've had on this trip was when it was out of our possession. Mallichore took it off us at Marabina. You saw what happened to *him*. We got it back, and you saw what nearly happened to us, and, I honestly believe, would have happened had not Dick discarded his coat, with the doubloon in the pocket, at the last minute. The coat was washed up. Algy and Ginger found it. Within half an hour they were face to face with death. At the crucial moment Pedro took the coin, and the evil influence went with it. I shot him within the hour. To the long list of casualties I think we can now add the names of Louis le Grande and his crew.'

'He talks of other doubloons,' reminded Algy.

'I know, and what happened here is now as clear as daylight,' returned Biggles swiftly. 'Dakeyne's crew knew the cursed doubloon was aboard, and wanted to get rid of it. He says so in his log. But somehow it had got mixed up with the others, and Louis wouldn't jettison the lot.'

'He must have done at the finish – or else they're still aboard,' asserted Algy.

'Aboard or ashore, I should say they're not far away from us at this moment,' declared Biggles.

'Where could they be?' cried Dick.

Biggles shrugged his shoulders. 'That's what we've got to find out. I believe Dakeyne was in the act of making a map of the hiding-place when he was killed. Dick's father found the paper on his desk. I've got it in my pocket. I haven't been able to make head nor tail of it, but now we are actually on the spot I will have another look at it.' He picked up the quill that still lay on the desk. 'Here is the pen he used,' he said, glancing up at the sky, just visible through the breach in the deck. 'We shall have to be getting back,' he went on quickly. 'It will be dark in another quarter of an hour, so we've no time for doubloon-hunting today, unless they happen to be handy, which seems doubtful. We've just time for a quick look round.'

The other drawers in the desk yielded three items of interest. In one lay what appeared to be a black tablecloth, neatly folded. Biggles was about to pass it over, and had half closed the drawer when a thought seemed to strike him. He reopened the drawer, took out the black material and, with a quick movement, shook it open. At once it became a flag, complete with loops for a lanyard – a black flag; a field of black with a white device, the device being a skeleton, holding, upraised, in its right hand, a dart; in the other, an hour-glass. Each foot rested on an initial letter. They read L D.

'By the red beard of Barbarossa!' exclaimed Biggles, 'fate has played a grim jest here. On the flag is Death, standing on the initials of the man who flew it; and here in the chair is death itself – the mortal remains of the same man. What a pity he can't return from the shades, if only for a moment, to see the joke.' Biggles tossed the flag to Dick. 'Bring it along,' he said. 'It's a unique trophy.'

In another drawer was a magnificent ruby ring, which Biggles slipped into his pocket with the casual observation that it seemed a pity to leave it lying about. In another were about a hundred silver coins. 'Pieces of eight,' he said laconically, picking one up and examining it. 'Find a bag or something to carry them in, Ginger. We had better take them with us in case Deutch happens to find the ship, which is by no means improbable if he starts crashing about in the bushes up above, looking for us.'

They made a quick examination of the chests, but they were all full of bolts of silks, satins, and other fine materials in which moths or other insects had played havoc, destroying their value. Afterwards they looked into the hold, but they found nothing more interesting than a number of barrels more or less full of mouldering sugar, coffee, and flour.

They would have liked to stay longer, for there were still many places to explore, but Biggles pointed to the darkening sky and ordered a retreat. 'Without any sort of illumination it isn't much use staying here,' he remarked. 'Moreover, I've no desire to spend the night with Louis. Let's get back to the islet; all being well, we can return first thing in the morning.'

But this was easier said than done, for they could find no means of regaining the hole through which they had fallen. Algy tried standing on Biggles's shoulders, but the rotten timber crumbled under his hands as soon as he put his weight on it, and they had to abandon the project. They began to understand the difficulty that Dick's father had experienced. In the end they found the hole he had made in the bows, and picking up their trophies, they crawled one by one out of the dim past into the twilit world of the present.

The boat was as they had left it, so, putting it on the water, they paddled back to the islet, and the fort which they had made their home.

'We'll make an early start in the morning,' declared Biggles as they enjoyed a frugal meal from their fast dwindling stores, helped by the remaining coconuts which provided both food and drink. 'But before we do any serious treasure-hunting,' he went on, 'I think it would be a wise move if we put this place in a better state to stand a siege. Sooner or later, whether Harvey comes back or not, Deutch and 'Frisco are bound to locate us, and if they decide to move their camp to the rocks opposite, 'Frisco, with his gun, would make it very awkward for us to get to and fro.

381

We'll lay in a supply of coconuts, and bring some more gunpowder over. We may need it if it comes to a show-down. If 'Frisco starts any rough stuff we could give him a dose of grape-shot,* which should make him think a bit. Another thing we shall have to do is mount guards. In fact, we had better start now; we should look a lot of fools if we let them catch us napping. A two-hour shift for everyone will see us through until morning. I think I'll just have another look at Dakeyne's map – if it is a map.'

He went over to one of the loopholes and spread the piece of yellow paper flat against a stone, where they all looked at it for a long time. At last Biggles shook his head. 'It must mean something,' he said. 'But if you can tell me what it is you're cleverer than I am.'

The others agreed that they could make nothing of it, so Biggles folded the paper and put it back into his pocket. 'I think we can do without those two unpleasant-looking fellows,' he said, pointing to the skeletons. 'It's time they went to Davy Jones, where they belong. Bear a hand everybody, to heave them overboard.'

The gruesome job was soon done, and Biggles turned to Dick. 'You'd better take the first watch,' he said. 'It's the easiest. Wake Ginger when the moon shows clear above the palms; that will be roughly in two hours' time.'

'Ay, ay, sir,' replied Dick briskly, and made his way up to the roof.

---

* Small metal balls put together in a bag and fired from a cannon, often with devastating effect.

Chapter 14

Dick Goes Ashore

For what seemed a long time Dick sat alone on the roof. At first he could hear the others talking down below, but after a while their conversation became intermittent, and then finally stopped altogether, so he assumed that they were sleeping. Silence fell, the breathless hush of a tropic night. The quivering of the palm fronds ceased, and even the gentle lap, lap, lap, of the ripples at the foot of the rock died away. The stars shone in the heavens with unbelievable luminosity, like lamps suspended from a purple ceiling. The moon crept over the horizon and began its upward journey, turning the sea into a lake of shimmering quicksilver, and the island into a mysterious world of vague black shadows. Across the deserted beach the black rocks crouched like monsters emerging from the ocean bed.

Dick leaned his musket against the rampart wall and regarded the scene with questioning, brooding eyes. It produced a queer sensation to think that on the very spot, wearing the same clothes and armed with the same weapons, an Elizabethan sentinel may have stood, doing sentry just as he was doing it now. Perhaps the gallant Drake himself had been there! Afterwards had come the buccaneers – the pirates. They must have known of the little fort, and used the creek, perhaps careened their ships on the coral strand inside the shelter of the headland. With all their lust and cruelty, they must have been romantic days in which to live; vaguely, he was sorry that they had gone. Treasure or no treasure, he would, he knew, rather

383

have been a member of Drake's stalwart crew, or even Dakeyne's, than sell papers in a London street. Louis le Grande! He whispered the words, rolling them off his tongue with relish. What days they were, when new lands remained to be discovered! What men they bred! What ships they built! Dimly, he perceived that although the days were gone the men remained, and many there were in town and city who would go back to them if they could.

A feeling of intense depression swept over him, for he knew that the gallant days of sail had gone for ever. Men themselves had done it; condemned themselves for ever to be slaves of iron and steel. What fools they were! To satisfy their longing, they messed about with little ships, around the harbours, at weekends. There was no romance in smoking funnels; his father had often told him so, and he realized it now. The voice of the throbbing screw had silenced for ever the creak of blocks, and the song of the breeze through straining sheets. The risks had gone, and with them, the joy of victory over them. Yes, it was a great pity, he reflected sadly.

Yet life was not so bad, after all, for he was luckier than most. Was it not true that within a short distance of where he stood a pirate's hoard remained? Doubloons! He said the word aloud. How much more satisfying it sounded than 'pound notes'. Paper money. Pah! What inspiration was there in paper? Thank goodness they weren't looking for a parcel of paper notes. Gold! That was the stuff. Solid metal with a healthy ring to it, not a feeble crackle, like notes. No wonder men went a-pirating when they used such money as that. Dakeyne must have collected quantities. Where was it now? Where had he put the doubloons? If he had buried them, how could they hope to find them? As Biggles had said, it would need an army of men to turn over all the rock and sand within a quarter of a mile of the galleon. It was a pity that Louis le Grande had not been more concise, had not finished the map he was making. He could still visualize the paper, but he could not associate it with anything he had seen. Were they on the wrong track after all? Suppose the lines on the slip of paper were just meaningless marks made by a dying man? It might well be so. In that case the secret of the treasure might still remain where he had hidden it. There was nothing in the candlestick, for Biggles had looked to see. What else was there an the desk? The pistol. There was nothing in that. The quill offered little hope. The doubloon! Louis might have scratched a message on the coin. They had not examined it very closely. That was the sort of thing a pirate might do, he reflected. What a pity Biggles had kicked it into the hole.

The more he thought about it the more he wished he had examined it more closely. In view of what he now knew, he would look at it through different eyes. What a triumph it would be if he solved the mystery where the others had failed! It would be a feather in his cap. How foolish it had been of Biggles to throw the coin away. He shouldn't have done it. After all, it was *his* coin.

The desire to examine it again for the marks he had now almost convinced himself were on it, became a mania, and he began to look towards the spot where it had been discarded. Another thought struck him. After all, it wasn't very far away. He might fetch it. There was nothing to prevent him. He could get into the boat and be there and back in ten minutes at the very outside. Nothing could happen in that time, he persuaded himself, although in his heart of hearts he knew that he had no right to leave his post. But everything was very quiet, and it was hard to believe that anything could happen before he got back.

At the end be made up his mind quickly, although somewhat guiltily. He crept to the top of the stairs that led down to the room where the others slept. All was quiet. He tiptoed back to the wall. Then, leaving his musket, but examining his pistol to make sure it was primed, he went quickly down the outside steps that led to the sea. In another minute he was in the canoe, paddling swiftly but silently towards the point.

He landed where they had gone ashore a few hours earlier, and tying the boat to a convenient crag, made his way swiftly up the rock. Reaching the top, he paused to look round. All was silent – rather too silent for his liking. In some queer way it reminded him of the silence in the galleon. Louis le Grande! He hoped his spirit did not walk. He shook himself angrily. What made him think about these things now? He had come to fetch the doubloon, but it was not so easy as he had thought it would be when he was standing on the islet with the others only a few yards away. He braced himself suddenly, annoyed by his nervousness. 'Dead men don't bite,' he muttered angrily, and set off towards the hole into which Biggles had kicked the coin, the hole in which he had nearly lost his life at the hands of the dreadful Pedro. He sped on, throwing furtive glances at the unexpected shadows cast by the moonlight. Some of them looked very human.

With his heart beating faster than usual he reached the hole. A swift glance around and he had dropped intó it, palms feeling lightly for the metal disk. He found it almost at once; with a gasp of relief his hand closed over it; and then, and not before, did he remember the superstition of the curse. Half fearfully, as though he could not bear to touch it more than he could help, he stood upright, and pushed the coin on to a flat piece of rock in order to free his hands while he climbed out.

Resting them on the ledge, he vaulted up, but his pistol caught on a jagged piece of rock and threw him back. More annoying still, for he was anxious to be gone, the weapon was pulled clean out of his belt and clattered to the bottom of the hole. With a muttered imprecation, for he dare not go without it, he dropped on to his hands and knees, groping swiftly, for the moonbeams fell aslant, and did not penetrate to where the pistol lay.

His questing hand closed over something, and as he felt its shape he stiffened, rigid, tense. Surely it was the doubloon! It felt just like it. But he had already put it outside! There could not be two. Could it have fallen back inside? Swiftly he stood up and looked over the ledge of rock on which he had put the coin. It was still there, gleaming softly in the moonlight. There could be no mistake. Then what was it he held in his hand? He opened it to see. It was a doubloon. Then there *were* two! But that was impossible! How . . . ? He began to tremble, and perspiration broke out on his forehead as his superstitious fears returned in force. The thing must be bewitched. What a fool he had been ever to touch it again – unless?

He caught his breath as another thought flashed into his brain. Quickly he stooped again, fingers scooping at the bottom of the hole. They closed over a handful of small round objects, and his mouth went dry as he felt their shape. Hardly able to breathe, he leaned against the side of the rock, and opening his trembling hand, stared wide-eyed at what it held! Doubloons! A dozen or more of them. He scraped with his foot, and heard the metallic ring of others. He was standing on doubloons! He had found Dakeyne's doubloons . . . *The* doubloons! The words seemed to ring in his ears. He forgot his pistol. He even forgot where he was and what he was doing. Breathing fast, again he dropped to his knees, fingers clawed. They sank into the golden pile. Were they really there, or was it all a dream? He felt again. No, it was no dream; they were real enough. He must tell the others about it at once.

Leaving the coins where they were, for without pockets he had no means of carrying them, he was about to leap joyfully out of the hole when a sound reached his ears that sent him cowering to the bottom again, his heart beating as though it would choke him, while his body turned as cold as the stones by which he crouched. It was the sound of a human voice, and there was no mistaking the guttural tones. The speaker was Deutch.

'I tell you they're round this headland somewhere,' he said in a surly voice.

'Aw shucks! What does it matter, anyway?' replied the voice of 'Frisco Jack. 'What's the hurry? There ain't no call to get nervy. We'll round the lot of 'em up tomorrow and bump 'em off.'

'I'd like to know what they're up to,' replied Deutch with an oath. Then he spoke again, in a voice charged with interest. 'What's that over there?'

Dick nearly swooned as rapid footsteps approached the hole; they seemed to stop on the very edge, and he braced himself for the blow which he felt was coming. But he did not move – possibly because it was beyond his physical strength to do so.

'Why, if it ain't the gold buck,' came 'Frisco's voice, tense with surprise. 'Now what do you make 'o that?'

'Blister their hides! They must have found the doubloons, and dropped one, or how else did this one git here?'

'Beats me!' murmured 'Frisco. 'Hold hard,' he went on quickly. 'I've got it. This is where Pedro got plugged. He had the doubloon, you recollect. He must 'a dropped it when he fell. That's it. This is where I found 'im. Look, there's his blood marks. Well, he's gone where doubloons won't be no use to 'im, so I might as well have it.'

'Hands off, 'Frisco! I found it; it's mine.' Deutch's voice had a hard, vindictive ring.

Came the American's voice again, bitter in its frigid hostility. 'Hey, what's biting you, Deutch?'

'Hand it over,' snarled Deutch, from which Dick,

shivering with horror in the hole, gathered that the American had picked up the coin.

'Frisco spoke again, fury blazing in his clipped words. 'You dirty rat! Pull a knife on me, would you, you—' His voice broke off in a choking gasp that ended in a horrid gurgling sound. There was a swishing and writhing on the rocks, punctuated with grunts accompanied by the sound of fiercely driven blows. Then silence.

Dick bit his lip to prevent himself from crying out aloud. He could visualize what was happening on the very edge of his hiding place. In a nightmare of horror he heard Deutch muttering, between deeply drawn breaths, 'I'll teach you, you—' each sentence concluding with an oath worse than the last.

At last, to Dick's unspeakable relief, the footsteps began to recede, but it was a good ten minutes before he dare move from his cramped position. Slowly he drew himself upright. His face, in the pallid moonlight, was ashen, but he did not know it. One glance was enough. His fears were realized. A yard or two away, the wan light shining whitely on his death-distorted features, lay 'Frisco Jack.

Dick did not wait to collect any doubloons. He did not stop to pick up his pistol. He waited for nothing. One leap and he was out of the hole, running for dear life towards the rock where he had left the boat. Several times he nearly fell, for his knees were strangely weak. He literally tumbled into the boat, and untying the painter with trembling hands, snatched up the paddle and sent it flashing through the water. Panting with excitement and exertion, he crossed the narrow channel, moored the boat – not without difficulty, so violently did he tremble – and dashed up the steps to the fort. He could hear the others talking before he reached the top. Apparently they heard him coming, for Biggles's voice, as hard as cracking ice, came down to him below the rampart wall.

'Halt there! Who goes?'

'It's me,' gasped Dick.

'All right; come aboard.'

Dick finished his journey. At the top he found Biggles waiting for him. His eyes were cold and his manner hostile. The others stood close behind him. 'Where the devil have you been?' he snapped.

Dick faltered. 'I've been ashore,' he panted. 'I've found—'

Biggles's voice cut in, crisp and curt. 'Never mind what you've found. You left your post!'

'But—'

'I don't want any excuses. Did you, or did you not, leave your post?'

'Yes, sir.'

'Then you ought to be thundering well ashamed of yourself. Are you?'

'Yes, sir.'

'Well, that's something, anyway. Fortunately no harm came of it, but if you ever do that again I'll tie a couple of cannon-balls to your feet and throw you overboard. Orders are orders – you understand?'

'Yes, sir.'

'Why did you do it?'

'I went to fetch the doubloon.'

Biggles took a quick pace backward. 'You *what?*'

'You see, I thought—'

'Wait a minute – wait a minute. Have you brought that accursed coin back here? If you have, you can take it ashore again, and as soon as you like, my lad.'

'No, Deutch has got it.'

'How do you know that?'

'He and 'Frisco were over there. I got into the hole and found the doubloon and put it on a rock while I got out. I bobbed down again when Deutch and 'Frisco came along. Deutch spotted the doubloon, but 'Frisco got it first and wouldn't give it up. They fought to see who should have it, and in the end Deutch knifed 'Frisco. He's lying over there on the rocks, dead. Deutch has gone off with the doubloon.'

Biggles turned to the others. His manner was slow and deliberate. 'Did you hear that?' he said in a strange voice. 'Another death to the score of Bawn's doubloon. By heavens, there's more than coincidence in this! Deutch is welcome to it; he's sealed his own fate or I've missed my mark.' He turned back to Dick. 'What were you doing all this time?'

'I was lying in the bottom of the hole; you see, I'd just found some more.'

'Some more what?'

'Doubloons.'

There was a brief silence. Biggles spoke. 'Did you say you'd found some more doubloons?' he asked incredulously.

'Yes.'

'How many?'

'Hundreds – maybe thousands,' declared Dick exultantly.

'Are you sure?'

'Certain! I held them in my hands.'

Biggles eyed Dick suspiciously. 'You didn't by any chance drop off to sleep and dream this, did you?'

Dick took a pace forward. 'Sleep!' he cried. 'I did not. I was scared stiff. I tell you I picked up the doubloons in handfuls.'

Biggles turned again to the others. 'Jumping alligators! He must have found the treasure,' he breathed. Then to Dick, 'Where is it?'

'In the hole where you kicked the doubloon – the same hole where I hid when Pedro was after me. We stood beside it this afternoon.'

Biggles rubbed his chin. 'Would you believe it?' he murmured. 'So *that's* where Louis dumped them when his

391

ship ran into the creek? And after all this time Bawn's doubloon got back amongst the others. There seems to be a sort of fate in this.' A light of understanding came suddenly into his eyes. 'Why, what fools we were!' he cried. 'I see it all now, although I should never have guessed it. Those two parallel lines on Louis's map were the boundaries of the inlet, with the holes in the rocks marked beside it. The one in which he put the gold was filled in solid. Well, well, it's easy to be wise after the event. What were Deutch and 'Frisco doing up there, Dick?'

'Looking for us, and talking.'

'Could you hear what they were saying?'

'They didn't say very much, but they were talking about rounding us up tomorrow and bumping us off.'

Biggles inclined his head. 'How very nice of them. Did they say just how they proposed to do that?'

'No, but they seemed pretty confident. They talked as if something was due to happen tomorrow that would make it easy.'

Biggles looked thoughtful. 'I don't quite see how that can be,' he said slowly, 'but it's as well to know what was in their minds. I should have thought that the boot was on the other foot. We were four against two; now we are four against one, assuming that Pedro is out of action.'

'He's dead,' put in Dick quickly. 'At least, I heard 'Frisco say that he had gone where doubloons wouldn't be much good to him.'

'Another victim to the doubloon,' said Biggles softly. 'Where is 'Frisco now, Dick?'

'He's lying over there beside the hole.'

'Then we'd better move him first thing in the morning, in case Deutch comes prowling about and finds the treasure – not that I think we have much to fear from him now. We can't do much in the dark, but we'll get busy as soon as it starts to get light; meanwhile, we'd better see about getting some rest. Ginger, take over guard, and don't go wandering ashore; you may not be so lucky as Dick was.'

Dick smiled at the faint sarcasm in Biggles's voice as he followed the others below and lay down to try to get some sleep. But it was a long time coming, and when at length it came he was haunted by dreams in which Dakeyne, Deutch, 'Frisco Jack, and the doubloons were hopelessly interwoven.

Chapter 15

The Attack

He awoke with a start, aware that he had slept. It was still dark, but he could see a vague form moving about the room. He sat up to see more clearly.

It was Biggles who, seeing him move, addressed him. 'Parade in five minutes. Full marching order.'

'It's very early, isn't it?'

'In these parts, it's the early buccaneer who catches the doubloons,' answered Biggles lightly. 'The stars are paling. Dawn will break in about five minutes. Hey, there, Ginger, show a leg! I want to get ashore before Deutch starts prowling about. Crack yourselves a nut apiece for breakfast.'

Ginger sat up, yawning. 'What the dickens have you been doing?' he inquired sleepily.

'Giving the battery the once-over; in other words, inspecting the guns.'

'Do you think we are likely to need them?'

'One never knows what one is likely to need when one goes a-pirating.'

'Where's Algy?'

'On the roof; doing guard and finishing his brekker. Jump to it; we go ashore in three minutes.'

Ginger sprang to his feet. 'My goodness, I'd forgotten about the doubloons! Are we going to fetch them?'

'We are. We should look a lot of silly asses if, having found them, Deutch found them, too, and hid them in another place. I'd rather they were under my eye. Ready?'

Ginger cracked a nut, took a quick drink of the milk, and breaking off a piece of the kernel, handed it to Dick. 'Ay, ay, sir,' he said.

'Then all aboard for the dollars. We've a lot to do today.'

Algy joined them at the top of the stairs. Already the sky was pale azure blue, with the rim of the sun just showing above the horizon. They could just see the lagoon, but there was no sign of Deutch, or the amphibian, from which they concluded that Harvey had not yet returned; so, each carrying a loaded musket, they made their way down the outside steps to the canoe.

In five minutes they were across, with their frail craft made fast.

'Dick and Ginger, stand fast,' ordered Biggles. 'Algy, come with me.'

'What's the idea?' inquired Dick.

'We've got a job to do. We'll call you as soon as it's done,' answered Biggles seriously. 'Come on, Algy.'

Dick sat down on a convenient piece of rock. He realized what the job was. A few minutes later he breathed a sigh of relief as he heard a loud splash on the far side of the headland, knowing that it was done. He had no desire to see 'Frisco again. 'Queer, isn't it?' he said to Ginger, who was sitting beside him. 'Gold always seems to be associated with dead men.'

'Because too many of the wrong sort of men try to get hold of it, I expect,' returned Ginger philosophically.

A hail from Biggles sent them hurrying up the rock, where they found him and Algy waiting for them.

'Now, Dick,' said Biggles, 'you found the doubloons, so it's only right and proper that you should lead us to the spot.'

With shining eyes Dick led the way to the hole in which he had twice taken refuge. 'There they are,' he said, pointing.

'My goodness! He's right,' declared Biggles, staring down into the hole.

They all laughed, a trifle hysterically.

Biggles jumped down and picked up a handful of doubloons. 'You're right, Dick,' he said, rather breathlessly. 'There must be thousands of them.'

'Let's take them across and count them,' suggested Dick.

Biggles climbed up out of the hole. 'Wait a minute,' he said. 'We mustn't lose our heads. If we take them across to the islet it means that we shall have to make that our headquarters, perhaps for a long time, in which case my common sense tells me that we ought to provision it. A rough sea might prevent us from crossing over here for days on end, and we should look a lot of silly asses sitting on a pile of gold with nothing to eat. We've got the day before us, so we may as well take things in order. Ginger, you collect a pile of nuts and carry them across. Algy, you go down into the galleon and find a way of getting some gunpowder to the boat for Ginger to ship across. We may need our muskets, and there isn't much powder over there. Dick, you go with him and fetch one of those old water-buckets. There are several lying about beside the cannon: they used to use them for carrying water to sluice out the guns. Bring it back here and we'll use it to transport the doubloons. I'll start getting them out of the hole.'

'What about Deutch?' asked Ginger.

'I think he will have more sense than to take on the four of us,' returned Biggles casually. 'But if he comes along looking for trouble he can have it. With that doubloon in his pocket he's as good as dead already. All right. Go to it, everybody.'

By the time the sun was well up the first part of their task was complete, and Algy and Ginger joined Biggles and Dick at the treasure hole.

'Got some nuts across, Ginger?' asked Biggles.

'Yes.'

'How about powder, Algy?'

'I've taken over the best part of a barrel; that should be enough to last us for a long time.'

'Good enough,' declared Biggles. 'All hands to ship the doubloons. I've only got about half of them out of the hole; they're heavier than you would believe. I think the best way to go to work is for you, Algy, and Ginger, to start shipping them across to the fort while Dick and I go on hauling them up.'

The shipment of the coins was a task to their liking, and they went to work with a will; but even so it took them longer than they expected, although, with most of the afternoon still before them, they were not particularly concerned with time. However, when at last the job was done, and they tossed into the bucket the last few coins that remained, Biggles estimated that between forty and fifty thousand doubloons, moidores, and ducats, with a sprinkling of oriental pieces, had been carried across to the fort.

'What you might call a good day's work,' he grinned, mopping the perspiration from his face. 'We'll take these last few across and have a rest; afterwards we'll decide what to do about Deutch. He's keeping very quiet, by the way. Dick, run up to the ridge and see if you can see anything of him.

He sat down near the others while Dick ran lightly up the barrier of rock that lay at right angles across the beach and obstructed their view in the direction of the lagoon.

Lightheartedly – he even stopped to examine a queer shaped shell on the way – Dick reached the ridge and glanced nonchalantly along the beach. For a moment he stared, thunderstruck into immobility, hardly able to believe his eyes; then he whirled round and raced back towards the others, leaping from rock to rock in a manner that was reckless, if not dangerous. And as he ran he shouted.

'Look out!' he yelled. 'Run for it! Quick!' He swerved towards the place where the boat was moored.

The others sprang to their feet in alarm. 'What is it?' cried Biggles.

'Soldiers! The soldiers from Marabina. Dozens of them,' answered Dick in a panic. 'They're coming this way, and they're only just over the other side of the rocks.'

Biggles waited for no more. He snatched up his musket and made a grab at the bucket that contained the remaining doubloons, but Algy, in his haste, tripped over it, and sent the yellow coins flying in all directions. Muttering at his carelessness, he started to pick them up, but Biggles made him desist.

'Never mind those,' he snapped. 'They are not worth stopping for. Down to the boat – come on.'

To the boat they dashed, pell-mell, infected by the panic in Dick's manner. Having got a flying start, he raced them to it, and was ready, paddle in hand, by the time they arrived. There was a wild scramble for places. Biggles snatched the paddle out of Dick's hands, used it to thrust the canoe clear, and then drove it deep into the water. Simultaneously, a chorus of yells from the top of the rocks told them that they had been seen. There was a moment's silence and then more excited shouts.

'They've found the doubloons we spilt,' grunted Biggles, as he put his weight behind the paddle.

He was right, and although he, and the others in the canoe, may not have realized it, the trivial incident of Algy accidentally upsetting the bucket may have saved their lives. Several of the soldiers were in the act of levelling their rifles when an astonished cry from one of their number attracted their attention to the coins. Some started to pick them up, whereupon those who were about to shoot – and the range was then point blank – seeing that they were likely to lose their share, threw down their rifles and joined in the mad scramble. Not even Deutch's furious cursing could stop them, and by the time they were satisfied that no more gold remained, the canoe was three parts of the way to the islet.

Deutch threw up the automatic he had taken from 'Frisco Jack and blazed away, but what with rage and exertion his aim was wild, and the bullets splashed harmlessly on the water. Some of the soldiers then fired, and one or two bullets came close enough to splash water into the canoe.

'Take a shot at them, Algy,' panted Biggles. 'It will rattle them even if you don't hit anybody.'

Algy's musket roared, and the vicious thud of the ball on the rocks had the desired effect. The soldiers dived for cover. They began firing again almost at once, but the brief respite had enabled Biggles to run the canoe alongside the landing place, where it was under the protection of the steps.

'Up you go,' cried Biggles. 'One at a time.'

For two or three seconds, as they crossed a shoulder of the rock, they again came into the field of fire of the watchers on the point, but they ran the gauntlet successfully. Biggles was the last, for he had had to make the canoe fast. 'Phew!' he muttered, as he dropped over the wall and crouched beside the others. 'That was warm work. Where the deuce did that mob come from?'

He crawled across to a loophole on the opposite side of the ramparts, one that overlooked the lagoon. His face was grave as he turned back to Algy. 'This is not so good,' he said seriously.

'What is it?'

'A boat. Looks like a sort of coastal craft, about the size of a trawler. Possibly it's a coastguard. What the dickens brought it here, I wonder? I've got it,' he went on quickly. 'Harvey! He went back to Marabina and told them we were here, and they've sent the boat after us. Either that, or Deutch asked for extra help to find the doubloons. Those thieving officials at Marabina are in on the deal.'

'That's it,' agreed Algy. 'The fellow in the pretty uniform is here with them; I saw him as we came across.'

'How many of them are there, do you think?'

'There can't be less than a score – probably more.

'That's how I figured it out. It looks as if it's a good thing we laid a few nuts in store, doesn't it? Hark!'

'There he is! It must be Harvey coming back,' cried Ginger. He pointed to a speck far out to sea, to the south-west.

'Yes, that's our machine,' said Biggles, shielding his eyes with his hand. 'It looks as if we've a tidy force opposed to us.'

Keeping under cover of the rampart wall, they watched the machine land, and then, peeping through various loopholes, they looked back at the point. The troops had withdrawn some distance, but they could see them being addressed by Deutch in the shade of the jungle.

'Hello! What's he going to do?' asked Biggles suddenly.

'Looks like a flag of truce,' answered Algy in a surprised voice.

With a dirty piece of white rag held high on a stick, Deutch advanced to the nearest point of the rock. 'Hi, you over there,' he bellowed.

Biggles spoke sharply to Algy. 'Keep me covered,' he said. 'Let drive at the first sign of dirty work.' Then he stood up. 'Hello yourself,' he answered.

'I've come to offer you a square deal,' shouted Deutch.

'What's your idea of a square deal?'

'You show us where you've hid the dough and we'll give you a passage back to Marabina.'

Biggles smiled. 'Thanks,' he called sarcastically. 'We'd sooner be where we are.'

'You mean you won't show us where you've hid the dibs?'

'Not a mother's son of 'em.'

'All right, my cock. You won't chirp so loud by the time I'm through with you; maybe I can find a way of making you talk.'

'Not forgetting that you've got to catch me first.'

Deutch cursed vindictively. 'I'll skin you alive when I lay hands on you,' he roared as he turned away, shaking his clenched fist. He rejoined the troops, and a minute later two or three detached themselves and set off at a run down the beach.

'I wonder what they're going to do?' murmured Algy.

'I should say they're going to fetch a boat from the coaster,' returned Biggles. 'They'll bring it back here and then try to storm us. I'm afraid we're in for a sticky time, but our only chance is to fight it out. Well, whatever happens, Deutch isn't getting those.' He pointed to the heap of doubloons that gleamed dully in a corner. 'If the worst comes to the worst, I'll heave the whole lot into the sea rather than he should get his hands on them. Come on, let's get busy and load every weapon we've got. We've a good card up our sleeves and we'll keep it there as long as we can. Deutch knows we've got muskets, but he doesn't know about these babies.' He touched one of the cannon with his toe. Then he smiled. 'As a soldier I've always been curious to see the effect of a charge of grape-shot, and it looks as if this is my chance,' he observed. 'Let's get the swivel-gun up here; I've got a feeling that it is going to upset Mr Deutch's calculations.'

'How can we fire the guns?' asked Algy suddenly. 'We haven't a match between us.'

'We can soon get over that difficulty,' answered Biggles promptly. 'When we're ready I'll snap a pistol into some loose powder with some pieces of dry rag in it. We shall have to keep a little fire going.

The sun blazed down as they rammed the powder into the guns. Algy picked up a cannon ball weighing perhaps five pounds. 'If this happens to hit anybody in the teeth there'll be no need for him to see a dentist,' he declared cheerfully, as he thrust it into a yawning muzzle.

The swivel-gun was dragged up from below, and with perspiration streaming from them, they aligned it on the channel. All the powder, shot, and small arms, including another cutlass and a pike, were brought up, and placed in handy positions. When it was done Biggles nodded approval as he glanced round. 'Well,' he observed, 'they may take us, but before they do there will be such a noise as should cheer the mouldering bones of Louis le Grande. By gosh! I'll tell you what! We'll fly his flag. It's many a day since the Jolly Roger flapped over the Main, and if it never flaps again we'll be the last to fly it.' He ran below and returned with the grim emblem of piracy. He picked up the pike, and after tying the flag to it, wedged the handle into the draining hole in the corner.

Dick regarded it with shining eyes. 'That's the stuff!' he cried approvingly. Then he burst into song:

> 'Fifteen men on the dead man's chest,
> Yo ho ho, and a bottle of rum.'

The others joined in the famous refrain, roaring it at the top of their voices.

> 'Drink and the devil had done for the rest,
> Yo ho ho, and a bottle of rum.'

Algy, looking through his loophole, saw the astonished faces of the soldiers peering out of the jungle. 'They think we've gone crazy,' he declared.

Biggles nodded. 'They're not far wrong, either,' he murmured drily. Then his eyes glinted. 'Avast there, pipe down,' he cried. 'Here comes the boat.'

A small boat had appeared from the direction of the lagoon; it was being rowed by four men, who kept close into the shore. It disappeared behind the headland, and presently the watchers, from their eyrie, saw Deutch's crew creeping down towards it.

'How many men can they get into that boat?' asked Algy.

'Not more than a dozen,' replied Biggles shortly. 'Here they come,' he added quickly, as the boat shot round the end of the point. It was low in the water under the weight of the men crowded into it. Four were rowing, urged on by Deutch who sat in the stern.

'Hold your fire until I give the word,' ordered Biggles.

He waited until the boat was half way across. Then, 'Fire!' he roared.

The four muskets blazed, their booming reports echoing again and again in the hills. Water splashed round the boat. A man collapsed, but the rowers continued to ply their oars. Biggles snatched up another musket. 'Rapid fire!' he yelled.

Under the fusillade of musketry, two more of the soldiers collapsed, one springing up and falling overboard; but the boat still surged towards the islet.

Biggles leapt to the brass swivel-gun, snatching up a piece of smouldering rag from the fire he had lighted for the purpose. There was a curious smile on his face as he brought the long barrel to bear. He dropped some loose powder on the touch-hole; then leapt aside as he fired it with the rag. A stream of flame and sparks spurted from the muzzle as the gun roared; a great cloud of smoke bellied outwards.

Had Biggles been serious when he said that he wanted to see the result of grape-shot, his wish was fulfilled. And it exceeded anything he imagined. In the first place, the recoil was terrific. He had rammed probably a hundred bullets into the gun. They struck the boat, and the water around it, in a murderous hail of lead. The water was churned into foam for an area of several square yards. The boat nearly overturned. Shouts and groans rose on the air. Inside the boat all was chaos. Only one of the rowers retained his oars, and these he was unable to use because of the turmoil. Above the uproar rose the frenzied cursing of Deutch. The bows of the boat, seemingly of their own volition, turned back towards the shore. The rower got his oars free and recommenced rowing furiously. A soldier snatched up another oar and helped him, using it as a paddle.

Biggles barely saw these things, for he was working like a madman reloading the gun. By the time he had finished the boat had nearly reached the sand near the point, but pressing home his advantage, he snatched up another piece of rag and fired the touch.

Boom! Another great cloud of smoke rolled turgidly towards the island.

When it had cleared somewhat they saw that the boat had overturned, and was lying awash in the gentle ripples on the beach. Two or three men were splashing in the water; others floated motion less. One was crawling up the sand. Three or four others, Deutch among them, were running for cover, and presently disappeared behind the rocks.

'Go on firing at the boat,' shouted Biggles. 'Try to knock some holes in her bottom.' Suiting the action to the word, he snatched up an undischarged musket and fired. A splinter of wood leapt from the upturned keel. Reloading, he fired again. For another five minutes they continued the fusillade before he gave the order to cease fire. 'That's given them something to think about, I fancy,' he observed with satisfaction. 'As Louis would say, there's confusion amongst them. Recharge all the muskets,' he added, as he set about reloading the gun that had done so much damage.

Algy grinned as he looked at him, for his face was black with powder smoke. 'As you say, that should have given them something to think about,' he agreed. 'Do you think they'll try it again?'

'There's no knowing what they'll try,' growled Biggles. 'Deutch is desperate for the doubloons, and he'll try everything before he gives up. If all else fails, he may try to starve us out, in which case, since we've no means of leaving the island, things may get awkward.'

'Talking about starving, what about cracking the odd nut?' suggested Dick. 'I'm hungry.'

A bullet splashed against the parapet.

'You'll get your own nut cracked if you don't keep it down,' Biggles told him grimly. 'I saw you dancing about while the fight was on as if there were no such things as bullets.'

Dick raised his eyebrows. 'Did they shoot at us?'

'I should jolly well think they did. The rest of the crowd, hidden amongst the rocks opposite, were sniping at us as fast as they could go. Don't forget that next time. All right; go below everybody and get a bite. I'll keep watch. Come up and take over when you've finished eating.'

The afternoon wore on, and by the time the others had finished, and Biggles had snatched a hasty meal, the sun was far down in the west. There was no sign of the enemy apart from an occasional shot that smacked harmlessly against the parapet, which served as a warning that the islet was being closely watched.

In the twilight four men made a dash towards the boat,

but they had no heart for their job and beat a quick retreat under the fusillade poured at them from the ramparts. Twilight deepened into night, but there was no further activity on the island.

'We shall have to keep strict watch tonight,' declared Biggles. 'We had better make our beds up here. Dick, no prowling about, remember.'

Dick shook his head vigorously. 'Don't you worry about that,' he said with an emphasis that made them all laugh.

Chapter 16

Warm Work

Dawn the following morning saw Algy doing duty as guard. A slight mist hung over the sea and shrouded the island in a soft, lavender-tinted mantle, but as the rays of the sun dispersed it, his sharply uttered, 'All hands to repel boarders' brought the others scrambling to their feet.

'What's happening?' demanded Biggles tersely, wide awake on the instant.

Algy pointed, and following the direction of his outstretched finger, the others saw the coaster, which was really a ketch fitted with an auxiliary engine, standing towards them over a flat sea that shimmered with all the hues of mother-of-pearl. With the island background, the tall mainmast reflected faithfully in the water, and the long ripple of the wake flashing like a jewelled chain, the boat made a delightful picture. 'A painted ship upon a painted ocean.' But Biggles saw no beauty in the scene, for her mission was all too clear.

'So that's the idea,' he murmured quietly. 'They're going to try to board us from the big boat. Unless I'm mistaken, this is where things start to warm up.'

'I can't see anybody, except the man at the wheel,' remarked Algy, one foot on the low parapet, leaning against his cutlass as he regarded the oncoming ship with brooding eyes.

'Don't be deceived by that. I imagine they are all below, out of reach of our shot – or so they think. They know all about the swivel-gun now, but they know nothing about

407

our heavy metal. If only we can aim straight we can still give them a jolt. Listen, chaps,' he went on earnestly. 'We've talked a lot about Louis le Grande, and we've played at being pirates, but there is going to be no fun about this. We're facing reality, even if the clock has been put back two hundred and fifty years. We've got to fight because we can do nothing else. It would be fatal to fall into Deutch's hands. We know too much, and he'd see to it that we didn't pop up at some future date to lay evidence against him for murder. "Dead men tell no tales" is his motto. It was Dakeyne's, under whose flag we are fighting, so we may as well make it ours. If Deutch wins, it will be a case of "Them as die'll be the lucky ones", as Long John Silver would say, so we'll fight as men were expected to fight in the days when the Jolly Roger flapped at the peak. That's all.' Stooping, he snapped his pistol in the little heap of powder he had prepared, and after the flash, stirred the rags it had ignited. 'Come on,' he added. 'Let's have the guns over to this side and stand by to give them a broadside.'

Dick helped to drag the heavy guns into position, and again the feeling came over him that he was living in the past; that he was doing something he had done before in some other age. But there was no time for contemplation.

'The skunks are taking good care to keep out of sight,' muttered Biggles, as he watched the approaching boat.

'What is the maximum range of these guns, do you think?' asked Algy.

'I haven't the foggiest notion,' confessed Biggles. 'I've handled a good many different weapons in my life, but not this sort. They were a bit before my time. All the same, I've taken a great fancy to them.'

'Try a sighting shot; we should be able to reach them now,' suggested Algy.

'Yes, I think we may as well open the ball,' agreed Biggles. 'Stand clear when I fire; she'll jump like a wild horse. Get ready to reload.' He crouched behind the gun, squinting through the small round hole that served as a crude sight. 'Get a light, Algy,' he ordered, as he made a slight adjustment in alignment.

Algy snatched up a piece of glowing rag on the end of his cutlass and stood ready.

'Fire!' shouted Biggles, jumping aside.

A long tongue of orange flame, followed instantly by a churning cloud of smoke, leapt out across the sea as the gun exploded like a thunderclap and jerked backwards under the power of the recoil. While the echoes were still reverberating in the hills a column of water spurted into the air beyond the boat, now about a quarter of a mile away.

'You're over her,' cried Algy, stooping down to peer under the smoke. 'Your line was good; a little less elevation and you'll hit her.'

'I'll get the hang of it in a minute,' answered Biggles, darting to the next gun, while Dick and Ginger started reloading the one he had just fired. Algy stood ready with the rag.

'Fire!'

Boom!

Again a stream of flame and smoke flashed towards the boat. There was a crash of timber and a cloud of splinters flew from her counter.

'Got her!' yelled Algy delightedly. 'Keep it up.'

'We've got to land one in her engine-room, or hole her at the water-line,' muttered Biggles. 'In the old days they could shoot at the rigging to put a ship out of action, but that doesn't work any longer – more's the pity. Now we've got the range we'll give her a broadside; it should put the wind up them, at any rate.'

Again Ginger and Dick reloaded feverishly while Biggles sighted the other guns.

'Everyone get some rag and stand by to fire,' he cried. 'Ready! *Fire!*'

The fort shook under the roar of the guns. A huge cloud of smoke completely hid the target. While it was clearing they all worked like madmen at reloading.

'Hurrah!' Algy's cheer was taken up by the others as the smoke cleared sufficiently for them to see the ship.

'You've got her mast,' shouted Dick, dancing in his excitement.

It was true. The mainmast trailed over the starboard quarter. This, of course, did not affect the boat as it would have done had it been under sail, but the extra resistance on one side caused her to yaw.* The crew had evidently realized it and were trying to correct the trouble, for three men were slashing furiously at the tangled cordage to clear it. Half the wooden superstructure had also been carried away, so it was clear that at least two shots had found their mark.

'Muskets!' roared Biggles. 'Try to drop those fellows who are clearing the tackle. If we can stop them it may foul the rudder.'

They opened up a brisk fire with their small-arms. One of the men dropped; another bolted. The third, with commendable courage – for the range was short – braved the fire and went on with his work.

Biggles dropped his musket, sprang to the swivel-gun, took quick aim, and fired. His aim was true. The deadly grape-shot swept the deck and sent splinters flying in all directions. The one survivor of the working party dropped, but after rolling about for a moment or two, he managed to get to his hands and knees and crawl away to cover.

Biggles was astonished at the effect caused by the gun,

* Turn unsteadily from side to side.

and he expressed it. 'It's more effective than shrapnel,' he declared. 'We stung her badly that time – look.'

The boat was now definitely veering off its course, although the helmsman, whom they could see crouching in the damaged superstructure, had got his rudder hard over.

'Ginger, Algy, go on firing the big stuff,' shouted Biggles. 'Don't wait for me. Load and fire as fast as you can. Dick, re-load all the muskets.'

They began a furious cannonade, Biggles using the swivel-gun, the others firing solid ball. The boat was hit several times; her planking was torn and furrowed; splinters lay everywhere, both about the decks and on the water, but in spite of their efforts, the helmsman managed to get his craft under control and it crept steadily nearer.

Biggles began to look anxious, for he saw that within a few minutes she would pass inside the field of fire of their guns, the muzzles of which were already depressed almost to their limits. Further, she had gone out to pass the islet on the seaward side, presumably to reach the steps, which Deutch had either seen or assumed were there, and time was lost while they dragged the guns to point in that direction.

On the other hand, the range was now point-blank, and a shot, when one went home, did a tremendous amount of damage, although, as the soldiers were still below deck, it was impossible to estimate the actual execution. Between the roar of the guns and the crash of striking shot, the gunners on the rocks could hear Deutch's furious cursing as he drove the crew on. Above the islet a mighty cloud of white smoke was mushrooming slowly into the air.

Biggles, perspiration streaming down through the grime on his face, tore off his shirt and flung it aside. 'Keep your heads down,' he shouted, as bullets began to whistle through the air or smack against the parapet. He dragged the swivel-gun into a fresh position and poured a withering hail of lead almost vertically into the coaster's deck. It was his last shot, for with that she crept within the zone of fire and began edging towards the landing steps. He saw that if she reached them the position would become desperate, but it was hard to see how it could be prevented. They had battered the ship to pieces, but her engines were still running; as he had said earlier on, had she been a sailing vessel she would have been out of action long before.

Algy snatched up a musket, took deliberate aim at the helmsman, and fired. A splinter of wood flew into the air near the fellow's head, causing him to duck, but did no further damage. Algy tossed the discharged weapon to Dick, who was panting with heat and excitement, and grabbed another. He fired again, and grunted his satisfaction as the man fell, howling, clutching at an arm that dangled uselessly.

'Hold your fire, everybody,' roared Biggles. 'Wait till they show themselves, then let them have it. Look out! Stand clear!'

He had seen that the vessel was now alongside the landing-stage, which was immediately under where they stood, crushing their canoe flat. While the others were still wondering what he was going to do, he had dragged one of the big guns round until the muzzle was pointing at the inside of the rampart wall, and flung a glowing rag across the touch-hole. The hot blast of the explosion made them stagger, gasping in the swirling smoke through which they saw that a large part of the wall had disappeared. The mass of masonry crashed down on the vessel's deck. Shouts and groans filled the air; bullets smacked viciously, or screamed as they richochetted off the rock.

Dick, fighting mad for the first time in his life, began

heaving cannon-balls through the breach in the wall, cheering hoarsely as he did so.

It gave Biggles an idea. 'Hi! Algy!' he yelled, straining at the gun he had just fired.

Algy saw what he was trying to do, and joined him. The others rushed to their assistance. Between them they trundled the gun to the edge of the fort. 'Right over!' roared Biggles.

For a moment the mass of iron hung poised on the brink; then it toppled over. With a frightful crash it landed on the deck of the vessel below; it went straight through the top deck as if the planking had been tissue paper, and disappeared from sight. The boat shuddered under the weight of the impact.

Deutch, with half a dozen men at his heels, appeared, making for the steps.

'Muskets!' yelled Biggles, snatching up the nearest. He took careful aim at Deutch and pulled the trigger. The hammer fell with a splutter of sparks as the weapon misfired. Deutch, by this time halfway up the steps, his teeth showing in an ugly snarl, threw up his automatic. Biggles hurled the musket at him. It struck him on the arm, knocking the weapon out of his hand. Deutch, without pausing in his rush, whipped out a knife. Biggles snatched up a pistol and fired; the shot missed Deutch but knocked over the man behind him. Pandemonium reigned. Biggles, looking frantically for another pistol, flinched as a weapon exploded in his ears, temporarily deafening him. He saw that Algy had fired it. Another of the attackers flung up his arms and went backwards, carrying one of his comrades off the steps with him as he fell. Deutch, mouthing like a maniac, came on and reached the top; two others were close behind.

Biggles, weaponless, looked round for one, and saw a cutlass lying where it had got knocked over in the fray. He

413

turned to get it, but his foot caught in the broken masonry of the wall, and he fell headlong. Deutch leapt at him like a wild cat. His arm jerked up, the knife flashing in the sun. Biggles wriggled like an eel to avoid the blow, but the sailor's legs were over his own, pinning them down. For a split second they remained thus, and then, at the precise moment that the knife began to descend, a pistol roared. Deutch stiffened, arm still upraised; it dropped to his side and he fell over, coughing.

Biggles flung him off and sprang to his feet. Dick, white as death, was crouching a yard away, a smoking pistol in his hand.

'Good work, Dick,' gasped Biggles, breathlessly, for it had been a narrow escape. He snatched up the cutlass. But during the second that he had been on the ground the whole position had changed. The sole survivor of the boarders, seeing Deutch fall and finding himself alone, waited for no more. He saw Biggles and Algy bearing down on him from either side, cutlasses in their hands. Flinging aside his rifle, he jumped clear off the rock into the sea. The few men left on the deck of the boat were working furiously to push it off.

'All right! Cease fire!' ordered Biggles, and looked about him.

Algy was leaning against the wall, his hat gone, his hair on end, perspiration streaming down his face as he reloaded his pistol. Dick was staring down at the ship, wild-eyed. Ginger, pale under a thick layer of black powder-dust, was sitting down, mopping blood off his cheek with a piece of his shirt.

'Are you hurt?' cried Biggles sharply.

'Nothing to write home about,' answered Ginger weakly. 'A bullet knocked off a piece of rock and it hit me in the face.'

Biggles looked back at the ship, now fifty yards away,

414

and making straight for the shore. 'They've had enough,' he said. 'By the shades of Morgan, Louis himself never saw a brisker five minutes than that.' He struck the top off a coconut with his cutlass and handed it to Ginger. 'Take a sip,' he invited.

'What I need is a bucket of water,' growled Ginger, as he staggered to his feet. 'I've never been so hot in my life. Where's the boat?'

'If you mean ours, it's sunk,' replied Biggles. 'It was crushed flat. If you mean theirs, they seem to be running it ashore. Those who are left have evidently had enough for one day. So have I, if it comes to that. Keep your heads down; some skunk might decide to take a last crack at us. Did anyone see Harvey in the fight? I was looking for him because he's the only one who can get away in our machine.'

'No, I didn't see him,' answered Algy.

'Nor I,' echoed the others.

'That's a nuisance. I'm afraid he'll make off in the machine before we can get to it,' muttered Biggles, with a worried frown. He walked to the opposite side of the fort and looked towards the lagoon. A movement on his left caught his eye, and he turned sharply seaward, staring incredulously. 'What the dickens is this?' he cried.

The others, sensing more danger, ran to his side. Less than a mile away, racing towards the island, her bows throwing up two tall feathers of spray, was a dark, slim, rakish-looking craft.

'Great Scott, it's a destroyer!' muttered Dick. 'If she's after us, we've got our work cut out, and no mistake.'

'She isn't. She's British,' cried Biggles excitedly. I can see her ensign.' He looked at the others. 'Trust the Navy to pop up when anything's going on,' he murmured. 'I don't know what they'll say when they see this mess; buccaneering is a bit out of date. Well, we can only wait and see. Frankly, I'm

415

not sorry to see her; a coconut diet may sound fine in books, but personally I'm pining to look a plate of ham and eggs in the face again.'

Leaning against the wall, they could see the destroyer's rail lined with inquisitive spectators, all looking in their direction.

'What about giving them three cheers?' suggested Ginger. 'That should let them know we're British, anyway.'

'Good idea,' agreed Biggles. 'Let 'em rip. Hip-hip—'

Raising their voices, they sent three rousing cheers floating over the water; but there was no answering cheer from the destroyer.

'Miserable blighters,' grumbled Algy.

'You've heard talk of the Silent Service; now you can see it,' grinned Biggles.

The destroyer's bow-wave dropped away suddenly as she slowed down. Before she had run to a standstill a boat was on the water, six pairs of oars flashing as it sped towards them. A dapper lieutenant in white ducks sat in the stern.

'Round the other side,' shouted Biggles, as he saw him looking for a landing-place.

A crisp word of command and the boat altered its course; it rounded the islet, and a moment later came to rest at the landing-stage. The officer stepped ashore, staring about him in astonishment at the signs of the conflict. The sailors in the boat grinned up at the four faces peering down at them.

The officer ran lightly up the steps and then stood still, an expression of comical astonishment on his face as his eyes ran over the guns and the four grotesque, powder-grimed figures. 'Just what do you think you're playing at?' he asked curtly.

Biggles frowned. 'Playing?' he queried. 'This sort of thing may be all fun and games to you, but I can assure you that

416

during the last hour some very strenuous work has been put in on this blistering rock. If you don't believe that, you try sticking cannon-balls down a muzzle-loader on a hot day.'

The other smiled faintly. The black flag caught his eye. 'Pirates, eh?' he murmured.

'Something of the sort,' agreed Biggles, carelessly.

'Sort of Treasure Island?'

'Precisely!' declared Biggles. 'Allow me to introduce myself. Captain Smollett, at your service. The gentleman on my left is Squire Trelawny; on my right – with the busted cheek – is Doctor Live-say and young Jim Hawkins.' He pointed to the huddled body of Deutch. 'And there's Long John Silver,' he added.

The other started. 'Is he dead?'

'I hope so,' answered Biggles frankly. 'He deserves to be, anyway. If he is it will save the hangman a job.'

The officer shook his head as if the affair was beyond him – as indeed it was. His manner suggested that he thought he was dealing with madmen. Did you get the treasure?' he inquired politely.

Biggles raised his eyebrows. 'Of course; otherwise the story would be all wrong, wouldn't it? There it is; help yourself to a doubloon or two for luck.'

The officer stepped forward, and Biggles, watching him, saw that he was about to pick up a doubloon that lay just under Deutch's pocket. He jumped forward and snatched it up. 'Not that one,' he said grimly. 'Touch that, and you'll never make another landfall. There is only one place for that particular piece.' With a quick jerk of his arm he sent Bawn's doubloon skimming through the air. For a brief moment the sunlight flashed on it as it dropped through space; then, with a tiny splash, it disappeared into the sea. Biggles breathed a sigh of relief as he turned back to the lieutenant. 'There's a story hanging to it,' he explained quietly.

417

The other nodded. 'I think you'd better come and tell it to Captain Crocker,' he said.

'That's a good idea,' agreed Biggles.

In single file they followed the officer down the steps into the boat.

Chapter 17

Explanations

'It was a bit of luck for us that you happened to be coming this way,' observed Biggles, as they sped towards the destroyer.

The officer smiled. 'Luck, do you call it?' he said. 'Do you think everyone is deaf? You made enough row to be heard over half the West Indies. We could see the smoke twenty miles away, and as we don't like wars starting on British islands – at least, not without knowing what they're about – we came along to see.'

Biggles laughed, and glanced at the destroyer's rail, lined with curious, expectant faces. He turned to speak to the others, but the expression on Dick's face caused the words to remain unsaid. His eyes were round, and his face was as white as a sheet under its grime. Suddenly he buried his face in his hands.

'Here, what's the matter, laddie?' cried Biggles sharply, thinking perhaps he had received a wound which he had tried to conceal.

Dick shook his head. 'It's nothing,' he said.

'Come on, out with it,' insisted Biggles.

'I thought – I saw – my father; up there on deck,' whispered Dick.

Biggles looked sharply at the little crowd lining the rails. A civilian, an elderly man with grey hair, was conspicuous.

'Who's that?' he asked the officer tensely.

But the lieutenant was looking at Dick. 'Your name isn't Denver by any chance, is it?' he asked quickly.

'Yes – Dick Denver,' answered Dick wonderingly.

'Well, that's about the last straw,' muttered the officer unbelievingly. 'We've got your father aboard. He went to the Admiral at Kingston with a wild tale about a treasure and a galleon, and the Admiral was so interested that he sent him out with us to locate the island. How in thunder did you get here?'

But Dick barely heard him. As the boat touched the steps that had been lowered, without waiting for permission he jumped on to them and raced to the top.

By the time the others reached the deck he was laughing and crying at once in the elderly man's arms, while a circle of officers and ratings looked on wonderingly.

'This certainly beats all the stories I've ever read into a cocked hat,' whispered Biggles to Algy, as the officer who had escorted them invited them to follow him to an awning on the after deck, where the commander was waiting.

Captain Crocker was a young man. With his officers behind him, he regarded the curiously garbed, battle-stained quartet with interest, suspicion, and some slight amusement. 'Sit down,' he said. 'I should like to know what's going on here. Who is in charge of this – er – party?'

Biggles stepped forward. 'I am,' he answered; 'but before I satisfy your very natural curiosity, may I make three suggestions, all of which have a considerable degree of urgency, or I would not make them now. First of all, a bucket or two of cold water for internal and external use; secondly, that you send a party to take charge of my aircraft, which you can see over there in the lagoon; and lastly, that you send a shore party to the rock we have just evacuated in order to take possession of a fairly valuable collection of gold coins which, as you will no doubt rightly assume, was the primary cause of the undignified bickering that was in progress at the moment of your opportune arrival. You see,' he explained, 'a few of the enemy have survived the engagement, and while I do not think it is probable, there is just a chance that they may make a final raid. If, at the same time, while your men are on the spot, they could dispose of some of the casualties which at present litter an otherwise pleasant spot, so much the better.'

The commander stared at Biggles. 'Do you mean to say that you've actually found a treasure?'

'There are about fifty thousand doubloons kicking about loose on that rock,' murmured Biggles evenly.

'Good heavens!'

'There you are, sir, I told you they were not far away,' cried Dick's father, who was present.

'As a matter of detail, sir, there are a lot of interesting things on this island,' observed Biggles quietly.

'Have you found the galleon that we've heard about?'

'Yes, I'll show you over it presently, if you like; but at the moment we are badly in need of some refreshment.'

The commander got up. 'Quite – quite,' he said. 'I'm still all at sea – but have a wash and a drink; then you can tell me about it. Meanwhile, I'll send parties to do as you suggest.'

'Thanks,' nodded Biggles.

While they were washing, Dick exchanged rapid explanations with his father who, it appeared, had survived the knife wound, but only after a long, painful illness. As soon as he was convalescent he had written a second letter to Dick, but by that time Dick was already on his way to the island, so he did not receive it. As soon as he – Dick's father – was well enough to travel he had worked a passage to Kingston, Jamaica, and there told his highly improbable story to the Admiral commanding the West Indian Station. The Admiral was sceptical about the treasure, but the story of the galleon, still intact, had aroused his curiosity, and he had dispatched a destroyer to investigate, with Dick's father to point out the island, and, when it was found, show the captain where the wreck lay hidden.

These things had only occurred during the last few days. On the previous evening they had picked up a wireless message, sent out by the Pan-American radio station at Marabina, to the effect that four British airmen were missing in the locality and it was for the aeroplane that the destroyer was really searching when the sound of heavy gun-fire was heard. Not a little astonished, she had steamed at full speed in the direction of the supposed battle, with the result that is now known. Dick's father was, of course, just as astonished to see Dick as Dick was to see him.

An hour later, after a square meal, they again forgathered under the awning. The Sikorsky had been towed to the destroyer, and now floated lightly close at hand on the limpid water. The doubloons lay in a pile near the commander's chair. Presently he joined them. 'There seem to have been some nice goings-on here,' he said seriously. 'Take your time and let me have the whole story.'

Whereupon, seated in a deck-chair with a drink at his elbow, Biggles told the tale of their adventures from beginning to end to a spellbound audience. The manner in which they had held the islet particularly intrigued the naval officers.

'It sounds more like a book than a true story,' observed the commander when Biggles had finished. 'By the way, this treasure will have to be regarded as Treasure Trove – that is, Crown property – anyway, until there has been a Court of Inquiry.'

'I know; I made provision for that before I left England,' replied Biggles. 'As a matter of fact, I have a document, issued by the Treasury with the concurrence of the Admiralty, stating that we are to take fifty per cent of anything we find, after deducting expenses. I think we shall be quite happy with our share.'

'I should think you ought to be, too,' smiled the commander. 'By the way, amongst the dead on the boat there is a fellow who looks like an Englishman. According to the papers in his pocket, his name was Harvey—'

'Ah! That's the chap who stole our machine at Marabina,' put in Biggles quickly. 'I wondered what happened to him. I imagine he went into partnership with Deutch.'

'Well, I'm taking some of my officers ashore. We are all anxious to see the old ship, and the fort on the rock. Naturally, we are professionally interested. Would you like to come and show us round?'

'With pleasure,' agreed Biggles. 'In fact, we'd like to have another look round ourselves.'

They spent the rest of the day ashore, exploring thoroughly the old fort and the interior of the once-stately galleon, with which the naval officers were entranced, declaring it to be of great historical importance. A guard was set over it, and only when it was too dark to see more did the party return to the destroyer, Dick taking with him Dakeyne's black flag, which he got permission to retain.

They spent the night on board the destroyer, but with the rising of the sun preparations were made for departure, Captain Crocker, who had reported the discovery by radio to his Admiral, having received a signal instructing him to proceed at once to headquarters. He offered to give the airmen a lift, but they declined, preferring to travel their own way. They arranged to meet at Kingston, however, where it was thought that the official inquiry would be held.

As the destroyer's anchor emerged from the blue water Biggles started the Sikorsky's engines. Aircraft and water-craft moved forward together, the destroyer slowly, the amphibian with ever increasing speed. The destroyer dipped her ensign as the aircraft forged ahead, but the salute of her siren was lost in the roar of the Sikorsky's motors as she soared into the air.

423

Ten minutes later, when Dick looked behind, Treasure Island was a blue line on the horizon.

There is little more to tell. After the Admiralty Court, held in the West Indies, where the discovery of the galleon and the treasure was a nine days' wonder, Dick, his father, and the three airmen took passage for London, where the final claims for the treasure had been lodged. It realized rather more than two hundred thousand pounds, of which one-half was held to be the property of the Crown. The remainder was divided between the adventurers in the proportions agreed upon.

Dick was in two minds whether to follow the sea or the air as a career; in the end, to please his father and follow the traditions of his family, he was entered as an apprentice in the Merchant Service. Today, in the cabin of 'Doubloon Dick', as he is called – for his story is well known – hangs a trophy that is the envy of every other apprentice in his ship. It is a black flag; the sinister banner of Louis Dakeyne, Louis le Grande, The Exterminator.

Also available in Red Fox

Biggles Story Collection 1

Biggles Learns to Fly

Biggles in the Camels are Coming

Biggles and The Rescue Flight

Biggles of The Fighter Squadron

Biggles & CO.

Biggles in Spain

Biggles in France

Biggles Defies the Swastika

Biggles in the Orient

Biggles Defends the Desert

Biggles Fails to Return

Biggles: Spitfire Parade

Biggles: Foreign Legionnaire

Biggles Flies East

Biggles Flies West

RED FOX STORY COLLECTIONS

This series of value-for-money paperbacks each comprise several of your favourite stories in a single volume! Whether you want to follow the action-packed adventures of Hal and Roger Hunt in THE ADVENTURE COLLECTION or discover the myths surrounding Arthur and his Knights of the Round Table in KING ARTHUR STORIES these bumper reads are full of epic adventures and magical mystery.

THE ADVENTURE COLLECTION
by Willard Price
Whale Adventure and African Adventure
0 09 926592 3 £4.99

BIGGLES STORY COLLECTION
by Captain W. E. Johns
Biggles in France
Biggles Defend the Desert
Biggles: Foreign Legionnaire
0 09 940154 1 £4.99

KING ARTHUR STORIES
by Rosemary Sutcliff
The Sword and the Circle
The Light Beyond the Forest
The Road to Camlann
0 09 940164 9 £4.99

Swallows and Amazons

Arthur Ransome

Titty drew a long breath that nearly choked her.
'It is…' she said.
The flag blowing in the wind at the masthead of the little boat was
black and on it in white were a skull and two crossed bones.
The four on the island stared at each other.

To John, Susan, Titty and Roger, being allowed to use the boat *Swallow* to go camping on the island is adventure enough. But they soon find themselves under attack from the fierce Amazon Pirates, Nancy and Peggy. And so begins a summer of battles, alliances, exploration and discovery.

By the winning author of the first Carnegie medal.

ISBN 0099503913   £5.99

EMIL and the DETECTIVES

ERICH KÄSTNER

'As a matter of fact,' said Emil, 'I'm keeping my eye on a thief.'
'What!' exclaimed the boy with the motor-horn. 'A thief? What has he
stolen? Who from?'
'Me,' said Emil, feeling quite important again.

If Mrs Tischbein had known the amazing adventures her son Emil would
have in Berlin, she'd never have let him go. Unfortunately, when his
seven pounds goes missing on the train journey, Emil is determined to
get it back...no mattter what trouble he may run into!

'This book is one of my favourites'
QUENTIN BLAKE
'This must be one of the most delicious children's books ever written'
DAILY EXPRESS

ISBN 0099413124 £4.99

THE WOLVES OF WILLOUGHBY CHASE

JOAN AIKEN

*She woke suddenly to find that the train had stopped with a jerk.
'Oh! What is it? Where are we?' she exclaimed before she could stop herself.
'No need to alarm yourself, miss,' said her companion. 'Wolves on the line,
most likely – they often have trouble of that kind hereabouts.'
'Wolves!' Sylvia stared at him in terror.*

After braving a treacherous journey through snow-covered wastes populated by packs of wild and hungry wolves, Sylvia joins her cousin Bonnie in the warmth and safety of Willoughby Chase. But with Bonnie's parents overseas and the evil Miss Slighcarp left in charge, the cousins soon find their human predators even harder to escape.

'Joan Aiken is such a spellbinder that it all rings true…'
THE STANDARD

ISBN 0099411865 £4.99

The Naughtiest Children I Know

Edited by *Anne Harvey*

My son Augustus, in the street, one day,
Was feeling quite exceptionally merry.
A stranger asked him: 'Can you show me, pray,
The quickest way to Brompton Cemetery?'
'The quickest way? You bet I can!' said Gus,
And pushed the fellow underneath a bus.

Whatever people say about my son,
He does enjoy his little bit of fun.

An A-Z of the naughtiest children ever! From untidy Amanda and Bad Boy Benjamin to Naughty Dan, Greedy George and Sulky Susan. They're all inside, so open up and see if there's a poem in here about you...

£5.99   009940866X

RED FOX STORY COLLECTIONS

If you are looking for a little animal magic then these brilliant bind-ups bring you stories of every creature, great and small. There are the fantastic creatures that Doctor Dolittle lives and works with in **DOCTOR DOLITTLE STORIES**, the bold and brave animals described in **ANIMAL STORIES** and there are three memorable tales of horse riding and friendship in **PONY STORIES**.

DOCTOR DOLITTLE STORIES
by Hugh Lofting
Selected stories from the Doctor Dolittle Books
0 09 926593 1 £4.99

ANIMAL STORIES
The Winged Colt of Casa Mia by Betsy Byars
Stories from Firefly Island by Benedict Blathwayt
Farthing Wood, The Adventure Begins
by Colin Dann
0 09 926583 4 £4.99

PONY STORIES
A Summer of Horses by
Carol Fenner
Fly-by-Night by K. M. Peyton
Three to Ride by Christine
Pullein-Thompson
0 09 940003 0 £4.99

RED FOX
SCHOOL STORIES COLLECTIONS

These brilliant bumper bind-ups are packed with top-grade tales of cool characters, treacherous teachers and some seriously sinister happenings in the classroom. School has never been this exciting, so get your hands on these cool collections - they'll be an education!

COOL SCHOOL STORIES
The Worst Kids in the World and
The Worst Kids in the World Best School Year Ever
by Barbara Robinson
Wasim in the Deep End by Chris Ashley
Follow that Bus! by Pat Hutchins
0 09 926585 0   £4.99

MORE COOL SCHOOL STORIES
Runners by Susan Gates
Graphicat by Marilyn Watts
The Present Takers by Aidan Chambers
0 09 940023 5   £4.99

NEW COOL SCHOOL STORIES
The Class that Went Wild by Ruth Thomas
My School is Cool by Catherine Sides
Triv in Pursuit by Michael Coleman
The Detention by Primrose Lovett
A Devilish Dare by Nick Corrin
0 09 941121 0   £4.99